P9-DEV-573

Praise for the novels of Jude Deveraux

"The mystery debut of bestselling romance author Deveraux…starts with an unhappily-ever-after—an unsolved murder. But its heroine, a romance novelist, has a better ending in mind. Fans of Deveraux and the cozy mystery genre will find common ground in this twisted tale of forgotten graves, small-town grudges, and new friends."
—*Kirkus Reviews* on *A Willing Murder*

"With three stories told two ways, this third book in Deveraux's Summerhouse series is emotional, imaginative, and gloriously silly."
—*Kirkus Reviews* on *As You Wish*

"Deveraux's charming novel has likable characters and life-affirming second chances galore."
—*Publishers Weekly* on *As You Wish*

"Jude Deveraux's writing is enchanting and exquisite."
—*BookPage*

"Deveraux's touch is gold."
—*Publishers Weekly*

"A steamy and delightfully outlandish retelling of a literary classic."
—*Kirkus Reviews* on *The Girl from Summer Hill*

"[A]n irresistibly delicious tale of love, passion, and the unknown."
—*Booklist* on *The Girl from Summer Hill*

"[A] sexy, lighthearted romp."
—*Kirkus Reviews* on *Ever After*

"Thoroughly enjoyable."
—*Publishers Weekly* (starred review) on *Ever After*

JUDE DEVERAUX

A Willing Murder

mira

If you purchased this book without a cover you should be aware
that this book is stolen property. It was reported as "unsold and
destroyed" to the publisher, and neither the author nor the
publisher has received any payment for this "stripped book."

mira

ISBN-13: 978-0-7783-0819-5

Recycling programs
for this product may
not exist in your area.

A Willing Murder

Copyright © 2018 by Deveraux Inc.

All rights reserved. Except for use in any review, the reproduction or
utilization of this work in whole or in part in any form by any electronic,
mechanical or other means, now known or hereafter invented, including
xerography, photocopying and recording, or in any information storage or
retrieval system, is forbidden without the written permission of the publisher,
MIRA Books, 22 Adelaide St. West, 40th Floor, Toronto, Ontario M5H 4E3,
Canada.

This is a work of fiction. Names, characters, places and incidents are
either the product of the author's imagination or are used fictitiously, and
any resemblance to actual persons, living or dead, business establishments,
events or locales is entirely coincidental.

® and TM are trademarks of Harlequin Enterprises Limited or its corporate
affiliates. Trademarks indicated with ® are registered in the United States Patent
and Trademark Office, the Canadian Intellectual Property Office and in other
countries.

For questions and comments about the quality of this book, please contact us at
CustomerService@Harlequin.com.

www.Harlequin.com

Printed in U.S.A.

Also from Jude Deveraux and MIRA Books

Medlar Mysteries

A JUSTIFIED MURDER

The Summerhouse Series

AS YOU WISH

For additional books by
New York Times bestselling author Jude Deveraux,
visit her website, www.jude-deveraux.com.

A Willing Murder

PROLOGUE

HE WAS WEARING THE CLOTHES HE'D FOUND in the back of the old truck. Filthy, with pieces of grass clinging to them, they smelled bad and scratched his skin. The baggy pants had fresh oil on them and stuck to him in places.

He didn't think anyone would notice the rusty old truck, but he was cautious by nature. He stopped in front of the house for just minutes as he unloaded the tree. It was in a five-gallon pot and heavy. Dirt slid up his arms, adding a new layer of grime to the shirt.

He left the tree on the lawn, then parked a block away in a vacant lot.

It was full night, but still, he hurried back as fast as his disguise allowed. He bent over and shuffled in the heavy-soled work shoes. They were too small and hurt his feet.

As he picked up the tree, he paused at the gate, listening. Night sounds: a TV in the distance, a child crying. All ordinary and nothing to worry about. When he was sure no one was near, he went around the side to the hole in the back. It hadn't been dug by him, but had been used to roast a pig and never filled in. There was still grease in places.

Immediately, he saw that the dirt had been disturbed. His heart leaped into his throat and pounded hard. His mind raced forward to what would be done if someone found out what had happened. It would be the end of his life, of his family's life.

"Happened," he said aloud. Yes, it had just *happened*. Not anyone's fault. It was something that couldn't be helped.

When he'd calmed himself enough to look closer, he saw that the dirt had moved from beneath. Not from an outside disturbance, but from inside. Underneath.

He refused to think what that meant. A vague question—*which one?*—ran through his mind, but he didn't try to find out.

The hole had been deep and they were small. Only a thin layer of dirt was over them, so there was still plenty of depth left for planting.

He hefted the tree out of the plastic pot and put it on top of what was barely covered. He adjusted it so it was on the exact spot that had been disturbed.

When he realized he didn't have a shovel, he cursed in annoyance. Maybe there was one in the truck, but that meant he'd have to make another trip in and out. He couldn't risk it.

Angry, he got down on his hands and knees and began clawing at the pile of soil. The hole had been there a long time and was littered with beer cans and broken glass. When he cut his hand, he wiped the blood on the old shirt.

Two times the earth shifted from beneath, but he ignored it. He was satisfied that he was planting a truly beautiful tree. It was a fitting monument to—to them.

When he was done, he patted the dirt down, then stood up. To make sure it was done right, he went around the tree again and again, stamping harder and harder, crushing what was buried beneath the soil.

By the time he finished, it was late. He left the backyard of the ramshackle house and walked down the street to the truck.

For a moment he thought it wasn't going to start, but it did. He drove it back to the owner's house, removed the old clothes from over his own and threw them in the back.

As he walked away, he smiled at the peaceful houses. His small town was such a nice place. In fact, maybe ridding it of undesirables had been a favor to the neighborhood. All he was sure of was that he was content to know that a lesson had been learned and nothing like that would ever happen again.

A few months later, the abandoned house was put up for rent. It was said that the last tenant and her daughter had packed up and run away in the night. No one liked the mother much, so they didn't mind. And besides, everyone in town knew the truth about her. Too bad about her daughter, though.

While he'd been waiting, he'd made a plan. He did some clever and elaborate dealings to buy the place under a name that had nothing to do with him.

Anonymously, he put the house under the care of a management company that kept it rented. The money was sent to a charity for battered women. They sent thank-you notes, but he never saw them.

The rental agreement stipulated that the beautiful royal poinciana tree in the backyard was never to be disturbed. It wasn't even allowed to be pruned. The tree grew and flourished and was remarked on by many people.

Gradually, the incident faded so deeply into the man's long-ago memory that he sometimes wondered if it had actually happened.

But then, one night as he was watching the local news on TV, he saw a picture of the house and the tree. A pretty young journalist was saying that Wyatt Construction had bought six houses on one street and they were going to completely remodel them. The reporter held the mic toward the owner, Jackson Wyatt, a tall, handsome, dark-haired young man.

"We're going to redo the houses from two feet down up to the rooftops," he said, his head turned in profile to the camera.

"You aren't going to take out that big poinciana, are you?" the reporter asked.

"We are, actually. The truth is, that tree's never been taken care of and it's full of termites. The next big storm will knock it down for sure, and it's going to land on a couple of houses—or maybe people."

"That's sad." She smiled at Jack.

"Yeah, it is." He smiled back.

The man threw the remote at the screen. How could this have happened? He owned that house! How could it have been *sold* to someone else?

It took him hours of digging through papers that had long ago been filed away to find the single sentence that released the house to be sold. He'd done such a good job of keeping himself disconnected from the property that when it had been confiscated, no one knew how to contact him.

His initial anger was replaced with fear. Logically, he doubted if he could be connected to what would be found when the tree—and what was beneath it—was dug up, but people in small towns had long memories. And they were always snooping. It was better to be cautious than sorry.

He made himself a fresh pot of coffee and began to think about what he had to do to stop this desecration from happening. He'd stop it no matter what it took—and he'd start with the guy from Wyatt Construction.

ONE

SARA WAS SITTING IN JACK'S DRAB, SUNLESS apartment on an old chair someone had given him. She let her shoulders droop and her head sag in an attempt to show every minute of her sixty-plus years of life. It wasn't helping that she'd been in boxing class at 6:00 a.m. When she moved her arm, she gave an involuntary gasp. She was sore from all those uppercuts her trainer had made her do.

As she watched Jack stumble about the dreary room on his crutches, she tried not to show how her heart was breaking for him.

To her, Jack was the grandson she should have had. She and his late grandfather, Callum Wyatt, had been born in the same year and had grown up living next door to each other. They'd always been in love, had always planned to marry, but because of things that Sara worked hard not to remember, that hadn't happened. Cal had stayed in little Lachlan and run his father's car repair shop, while Sara had, as Cal used to say, "conquered the world." It was a gross exaggeration, but it had made Sara laugh, so Cal was content.

Jack was her compensation for the past. Since he was eighteen, Sara had been a silent partner in his construction business and they'd spent a lot of time together. When Sara retired, she never thought of going anywhere other than where Jack was. And right now, she didn't feel even a smidgen of guilt about conspiring with his mother and sister to get him to move into her big house with her. Someone needed to take care of Jackson Charles Wyatt because *he* certainly wasn't doing it!

It looked like the pain she was feeling was worth it because Jack was at last losing that expression she'd seen so many times on Cal—head back just a fraction, chin out, lower lip rigid. "You can't make me do it." His mother said those were the first words Jack spoke. Full sentence, no piddling around with just one word, but the entire statement said at once. And said fiercely.

Now here he was, thirty-one years old, six feet two inches of mostly muscle, his leg in a cast and leaning on crutches—and he looked just like that little kid.

Yes, he was balking at making the move, but Sara had a trick up her sleeve. She'd just told him that her niece was coming to visit. "I can't help it," Sara said, "I'm nervous about her being here."

"Then tell her not to come."

His words were harsh, but she could tell that he was softening. Maybe it was the stairs. His apartment was on the second floor of an old house he'd bought years ago. It was a struggle to carry groceries up the outside stairs while on crutches.

"You must make rules for her to follow." Jack was frowning.

Sara turned away to hide her smile. His tone was just like his grandfather's. Sara used to tell Cal he should try out to play Moses. Stern, lecturing, ready to give out orders.

Sara tried to slump more. *Look old!* she commanded herself. "It's just that I've lived alone for so long that I don't know how to handle a visitor." She gave a sad little sigh and looked at Jack for sympathy. She saw his lashes flicker. Inside, he was as soft as his grandfather.

"She's my niece, but I haven't been around her since she was a child," Sara continued. "She was so sweet and funny then. And very smart. I've seen lots of photos of her, but…" She gave another sigh. "I just don't know how she's going to be to *live* with. Will she Tweet and text me rather than actually speaking?" She gave a genuine gasp of horror. "What if she…if she says 'amazing' in every sentence? How will I stand it? Will she—?"

She broke off as Jack hobbled to the couch and heaved himself down. He was a strong young man and shouldn't have that much trouble with a cast and crutches. But she wasn't worried about him physically. What Sara was concerned about was Jack's mental state. The wreck that smashed his leg had killed his half brother. As Jack was taken to the hospital, he kept saying that it was all his fault. He'd been drinking, so he let Evan drive. Jack had fallen asleep so hard that he didn't wake up until the truck was flipping around and around through the air. He kept saying, "If only I'd stayed awake… If only I'd driven…"

It was Jack's deep sense of guilt and his grief that Sara was worried about. She was determined to do whatever was necessary to get him to stay with her in her huge house. She wanted to make sure that he didn't do…well, do something dumb.

Jack's mother had planned it with Sara. "He won't listen to me," Heather said.

Her eyes were red from days of crying. Evan hadn't been her child but she'd loved him. At the funeral, someone said that Heather had been a better mother to Evan than his own had.

But Sara hadn't been able to come up with anything that wouldn't make Jack dig in his heels and refuse to move. "I'm worried about you" was sure to make him say no.

Then, last evening, she got an email from her beloved niece, Kate. She said she had a job in Lachlan and asked if she could please stay with Sara until she got a place of her own.

The thought of her niece coming made Sara so happy that she turned on some old blues music and danced from one room to another. The house was too big, too empty, and besides, retirement sucked. What was she to do with her *mind* in retirement? She couldn't think of anything better than having her lively young niece to stay. There was a self-contained apartment on the west side of the house and it opened into a little courtyard with a fountain of a girl dancing in the rain. Kate would probably love it. Maybe she'd like everything so much that she'd stay permanently. Maybe the two of them could do things together. Go places.

Maybe— As always, Sara's mind had taken off like a freight train on jet fuel. An hour later, she'd planned three trips she and her niece could take together.

Later, when she stepped into her big, glass-surrounded shower, she thought of Ivy—who was Kate's age—helping to decorate the apartment. Right now there was only a queen-size bed in there, and the living room didn't have so much as a chair.

As she shampooed her hair, she thought how Ivy could— Sara halted. *Ivy.* Jack's half sister. He shared a father with Evan and a mother with Ivy. And they had all grown up together.

"Eureka!" Sara shouted as she rinsed her hair. Kate's visit might be the key to getting Jack to stay with her. He could take the bedroom by the garage. When he'd remodeled the house, he'd made that room quite nice. There was no furniture in it, either, but one trip to a store and…

By the time Sara got out of the shower, she was hatching a plan. Once she got Jack out of his second-story apartment, she and Heather—and Kate—would make sure he didn't let his grief overcome him.

As she looked across Jack's dull little apartment, Sara said, "I just want to feel *safe*." She was slumped so far down in the awful old chair that her neck was practically on the seat cushion. Jack had always been one to help a person in need—as long as it wasn't him who needed it.

"You don't think she's after…?" He trailed off.

"Money?" Sara shrugged. "Maybe. I'm an older woman who can pay her bills. I'm a prime target for every scammer on the planet." She drew in her breath. Was that too much for him to believe? But no, Jack nodded in agreement. It took work for Sara not to sit up straight and declare that she could take care of herself. "I'm sure she won't stay for long."

When she saw that Jack was still hesitating, she decided to give his male ego a push. She used the arm of the chair to help herself up. Since her trainer had made her quads so sore that it hurt to stand, her wince was genuine. "I can see that you don't want to do this." There was so much martyred suffering in her voice that she thought he'd laugh at her. But he didn't. "You don't have to do anything. I'll hire someone to help me."

"*Hire* someone?" Jack grabbed his crutches and nearly fell as he stood up with them. "All right. You win." He sounded disgusted. "You have any furniture for the room?"

"I thought maybe you'd go with me down to Baer's to see Rico and pick out a few pieces. I need some for Kate's rooms, too."

"I don't know anything about furniture. Ivy is the one—"

"What a great idea! So clever of you to think of her. And I do believe that Ivy said she has the morning off." Sara pulled her cell from her handbag. "I'll text her to meet us there. Okay if she brings your mom?"

Jack was glaring down at her. "It sounds like all of you planned this. And you certainly look like you're feeling better. How was your boxing lesson this morning?"

"Brutal. Are you ready to go?"

"No. I need to pack. I'll stop by on Saturday. Or Sunday, maybe."

"You don't need to pack anything. Every piece of clothing you own has concrete splatters or paint on it."

"That's because I spent the last year working on that old house you bought. You kept adding so much that I didn't have time to go *shopping*." His eyes were narrowed. He was Moses being defied.

Sara went to the door. "That's all right. Your mom picked up a few things for you. Can we go now? If we get there early enough, Rico can schedule delivery for tomorrow."

Jack was looking like a horse that was going to balk at the starting gate.

She gritted her teeth. Real men could be as stubborn as the ones she put in her novels. "Did I tell you that my niece is five foot seven and has dark red hair? And green eyes? She was voted the prettiest girl in her high-school class."

"That makes no difference. I'm not looking for—" He took a breath. "Actual green or brownish green?"

"Emeralds are jealous," Sara said without a hint of humor.

Jack glanced around the apartment, then back at Sara. "I don't think I can fit in that car of yours."

"Don't flatter yourself. You're not that big and MINI Coopers are roomy inside. Wait until you see how many lamps I can jam in there." She held open the door. "You go first. If you fall, I don't want you landing on me."

"Because you're so old and fragile?" He stepped past her. "Fragile as a water buffalo," he muttered as he struggled down the steep flight of stairs. "Just so you know, I'm only doing this because you can cook."

"That is *not* part of this deal," Sara said, but she was smiling—and offering up a prayer of thanks. Neither she nor Jack were going to be alone. Life was good.

TWO

WHEN KATE MEDLAR SAW THE BIG GREEN
highway sign that said Lachlan was two exits away,
she took the nearest exit. At the wide T in the road,
she hesitated. She didn't know which way to go. Of
course, the guy behind her blew his horn. Laid on it.
It seemed that he was so frantic to get somewhere that
a twelve-second delay put him in a rage.

She turned right because it was easier and the other
car sped forward. As he passed, the driver gave her the
finger and mouthed the "call you next Tuesday" word.

And people wondered why there were shots fired between cars, she thought. There was a little diner ahead
and she pulled into the gravel parking lot. Inside, she
took a booth by the window so she could watch her car.
After all, everything she owned was stuffed inside it.

When the waitress came, Kate ordered an egg-white omelet, a single slice of whole wheat toast and black coffee. No sauce, no butter, no cheese, no flavor. Long ago, she'd learned that she had *not* inherited her mother's ability to eat fried chicken and doughnuts and remain as thin as a broom handle.

It was one of Kate's complaints about the unfairness of this "I'm fat, you're not" that had brought about what she'd come to think of as The Great Reveal.

Usually, her mother made no comment on Kate's weight complaints, but three months ago, she'd said, "That's because you're like her. That writer woman."

The waitress poured the coffee and Kate sipped. When she'd questioned her mother, she was told that "her" was an aunt she'd never heard of: her late father's only sibling, Sara.

Kate combined the first name and her own last one with the label of "writer woman."

"Sara Medlar?" she asked in disbelief. She'd been sitting on a stool at the kitchen bar in the little house outside Chicago that she and her mother shared. Ava had been standing at the stove, her back to her daughter.

"*The* Sara Medlar?" Kate repeated, louder. "The writer whose name is on half the paperbacks in the grocery stores? She's my father's sister?"

Ava didn't turn around but gave a curt nod.

"I knew the last name was the same, but I never dreamed there was a connection." Kate felt like she should get angry. Shouldn't she start shouting about the injustice of not having been told this before? But she knew that directing anger at her mother never worked. Besides, the news was oh, so intriguing!

Until that moment the only relatives she'd known

about were her mother's three older brothers. Horrible old men!

Kate's brain skipped the drama that she was being cheated out of and she said, as calmly as she could, "Why haven't you told me this before?"

Ava shrugged. "She's famous. She wanted nothing to do with us after dear Randal left."

As always, at the mention of her husband, tears came to Ava's eyes. She'd never made an attempt to "move on" from her beloved husband's early death.

Kate knew when to back off. Her father, Randal Medlar, had died when Kate was just four years old and she remembered nothing of him. Over the years, she'd tried to get her mother to tell her about him. But Ava's memories were more deification than about a real man. Kate wanted to know about *him*. What made him laugh? What talents did he have? But she could never get answers out of her mother.

To hear that there was someone else who knew her father made her so curious that it was like a fire had been lit inside her. That night she didn't sleep but stayed on her computer, researching the author Sara Medlar.

There was the usual hype around her glorious life and speculations about how she wrote—pen or keyboard?—but no mention of her deceased brother. Kate skipped all that. What she wanted to know was where Sara and her brother had grown up. It took some work, but eventually she came up with the city of Lachlan, Florida.

Further digging, some of it into a paid site that found missing people, said that Sara Medlar had retired from writing and recently moved back to Lachlan.

"Eureka!" Kate said, then began to research the town. She soon found what she was looking for: a local real estate office. Kate had been selling real estate for the two years since she'd graduated from college and she loved it.

There was only one real estate office in Lachlan and it was owned by a woman named Tayla Kirkwood. There was an excellent website, and over the next few days, Kate read it avidly and came to greatly admire Mrs. Kirkwood. She'd spent the past twenty years bringing the derelict town back to life. When Tayla was growing up in Lachlan—at approximately the same time as Kate's father—it had been a peaceful, tight-knit little Florida community. But Tayla had married and moved away. While she was gone, Fort Lauderdale had expanded until it had consumed the town. People moved out; stores closed.

After Tayla was widowed, she returned to find that Lachlan was nearly a ghost town. Several lovely old houses had been torn down.

Angry and determined, Tayla worked to bring the town back to life. She bought and remodeled stores in the downtown area and brought in high-end businesses that drew tourists and shoppers from Fort Lauderdale.

The transformation of Lachlan under Tayla's supervision was admirable, Kate thought as the waitress put a plain egg-white omelet in front of her. "Want some butter and jam with that?"

"I wish," Kate said.

"I hear you on that!" the waitress said as she went back to the counter.

The eggs were tasteless, the toast dry. But it didn't

matter—all Kate could think about was the new life she was about to start.

After weeks of reading and researching, Kate had written Mrs. Kirkwood a letter. She explained who she was, complimented her lavishly and said she would like to be considered for a job there.

The reply came back almost instantly:

Yes! I've done a lot, but Lachlan still needs much more work. There's a whole section of the town that's practically a slum. I'd love to have your help. That you're a hometown girl who has come back will mean a lot.

Tayla made Kate feel wanted and needed. And truthfully, becoming part of bringing a town back to life excited her. It was better than selling the same suburban homes over and over.

After Kate had the job offer, she asked Tayla for a favor. Would she please see that a letter got to her aunt Sara Medlar? Kate figured that sending a note through Sara's publishing house was no guarantee that it would ever reach her. Tayla had agreed.

Kate wrote a simple letter to her aunt saying that she had a job in Lachlan and could she possibly stay with her for a few days while she got settled. She didn't mention that she'd only recently found out Sara existed, as that might be a disparagement of her mother.

The response Kate received was enthusiastic and welcoming:

You must stay with me until you find a place of your own. There is a self-contained apartment on the side of my house and it's yours for as long as you want it.

It had all been easy, actually. She had a job and a place to live. The only thing left was to deal with her mother. Ava Medlar's nerves and fears, not to mention her odious older brothers, had been a big part of Kate's twenty-three years of life.

She gathered up her courage and told her mother what she was going to do.

Ava had *not* reacted as Kate thought she would. To Kate's surprise, she'd said, "That's a good idea. You can help her. The poor thing had to give up writing because her mind couldn't do it anymore. Not that her books ever had any literary merit, but she does need some brainpower to pump them out. And it's good that you'll be living with her. She has a mansion and lots of servants. You need to make sure that none of them are stealing her blind."

Kate was shocked that her mother knew so much about the sister-in-law she'd never once mentioned. How? When? Why? *All* her questions were answered with variations of the fact that Sara Medlar had cut them out of her life when her brother died. It wasn't Ava's doing, but the aunt's. And Ava had thought it was better to never tell her daughter about a woman who wanted nothing to do with them. "To save you more heartache," she said.

Ava's story was so dire that Kate began to doubt her plan to stay with her famous aunt and move to Lachlan. But by then she and Tayla were exchanging daily emails and sharing photos and telling about their daily activities. Cyber friends.

Kate told Tayla of her hesitation. Maybe it would be better if she rented an apartment and just visited her old aunt.

Tayla wrote back that she had a listing for a second-floor apartment that would be perfect for her. Coincidentally, it was vacant because the young man who used to live there had just moved in with her aunt Sara. "'She must be lonely living in that big house and Jack has always had a way with women,'" Kate said, reading the email aloud to her mother. "'Such a personable young man! And rumor has it that Sara has started financing his business. It looks like it's working out well for both of them.'"

When she'd finished reading, Ava had given her the "I told you so" look. Kate began to think her aunt needed her protection. Who knew all the ways this Jack character might be planning to take advantage of Sara? She would stay with her aunt.

The next day Ava helped Kate clean out her room.

Three days later, Kate was on her way. The goodbye to her mother had been tearful. It had always been just the two of them and Kate was the strong one. By necessity she'd had to cope with her mother's bouts of depression over the loss of her husband. Kate had had to learn how to take care of herself.

"You'll be all right?" she asked her mother as she got into her car. "You won't let the uncles bully you?"

"I'll be fine. You'll email me?"

"Every day. Just look at the green message app on your phone. Check for texts from me."

Ava, biting her lip to stave off the tears, said, "Don't let her be nasty to you. Stand up to her. She has a horrible temper. She used to scare me half to death."

This was the first Kate had heard of a temper. "She—?"

"And put her on a diet." Ava shut the car door. "Two hundred pounds is too much for her. She's not even five feet tall. If she lost weight, she might not be so bad-tempered all the time." Ava stepped back and blew a kiss. "I love you. Have a good time." She hurried back into the house as Kate drove away.

For the first day of the drive, Kate kept muttering, "What the hell have I done?"

Now she was almost there, and her bravado was draining. New town, new job, new home with a new relative.

What was that list of the ten most stressful events in a person's life? She was facing at least four of them.

She paid and left the diner.

At her car, she halted. "I can do this," she told herself. "I have a job. I even have a friend in Tayla. And I'm…" She swallowed. "I'm staying with, uh…" She took a breath. "With a senile old aunt who has a fierce temper and is living with some guy who's conned her into buying him a business. I *can* do this." She got in her car. "And if I can't, I can run home to mommy. As a failure."

She got back on the highway, and when the exit for Lachlan came up, she went down the ramp. But her heart was pounding so hard that she had to pull to the side of the road, lean back and try to calm herself.

It would be courteous to first go to her aunt's house. Or rather, her mansion, as her mother called it. But when Kate put the street address into the GPS system, it said there was no such place. She had a map but it didn't show Stewart Lane, either.

That's bad, she thought, but felt relieved. She'd have to go to Tayla's office first, meet her friend in person and ask directions.

The GPS said that the office was only a mile and a half away. An omen, she thought, and pulled back onto the road.

Her first sight of Lachlan made her draw in her breath. She'd seen photos but they didn't do the pretty town justice.

To her right was a fire station, redbrick with two open garage doors. Some muscular men were washing a big red fire engine, a dalmatian nearby. "Like something out of Disney." She saw the blond fireman, the youngest one, pause, rag in hand, and look at her. His wet T-shirt clung to him.

The man next to him hit him with his elbow, but the fireman didn't stop staring. When he smiled at Kate, she smiled back.

"I just might like it here," she murmured as she pulled into the town hall parking lot. Tayla's office was beside it.

She got out and looked around. Across the road from the brick building was a large green area, with trees and benches and a wide oval track. There were joggers and people walking, dogs chasing Frisbees and three families having picnics.

How lovely, she thought, and remembered the photos of the town as it was when Tayla had returned to Lachlan. The green area had once been filled with buildings that had been hit hard by Hurricane Andrew in 1992.

The severely damaged buildings had been repaired, but no one had cared enough about Lachlan to make them beautiful. Ugly concrete block stores dominated.

Tayla had torn down and rebuilt to create a recreation area smack in the middle of town. To get people downtown for something other than shopping, she'd told Kate in an email. But, of course, once they're near all those lovely stores, they'll buy things.

Kate had laughed at that. She'd majored in business in college and she agreed with Tayla. Keep the money moving!

Tayla's office was an old house that had been tastefully converted. It was one story with a tall, pitched roof and a couple of dormers. A long porch extended across the front. The two large windows and a wood-framed glass door were a concession to business.

The windows had the current listings taped to them. Kate was too much of a businesswoman not to stop and look at them. There were three fixer-uppers that had peeling paint and sagging roofs, a lovely Victorian-style house and some nice starter homes.

Smiling, Kate stepped back. Judging from the photos, they could use some staging and the yards needed cleaning. Yes, she could work with that.

She opened the door and stepped inside. Immediately, Kate liked the place. The ceiling went up to the roof, exposing the rafters. The dormers let in light that filled the office. The waiting room was furnished with modern, good-quality leather-and-chrome chairs.

No people were to be seen.

"Hello?" she called. No answer. There was a tall counter and Kate picked up one of the brochures that Tayla had sent her. It told what she'd done to the town, with impressive before and after photos. At the bottom was a stamp-sized photo of Tayla with her short gray hair, very stylish, very of-the-moment.

In the back, a door opened and a woman came around the corner. She was older than Kate, late twenties maybe, shorter, and carried a few extra pounds. "Oh, sorry. I didn't hear anyone come in. Chris is usually here, but today—" She broke off as she stared. "You must be Kate."

"I am. Is Tayla here?"

"No. She has some showings in Weston. The couple wanted to be near big stores and flashy streets. We're too quiet for them. Their loss. She won't be back for hours. She said you wouldn't be here until tomorrow."

"I didn't think I would be. I was going to go to my aunt's today but my GPS can't find Stewart Lane."

"I guess it's too tiny to put in the system. I'm Melissa. Want some coffee? Tea? Water from the faucet?"

Kate smiled. "Water sounds good."

"Come on, then, and I'll show you around."

It took only minutes to see the place, and Melissa showed Kate her office. It was a good size, with a window that looked out to the big circle, where people picnicked.

"Try it," Melissa said, nodding toward the tan leather chair. "Tayla ordered it just for you. I tried to get her to buy it in red but she wouldn't."

"Good. I like this one." She sat down and swiveled around in a full circle: L-shaped desk, wall, window. It was an excellent area.

Melissa was leaning against the door frame, cup in hand. "You know, you look a bit like your aunt. I've only seen her once, but I think your faces are shaped the same."

When she paused, Kate knew Melissa was waiting for a reply, but she said nothing. She'd seen a publicity shot of her aunt on the back of her books but she had no idea what she looked like every day.

"If you don't know where Stewart Lane is, then you haven't seen her house, have you?"

"No. Is it great?"

"Mmmm." Melissa rolled her eyes. "Magnificent. Jack spent over a year redoing it."

Again, Melissa paused and Kate had the idea she was supposed to ask something. About her aunt? The house? Ah. "Who is Jack?"

Melissa smiled in a way that let Kate know she'd got it right. "The man women dream about. Gorgeous, built, deep voice. He's charmed Ms. Medlar into letting him move in with her. Rent-free."

Kate turned around in the chair so her back was to Melissa. One thing she'd learned in her life was not to reveal too much. With autocratic, domineering, "stick their noses into everything" uncles like hers, she and her mother knew how to keep quiet. She was *not* going to tell this snooping woman that when it came to her aunt, she knew nothing about anything.

When she turned around, Kate was smiling. "Jack is in business with my aunt and his stay with her is only temporary."

"Oh." Melissa seemed to be deflated by this news. She straightened. "When he moves out, would you please give him my info? I'll work with him on finding any house he wants."

When Kate stood up, Melissa looked her up and down, as though she was the competition. *Puh-lease*, Kate thought. She'd never been one for catfights over men.

"I'll do that." Kate looked at her watch. "I have to

go." She picked up her handbag and hurried toward the front door. As she opened it, she looked back at Melissa. "I'll be here first thing tomorrow. At eight. Please tell Tayla. Or no, I'll text her. It was very nice meeting you."

Kate quickly exited, her sensible-heeled shoes clicking on the wooden porch. When she got in her car, she saw Melissa watching from the window. Kate waved and smiled, then drove away.

She went around the central green area to park off the street, behind some shops. She put her head down on the steering wheel. It looked like her mother was right, that Aunt Sara was being exploited by some hunk of a guy—and *she* was going to have to deal with it. Was it too late to run home?

She leaned back in the seat and tried to get herself together. *Damn!* she thought. She forgot to get directions to Aunt Sara's house—but then, Melissa hadn't exactly volunteered to tell her. Okay, so she'd explore the town and ask someone. Besides, she shouldn't arrive empty-handed. She needed to buy a thank-you gift. Flowers? Candy? A diamond tiara?

Telling herself to cut the sarcasm, she picked up her map. "Distributed by the town of Lachlan, Florida, courtesy of Kirkwood Realty" was written on the back.

She was on Eden Bay Lane, and The Flower Pot, a florist shop, was nearby. She could get flowers there, and chocolates across the street. But considering her aunt's weight problems, maybe she should get her a book instead. Two blocks away was a large bookstore.

She got out of the car and went to the florist. It was an enchanting little shop and it smelled divine. A young woman helped her choose a huge bouquet of flowers and wrapped them in peach-colored tissue paper. Kate asked her for directions to Stewart Lane but she said she lived in Sunrise and had no idea where it was.

Not far away was a fruit shop, with bins of beautifully ripe fruit displayed in front.

Better than chocolate, she thought. He had baskets for sale and she chose a large one and filled it.

Kate started toward her car with her arms full, the flowers half covering her face. "Weston, Sunrise," she muttered as she walked along the sidewalk. As a Realtor, she'd be driving people around to these places and she needed to know where they were.

As she stepped off the curb, she remembered that she'd forgotten to ask the man with the fruit where Stewart Lane was. Suddenly, there was the sound of squealing brakes. A strong hand grabbed her arm and pulled her back. She jolted hard into a man's body and he caught the flowers and basket before they fell.

Kate turned to see a woman in a car just inches from where she'd been. The driver was angry and yelling, hands gesturing. In the back seat were two wide-eyed children.

"Sorry," Kate said. "Sorry, sorry."

The woman drove past and Kate finally turned to see who had saved her. The man was in his thirties, tall, slim, dark blond hair, blue eyes. Extremely handsome. "I…" she began as she took the flowers from him, but he kept the heavy basket.

"I'm Alastair Stewart," he said.

"Kate Medlar." Her voice was a bit shaky, since she'd nearly been run over by a car. "Thank you so much for what you did, but I should go. I have things to do." But when she took a step, her legs wobbled.

"Allow me." He held out his bent arm for her to take. "I think you need to sit down so you can recover from the dangers of speedy little Lachlan."

She nodded, shifted the flowers that had blocked her view, then took his arm. They crossed the road and he opened a door into a bakery. Inside was a long case filled with delicious, high-calorie, forbidden foods. To the left were tables, several with people looking at them in curiosity.

He led her through a doorway at the side of the bakery to enter an old-fashioned tea shop named Mitford's. Little tables with pink cloths and flowered tea sets filled the sunlit room.

Alastair set the basket on the counter and turned to the woman in the apron. "Bessie, would you please introduce me to this young woman?"

She was short, stout, with a head full of gray curls. "This is Alastair Stewart. Born and bred here in Lachlan. Lived here until the world offered him money and glamour, then he left us to chase after the gold."

Alastair shook his head. "That's not the version I wanted to hear. Just tell her of my sparkling character and my reliability, and that I'm not some unknown vagrant who hits on pretty girls."

Bess's eyes were laughing as she looked at Kate. "He and my daughter used to swim naked together. Remember that time—?"

"No, I don't," Alastair said loudly. He took Kate's arm and led her to a table by a window. "Sorry about that. My intention was to present myself as trustworthy. A pillar of the community, et cetera. And by the way, her daughter and I were two years old when we were skinny-dipping."

Kate sat down, the flowers still in her arms.

"May I take those?" he asked.

She had to look up at him. Way up. He was six-three or -four. She handed him the flowers and he took them to the counter to Bessie. Kate watched them talk, and whatever Alastair said, it made Bessie laugh.

He returned to the table. "I ordered a pot of Darjeeling and a couple of Bessie's orange-peel scones. I hope that was all right."

"Very nice." She could skip dinner to make up for the calories.

For a moment he looked at her in silence, then his eyes lit up. "You aren't by chance Tayla's new employee, are you?"

"I am."

"And your name is Katherine."

"It's just Kate. I was told that when I was born I let out such a yell that my father said I needed taming. As in *The Taming of the Shrew*."

Alastair smiled. "Your father. That would be Sara's little brother, Randal."

Hearing this so excited Kate she almost shouted. "You *knew* him?" She glanced at the other customers. "Sorry. I've never met anyone who knew my father."

"I didn't. He was before my time, but there are people in town who did know him. I'm sure Tayla did. She and Sara were in the same class in high school."

"Were they?" Tayla hadn't mentioned that in her emails.

A young waitress put a pot of tea on their table and two delicious-looking scones. Alastair poured. "So how is Sara?"

Kate hadn't wanted to confide in Melissa, but

Alastair was different. Maybe he'd been right in the way he introduced himself. It was making her feel secure. "I haven't seen her since I was four years old. What do you know about the man who's living with her?"

Alastair frowned. "I hadn't heard about that. What's his name?"

"Jack something."

Alastair's frown disappeared. "That would be Jack Wyatt. That makes sense. How's your scone?"

"Excellent." She was waiting for him to go on, and he seemed to get the hint.

"The Medlars and Wyatts used to live next door to each other. Will you think less of me if I say it was in the, uh, least financially secure part of town?"

"I'm a Realtor. Nothing about houses shocks me." She remembered Tayla saying that Lachlan had a slum area.

"The connection goes back a long way. You said Jack has moved into the house with her?"

"That's what I was told. I'm just worried about my aunt, as she's there alone."

Alastair looked down at his half-eaten scone.

"What aren't you telling me?" she asked.

"I don't like to spread gossip, but my grandfather was a judge. He lived with us, so Mom and I had to endlessly hear about Jack's father, Roy. He was in and out of jail from the time he was a teenager. He fought with everybody, had problems with drugs and alcohol. He nearly drove my grandfather mad. Roy died a few years ago when he wrapped his truck around a tree. I've never heard that Jack is like him, but just recently—" He stopped talking.

"My elderly aunt is involved in this, so I'd like to know about this man."

"Jack was in a car crash and his brother was killed. I heard that Jack was drunk."

Kate fell back against her chair.

Alastair gave a sigh. "Now I've ruined it. You look like you want to leave Lachlan and never return."

Kate finished her cup of tea and poured herself another one. "Part of me wants to run, but another part wants to protect my aunt. She's my only connection to a father I don't remember. But besides family, I have a job here. I like what Tayla has done and she said there's more to do. I want to help."

Alastair's handsome face broke into a slow smile that widened into a grin. "What a day this has been! This morning I was looking into moving back to Lachlan. And now I've met the prettiest girl to arrive here since Elizabeth Taylor passed through in the fifties."

His compliment was so outrageous—and so untrue—that she laughed.

"Wait a minute! If you're going to be living with your aunt, and Jack Wyatt is there, too, I don't have a chance. I don't understand it, but all women fall for him." Bessie was putting a teapot on a nearby table.

"Bess?" Alastair said. "What do you think of Jack Wyatt?"

She rolled her eyes. "Just as scrumptious as his father."

"But without the prison stripes," a woman at the next table said and they laughed.

"Come on, ladies, help me out here. I'm marketing him as ugly and dumb." That comment only increased their laughter.

Alastair turned back to Kate and lowered his voice. "Seriously, I'll help in any way I can. I work with money, so if you have any questions or suspicions, let me know. I'll gladly go over Sara's accounts to see if anything, shall we say, unusual is going on."

Kate nodded. "I'm not so bad with numbers, either. I'll see what I can find out."

"I like you more with every word you speak."

She smiled at him. "You don't have to worry about this guy Jack and me. I've never been attracted to the leather-jacket, motorcycle-riding type of guy."

"Then I do have a chance?"

"Maybe."

"I'll take that. Could we have dinner on Saturday night?"

"That would be nice."

He paid the check and she noticed that he left a generous tip. Just as he said about her, she was liking him more with every minute.

They went to the counter, Bessie handed the flowers and the basket to Alastair, and they left.

"Where's your car?" he asked. "I'll carry these to it."

They walked together the half a block to Kate's car and put everything in the back.

"Where to now?" he asked.

"It's time to meet my aunt. I'm not sure how to get there, since the GPS in my car told me Stewart Lane doesn't exist."

"The house and lane are right where my grandfather built them."

"Oh." Kate was embarrassed that she hadn't connected the names. "I've heard the house is beautiful. It must have broken your heart to sell it."

"Not at all. Seventy-five hundred square feet to maintain is not my idea of paradise. Carved moldings, marble floors, fifty-pound solid doors and— Are you all right?"

She was smiling in a dreamy way. "The house sounds wonderful!"

"My mother thought so. I had a hard time persuading her to sell it and move into a condo near the ocean. She says she hates it but it's very nice. Clean."

"I bet I've sold twenty just like it."

There was so much contempt in her voice that Alastair laughed. "Just some advice—don't mention the Stewart house to your new boss."

"Tayla?"

"Yes. My mother promised to let Tayla sell the house. But when she got there with the paperwork, Mother had already sold it to your aunt. The entire purchase price—which, by the way, was a healthy seven figures—had been wired into my mother's bank account. And all the papers had been signed."

"And your mother got out of paying Realtor fees," Kate said.

"She did. It seems that when your aunt wants something, she goes after it."

"Or her manager does."

"I didn't know she had one," Alastair said.

"I'm not sure she does, but according to my mother, Aunt Sara isn't in good health, so I assume she has people to handle those sorts of things. Maybe this guy Jack…" She trailed off in thought again, worried for her aging aunt.

"Sorry to hear that about her health. Too bad my mother isn't nearby to give her tennis lessons. But do let me know what you need." Alastair reached into his pocket and pulled out his cell phone. "Maybe you'd give me your phone number?"

Kate tapped it in for him, he sent her a text and it was done.

His eyes grew serious. "I mean what I say. If you need anything, call me at any time. I never turn my phone off and it's always with me."

"Thank you," she said.

His smile returned and he stepped back. "Okay, I'll pull up in front and you can follow me. That way I'll have ten more minutes with you before you fall into the clutches of the spectacular Wyatt kid."

"He's just a boy?"

"He's younger than me, so that's how I see him."

She smiled. "Young, dumb, ugly. I think I'll recognize him."

"Maybe when I see you again, you can tell me all about what's been done to my family home."

"If I do stay there, I'll invite you in to see the place."

"Alastair!" a tall, big man shouted from the opposite side of the parking lot. "We need to get together."

"Oh, no," he muttered. "My former high-school buddy. He only wants to talk about when we were sports stars. He drinks now and…" He turned. "Can't now, Dan," he called out. "Kate and I are going to my house." He looked back at her.

"That sounded like you and I are a couple."

Alastair smiled. "I thought I did rather well with that bit of subterfuge. That makes one fewer male I'll have to fight to win you—not that Dan stays sober long enough to do battle." He waved his hand in dismissal.

"I'll get my car. How about if you follow me around town for a look at my beloved Lachlan?"

"I'd like that. Lead on!"

THREE

KATE FOLLOWED ALASTAIR IN HIS SLEEK blue BMW out of the downtown into the suburban area. It was pristine. Pretty houses with even prettier gardens. The houses all had a Florida flavor: porches, verandas, a strong Spanish influence. Big trees, especially palms, moved in the breeze. Here and there were small specialty shops. There was a café with outdoor tables under umbrellas. She could see why people who lived in busy Fort Lauderdale would come here to spend an afternoon and leisurely shop and dine. And, of course, tourists would love to see a glimpse of "old Florida."

Even though they weren't going on a direct route, she tried to memorize the street names—work was always on her mind. On the floor of the passenger side of her car was a box of business cards she'd had printed.

It would be presumptuous to hand them out before she'd met Tayla, but she'd been tempted in the tea shop.

They drove down Coral Gate, Palm Bay, then around Lime Key Circle before finally turning onto Stewart Lane. Kate saw why her GPS hadn't listed it. It was so private that the US Postal Service probably classified it as a driveway.

There was what looked to be a tiny guesthouse at the end of the road. Past it, the main house was nestled behind old, tall palm trees. To someone who'd survived many Chicago winters, it was an exotic landscape.

As Alastair drove slowly around the paved, circular drive, she saw him watching her in his rearview mirror. No matter what he said, he must have felt bad at losing his ancestral home.

It was a truly beautiful house—long, low and as Spanish as if it was in Barcelona. There was a bay with round-topped windows at one side, a magnificent front door with huge iron handles and more tall windows at the far end.

Alastair stopped his car but stayed inside. Kate turned off the ignition, got out and went to him.

He rolled down the window. "I'll leave you here. Everyone in town knows that Ms. Medlar likes her privacy. You don't enter unless you're invited."

She thought how all the stories of rich old women being bamboozled by their employees involved isolation. "Thanks for telling me. And wish me luck."

"That I do. Looks like they're expecting you. The front door is open."

She looked toward the entrance and saw a three-inch gap left by the open door.

"So it is." She stepped back from his car.

"Mind if I call you tonight to see how things went?" he asked.

"Please do."

He smiled at her in encouragement, then slowly drove back down the drive. Kate got the flowers and fruit out of her car, went to the front door, straightened her shoulders and rang the bell.

No response. She waited, did it again, waited. Still no one.

Tentatively, she pushed the door wide-open. "Hello?"

She stepped into a beautiful foyer with a triple tray ceiling. A crystal chandelier hung above a marble floor that was a swirl of cream and pale coffee. She put the flowers and fruit basket on a stone-topped table that was against the wall.

In front of her was a pretty living room with a big blue Oriental rug, double couches of light blue and two chairs in navy toile.

As she stepped forward, what struck her the strongest was the light. In every direction she looked, there were floor-to-ceiling windows. Outside were palm trees and a wide body of water. Beautiful! To her left was a hall with a skylight. To her right were closed double doors that she thought probably led to the master suite.

Was her aunt Sara in there? Possibly with a caretaker? Or maybe a nurse?

The house was silent but it didn't feel empty. But then, with that much light, it couldn't feel anything but part of the world.

She went toward the hallway, walking quietly. She knew she was snooping but her love of houses was an irresistible force. There was a dining room with an antique table, and chairs upholstered in a pretty print of flowers and vines.

The kitchen was big and cheerful. From the appliances and the trays full of oils and the giant spice rack, it looked like someone liked to cook.

Across from the kitchen was a glass wall that enclosed a breakfast table. The view was of a big swimming pool and a paved courtyard, plus a screened-in area.

Open to the kitchen was a large family room with a TV the size of a highway billboard. There was a huge couch with colorful pillows.

To the left was a pair of open double doors. "Is anyone here?" she asked.

When there was no answer, she went into what appeared to be a suite, possibly the one her aunt said would be Kate's. One end of the living room was all glass and looked out to see a bit of lawn and the pretty canal. A gray-green iguana that had to be six feet long was lying under a clump of palms. Near him were four smaller bright green lizards. Two long-legged white birds—the kind she'd seen only in zoos—were pecking at the grass. They all turned to look at Kate, seeming to ask why she was in their territory. Unafraid, unmoving.

"Well, Kate," she said aloud, "you're not in Kansas anymore."

Down the hall, she passed two walk-in closets that flanked a bathroom tiled in shades of cream. At the end was a bedroom with a white bed with a light blue spread. The French doors at the far end had blinds on them. When she lifted one, she saw a walled courtyard. Very private. It had a brick-paved floor, and there were big flower beds full of plants that in Chicago could only be grown indoors. In the center was a fountain with a dark green sculpture of a girl dancing in the rain. It was so pretty that it took her minutes to take it all in. This courtyard was off what could possibly be *her* bedroom.

In the far corner was a raised flower bed filled with thick palms that had long, slender tendrils. Below it, in the shade, was a man in a T-shirt stretched out on a chaise longue. He had in earbuds and a light blanket covering his legs. His eyes were closed.

She was sure he was Jack Wyatt—and it was easy to see what people seemed to like about him. Black hair that was on the long side, black whiskers, sharp cheekbones. He did indeed look like a very handsome criminal.

Not her type at all.

When she opened the door, it made no sound, but that didn't matter. If he hadn't heard the doorbell over whatever he was listening to, he wouldn't hear a door.

As soon as she stepped outside, she heard an odd sound, like something pounding. She couldn't identify it.

As she walked toward the man, she wondered what to say to him. *Are you exploiting my aunt? Taking the poor woman for all she's worth?* Not a good introduction. She needed to find out the truth before she started making accusations.

When she was two feet away, he turned to look at her. He had very dark eyes. "You must be Kate. Sorry I didn't make it to the door." He removed the earbuds. "But I left it unlocked for you."

The pounding continued. There was a chair nearby

and Kate sat down. "Is this the apartment I'm supposed to take?" She motioned to the doors.

"Yeah. You like it?"

"Very much."

"Sara will be glad. She drove everyone mad planning it. You have any trouble finding the place?"

"I met Alastair Stewart in town and followed him in my car."

Jack gave a little smile. "I heard he was back. Did he ask you on a date yet?"

"He did, actually. We go out on Saturday." Kate settled back in the chair.

Something about the warm, balmy air was peaceful. And oddly, this man made her feel calm—the exact opposite of Alastair.

"I knew he wouldn't waste any time. He's a good guy, though. A little too old and a little too perfect, but he's okay. Who else did you meet?"

"Melissa at Tayla's office."

He gave a snort of laughter. "If you sell houses and get along with Tayla, she'll be jealous."

"She already is—because of you. If you're Jack, that is."

"I am and you're right. She follows me around town. Who else?"

The pounding kept on. It wasn't a regular rhythm. It went fast, stopped, then slowed. "Bessie at the tea shop."

"She loves all things Stewart. Thinks they're royalty."

"I can see that." Kate closed her eyes and held her face up to the warmth.

Contrary to what she'd dreaded, she felt like she was

talking to someone she'd known for a long time. "How is my aunt?" She prepared herself to hear the worst.

"Sounds like she's doing well."

"What does that mean?"

When he looked at her, he seemed to be puzzled by her expression. But then he turned back to face the fountain. "Today she's hitting something besides me."

"Oh." Kate's eyes widened. "Does she hit you because of her bad temper?"

Jack looked shocked. "Bad temper? What in the world have you been told about her?"

Kate didn't answer.

"I know that look! It's just like hers. You aren't going to tell me, so you'll just have to go and meet her for yourself. Go back through those doors and out through the living room. I'd go with you, but—" He tossed the blanket back to expose his left leg, which was in a cast that reached above his knee.

His drunken car wreck, Kate thought, but didn't say. She went through the apartment, then outside past an outdoor kitchen. The swimming pool was in front of her and to the right—under the deep roof overhang, she saw a woman from the back. She was wearing red boxing gloves and slamming away at a big leather bag. Her pounding reverberated through the house.

The woman was short, trim and obviously strong. She had blond hair that was wet with sweat in the back. Who was this? she wondered. A caretaker for her aunt Sara?

Kate was about to speak when one of the sliding doors between her and the woman was thrown open.

Jack stood there, leaning on crutches, and he was looking at the woman. "Juan just called and that big poinciana came down. I have to go see about it. You want to shoot it?"

"Damn right I do! Oh." She saw Kate and halted, staring at her.

Jack hobbled to the woman—he wasn't good on the crutches—and she held out her arms so he could pull off her big boxing gloves. "Kate, Sara. Sara, Kate." He looked to Kate. "You wanna go with us?"

"You're Sara?" Kate asked. The woman was older but she certainly didn't look to be in her late sixties. "But I thought… I mean…"

Sara nodded. "Ava told you about me, right?"

"Yes. She said—"

"Can you two do this later? If that tree hit the roof, I need to get the men to fix it. It might rain today."

"It's Florida," Sara said. "It's always about to rain. Maybe Kate wants to freshen up or maybe I should stay here so we can talk. Or—"

Jack turned his back on them and started into the house. "Stay here and write a novel about it for all I care. I'm going to go see the damages. I bet those roots are huge. I'll take some cell-phone photos for you."

"Cell phone! You blasphemer," Sara called out, then looked at Kate. "If you want to stay here and get acquainted, we can."

"Houses, fallen trees. They're right up my alley," Kate said. "Let's go. We have plenty of time to catch up."

Sara's eyes lit up and she smiled big. "Wait for us," she called after Jack. "I have to get my camera."

"I'll wait five minutes," Jack replied from inside the house. "Then I'm leaving."

"It'll take him ten minutes to get into the truck."

Sara hesitated only a second, then started running into the house.

Kate didn't know whether to follow her or try to find the garage. She went after her aunt.

The double doors leading into Sara's bedroom were open, so she followed her aunt in. To the right was the bathroom and Sara's voice came from there. "I've got to peel off these sweaty clothes. Would you get my camera? Everything is in that black backpack by the bed."

Kate went into the bedroom, which was all soft blues and pale greens, with an off-white carpet. There was a glassed-in sitting area that looked out to the canal.

"Done!" Sara said from the hall.

She had on black pants and a pink polo shirt, and she looked good. Kate grabbed the camera bag and hurried into the foyer.

Jack had dropped the flowers into a vase full of water. He was leaning on his crutches and rummaging through the fruit basket Kate had brought. He held up an orange in an almost threatening way. "This is the basis of our Florida economy."

"Quit complaining and let's go," Sara said. "Or are you waiting for me to pick you up and put you in the truck?"

"There are some women who'd like that." Jack was stuffing the pockets of his baggy pants full of fruit. "I'll save these for later and maybe Kate will want some."

"If you want a bunch of bananas or whatever," Sara said, "you could always go to the grocery and get some."

Kate was standing back and watching them. Nothing could be more different from what she'd expected.

Jack didn't seem like the predator she'd thought he was, and her aunt Sara didn't seem anywhere near ill or senile. She certainly wasn't overweight, as Kate had been expecting. And she didn't appear to have lost any of her intelligence.

But it was too early to make conclusions. Jack had opened the garage door to reveal a Chevy pickup so ratty it looked like it had been used to haul gravel for state roads.

Sara opened the passenger door. "You get the middle."

"That's so she can shoot out the window." Jack tossed his crutches into the back, then struggled to get up and into the cab.

Kate scrambled in and Sara took the other side.

As he pulled out, the three of them were silent—and it was awkward. There was such a newness about them, a feeling of knowing so little about one another that they couldn't begin. *I was born in...?* Did she start there?

"So," Kate said, "are you two lovers?" It was such a ridiculous question that she hoped to make them laugh. But when they were silent, she began to wonder if her sense of humor wasn't the same as theirs.

Sara was the first to laugh, then Jack gave a chuckle.

"I'm more like his babysitter," Sara said with a grin, and Kate was pleased.

"Hey—you want me to move out, just let me know," Jack said.

"Then who would eat all the fruit?" Kate asked.

"Oh, no," Jack groaned. "There can't be *two* of you. I didn't think the world could hold more than one."

Kate stared at his profile.

"Two people who make jokes about everything," he explained.

"When you grow up without humor, you need to make your own." The second she said it, Kate knew it was a mistake. Too serious, too soon. What was the matter with her today? She needed to change the subject quickly. "So where are we going?"

"We bought—"

"We bought—"

Jack and Sara spoke in unison. He nodded for Sara to go ahead. "You're the storyteller."

"We bought six houses before Tayla could devour them and dehumanize them," Sara said. "I'm thinking of parking pickups in front of ours. We'll put plastic in the beds. Redneck swimming pools."

"My job is with Tayla," Kate said seriously, "and I like what she's done with the town."

"So does she," Jack said, nodding toward Sara. "But she and Tayla aren't besties."

"Understatement," Sara muttered.

When Kate looked at her in question, Sara waved her hand. "Old high-school feud that never died."

"At least not from your side," Jack said.

"Anyway," Sara said, "Jack and I are going to design the remodels on the houses we bought and his crew will do the work, then Ivy will decorate."

"Ivy?"

"My half sister." There was a quiet tone to his voice.

Kate started to say something but she glanced at his cast. His brother had been killed in that crash.

Kate's handbag was between her and Jack. When she felt her phone buzz and looked at the ID, she took it out of the side pocket. "I have to take this. It's my mother and she'll worry." *And if I don't answer, she will drive me insane*, she thought.

"Mom!" she said with exaggerated cheerfulness. "How are you?"

Ava erupted loudly, and in rapid-fire. "How are *you*? Has she yelled at you yet? Is she bedridden? Are her servants stealing everything? Do you have a clean room? Maybe you should get an apartment and I'll come stay with you."

To Kate's horror, she could see by the rigid faces of Sara and Jack that they could hear every word. "Mom!" she said loudly. "I'm fine."

"Don't let her bully you. That's what she always did to me. She likes to get her way and—"

Kate knew she *had* to distract her mother. "I met a man. I really like him. He's—"

"Through *her*? I don't think—"

"No!" Kate kept her eyes straight ahead, although she was seeing nothing. She couldn't hang up on her mother. Doing that would send her into a depression. "His name is Alastair Stewart and he's gorgeous. Like a tall blond Viking. You'd really like him."

Ava gasped. "You talked to a stranger?"

"Not until after he'd had people introduce him to me. He grew up here and everyone knows him."

"Wait! Did you say Stewart? Your father told me about them. The family owns that town."

Kate blinked a few times. Her mother *never* mentioned her father in that casual way. "Yes, it's the same family."

"Do you have a date with him?"

"This Saturday. He doesn't live here now but he's thinking of moving back."

"That's good," Ava said. "He'll be a safety net for you when *she* gets too bad."

"Uh, listen, Mom, I need to go. I start my job tomorrow and I need to look over the listings. I love you!"

"Yes, but, Katie, honey, I need to be sure that you're safe."

"I am very safe. Bye, Mom." She touched the button, turned off the sound and put her phone away.

Kate stared out the truck window. She was embarrassed down to her bone marrow. "I, uh, I apologize for—"

"No need," Sara said brightly. "I know your mother quite well. What do you think of this part of town?"

Quite well? Why had she never been told any of this? It took Kate a minute to recover enough to be able to see what was around them. It was difficult to believe that this was part of the perfectly manicured Lachlan that she'd seen. Houses with broken porches, roofs with blue plastic covering holes, weeds, two dogs fighting, crumbling sidewalks. This wasn't the result of a hurricane, just plain old-fashioned poverty.

"This area is where Jack's grandfather and I grew up," Sara said. "We were next-door neighbors."

Jack and Sara smiled at each other across Kate in a way that showed they shared both memories and secrets.

"We're here," Sara said as Jack pulled into a weed-infested driveway. The house was in bad repair but Kate could see its potential. Add a little entry porch, repair the windows, paint…it could be nice.

Sara picked up her big black camera bag, got out of the truck and went past the house to the back.

Kate started to get out but Jack turned to her. He looked serious.

"I don't think you should take more calls from your mother in front of Sara. She doesn't need to hear more of that."

He looked like he was bracing himself for a fight, but Kate said, "I agree. I feel bad that she heard that. It won't happen again."

Jack seemed surprised at her answer, and he gave a smile. "Bet you think this place should be bulldozed."

"Are you kidding? I could make that house so cute that one look at it and you'd turn into a girl."

When Jack laughed, it was so contagious that Kate joined him. She was startled to see Sara in the driveway photographing them through the windshield.

"Don't mind her. She's always doing that. She's trying to replace writing novels with a photography obsession. She needs to be addicted to something." He struggled to get out of the truck and winced when his left leg hit the ground.

Kate got out the other side, still smiling. Maybe it was from a lifetime of dealing with her mother's up-and-down moods, but she was glad that no one was angry at her. Her mother's comments must have stung Sara, but she'd been nice about it.

She followed Jack down the driveway and to the back of the house, then halted when she saw the tree. It was huge. Not big—enormous. It was on its side, delicate greenery spread on the ground. It was lushly covered in beautiful red blooms. The wide, shallow roots were standing upright, taller than a person. Sara was moving around it, taking what seemed to be a thousand photos.

"Shame." Jack was looking at the tree. "I knew it was in bad shape, but still..."

"Even now, it's beautiful."

"It is. But the rain and disease were too much for the old lady." He turned. "At least it missed the house. Small favors."

Sara returned to the roots and the wide, deep hole it had made. "Kate, would you mind stepping down in there so I can get a size comparison? I'd ask him, but..." She shrugged.

"She wants you because you're smaller than me, so the thing will look bigger," Jack said. "She likes dramatic photos."

Kate replied before Sara did. "More likely, you're so clumsy that you'd fall face-first into the roots. We'd have to use a block and tackle to get you out." She had to almost jump down into the hole, as it was deeper than her knees.

Sara was looking at her niece oddly, as though she couldn't believe what she'd just said.

"You're ridiculing a wounded man," Jack said. "Before this—" he tapped his cast "—I could pole-vault that thing."

Smiling, Kate started through the mud but it was so deep that it went over her sandals. She pulled them off, then tossed them toward Jack. He caught one—and got mud over his hand and arm. "Thanks a lot, Red."

She blinked at the nickname, even though it was a familiar one. Red-haired people were always called Red by someone.

While Jack was hobbling away to get the other sandal, Kate moved closer to the roots. On the last step, the mud sucked at her bare feet and made her fall forward. She barely missed having her face smack into the tree roots. As it was, her movement loosened a bunch of dirt and gravel. She crossed her arms over her head to keep from getting hit as it poured down the slope.

With the giant tree root behind her, she stepped back until she could feel it touching her. More dirt and gravel fell. She looked at Sara with her camera. "I hope you can do this fast or I might find myself buried in here. My hair is already caught on something." She reached up to loosen it, but it was wrapped tightly. Whatever was holding it didn't feel like a tree branch, but was smooth and hard.

"I'm very fast." Sara clicked, then stepped to the left. Suddenly, she stopped, moved the camera from her eye and looked at Kate. "Stand right there and don't move." Her voice sounded as though she was warning someone crossing a minefield.

"Is everything all right?" Kate asked.

"Don't move!"

Jack had picked up Kate's other sandal. At Sara's tone he pivoted on his crutches to look at her, then stared, wide-eyed, his face drained of color. "Stand very still," he said softly. There was a tone of reassurance in his voice, one that said, "Trust me."

Kate obeyed both of them. She froze where she was. Rigid.

She watched as Jack moved to the edge of the pit and seemed about to climb inside it.

"You can't—" the women said in unison.

Jack didn't take his eyes off Kate and plastered on a smile of reassurance. "You're too small to go." His words were directed at Sara. "The mud would swallow you whole, so I'm going."

Kate didn't move as Jack made his way toward her. He stopped inches in front of her, put his muddy crutches under his arms and reached out to her hair.

He said, "I'm going to untangle you," as calmly as though whatever was holding her was an autumn leaf.

Sara had her phone out and placed a call. "Daryl, you need to come here now." She gave the address. "Yes, *now*!" She listened. "I don't give a damn where you're going tonight or how many medals they pin on you. *Now!* Got it?"

Kate was looking at Jack, his face inches from hers. He had a hand on each side of her head, his fingers getting her hair away from whatever was holding it. "You forgot to shave this morning."

"It's not Sunday. I bet Stewart shaves every day."

"Of course." She was trying to keep her voice from shaking. *What* was in her hair? A snake? Some giant Florida bug? Every Indiana Jones movie ran through her mind. It couldn't be an alligator, could it?

"There," Jack said. "All done."

"Did you kill it?"

"That was done by someone other than me."

"What does that mean?"

He turned on his crutches, expecting her to follow, but Kate looked back at the tree roots and gasped. Where her hair had just been tangled was a human skull and near it was another one. There were other bones protruding from the dirt. Two entire skeletons were exposed. The big tree had wrapped roots around the bones like loving fingers holding them to her.

"Jack," Sara said.

He looked back at Kate, took a step toward her.

He handed her a crutch, then put his arm around her shoulders. "Would you mind helping me out of here?"

She knew he didn't need help but her heart was pounding so hard she was glad for his steadying arm.

With Jack's crutches, his unbending leg and Kate's bare feet, it made slow going in the mud. When they got out of the hole, Kate sat down and cleaned her hands on the grass. Jack sat beside her.

They were both staring at the skulls and bones embedded in the tree roots. It was an eerie sight. The tree seemed to own the bones, to hug them, caress them... protect them. If someone tried to remove them, the tree looked as though it would swallow them whole.

Sara came to stand behind them, her camera constantly clicking. She paused only to change batteries. "Daryl is on his way." In the next second they heard a siren in the distance. "Damn him! He'll have the whole town coming to see what's going on."

"Who were they?" Kate whispered, her eyes on the bones.

"No idea," Jack said. "It looks like the tree was planted on top of—of them."

Sara sat down beside Kate and held out her camera. "Look at this." She had enlarged the playback on the screen to show the skull that had been tangled in Kate's hair. "Is that what I think it is?"

Jack took the camera and he and Kate put their heads together to look at it. "There's a hole," Kate said.

"In the side of the skull. Looks like it was hit with something," Jack said.

"Could have been the tree," Kate said.

Sara and Jack looked at her. None of them believed that.

Jack frowned. "The two of you aren't going to turn into scream queens, are you?" He held up the camera. "If so, quick! Show me where the video is so I can put you on YouTube."

"Not funny," Sara said. The siren could be heard at the front of the house and was then turned off. "Sheriff's here."

Kate got up and helped Jack with his muddy crutches, and they walked to the front.

A dark-green-and-white car, Broward County Sheriff's Department, Lachlan, Florida, painted on the side, was parked beside Jack's old truck.

A man wearing a tuxedo got out. He was fiftyish, medium height, sparse hair, a belly. He was frowning so deep his face was scrunched up. "I'm supposed to be in Miami in thirty minutes. This better be good." His voice was a growl and it was aimed at Sara.

"It is," Sara said. "Come and look."

As he walked past Jack, he said, "You managing to stay sober, Wyatt?"

Kate saw Jack's face turn to such rage that he looked like he might hit the sheriff. She stepped between them. "Hi! I'm Kate, Sara's niece. It was so kind of you to come here to see what we found." She slipped her arm through his tux sleeve. "You make me feel like we're going to a party."

It took the man a moment to change moods, but he smiled at her and put his hand over hers. "You must be Randal Medlar's daughter."

"I am." She was startled at hearing the name, but she smiled as warmly as she could manage. When they reached the edge of the hole, she dropped his arm.

Sara was looking as though she might start laughing

at what Kate had done. But Jack was glowering like a villain in an action movie.

"There's the problem." Kate motioned toward the tall tree roots.

Daryl stared at it, seeming to be unsure of what he was seeing. But after a moment, he looked at Sara. "Somebody planted a tree over an old burial ground. Happens all the time. I'll send the coroner over tomorrow to remove the bones and rebury them somewhere." He turned away as though he meant to leave.

"One of the skulls has a hole in it," Sara said. "Like someone was hit over the head with a weapon."

"Sara." The man sounded as though he was talking to a child. "You aren't trying to make this into one of those books you write, are you? *Love Under the Tree Roots.* Something like that?" His face was a smirk.

Jack, his anger now under control, was standing by Sara. When she started to speak, he clamped a hand onto her shoulder.

The sheriff straightened his cuffs and looked back at Kate. "I think I should introduce myself. I'm Sheriff Daryl Flynn. My mother was a Kirkwood."

Kate could tell this meant something locally. "Like Tayla," she said. "I work for her."

"She's my mother's cousin and she's been good for this town. You're the girl that Alastair Stewart asked out, aren't you?"

Kate nodded, amazed at the speed of the local gossip.

"That's good. A pretty girl like you might make sure he moves back here. He'd give this town back its sense of class." He cut his eyes at Sara. "Too bad about the house being taken away from the family."

Kate drew in her breath. No house was "taken" from anyone.

"You didn't hear?" Sara said. Jack still had his hand on her shoulder. "I'm planning to give the house back to him because he's, you know, a Stewart and I'm just a Medlar. It will be my honor to do so."

The sheriff looked like he wasn't sure if she was kidding or not. "I have to go. I'm to give the toast tonight, so I can't be late." He took Kate's hand and held it with both of his. "You'd do well to stick with a Stewart." He gave a quick look at Jack, making it clear who she was to stay away from. "A connection with a Stewart might mean you could make something of yourself in this town."

Kate gave a girlish little laugh. "In spite of the fact that I'm a Medlar?"

The sheriff smiled at that and, still holding her hand, looked at Sara. "You got a smart one here. Catches on fast. You could learn from her." He released Kate's hand and started for his car. "I'll send the coroner—or somebody—first thing tomorrow. Have a good night." He gave a contemptuous look at Jack, got into his car and started the engine.

When Sara made a movement, Jack dropped his crutches to the ground and grabbed her about the waist, her back to his front.

"Let me hit him," Sara said. "Just one good right. Please. What made me come back to this town? It's still high school here."

Jack held her until the sheriff drove out of sight. "Why don't you take some photos inside the house? There's only about an hour's worth of light left."

Sara didn't say anything and went into the house.

"Is she going to be okay?" Kate asked.

"Sure," Jack said. "She just needs time alone to calm down. She's had years of signing autographs and giving interviews, so it's culture shock for her to come back here and be considered less than best. But to be fair to Lachlan, very few of those old-time bigots are left. Unfortunately, one of them happens to be the sheriff."

He went through Sara's backpack and withdrew a small camera. It was black with a silver top and it had dials and buttons on it.

"That looks like something James Bond would use."

Jack grinned. "That's what I thought when I first saw it. But it's modern and it's digital. I want to take some close-ups of those skulls." He looked down at her muddy feet. "Mind helping me?"

"Not at all."

"Not superstitiously scared?"

"Minds like the sheriff's scare me more than bones."

He nodded in agreement as he lowered himself into the big pit, then helped her down.

When they reached the roots, she watched him adjust the knobs and buttons. "I got the idea that you didn't know how to work a camera."

"Please don't tell Sara that I know aperture from shutter speed."

"She'll be jealous?"

"Worse. She'll put me to work. I'll be made into her camera assistant and have to carry fifty-pound bags full of lenses. Last time she told me to shoot something, I left the lens cap on. I said I'd better just use my cell phone. That sends her into a ten-minute lecture."

He picked up his crutches, handed her one, leaned

on the other and began taking pictures. The light was fading fast.

Kate knew he was trying to put humor in the atmosphere after what the sheriff had said, but she wanted to know more. "It seems that you and I, the Wyatts and the Medlars, are the lowest in this town."

Jack gave a smile, but it was forced and there was a muscle working in his jaw. "We are. I grew up with Henry Lowell as my stepfather, but that didn't erase—"

"Your father? Alastair told me about him." She could see that Jack didn't like that and she tried to cover herself. "Alastair had nothing but good to say about you. Except that you were ugly."

Jack didn't smile. "I'm certainly not a blond Viking."

"I exaggerated all that to distract my mother." She lowered her voice. "My mother's memory of Aunt Sara doesn't seem to fit with the way she is now."

"If you thought Sara was a pain, why did you come? For her money?"

Kate cut him a look that made him laugh. "Actually, I wanted to learn more about my father. I only recently found out that he had a sister. Money and being famous had nothing to do with it. And besides, I needed a change. It just all seemed to fall into place at the right time." She paused. "What's that?"

Jack had his eye to the viewfinder. "What's what?"

"There. To your left. Sticking out of the mud."

He looked but saw nothing, but then the light from his angle was different. Kate, still holding his crutch, made her way to the far side. "When we get back, I'm going to soak my feet in a pot of hot water. It'll take hours to get the mud out from under my toenails."

Bending, she used her thumb and index finger to pick up what she'd seen. It was hard to tell what it was. She slogged back to Jack.

"Skeletons don't scare you but mud does?"

"Last night it took me two hours to file and polish my nails, so yes, mud turns me off."

Jack took the thing from her fingers, put it against his T-shirt and rolled it around to clean it. "Sure you didn't drop this when you ran out of here after I untangled your hair? What did you think had you? An alligator?"

"Of course not!" she said much too quickly.

He was obviously amused by that. "They don't climb trees. They—" He looked at what he'd cleaned. In an instant, the expression on his face changed from teasing to pure, unrestrained horror.

"What is it?"

Jack just stood there. Silent and staring.

She had to open his fingers to see what was in them. She held up a gold chain and on the end was a charm that formed the letters *CM*.

"Cheryl Morris," he whispered. "And I loved her." Turning, he started toward the side of the pit.

Four

KATE WAS BEHIND JACK AS HE GOT OUT OF the hole. As soon as he stepped onto the grass, his shoulders fell down. He struggled to walk away from the tree roots and what they contained. But he got only a few feet before he slumped down onto the crutches. If it hadn't been for them, he would have fallen.

She saw his shoulders begin to shake. He was crying. The brother he'd so recently lost and now his connection to what they'd found in the tree were breaking him.

If there was one thing Kate knew about, it was grief. She'd dealt with her mother's since she was four years old. She'd had to learn how to comfort her mother, how to steer her toward the bedroom so she didn't lie down on the floor and curl up.

She didn't know this man well, but she could see

that he needed help. Sara was inside the house, her camera aimed at places that the setting sun was hitting. Kate rapped on the window and motioned for her to come out.

Sara put her arm through her camera strap as she ran to the door.

Outside, she went to Kate, who nodded toward Jack. He was leaning on his crutches and he looked in danger of collapsing. "He knows who it was. Someone he loved."

That was all the explanation Sara needed to make her run to Jack, Kate beside her. The look on his face was something Kate had seen too many times. Grief was an emotion that took over a person's body and mind. It pulled at your soul until it was the only thing that existed. There was nothing else, no one else, just the deep, all-consuming grief.

Sara put her arm around his waist and spread her hand wide on his stomach. It was as if she wanted to take his pain into herself. Her face seemed to age as tears began to roll down her cheeks.

Kate knew Sara's feeling of helplessness. She'd felt the kind of love that wanted to share someone else's pain but couldn't. She put her arm around Jack's shoulders and her hand on his heart. Slow, deep beats. It was as though his heart was trying to decide whether or not to continue. Did it gladly and gratefully give over to that oily, drowning, devouring grayness that was grief? It wanted Jack to say, "Take me. I'm yours. Do with me as you will."

Kate knew it was up to her to direct the two of them. They needed to sit down before they fell. She pulled, pushed, maneuvered. Sara clung to Jack, her small body almost merging with his. Whatever the actuality of their relationship, there was a bond between them that was so strong they were almost one person.

There was a concrete porch and steps at the back of the house and Kate managed to get them there. She helped Jack sit, Sara still clinging to him, and Kate took the other side.

The three of them were close together, tight, bodies mashed side by side, needing the warmth, the sharing of humanness. Needing not to be *alone*. It was going to take some time for Jack to come back to now, back to reality. He had to let go of that pull to another world where pain no longer existed.

As Kate waited, she watched the fading light illuminate the tree in front of them. The sun hit the red blossoms and seemed to catch fire. It was the magnificent tree's last blaze in her long life. Tomorrow she would fade. Tomorrow she'd give up the secrets she'd held inside her for so very long.

The light was red, then yellow, then red again, and the tree was as flamboyant, as spectacular, as any fireworks.

When the show at last died out, Kate could feel Jack's body beginning to strengthen. His soul was returning to his body. The grief was there—would always and forever be there—but for now, it was retreating. She knew that it would return, slowly coming from inside him, to hover and plead. "Come with me," it would say. "Let me take you away from this pain. Let me give you peace."

But for now, the Gray Lady of Grief was retreating back inside him.

Kate reached into her pocket, pulled out the necklace and held it out so Sara could see it. "This was in the mud."

Sara kept her tight hold on Jack. She was the medicine he needed, and until she saw that it had taken effect, she wasn't going to release him.

He pulled his arm from between him and Kate and took the necklace. "Twenty years ago, when I was eleven years old, I gave this to Cheryl Morris for her sixteenth birthday."

Neither Sara nor Kate spoke. This was a pivotal moment. Would he talk? Would he release a piece of what was tearing his insides out?

It was growing dark and the Florida night sounds were beginning. But there was no rush as the three of them sat at the top of the hard, cold concrete steps.

"I don't know why I didn't realize who it was when I first saw the…" He looked at the tree on its side. "But they left town. Everyone said that. Why didn't I know?"

Kate and Sara waited in silence for him to stop accusing himself and go on.

"That winter I was court-ordered to spend every weekend with Roy," Jack said softly. "I lived with the man who was my true father, but Roy was…"

"I know," Kate said. "Biological."

"It was all right because—because…"

Kate could feel him weakening.

Sara sat up straighter and took Jack's hand. "Because Evan was there. He was about seven then, wasn't he?"

"Yes. But he wasn't there that summer. Krystal and Roy were fighting, so she'd taken my brother to her parents in Colorado."

Kate guessed that Krystal was Roy's second wife and Evan's mother.

"I was bored and alone," Jack continued. "Roy was always working on cars, and always angry at me because I wasn't interested in them. I was, but I didn't want to be around his constant belittling of me. I rode my bike to get away from him."

"To here?" Kate asked.

Jack took a while to answer. "Cheryl is why I wanted to buy this house." He looked at Sara. "It took me a year and lots of lawyer hours to get it. Remember?"

"Yes," Sara said. "I told you to give it up but you wouldn't." She paused. "What was Cheryl like?"

"She was the prettiest girl in our school. Petite and blonde, with big blue eyes. And she was nice to everyone. And really smart. People liked her." He took a breath. "She used to say that I saved her life."

He looked back at the tree, the blazing color now gone. The approaching night had taken away its last bit of spirit. "I was riding past her house and I heard what I thought was a scream. I went to see what was wrong."

Jack shook his head in memory. "This place always was a dump. The landlord was a bastard. Squeezed a penny until it squealed. There was some dangerous iron equipment in the back. Farm machinery, I think. Rusted and sharp. Cheryl had been hanging out clothes to dry when the pole gave way. She was tangled in the rope and the pole was across her legs. She couldn't get out."

"You saved her," Kate said.

"I wanted to think so," Jack said. "Roy had been on my case that morning telling me I was a worthless piece of crap, so I needed to feel like a hero. Cheryl invited me in once I'd freed her and gave me lemonade and cookies."

With every word he spoke, Jack seemed to regain energy. The pleasant memories were replacing what they knew had happened to the young woman.

"We became friends," he said. "Her mother was always gone and I wished Roy was, so we spent most of the summer together." Jack gave a snort. "And I was young enough that she considered me safe. Cheryl was so pretty that all the guys were after her, but she refused to go out with any of them—which made them try even harder."

"And, of course, the girls were jealous," Sara said.

"I'm sure they were but I was eleven. What did I know? All I cared about was that for one whole summer, Cheryl Morris, the prettiest girl in school, maybe in the whole world, was *mine*."

"What did you two do?" Kate asked.

Jack lifted his chin. "Cheryl wanted to be a newscaster. Not a journalist. She dreamed of being on TV and 'keeping the world informed.' That's what she called it. We worked on that."

Sara and Kate were silent as they waited for him to continue.

"My dad, my *real* father, Henry, had a video camera. I asked him if I could borrow it and he said yes. Henry was always kind and…"

When Jack trailed off, Kate felt the bad memories threatening to take over. She guessed that Henry was yet another loved one who had been taken from this man. "What did you do with the camera?"

Jack got himself under control. "Filmed her. She wrote newscasts, read them, and I recorded it all. She wrote tragedies and funny stories, everything. She wrote parodies of the people in town, then did them in accents. I'd laugh so hard I'd fall down. She wanted to learn how to report any story with a straight face."

As he remembered, Jack smiled. "She got really good at it but I tried to trip her up. I used to stand behind the camera and make faces at her. I would switch what she'd written with some comedy routine and see if she could keep from laughing. One time I replaced her story with tongue twisters. She read them perfectly, but afterward she knuckled my scalp so hard it was sore for two days."

"You did love her," Sara said.

"Oh, yeah. I did."

Jack held the necklace out on his open palm. "Her birthday was just days before school was to start. I asked her what kind of party she was going to have. That made her laugh. She said that people like her never had birthday parties."

He paused. "I knew what she meant. She had the kind of life I would have had. But my mother had the good sense to divorce my worthless father and marry Henry Lowell. Men like Roy Wyatt didn't waste money on birthday cakes for kids."

"So you gave her a party?" Kate asked.

"I did." He smiled. "I wanted to buy her an engagement ring but I thought it was a bit early for that."

"A tad," Kate said. "You got her the necklace?"

"Yes. I used all my savings from years of grandparent gifts and went to the local jewelry store. Mr. Hall was selling necklaces with initials on them." Jack chuckled. "I had a hard time deciding if I should give her my initials or hers. Mr. Hall persuaded me that my young lady would probably prefer her own name around her neck."

"Did you have guests at the party?" Kate asked.

"Absolutely not! When it came to Cheryl, I was totally selfish. Just us. That's all I wanted. I bought a little cake from the bakery but didn't put a name on it. The women there were curious, so I said it was for my father."

Jack closed his eyes for a moment. "Cheryl and I sat right here, on these steps, and had our own little party. She loved the necklace and said she'd wear it forever. I made a video of her cutting the cake. She acted like it was a newscast." He held up his hand like headlines. "'Cheryl Morris's sixteenth birthday rocks the world. World peace is declared.' She was very funny."

Jack's voice had a catch in it. "What happened was all my fault. I think the bakery told Roy that I'd bought a cake. Whatever happened, he came looking for me. I was so excited about her birthday that I'd left my bike at the front of the house. Roy saw it."

He hesitated. "Cheryl and I were eating cake and laughing when Roy showed up. He was a real a-hole. He'd had just enough beers to put him in the stage of ridiculing us. A few more and he would have been using his fists."

"He made fun of you," Sara said. It wasn't a question.

"He humiliated us. Said we were fooling around with each other. He…" Jack let out a breath. "At the time, I didn't know what he meant, but I remember his words. He said that it looked like Cheryl was going to be just like her mother. He looked her up and down and said he'd sure like to be her first customer. Then he looked at me and said that maybe it was too late to be number one."

"Yeow," Kate said. "Nasty!"

"Roy was," Sara said. "He never missed an opportunity to hurt someone."

"Cheryl ran into the house and slammed the door. Roy…" Jack took a moment to calm himself. "When he left, Roy backed his truck over my bike. He said he had enough problems without me knocking up the town slut's daughter. He said I was never to see her again."

Kate swallowed. "And all this when you were eleven years old."

"What happened after that?" Sara asked.

"I called my mom and she came and got me. I said I never wanted to see Roy again. When Cheryl didn't show up at school, I thought it was because of me. The next Saturday, I walked to her house."

"But she wasn't here," Sara said.

"The storyteller knows." Jack affectionately kissed the top of her head. "Cheryl and her mother were gone. The house was locked but I could see that the inside was a mess and it was empty. I walked all the way to the sheriff's office and told old Captain Edison that my friend had been kidnapped."

"He was a nice man," Sara said.

"He was," Jack agreed. "The deputies were laughing at me, but Captain Edison treated me with respect. He let me ride in the front seat of his patrol car and we came here, to this house. I don't remember how he did it, but he got the door open and we went inside. The house had been ransacked. Clothes, personal items, kitchen things—they were all gone."

"What about Henry's camera?" Sara asked.

"Gone. Captain Edison told me that sometimes there were things in adult's lives that made them need to leave a place quickly. He figured that's what happened here. And he said that Roy had…" Jack stopped talking.

"What did he do?" Sara asked.

"The captain was kind but I didn't understand it all then. He said that Roy had told him Cheryl was trying to do unlawful things to his underage son. He said Roy yelled that the Lachlan sheriff's department was so busy spying on *him* that they ignored abuse that was going on right under their noses."

"That poor girl," Kate said.

"That sounds like something Roy would do," Sara said. "He always said that everyone was worse than he was—but they weren't. Did he spread gossip about young Cheryl?"

Jack took a deep breath. "Probably so, but no one said anything to me. I think gossip was why Captain Edison thought it made sense that they'd left town in a hurry."

"What happened after that?" Kate asked.

"Nothing—except that my life changed. I told Dad—Henry—that I'd lost the camera. To pay for it, I started working for him at his construction company. That's when I found out that I loved building things. It was because of Cheryl that I found my life's work. Renewing these old houses has been good for me, and Dad taught me everything. He—" Jack gave himself a few moments to quiet himself. "After Roy died, I found the video camera in the back of a closet in his house."

Both Kate and Sara gasped.

"That means he went back," Kate said.

"To that dear, innocent girl," Sara said.

"I've often thought that *he* was the reason Cheryl and her mother left town."

But Cheryl and her mother didn't leave, Kate realized as they stared quietly at the shadows made by the fallen tree. They had been killed, then irreverently and cruelly dumped into the ground behind their house. A tree was planted over them, hiding all evidence that they had ever existed. No one had discovered them for twenty years. Worse was that no one had even tried to find them. Except for an eleven-year-old boy who was patted on the head and told to forget about a girl he'd grown to love.

"Do you think that Roy—" Kate couldn't finish her sentence. Was it possible that Jack's father had murdered Cheryl and her mother? For that matter, *was* the second skeleton the mother?

Jack said, "I think—" but cut himself off. In front of them appeared three flashlight beams heading for the tree roots. Young voices came to them.

"Kids," Jack muttered, then grabbed his crutches and disappeared behind the big branches toward the beams.

Sara and Kate were left sitting on the porch. "Thank you," Sara said. "No one has been able to get through to Jack since Evan died. His mother and I've tried, but he is one stubborn boy."

"It's the same with my mother. Ever since my father died, she's been grieving." She hesitated. "I'd like to hear about my father."

"Sure," Sara said.

Kate waited but she said nothing else. "Was he—?"

Jack appeared out of the dark. "Flynn told his wife about the skeletons, she called every person she knows and now the whole damn town is planning to come see them tonight. They're bringing coolers full of beer. Like it's some kind of party."

"They'll want to take souvenirs," Sara said. "Small bones that they think no one will miss."

Jack took his cell out of his pocket and quick-dialed a number. "Gary? So you've heard. I want your entire team over here immediately." He listened. "Yes. All of them, and bring the dogs. I want barriers set up, and put up those big motion-detector lights, too. As many as you have. That all? Send someone to buy some more, but I want *you* here fast. Yeah, I'll pay time and a half."

Jack put his phone back into his pocket and looked at Kate. "Gary heads the security team I use for my construction jobs. He's on his way, and his men will be here soon with barriers and whatever else they need." Jack left as fast as he could, wanting to meet Gary at the front as soon as he arrived. And he needed to send any other gawkers away.

Sara got up. "This has been a long day. Do you mind if we postpone talking about Randal until a less hectic time? I'm pretty worn-out right now."

"Of course." Kate stood up. "I have to be at work at eight tomorrow morning, so I need to get some rest, too."

They heard the crunch of gravel, headlights appeared, then they heard Jack talking to someone.

"Do you know how to drive a pickup?" Sara asked.

"Yes."

Sara took Kate's arm and leaned on it. "I think Jack will want to stay here. After all his soul-baring to two women, I think he needs men and dogs and all things male."

Kate smiled. "Probably so. Personally, I could use a meal, a hot shower and a couple of episodes of *Madam Secretary*."

Sara laughed. "Me, too. Let's go home."

Kate liked the sound of that word.

FIVE

WHEN KATE ARRIVED AT THE REAL ESTATE office the next morning, there were a dozen reporters waiting for her, all of them firing questions.

"How many bodies were there?"

"Was it a massacre?"

"Murder or suicide?"

"How long have you known Jack Wyatt? Was he involved in the crime?"

Kate did her best to push through the crowd and get inside.

Melissa was waiting for her at the door with excited eyes. "They were here at six a.m. Did you really find a dozen bodies? Were you *with Jack*? Were you frightened? Did he, uh, comfort you?"

What the woman was saying was so far from reality that Kate couldn't reply. Tayla's office was straight ahead, and Kate wanted to see her friend. She gave a single knock, went in, closed the door and leaned on it.

Tayla had her back to her and was looking at a computer screen of current listings. "Bad, isn't it?"

"Horrible," Kate said.

Tayla turned and smiled. "Nothing like catastrophe to bond people, is there?" She was tall, slim, and had beautiful gray hair. She was a handsome woman, quite regal-looking, and Kate could see why the sheriff bragged that he was "a Kirkwood." They obviously had good genes.

She motioned to the chair in front of her desk. Kate took it, and they looked at each other.

"You look like your father," Tayla said.

"Do I?" Kate's eyes lit up. "I know nothing about him."

"A charmer, a sweet talker. Could get anyone to do anything he wanted. If he hadn't been younger than me, I would have gone after him." She paused. "Now, tell me what caused all *this*?" She waved her hand to indicate what was happening outside the office.

"There were two skeletons in the roots of a tree that came down on one of Jack's properties."

"That's it?"

"Yes," Kate said. She wasn't about to hint that they thought they knew who the victims were.

"So how was Sheriff Flynn?"

Kate remembered that the man was related to Tayla. She needed to be tactful. "He… He, uh…"

Tayla leaned forward. "He's a terrible bigot, isn't he?"

"He's number four. Not even close to my three uncles," Kate said, completely deadpan.

The women laughed together.

"Relatives, right?" Tayla said. "You can't choose them. Was he awful to Jack?"

"Dreadful. Sara wanted to punch him, but Jack stopped her."

"Oh, yes. Her boxing. Jack should have let her. Daryl would have been too embarrassed to tell anyone who hit him." Tayla grew serious. "What are we going to do about these?" She picked up a dozen yellow message slips off her desk. "These are requests for you—no one else will do—to show them houses. But I'm betting most of them are reporters trying to get some one-on-one time to question you. All the media think you and Sara and Jack know a lot more than you're telling."

Kate made her face blank. She'd learned early on to conceal what she was thinking.

Tayla leaned back in her chair. "That's your private life and it's none of my business. I had a couple of houses for you to show today, but under the circumstances I think you shouldn't leave the office. Why don't you spend today going over the local listings? Familiarize yourself with them."

In the last week Kate had been over them so often that she knew the square footage of every house for sale in Lachlan. But she didn't say that. She knew when she was being dismissed. "Good idea." She left Tayla's office and went to her own.

The reporters stayed outside, and when Kate went to the kitchenette, they spotted her and came alive like bees when their hive was disturbed. It was going to be a difficult day.

"And Cheryl wanted to be part of that," Kate muttered as she made herself a cup of tea.

At ten, she finally checked her phone. She'd been too cowardly to do it before but now scrolled through the list of missed calls: reporter, reporter, her mother, Alastair. Four more reporters, her mother, Alastair, three reporters. She wasn't about to return the calls of the reporters and she didn't want Alastair to hear the agitation in her voice.

That left her mother, and Kate knew she couldn't postpone that. She braced herself for hysterics, but there were none. All Ava wanted to know was how Sara was treating her.

Images of tears and laughter ran through Kate's mind. What a lot they'd been through in the last twenty-four hours! *We*, she thought and smiled. She reassured her mother that Sara had been quite courteous. "Mom, did you hear about Lachlan on the news?"

"Oh, yes. Skeletons in a tree, right? Small towns are full of creepy crimes like that. Always secretive. Not like in a city, where they just shoot you out in the open and leave your body on the street where people can find it."

"That's one way to look at it," Kate said, eyebrows raised. "I better go. I'm at work."

"Oh, sure. Make a good impression. Bye."

Kate stared at her phone for a moment. What a truly surprising response her mother had given. But then, her mother had been surprising her a lot lately. And when she thought about it, there hadn't been one of her multiday depressions in months.

Next, she called Alastair, but she got voice mail. "I'm sorry I didn't get back to you, but you may have heard that I've been busy. Today I'm fighting off re-porters. I'll try to call you this evening. Oh. This is Kate Medlar."

At three, Tayla said that a security company had called and Kate was needed at home. By then everyone had given up trying to work. Kate slipped out the back way and ran to her car. She made two wrong turns, but she finally found Stewart Lane—and wasn't surprised to see two armed guards at the entrance to the road. When the reporters sitting there saw her, they jumped up, but the guards waved her through.

The front door was unlocked and she saw Sara sit-ting outside in the shade of her screened-in area. Kate joined her. "How are you holding up?"

Sara put down her pen and notebook. "Not bad, considering. Help yourself." She nodded to a pitcher of what looked to be iced green tea.

Kate poured herself a tall glass and sat down on one end of the couch. "Where's Jack?"

"Getting dressed. He didn't get back until six this morning, took a bath, then went straight to bed. I had to wake him up to tell him that the sheriff's coming at four."

Kate groaned. "Mind if I borrow your boxing gloves?"

Sara smiled. "He won't be alone. Some big shot from the Broward County sheriff's office is coming with him. It seems that they not only have information, they believe they have answers."

"You're kidding."

"Wish I were."

Kate sipped her tea and looked at the pool. It had a big spa at one end.

"Do you swim?" Sara asked.

"Not well," Kate said. "What about you?"

"Not a stroke. When Jack isn't on crutches, he does laps. Sometimes Gil and his son use the pool."

"Gil?"

"Jack's foreman. You'll meet him soon. Everyone will want to meet you. What's that look for?"

"I was thinking how normal all this sounds. Relatives, friends. Steps and halves."

"Not what your life has been like?"

"Far from it," Kate said but then smiled. "Except in college. I *loved* college."

"Me, too!" Sara said. "I—" She broke off when Jack opened the door and came outside.

His hair was wet, his clothes clean, and he was frowning. "Tell me that isn't your sour old green tea."

"It isn't my sour old green tea," Sara said by rote.

Jack poured himself a glass, took a drink, made a face, then sat down on the opposite end of the couch from Kate. "You look tired."

"Thanks," she said. "Hard to believe I don't look my best when the last two days have been so much fun."

"You talk to anyone?" he asked, his eyes on his glass.

"Not really. I just told people about the necklace and how Cheryl wanted to be a newscaster and that your father stole the camera and maybe he killed her. Not much."

Jack was blinking at her, eyes wide.

Sara laughed. "You deserved that. We want to hear what happened after we left last night."

"Nothing," Jack said. "Guys from the county came and I told them Cheryl's name. I gave them the necklace and said I'd given it to her. I told them about knowing her when I was a kid and that we were friends. I thought those were all the facts they needed to know."

"Nothing about Roy?" Sara asked.

"I didn't see any reason to bring him into it."

"Roy might have—" Sara began but then stopped.

"I know," he said sharply. "No, I didn't tell them that they'll probably find out that my biological father is a murder suspect. And I don't plan on mentioning it unless I have to. Is there any fruit left?"

Kate said she'd get the basket. She took her time in the kitchen while making up a tray. Cheese was in the fridge, crackers in the pantry, and the basket was full of fruit. She sliced and arranged it and took it outside.

"This is great," Jack said. "Look what she did." He was admiring the food as if it was a feast. "Mustard. And olives. Okay, so what size ring do you want?" His mouth was full.

"Too late," Kate said. "Alastair has already sized me for a family heirloom."

Jack halted, crumbs on his chin, and stared.

Sara and Kate laughed in unison.

Jack groaned. "Yet again, I find myself living in a house full of women. All jokes are at *my* expense. I'm going to get a beer." He hobbled away on his crutches.

When he was gone, Kate said, "He seems to have perked up since last night."

"Thanks to you. But I doubt if his good mood lasts long. This has hit him hard, and he isn't over Evan's death by a long shot."

"Were there any DUI charges brought against Jack?"

"Why should there be? Evan was driving."

"I thought…" Kate trailed off.

"Jack was in a bar celebrating that he finally got those houses, and he drank too much. He called Evan, his beloved brother, to say how happy he was. Jack was going to get a ride home, but Evan said he'd come get him even though it was after midnight. Evan drove Jack's truck. Jack fell asleep, and…that was it. He woke up when the truck was turning over. Evan was killed instantly." Sara grimaced. "The brake fluid had drained out and Jack thinks it was because he'd driven over some rocks that day. *His* fault."

"I misunderstood," Kate said. "I'm sorry."

"Gossip. It all goes back to Roy. People are waiting to see if Jack is going to be like him."

"He doesn't seem to be headed in that direction."

Sara grinned as though she'd just heard the greatest compliment ever. Jack appeared with a cold can of beer and four kinds of deli meat.

"You need French bread with that," Kate said.

"That's what I say, but in this house, there's no bread and no sugar."

"Whole Foods is on University," Sara said. "Brand-new and big. They let anybody in, even males."

Jack ignored her comment. "So why aren't you looking at your photos?"

"It didn't seem fair to see them first. As soon as we get rid of the lawmen, I think we should put them on the big TV and look at them together."

"Did you tell the county guys that you'd taken hundreds of photos of the site?" he asked.

"Darn! I forgot to mention that. But I'm sure they have a photographer of their own."

Jack looked at Kate. "They won't be as good as our Sara's. Did you try some of this ham?"

"That is hundreds of calories a bite. I'll stick with the fruit."

"Which is all sugar," Sara said. "Might as well be eating cane sugar with a spoon. You should—"

The doorbell rang.

"Thank you, Lord!" Jack said. "Saved from hearing more about fructose and grams of carbs. If this guy gets too boring, tell him about the glycemic index. He'll leave before you even get to the horror of foods that grow underground. The evil of carrots!"

"That's what I have to put up with," Sara said as she got up to answer the door, but she was smiling as she left the room.

"I guess we better go." Jack stood up and finished his beer. "Are you going to play Little Miss Hostess again?"

"Only if you do your bad-boy act and try to start a fight."

"Deal."

They went inside the house to the living room.

Sheriff Flynn and Sara were with a tall man of Cuban descent who was wearing a suit. He was in his forties, looked to be in good shape, and he was holding a laptop computer and a file folder. From the way he stood in front of Flynn, the man was clearly the boss.

"This is Detective Cotilla," Sara said, her face serious as he reached out to shake hands with Jack and Kate.

Cotilla turned back to Sara. "I just want to say, ma'am, that my wife loves your books. I think she has all of them. I had to build a bookcase just to hold your novels."

"Thank you." Sara managed a small smile.

"I guess we should get to it. Could we sit down?" the detective asked. "I have things to show you."

"Would anyone like something to drink?" Kate asked. "We have—"

"No, thanks," Detective Cotilla said. "We won't take a lot of your time." He and Daryl sat on one of the blue sofas, while Jack, Sara and Kate sat across from them on the other one.

The detective put the computer on the table and opened the file folder. "District Chief Edison—I believe that, locally, he was referred to as 'Captain'— kept excellent records and we pulled all of them." He looked at Jack with an intense stare. "You were quite young, so I doubt if you know all of what went on."

"Some of it," Jack said. He was leaning against the cushions, his arms spread across the back, looking as though he hadn't a care in the world. But Kate was close enough that she felt him tense up.

Detective Cotilla held up the folder. "I have copies of the reports that Captain Edison wrote about your case."

"My case?" Jack asked.

"The one your father filed about you," Detective Cotilla clarified.

Jack didn't reply, just nodded.

Daryl Flynn was watching in silence, a smile on his face that was very near to being a smirk.

"Everything is from the summer of 1997. The first report is of Roy Wyatt accusing Cheryl Morris of molesting his eleven-year-old son."

Again, Jack nodded, but he said nothing.

Sara took the paper and Kate leaned toward her to read it. It was written in the police procedural way, telling only the facts, but it managed to convey Roy's anger. Jack had told the same story, but this time, the sympathy went to Roy. He was portrayed as an angry man who was looking out for the well-being of his young son.

Sara handed the paper to Jack, but he didn't take it. She put it on the table.

The second report told of Captain Edison going to the site with a very agitated boy, Jack Wyatt, to check on his "girlfriend." The report told of the house having been cleaned out, as though the tenants had left in a hurry. There was mention of the boy's distress and it was noted that, contrary to what the father had said, the boy didn't seem to have been abused.

"He wasn't abused," Kate said. Jack wasn't defending himself and Sara was silent, so she spoke up.

But Sara put her hand on her niece's arm. "What else do you have?"

Detective Cotilla held out another report. "As I said, Captain Edison was a very thorough man. After the boy—" he glanced at Jack "—came to him, the captain revisited Roy Wyatt. He wanted a clearer picture of what had gone on that summer." He handed the women the pages.

Captain Edison wrote that when he told what he'd found, Roy got very angry. He said that yes, he'd gone back to the Morris house and demanded that Cheryl stay away from his son. He said Cheryl had given him a cock-and-bull story about her and Jack taking pictures of each other. She even showed him a camera that had Henry Lowell's name etched on the side.

Roy said he demanded the return of the camera and all the film that had been shot with it. The young woman gave all of it to him and he left.

The captain said Roy stated that when he returned home he watched the films and was sickened. He wanted to take it all to the sheriff, but he didn't want to humiliate his son by letting others see what had been done to him. But to prove what he was saying, Roy had cut pieces of the videos out and put them on DVD, which he turned over to Captain Edison.

Jack was still leaning back, still refusing to participate in what was going on. But when Sara handed him the third paper, he read it.

They all saw the blood creep up Jack's neck and into his face.

When Kate and Sara leaned back onto the cushions beside Jack, the three of them presented a unified front.

Jack handed the paper to Kate and she put it on the table. Sara nodded toward the computer. "I guess you have the DVD that Roy made."

"Yes, we do." Detective Cotilla flipped open the laptop and turned it on. "Sorry, but there's no sound."

The first video was of an eleven-year-old Jack sitting at a table staring at the camera. He was a *very* pretty boy. Dark hair with curls, thick eyelashes and eyebrows, full lips.

Kate turned to look at him but he was staring at the screen.

They saw the back of a blonde female head go to him and kiss his cheek. When she walked away, her face couldn't be seen, but Jack looked like he was about to melt. Young love was in his eyes. It would have been sweet except for what they knew had happened.

The next clip was a profile of Cheryl. Just her cheek could be seen, but her body was in clear view. She was built! A tight red skirt hugged her curvy backside and showed off her little waist. She had on dark hose and four-inch heels.

She was bending over Jack, who was curled up on the floor. The lack of sound didn't hide the fact that he was saying, "No! No!" From Jack's story, they knew he was laughing, but in the video, it looked like he was begging her to stop—but she wouldn't.

The third clip was the worst. It showed Cheryl sitting behind an old table, talking to the camera. She was pretty, yes, but what made Kate involuntarily suck in her breath was that the girl looked to be in her late twenties, maybe older. She had on a lot of makeup. Her shoulder-length hair had been twisted back into a soft chignon, and she wore pearl earrings. Her white shirt didn't hide her impressive bust.

No one seeing the film would believe she was just fifteen years old.

When she stopped talking, her pretty face turned to anger. Or, actually, rage. She stood up and again they saw the curves of her. No wonder the boys were after her! Kate thought.

The camera recorded her stalking forward in her very tall heels. Her arm shot out.

In the next second, she pulled young Jack into view. She had him in a scissor hold, his head smashed against her breast. She rubbed the top of his head hard with her knuckles. The boy struggled to get away, but she held him and kept rubbing.

The video ended abruptly and Detective Cotilla put down the lid. He waited a moment, then handed Kate the fourth report.

This time, Jack read it with them. Captain Edison wrote that he was disgusted by what he'd seen and he wished Cheryl Morris hadn't run away. He would very much like to arrest her for corrupting a minor. But all he could do was send her photo to a few surrounding states and hope to find her.

After that were five yearly notes saying that there was no news of either of the women.

They put down the papers and looked at Detective Cotilla.

"That's it," he said. "That's all of what happened." He looked at Jack. "I've read your father's rap sheet, and based on what I've seen of his temper, I think he saw the films and he went back. There was probably a fight and it got out of hand."

He waited for Jack to reply but he said nothing. "We know that the mother of this, uh…Cheryl—" he seemed to be sickened by saying her name "—supplemented her income with prostitution. Her daughter didn't have a good role model, but even so, what she did to a young boy…"

As he looked at Jack with pity, he withdrew a business card from his jacket pocket and held it out to him.

Jack didn't take it.

Detective Cotilla put it on the coffee table and Kate picked it up. It was the name and address of a clinic that dealt with adults who had been the victims of child sexual abuse.

"Things like this affect your whole life," Detective Cotilla said with sympathy. "You're what? Past thirty and not married? If you get help, maybe you could—"

Abruptly, Sara stood up. "Thank you both for coming," she said loudly. "We'll keep these documents and go over them." She held her arm out to point them toward the way out.

The detective went to the door, but Flynn held back. He was looking at Jack.

His smirk was gone and he seemed to be sympathetic. "Could have been worse than with that girl. I know a lot of men in this town were waiting for her to follow her mother. Roy told me that—"

Jack came up off the couch, his eyes blazing anger.

Kate stepped between the two men. As before, she put her arm through the sheriff's. "How was your dinner? I bet your speech was enlightening."

The sheriff seemed to be glad for a face-saving way to get away from Jack. He quickened his pace to get to the door. "It wasn't really a speech but the applause was good. It's nice to be appreciated for all I do." He glanced over his shoulder at Jack, who was still standing at the end of the couch.

When they were gone, they went back outside into the lovely Florida weather. Jack started eating, but Kate and Sara just stared into space in silence.

It was all so twisted, Kate thought. It looked like there was going to be no further investigation, which meant that Roy Wyatt's lies were going to win. Based on what she'd seen of the gossip in Lachlan, it wouldn't be long before everyone knew all the facts. Roy's death would end anyone's curiosity about whether he did or didn't do it. It was going to be Jack who would suffer. He'd be labeled as the son of a murderer. Even worse was that it would be said that Roy was right in killing Cheryl Morris. She was the girl everyone thought was so good, but who was actually a child molester. Kate could imagine the videos going viral. There'd be Cheryl dressed up like someone double her age and wrestling a very pretty little boy who kept saying no.

Jack's protests wouldn't drown out a viral video. Besides, didn't victims often side with their abusers?

She looked at Jack and Sara. His jaw muscle was working and Sara's face showed her growing sadness. Kate worried that she might be like her mother and never get out of it.

She took a breath. They couldn't let this beat them. "You sure were the prettiest little boy I ever saw."

Jack looked startled. "When did you see me?"

Sara smiled in a way that let him know she wasn't answering that. "For years, he looked like an angel. But then he reached puberty and he went through a gangly stage. He was too tall, too thin, and he had skin problems. But he turned out rather nice."

Kate looked at Jack like she was a judge in a cattle show. "He's okay now, but the kid… Wow."

Jack's face was beginning to relax. "Cheryl was the beauty."

"Even when I did TV, I didn't wear that much makeup," Sara said. "I can't walk in heels that high."

"She was five foot two and she would have worn stilts if she could get away with it," Jack said.

"The head rub?" Kate asked. "Was that when you gave her the tongue twisters? Rubber baby buggy bumpers? That sort of thing?"

"Yeah. And Peter Piper."

"Roy must have…" Kate didn't want to complete that thought.

Sara picked up a piece of cheese. "He probably went to her house and made a pass at her. Wonder what she did to get him to go away?"

"You can be sure that just the word *no* didn't do it," Jack said.

"I guess the 'cock-and-bull story' she told him was about being a newscaster. And she showed videos as proof." For all that Kate had tried to lighten the mood, she was thinking about what that poor girl must have gone through.

"He took the camera and all the films away from her," Jack said.

"When Roy saw that you'd given her something with Henry's name on it, he probably went berserk," Sara said. "He was always insanely jealous of Henry. Cal told me of Roy's threats and complaints about Henry. Sheer jealousy."

"Who's Cal?" Kate asked.

Jack smiled. "My grandfather. The love of our Sara's life. He's why she puts up with me."

Kate looked at Sara questioningly.

"All true." Sara waved her hand. "That doesn't matter. The problem now is that Jack is going to be the one who is persecuted."

Kate nodded. "He'll have to bear the brunt of the rumors that will fly. A father who is a murderer." She sighed. "And he may be thought to be so damaged that he's impotent."

Jack spit out a mouthful of Sara's green tea. "Like hell I am!"

"I think you might have to prove that," Kate said.

"Anytime you want to, baby," he said with hot eyes.

"Not to me, you idiot, but to the whole town."

"Could you two stop playing a scene from one of my romance novels and think about this seriously?" Sara said.

"Jack *is* going to have this dumped on his head. The question is…what are *we* going to do about this?"

"I don't see anything we can do," he said. "Obviously, I can't stay in this town. But then, I've always thought I'd like Seattle. Or maybe I'll move to New Mexico. High mountain desert."

Kate and Sara were staring at each other. When they seemed to reach an agreement, they looked at Jack.

"Did I miss something? What are you two thinking? Anybody want a beer?"

"Sit," Sara ordered.

Jack didn't move.

She stared at him. "Do you really and truly believe that your father killed two women, buried them, then planted a tree over their bodies? And that he kept a secret like that until the day he died?"

"No," Jack said. "He might get into a bar fight and smash a head, but…" He took a breath. "If he'd killed Cheryl, it would have been by accident and he wouldn't have had the calm calculation that he needed to cover it up. He sure as hell wouldn't have kept his mouth shut."

"Which he had to do," Kate said. "My impression of your father is that he tended toward flamboyance rather than coldly hiding two murders."

"He certainly never planted a tree in his life," Jack said.

"So…" Sara said. "We agree that Roy probably didn't hide two murders and he certainly didn't plant a tree. However, I think that he did do something to that poor girl that he wanted to hide. He was so worried that she'd report him that he tried to discredit her before she told on him. I think that's the real reason he edited the videos to make her look bad."

"You mean he wasn't doing all that to save the honor of his son?" Jack was sneering.

Sara turned to him. "Was Roy good enough with a computer to do that kind of editing?"

"I don't know," Jack said. "Maybe. But you know Donna. She would have helped him bury the bodies. She worked with the parks department and she did a lot with computers."

"Donna?" Kate asked.

"Roy's mother," Sara said quickly.

"Wait," Kate said. "If she was Roy's mother, then she was Cal's wife." She looked at Sara. "If you loved Cal, why didn't *you* marry him?"

"The question we all ask," Jack said. "Everyone in this town wants to know the answer to that one."

Sara shook her head. "Neither of you two could *ever* write a novel. You need to stay on point. If Roy didn't kill Cheryl, *who did*?"

They were silent for a moment.

Jack said, "If I say that *we* should try to solve this twenty-year-old murder—which, by the way, is impossible to do—can we order in pizza?"

"Four kinds of cheese," Sara said.

"Just sauce and a very thin crust for me," Kate said.

Jack took out his cell. "I want everything but anchovies." He called and ordered, then they looked at one another in silence.

"Where do we begin?" Kate asked.

"With her," Sara said. "With Cheryl. What was going on in her life that backfired so much that someone wanted to kill her?"

Jack leaned forward. "Aren't you two forgetting something?" There was no reply. "Cheryl's *mother*. If she's the second skeleton, that is. From the sound of it, she slept with several men in town. Maybe she blackmailed one of them, then got greedy. Wanted more than they were willing to give and they got fed up."

"Are you saying her death was her own fault?" Kate said. "Are you really going to blame the *victim*? It's more likely that one of the slimy bastards who took advantage of her financial problems got scared and did away with her."

"Or that," Jack said.

"You both make good points," Sara said. "So where do you two think we should start?"

"With Cheryl," Kate said.

"The mother, Verna," Jack said. "Cheryl was so young that I believe she was collateral damage."

"Beautiful young girl who was wanted by lots of boys and men but she told them no," Sara said. "That must have generated a great deal of anger. Then there was Verna, who wasn't saying no to any man who had a checkbook."

"Or woman," Jack said.

Kate rolled her eyes.

Sara stood up. "I need a notebook. We have to figure out what we know and what we need to find out." She looked at Jack. "I want you to think back to your time with Cheryl. When you weren't drooling over the girl and/or trying to mess up her work, who did she talk about? Did *any* of those randy boys in high school interest her?"

"None of them," he said.

"She only liked *you*?" Kate said. "A gorgeous fifteen-year-old girl was only interested in an eleven-year-old boy who looked like an Italian castrato? And if you don't know, that's a—"

Jack put his hand up. "Don't translate. I get it. Let me think about this. It was a while ago."

"I'm going to change clothes," Kate said.

"I'm going to get the photos," Sara said.

"And I'm going to enjoy the quiet," Jack said.

Six

KATE WOKE THE NEXT DAY BUT SHE DIDN'T
get out of bed. The sun was peeping through the white
plantation shutters in little gold slivers. She was in
Florida! The state that late-night talk-show hosts liked
to ridicule, but people dreamed of going to. Palm trees
and alligators, lots of Cuban cheek kissing, people
who'd never seen snow.

She could hear voices in the house, so the others
were up and about—and she wanted to see them. She
was still marveling at her aunt Sara. Not at all as she'd
expected! And Jack… Laughter and tears. Far from
boring.

When she heard a pan clatter, she got up. Last night
Tayla had sent an email saying that the reporters were
still surrounding the office. She thought it would be
better if Kate stayed away until after Tuesday, when
this matter would be closed.

They'd been looking at Sara's excellent photos on the giant TV and had taped some photos on the walls. Kate read the email aloud.

"Ask her why the hell she thinks it's going to end by Tuesday." Sara's harsh tone made Kate blink in surprise.

Kate sent an email to ask Tayla if she'd heard anything about the case closing. The reply came right away. Tayla said that the sheriff had decided to bury the skeletons at 10:00 a.m. on Tuesday. She said there would be a short service at the grave site and anyone who wanted to attend could. The two women would be buried at county expense.

The date of "closure" seemed to be proof that there was going to be no further investigation into the murders.

Kate replied to Tayla that she'd be there Wednesday morning, then clicked off her phone. The news had seemed to take the heart out of all three of them. They'd turned off the TV and separated to go to bed.

As Kate dressed in leggings and a tunic this morning, she remembered that they'd declared they were going to investigate the murders. But *how*? Where did a person start? The only police files they had—and all they were likely to get—just about declared that the late Roy Wyatt had killed the women. And that he was a hero who had been defending his young son.

Kate took a few minutes to look at the suite of rooms Aunt Sara had put her in. Her clothes didn't fill even a quarter of one of the two closets. Her bed had a linen headboard, and the sheets and pillowcases were Porthault. The living room was divine, all blue and white, with silver accents. After last night she knew that the pictures on the walls were Sara's photos. Kate's favorite was a sunrise over temples. It must have been taken from a hot air balloon.

She opened the doors into the house. Jack was sitting on a bar stool and eating breakfast, while Sara was moving about the kitchen. The smell of bacon was delicious.

"Good morning," Sara said. "Want some eggs?"

"Sure," Kate said. "Anything I can do to help?"

"Stay out of her way." Jack pushed forward a plate of what looked to be bacon wrapped around cheese sticks.

"Too many calories for me." Kate took the stool next to him.

For a moment they were quiet. Last night's news was hanging over them. Did they let the burial take place and go about their everyday lives? Or did they… Do what? Where did they begin?

"What I want to know…" Jack picked up his crutches and went to the coffeepot. He held it up toward Kate and she nodded. "Is who tore the house apart. When I saw it, it was a mess. Even their toaster was gone."

She took the cup of coffee he handed her, then nodded when he got a carton of milk out of the fridge. "What was the house like inside usually?"

"It was nice. Very clean." Smiling, he sat back down. "The only time I saw Cheryl in jeans was one Saturday morning when I got there early for our newscaster session. She—"

"How much early?" Sara asked.

He gave a sideways grin. "Three hours. Or so."

"Cheryl was a saint to put up with you," Kate said. "Go on."

"I knocked but no one answered. I was about to

leave when she opened the door. I thought she was like a spy because she looked around to see if anyone was watching. Then she grabbed me by the collar, pulled me in and shut the door." Jack ate two more bacon-and-cheese pieces and kept on smiling at the memory.

"And?" Sara asked impatiently.

"Nothing. I thought she looked really pretty."

"As opposed to the way you usually saw her?" Kate asked.

Jack looked from one woman to the other, both staring at him. "That day, she looked different. That's how my eleven-year-old mind saw her. Younger. More like a kid."

"I bet she didn't have any makeup on," Kate said.

"I agree." Sara cracked eggs into a bowl. "Please tell me she didn't wear her newscaster face to school."

Jack shrugged. "Don't know, but she always looked perfect."

Again Sara and Kate just stared at him, waiting for him to go on.

Jack put down his coffee. "Cheryl never looked like the other girls. She didn't wear the same clothes as they did. And don't ask me what she wore. You'll have to get someone else to explain that. My point is that on that Saturday, Cheryl was cleaning her house."

"Where was her mother?" Sara asked.

"I have no idea. I never saw her."

"Not once in the whole summer?" Kate asked.

"She was there, I guess. A couple of times Cheryl said we had to be very quiet because her mother was sleeping. But Cheryl always ran me off when it was time to wake her mother."

"Sleeping during the day because of her night, uh, job," Kate said.

"I guess so." Jack quit smiling. "So back to my original question—who tore the house apart? Who took the toaster that Cheryl had just bought? The pillows off the couch?" He took a drink. "All her clothes were gone. They even took her red makeup case and that was precious to her."

Sara's head came up. "What did it look like?"

"A little suitcase." He motioned with the size.

"Ah, that would be an old-fashioned train case," Sara said.

"Cheryl loved that case. It had all her makeup in it. She bought it at a garage sale and she called it by some man's name."

"Mark Cross," Sara guessed.

Jack grinned. "That's it. She'd say, 'Go get Mark' and I'd take the case to her and she'd fix her face."

Sara and Kate looked at each other.

Kate spoke first. "Why would a mother make her teenage daughter dress up like a…a…all the time? Was she preparing her to follow in her, uh, footsteps?"

Sara put eggs in the skillet. "You ever see that early Brooke Shields movie, *Pretty Baby*? She was a beautiful child and she was literally offered up on a platter to the highest bidder. For her virginity."

"Maybe that's why Cheryl never went on dates with guys her own age," Kate said. "She was being 'saved.'"

Sara grimaced. "Her mother would have had to keep strict control. With testosterone-laden boys all around and Cheryl's teenage hormones, she wouldn't last long."

Kate nodded. "She'd have to—"

"Stop it!" Jack said in anger. "You two sound like Salem witch hunters. You're ready to burn mother *and* daughter at the stake." He glared at Kate. "Now who's blaming the victim?" He didn't wait for an answer because the doorbell rang and he hurried to answer it.

Sara put a plate of scrambled eggs in front of Kate and lowered her voice. "We're going to have to be careful with what we say around Jack. First loves can do no wrong."

"Cheryl's mother was supplementing her income with prostitution. That had to have an effect on her daughter. And Verna slept all day. Drugs maybe? Or alcohol?"

"Possibly. But maybe it was just exhaustion."

"Lucky her," Kate mumbled and Sara laughed. "I was thinking that whoever killed them probably left town. How would we find them?"

"That won't be a problem. If our investigation leads to someone who now lives in Montenegro or wherever, then we'll go there." She looked at Kate. "Then you and I will go shopping in Venice."

"Oh," Kate said, wide-eyed. They heard a man talking to Jack. "Who's that?"

"Gil."

"The foreman?"

"Yes." Sara smiled. "Good memory! I can never remember names. I'm good with faces, but names elude me."

"When you have as many relatives as I do, you have to memorize lots of names."

Sara frowned. "Are your uncles still as obnoxious as they used to be?"

"They get worse every year." She paused. "They want Mom and me to move in with them."

"And let me guess. Your mother's income—and yours—would go into the community pot."

"Exactly," Kate said.

"I think I'm seeing why Ava let you come here."

"It was my decision," Kate said defensively.

"Anyway, Jack texted Gil last night. He thought Gil might have been in the same class as Cheryl and he was. Gil said he'd come over as soon as he got the men started on the job. He—"

She broke off when Jack entered with another man and introduced him.

Gilbert Underhill was shorter than Jack and as pale as Jack was dark. Gil was young but he had little hair, and for all that his T-shirt showed muscle, he had a round, almost cuddly look to him. Kate liked him immediately.

Jack looked at Gil and Kate smiling at each other. "She's taken. Alastair Stewart has stolen her eternal love. She has room for no other man."

"Not true. I'm free for whatever life holds." Kate nodded at the book in Gil's hand. "Is that a yearbook?"

"It is."

She motioned to the stool beside her, the one Jack had vacated.

With an eye roll at his seat being usurped, Jack poured Gil a coffee and got the sugar bowl. It looked like something he'd done before. He took the stool on the end and Sara sat beside Kate.

Jack flipped through the yearbook to Cheryl's class. "There she is!"

Kate and Sara peered in disbelief at the girl he had

his finger on. She was quite plain-faced, with frizzy hair and a look of "Woe is Me, the World is an Awful Place."

"That's Cheryl?" Kate asked.

"No, of course not." Jack turned the pages. "Here's Cheryl."

All the other photos looked like regular kids with bad hair, but Cheryl Morris was perfect. Hair, makeup, smile, pose. Flawless. And *old*. She looked to be in her twenties.

"Wow," Kate said. "I wish I looked that good now."

"I like red hair." Gil didn't look up from the book.

"Do you? You don't think it's too loud? It's my natural color but I was thinking of putting some blond streaks in it. What do you think?"

"I like it just the way it is." Gil turned to look at her. They were very close.

"Do you have to flirt with *every* male?" Jack snapped. "Stewart, Flynn and now Gil?"

Before Kate could reply, Sara spoke loudly. "So who's the first girl you pointed out?"

Jack looked back at the book. "Last night I remembered that one day when I was there Cheryl was washing some girl's hair. I told Gil and he found her."

"Ah," Sara and Kate said in unison.

"*Not* like that!" Jack's teeth were clenched. "Gil, help me out here. These two think only bad of Cheryl."

"That's not true," Sara said. "Her mother, yes, but not Cheryl."

Jack threw up his hands. "What is with you women? You'd be more forgiving if you found out Verna was an ax murderer. But—"

"I do tend to admire Lizzie Borden," Kate said.

Jack shot her a look and continued. "But screwing men for money and you act like she's the devil incarnate."

"She's stealing our strength," Sara said. "She's giving men what they want so other women can't use it to threaten them to take out the garbage. Loose women undermine the only real power women have over men."

Jack started to protest, but then he saw the twinkle in Sara's eyes. "So this is about garbage?"

Sara looked at Kate, then back. "More or less."

When Jack laughed, Sara grinned at Kate. Gil turned back to the book and the plain girl. "Elaine Langley. She married Jim Pendal. They moved away and I haven't seen either of them since high school."

"I knew his dad," Sara said. "Very nice family. I guess. They seemed to be."

Gil turned the pages to show Jim's photo. He was a handsome young man.

No one said what they were all thinking: that girl and this boy were *not* a physical match.

"Elaine was real smart," Gil said into the silence.

"I think *he* is the smart one," Kate said. "A man who can look past the exterior is brilliant."

"Then why are you so worried about the color of your hair?" Jack shot back.

"Because most men *aren't* smart," Kate said.

"I think—" Jack began.

"What do *you* remember about Cheryl?" Sara loudly asked Gil. "And let's move to the couches."

When they were settled, Gil said, "I haven't thought of anything else since Jack called me. Cheryl and I were in the same class, but she was above my league."

"That's hard to believe," Sara said. "You were a football star and your parents live on the west side of town. Cheryl lived—" She waved her hand. "You know."

"Sometimes in school things like that get lost. Cheryl was smart and the teachers loved her. And she wore nice clothes all the time. It was like she lived in a world all her own. She was different from the rest of us."

"Who were her friends?" Sara asked. "In my experience, high-school girls travel in packs. Snarling, sneering, dangerous little packs."

"Were you part of one?" Jack asked.

Sara smiled. "Not at all. I'm an outsider and I've always been one." She looked at Kate in question.

"Sorry. I had lots of friends. Very much *not* an outsider." She looked at Jack but he said nothing. But then, she already knew. Good-looking, athletic boys ruled high schools everywhere.

"Those girls used to scare me to death," Gil said. "But I don't think I ever saw Cheryl with anyone else."

"What about in a couple?" Kate asked. "Boyfriends?"

"Definitely no." Gil looked a bit embarrassed. "Unfortunately, there was a lot of locker talk about her. She was so damn pretty. And that body! I had—" He cleared his throat. "I had a dream or two about her."

"Any actual conversations with her?" Sara asked.

"Only once. I was about fifteen, and we'd had a late football practice. I went to the front of the school to meet my dad. Cheryl was there waiting for her mom to pick her up." He paused. "I was always awkward around girls, but it was just us there. I asked her if she'd go to the school dance with me that weekend." He smiled. "She was really nice. She said she wasn't free, but if she were, I'd be the boy she most wanted to go out with. She said, 'You're my second favorite.' That's when her mother showed up."

Gil shook his head. "Now, *there* was a hard-core mom. She looked at me as if I'd tried to rip her daughter's clothes off. She got out of the car and marched over to me like she was going into battle. I swear that if she'd had a gun, she would have shot me. But then, at fifteen I was six feet tall. Bigfoot in person."

Sara laughed. "What exactly did her mother say?"

"The usual, that she knew boys my age had only one thing in mind and that I'd better *never* get near her daughter."

"What did Cheryl say?" Kate asked.

"Not a word. I still remember my shock at it all. I don't want to brag, but mothers were usually nice to me."

"Why not?" Sara asked. "You were a catch—star athlete, smart, salt-of-the-earth personality."

"You make me sound dull," Gil said.

"You're a single father who works hard," Sara said. "Nothing dull about that."

"Another saint," Jack said. "Tell them about Cheryl's mother. They're interested in her profession."

Gil's face turned a rosy pink.

"It looks like you know about Mrs. Morris's, uh, 'outside job,'" Sara said.

Gil nodded.

"What do you know about it? Especially *who*," Sara said.

"I didn't know about her until later, but back then, my dad told me to stay away from both of them."

"*Both* of them?" Jack said. "What does that mean?"

"I don't know. If Dad were alive, he could tell us, but he's not, so…"

"But you have no idea who she…associated with?"

"None at all." Gil looked at Jack. "I think you should know that there's a lot of gossip around town."

"I know. It's about Roy."

"We were told that he's the suspect, but we don't think he's guilty," Sara said. "But how do you get an alibi for twenty years ago?"

Jack leaned back against the couch. "I bet Grans knows where her precious son was on every day of his life." He looked at Sara. "Why don't you pop over to her house and have a chat?"

"Got a flamethrower I can take with me?" Sara's upper lip was curled.

Kate looked over to Jack, who shrugged. It didn't take much to put together that Sara wouldn't have a close relationship with the woman who was married to the man she loved.

"I think that's my cue to leave," Gil said. "Keep the yearbook as long as you need it, but I don't think it'll be much help. There's just the one posed photo of Cheryl. It doesn't show *her*. When she used to hurry down the hallways, every male in the building would stop to watch her. She really was an unusual girl."

Sara leaned forward. "She had all that male attention but she *always* said no?"

"If she was dating, I don't think it was anyone in Lachlan."

"Who you knew about," Sara said. "On the videos, she could have passed for thirty. Maybe there was an older man. Or a married one."

"I don't think that Verna would have allowed that," Gil said.

"Maybe not," Sara replied. "I wonder if Verna wanted something, and that's why she worked so much."

"Yeah," Gil said. "She wanted her daughter near her forever."

At that, they all drew in their breaths. It was what had been given to both of them.

Seven

AFTER GIL LEFT, THE THREE OF THEM MOVED back to the kitchen together and were silent. Kate ate her eggs while Sara cooked an endless supply of bacon-wrapped cheese sticks. Jack ate them while trying to scratch under his cast.

The words *now what?* might as well have been a neon sign flashing above their heads.

"If we could just find someone who *knew* her," Kate said.

"Who am I?" Jack asked. "The Invisible Man? I knew Cheryl better than anyone."

"Okay, then who hated her enough to murder her and her mother?" Kate said, but Jack had no answer.

"Or loved them enough." Sara slid another pan full of bits onto Jack's plate.

"Love. Hate. They're the same deep level of emotions."

"I think it had to be love," Jack said.

Sara halted, the granite-topped counter between them. "We can talk to Elaine Langley, but Cheryl seemed to be such a loner that I wonder if it will lead anywhere. But *someone* must have known them. People don't live in isolation in this town—or anywhere, for that matter. All we've looked at is the school. Who lived in the houses around theirs?"

"They were rentals," Jack said. "Two-week snowbirds. In and out. Nonpaying visitors."

"What does that mean?" Kate asked.

"August heat is the price Floridians pay for the perfection of February. Snowbirds are people who show up just during the winter. They get the good without paying for it."

"But then they go away," Sara said quickly. "We need to find people to talk to. Who might have known them on an *adult* level?"

Jack popped another bacon bit into his mouth. "Let's call all the husbands and ask if they were ever one of Verna's customers."

"Right, no problem," Kate said with a roll of her eyes. "And all the high-school boys, while we're at it. Maybe one of them thought he couldn't survive hearing the word *no*."

"Cheryl told Gil he was her 'second favorite,'" Sara said. "So who was first?"

"Flynn," Jack said. The women gave small smiles, but there was no real humor.

Kate got up to get some of the photos Sara had run off. The two skeletons were vivid against the dirt of the tree roots. She tapped the picture that clearly showed a hole in one skull. "This isn't fair. That girl had ambition. She knew what she wanted. Most teen-agers have no idea, but Cheryl had goals and worked toward them."

"Maybe Verna's second job was meant to raise money for her daughter. College is expensive," Sara said.

"I think her dad was going to help with that," Jack said. He looked up to see the women glaring at him.

"Who was Cheryl's father?" Sara's voice was al-most a threat.

"No idea," Jack said. "One time Cheryl said her mother's friend had bought her some diamond earrings. I guess to my kid mind that meant 'father.' But now I think that probably wasn't what she meant."

"I'd like to hypnotize you to get every bit of infor-mation of that time out of you," Sara said.

"You'd be embarrassed," he said. "Like Gil said, I also had, uh, dreams about Cheryl."

"At *eleven*?" Kate said.

Sara was cleaning the countertops. "I wouldn't be shocked at all. Sex was part of what I used to write about. Knees, hands, mouths, where what went when. Sometimes I had to use action figures to keep body parts straight. After that, I don't embarrass easily."

Kate ate one of Jack's million-calorie cheesy bacon bits. "I've been meaning to tell you how much I like your books. I had to sneak to read them or Mom would have been angry."

"When you were *eleven*?" Jack mocked her tone.

"No. Last month. My mother believes I'm a virgin."

"*I* think you're a virgin," Jack said.

"More of your fanciful dreams?" Kate said. "Speak-ing of sublime sexual fantasies, would you mind if I invited Alastair Stewart to the house? He'd like to see what you've done with it."

"Everyone in Lachlan wants to see this house," Jack said. "But it's private."

"Don't let me forget to send Detective Cotilla an autographed book."

"You should hold a big autographing and clean out the garage," Jack said. "There must be a hundred boxes in there. Wish I could give a book to Cheryl." He halted, the last bacon bit on the way to his mouth.

Kate's eyes opened wide, and Sara froze, dishcloth in hand. They looked at one another.

"An autographing in memory of Cheryl and Verna Morris," Jack said.

"And when they come to meet the world-famous, reclusive author Sara Medlar, we'll ask them questions," Kate said.

Sara groaned. "I liked the idea up until now, but I don't relish being the bait."

Jack held out the last bacon-and-cheese to Kate and she took it.

"The funeral is Tuesday," Kate said. "It's Friday. Is there time to arrange something? And what about the funeral itself? Where does the county bury unwanted people?"

"*Unwanted.* What an awful word!" Sara looked at Jack. "Think your mom and Ivy could arrange a nice funeral? Lots of flowers? My expense?"

"Of course," Jack said.

"And a memorial service held in this house?" Kate asked. "Food, et cetera?"

Sara nodded, but she looked like she was agreeing to her execution.

Jack spoke up. "People will come if there's food but how do we weed out the ones who know nothing about Cheryl or her mom?"

"Good point," Kate said. "What man is going to say that he was insane with lust for the sweet, innocent Cheryl? Or was a client of Verna?"

Sara walked around the counter. "If you offer people something they really, really want, you can usually get them to give you something *you* want."

"I don't mean to be a downer," Kate said, "but a pretty house and a free book aren't going to make people confess to murder."

"Jack!" Sara said. "How much do people of this town want to see what you did to the Stewart Mansion?"

"An arm's worth. And maybe a leg. Definitely give up their firstborn."

Kate opened her mouth to ask why, but Sara put up her hand. "The Stewart family used to own all the land that the town's built on. Take it from someone who's written eleven medieval novels, this place was a fiefdom. Old Judge Stewart was a tyrant—but he was a good despot. Fair and just, as well as ruthless."

She took a step away. "His son was in my class in high school. Nice guy, but he wimped out and married a snob of a girl from old money. It was the judge's idea. He wanted to upgrade the family name."

"She's talking about your Viking's parents." Jack was smiling.

"People in glass houses," Kate snapped, then looked at Sara. "You're saying the peasants would dearly love to see the castle."

"Exactly!" Sara said.

"So we lower the drawbridge and let the great unwashed enter," Jack said. "Then what?"

"We can't let just anyone in," Kate said. "Even for a memorial service, it would be worse than an open house at a mansion. *We* have to vet people." She got off the stool. "It must be invitation-only. We send out invitations to Cheryl's classmates and to anyone we can find who knew Verna. Surely someone in town knew them well enough to know their secrets."

"Mom," Jack said and they looked at him. "She runs the Lachlan High School Alumni Association. She has addresses of people who attended in what year."

"All right," Sara said. "This is good. But how do we get them to *talk*?"

"Charge them," Jack said. He was rubbing hard under his cast. "In order to get in to view the castle, get a free autographed book and lots of cheese and bacon, they have to tell what they know about the Morris girls."

Kate and Sara were staring at him.

"A pirate with a brain," Kate said. "Will wonders never cease?"

It was such an odd remark that they laughed. This was something they could *do*. Not sit and accept what was being handed out to them, but an action. At the very least, it would honor two women whose lives had been cut short.

"We can try," Kate said and they agreed.

Jack took out his phone, called his mother and filled her in.

"Of course I'll do it," she said. "What's Sara's niece like?"

"Stop trying to matchmake." Jack was watching

Kate put pans in the dishwasher. "Ol' Alastair Stewart has already laid claim to her."

"Is that jealousy I hear?"

Jack didn't answer. "Could you go to the funeral home and set this up?"

"For Tuesday morning at ten, right? I guess you guys got the sheriff's permission for all this, didn't you?" When her son was silent, Heather groaned. "Really, Jack! That man thinks he's the king of this town. You can't put on a huge funeral and a memorial service for the victims in his case and not tell him. He'll be so mad he'll give you speeding tickets for walking too fast."

"The pirate's mother isn't dumb," he said.

"What does that mean?"

"Nothing. It's just Kate's sense of humor. She likes to make fun of me."

Kate rolled her eyes.

"Oh?" Heather sounded like she was ready to defend her son.

"It's not like that. She can be pretty funny. I'm a pirate and her boyfriend is a Viking."

"When do I meet her?" Heather asked eagerly.

"As soon as you show up with the current names and addresses of Cheryl Morris's classmates."

"Like they keep me up-to-date. Ha! Half the emails I send them get that Mailer-Daemon thing. What does that mean, anyway? Wait! I know. I'll call Janet."

"Who?"

"Janet Beeson. Church secretary. She's good at finding people."

"Get whoever you need to. I better go. I have to tell Sara and Kate that we have to go to the sheriff."

"And Kate," Heather said softly. "I'll be over as soon as I can. Love you."

"Back at you."

They hung up. Jack didn't need to tell the women what his mother had said as they'd listened to it all.

"We'll go see Flynn right away and get him to postpone the funeral. We need more time." Sara looked at Jack. He and the sheriff weren't exactly buddies. "Maybe you…"

"Should stay home and wash my truck?"

Before Sara could speak, Kate said, "Stay home and try to remember everything you can about Cheryl and her mother."

"I think I can do that best beside the pool."

Kate wished she could stay with him, but she didn't say so. She changed into a dress, and Sara into pants and a blouse—nice clothes for visiting the sheriff. After Sara talked to Heather and gave permission to set up a research team in her house, she and Kate got in the bright yellow MINI Cooper and headed into town. Kate drove. "Mind if I ask you a personal question?"

Sara gripped the armrest hard. "Sure. Go ahead."

Kate grimaced at her aunt's obvious reluctance to talk of personal matters. "My mother said you used to weigh a lot."

"I did." Sara's relief made her exhale so hard the papers on her lap fluttered. "I lost it. Turn here."

Kate pulled into the parking lot and they got out. "I gain weight really easily and Mom said I get it from your side of the family."

"She still eating brownies before she goes to bed?"

It was disconcerting to hear someone talk of what Kate thought only she knew.

"Yes."

"With maraschino cherries in them?"

"Oh, yes." Kate's voice was full of longing as she held the door open for Sara. "And almonds."

"However did you resist them? I know I wasn't able to."

"An evil thing called a scale."

"The Medlar iron lady. Pure torture."

They stopped in front of the desk and a tall, good-looking young man in a brown uniform with a deputy badge pinned to his chest asked how he could help them. He was trying to hide it, but he was blinking at Sara as if she was a movie star.

Suddenly, Sara was smiling and sounding as though the deputy was the most interesting person she'd ever met.

He was glowing under the attention. "I'm sure he's not busy. Come on and I'll show you in." They followed him.

Kate whispered to Sara, "If you'd given him an autographed book, he might have fainted."

"Then he'd go online and say that he didn't like the scene on page 268. The rest of the book was great, but he gave it one star because *that* scene reminded him of something bad that happened to him when he was a kid. Or worse, he found something that wasn't politically correct."

She sounded so fatalistic that Kate started to ask questions—but then they saw the sheriff. They'd caught him eating a doughnut and he didn't like being found out.

Kate expected Sara to use her charming persona, as she'd done with the deputy, but she didn't. Maybe the contemptible things the sheriff had said before were too much for her.

They sat down and looked at him across his big wooden desk.

"We want to postpone the funeral to next Friday." Sara's tone had no softness to it; she was meeting with an enemy.

"No," Sheriff Flynn replied in the same tone. "Anything else?"

When Sara started to speak again, Kate put her hand on her aunt's forearm. "We'd like to put on a memorial service for them," Kate said with a smile. "And Aunt Sara wants to pay for a funeral and a burial site. They deserve that, don't you think?"

The sheriff turned his chair a bit, as though he was dismissing Sara. "I have to think of the whole town— not just a couple of women no one remembers."

"You—" Sara's voice was angry, but Kate dug her fingers into her arm.

"I'm new here," she said. "Could you please explain to me what's going on?" She batted her lashes at him.

Frowning, he seemed to debate whether or not to say more. "I know I'm being seen as the bad guy in all this, but I'm trying to protect young Jack." He ignored the snort of derision that Sara gave. "Roy and I are the same age, and when we were in school, he was the kind of jerk who thought it was funny to shut little kids in lockers. A real bully. Contrary to what some people think—" he cut his eyes at Sara "—I have a reason for being so hard on Jack. I don't want him to become like his father."

He narrowed his eyes at Kate, emphasizing what he wanted to say. "Right now the gossip around this town is strong. Roy Wyatt had a big mouth and several people remember him bragging that he had 'set those Morris women straight.' Everyone—including me—thought he meant he'd made them leave town. Too many people knew about Verna, so nobody complained when she took her daughter and ran off in the middle of the night."

The sheriff leaned forward. "They're not saying that anymore. Now they're asking what else Roy could have meant. And maybe it's not a coincidence that Roy's son bought the property where the bodies were found. I'm being stopped on the street and asked why I haven't brought Jack in for questioning. And…" He paused. "They're asking what *really* happened that caused Evan to be killed. They're saying that maybe Jack was drunk and it was actually him doing the driving."

The sheriff turned his chair around. "The longer it takes to lay those bodies to rest, the stronger the gossip will be. I don't know how many copies of those videos are out there, but heaven help Jack if one of them goes viral. It would change his life. *That's* why I want to get those bones in the ground ASAP."

What the sheriff said was making Kate feel queasy. She swallowed. "But a memorial service?" she asked. "Something simple? Maybe it will help."

He took time to consider. "It might be good if you put that on. Give people something else to think about. And it'll keep Jack busy. I don't want that temper of his getting him thrown in my jail."

He looked at his watch. "I have to go. Work with the secretary to set up a funeral. And keep me informed of everything." He leaned back in his chair, his face saying that was the end. No more questions; no more answers; they were to leave.

EIGHT

KATE AND SARA DIDN'T SPEAK AS THEY walked to the car. What the sheriff had said was hanging over them.

"Mind if we stop at the café and get something to drink?" Sara asked.

"That would be nice."

Sara gave directions of where to park and they walked a couple of blocks to a little restaurant. There were outdoor tables under shade umbrellas. They took one and ordered iced tea.

Kate broke the silence. "The town must be really different from when you grew up here."

"This used to be a grocery store. Cal and I rode our bikes over here." Sara was moving her straw up and down in her drink.

"Cal. Jack's grandfather and the love of your—"

Sara looked up. "I feel really bad about all that's happened. It wasn't what I'd planned. I thought you and I would be going sightseeing. We'd get on one of those big air boats and search out alligators. Or drive north to see what Disney is doing. There's a butterfly farm nearby. But…" She looked back at her tea. "I didn't mean for you to be plunged into all the sordid little bits of this town."

Kate took her time in replying. "There's something I really want to know about my parents." When Sara looked about for the waiter, Kate lowered her voice. "I know you don't want to tell me about my father, but— Don't look so shocked. Every time I mention him, you look like you want to run away and hide. Right now I want an honest—and I mean truthful even if it's bad— answer to one question." She waited for Sara's terse nod of agreement. "I want to know if my mother loved my father as much as she says she did. Or is it an illusion she made up?"

Sara's relief made her smile broadly. "Your mother was madly in love with my brother. If Randal had told her to walk off a cliff, she wouldn't have hesitated. She adored him. It was close to worship."

"And my father?"

Sara took a deep breath. "Randal was always a bit of a, uh, scoundrel. But he loved your mother as much as I ever saw him love anyone. Except for *you*! You were so much like him and he was so very proud of you. He used to brag on you until it was embarrassing. But then, you did everything earlier than the other kids, so you deserved it. I agreed with him."

Sara leaned back in her chair. "You look so much

like him that it startles me. You even move your hands like him."

"Do I?" Kate said. "Do you have any photos?"

"A few. They're in one of the boxes in the garage. We can dig them out."

"I'd like that." Kate finished her tea. "Maybe we should go back now and see what mess Jack has made of everything."

"I think you and I should talk about all this now." Sara motioned for refills. "I hate to admit it, but there's a lot to what Flynn said. Maybe we should just put on a quiet, respectful funeral for the two women and leave it at that. No digging into the past, no trying to find out who, what and why about them."

"You think that leaving it alone will clear Jack's name?"

"I don't know. I thought that with all the influx of so many new people that the old disputes would be forgotten." She gave Kate a hard look. "Digging into the past is going to bring up some ugly secrets."

"Are you afraid we might find out that Roy actually did kill them?"

"That's one of my worries. He really was a piece of work. He was jealous of Jack from the day he was born and—" Sara quit talking and looked away.

"Is there any chance that Jack *was* driving the truck when Evan was killed?"

"No!" Sara said immediately. But then, after a quiet moment, she went on, "They didn't put on their seat belts, and they were tossed around so much…" She looked at Kate. "The truth? It could have been either of them driving. No one saw them get into the truck."

"So it's just Jack's word."

"Yes," Sara said. "I want to thank you for what you did for him, for *us*, the night we found the bodies. His mother said that no one has been able to get Jack to talk about what happened. There was only four years age difference between him and Evan, but Jack was always the big brother. He protected him from Roy. But then, Evan handled their father better."

"Without the temper the sheriff spoke of?"

"Oh, yeah," Sara said. "To see Jack and Roy go at each other was a scary sight. Like two wild animals, all teeth and claws. No ground rules, nothing held back. The things they said to each other made me sick to my stomach."

"Sounds like Roy could have murdered people."

"I think so. But that's never been the question. That he didn't brag about it is what makes me doubt. Kate?"

"Yes?"

"I wonder if maybe you should go home for a while. Just until this settles down. If your mother knew that I let you become involved in what may be a murder investigation, she'd be, uh, less than pleasant about it."

"Are you kidding? If my mother knew I was part of this, she'd call the FBI. No! Worse. She'd send the uncles after you."

Instantly, Sara's face turned as pale as an opal.

Kate leaned forward. "When I was growing up, the only relatives I had were the uncles, their holier-than-thou wives and their creepy kids. My mother is a martyr to the memory of her late husband. These last days have been the most... I don't know how to describe them. Interesting? Exciting? Maybe *fulfilling* is the right word. I feel like I'm doing something real and worthwhile. That poor girl! She had such dreams, but they were taken from her."

Sara was smiling. "And the mother?"

Kate glanced at the other tables. "Between you and me, I think there are more important things in a woman's life than what she does with her genitalia."

Sara laughed so loud the other customers turned to look at her. "Oh, Kate," she said, "you and I are going to get along fine. The only question left is how much we should tell Jack of what the sheriff said."

"Every word of it," Kate said. "Only, let *me* tell him. You'll be so sad that Jack might go after the sheriff with his crutches." She started to get up but Sara took her arm.

"Someone *murdered* them and was cold enough to plant a tree over the top of them. Are you *sure* you want to look into that?"

"The person who planted that damn tree interests me less than clearing the names of the innocent. Cheryl wasn't a pedophile; Verna wasn't pimping her daughter; Jack didn't drive drunk. I want everyone to know the truth about them. *That* is my goal. What about you?"

"I agree," Sara said. "Has anyone ever told you that you are a truly remarkable human being?"

"Other than my mother, no one." Kate got up and started toward the car.

"And you're as fearless as my lying, thieving skunk of a brother," Sara muttered as she followed Kate. "If I had any sense, I'd lock you up now."

NINE

SARA AND KATE RETURNED TO FIND THE guards had been sent away and the house was a zone of controlled chaos. The big dining table seemed to be the command center, with people seated with laptops. The curtains were closed against the sunlight. The kitchen counter had half a dozen plastic-wrapped casseroles and three coffeepots going. There were a dozen people wandering around, most of them talking on their cell phones.

"Do you know these people?" Kate asked.

"Only one of them." Sara was grimacing.

"Here you are!" A tall, slim, pretty woman stopped in front of them, her eyes on Kate. Sara might as well have been invisible.

"This is Jack's mother, Heather." Sara slipped through the people to flee into her bedroom.

Heather stood beside Kate. "I bet she hates this many people in her home. Sorry, but I couldn't help it. I put in a call to one person and…" She shrugged. "They all showed up. They're searching out people who knew the Morris ladies."

"Plus, there's the pull of getting to see Sara's house."

"Very true," Heather said.

Kate looked at her. "We heard some really nasty gossip from the sheriff."

"I know," Heather said. "Jack's been told. He—"

"Where is he?"

"Hiding somewhere. Drawing into himself. Escaping. I don't know what to—"

"Excuse me," Kate said. "Too much tea." She made her way past the people into her suite, closing the doors behind her. She hurried into her bedroom and out through the doors to the little courtyard with the dancing-girl fountain. As she thought, Jack was there, sitting in silence. She took a chair beside him. "So who told you?"

"The deputy at the desk, Pete, is a friend of mine. He likes to eavesdrop. What took you so long to get back?"

"Aunt Sara and I stopped at a restaurant. She asked me if I wanted to run back home to Mommy."

"Sounds like a sensible idea. When do you leave?"

"As soon as she tells me everything I want to know about my father."

"Looks like you're staying here for this century."

"Guess so. How are we going to do this?"

"Do what?"

She glared at him.

He smiled. "I guess people will send us stories."

"'I liked Cheryl Morris so much that I killed her.' That kind of story?"

Jack gave a one-sided smile and scratched at his leg. "You have any better ideas?"

"I might. Can you really build things? Like with saws and hammers?"

He looked at her in amusement. "When Sara bought this house, it hadn't been touched in twenty-one years. This courtyard? The pavers had crumbled. There was a hole in the roof of your bedroom. Termites had eaten half of your living room. Sara's bedroom was—"

"Okay. I get it. Strong Man Jack. Anyway, when we left the restaurant, I saw an ATM machine set back in a wall. Those things are opened from the inside so money can be put in them. And they have cameras that take photos of everyone who makes a transaction."

"What does that have to do with a murder?"

"I thought of secrecy. What if people were to put their stories in a kind of ATM and were told that the papers will go directly into the coffins? Maybe people would reveal more if they believed their stories were to be kept secret."

Jack stared at her. "But a camera would record who put what in the box. And, of course, the stories would be opened and read."

"Of course. I don't expect anyone to admit to murder, but Cheryl and her mother were unusual people. Surely someone didn't like them."

"A few wives, maybe?"

"And all the boys Cheryl said no to," Kate said. "Could you build something like that? Somewhere for the papers to go?"

"Easily, but I'd have to go to the shop to do it."

"And miss all the fun here? Poor you." There was the sound of laughter coming from the dining room. When Kate turned, she saw that the sliding glass doors had extraordinarily heavy accordion shades drawn across them. "What are those?"

"Hurricane shutters," Jack said with a grin.

Kate laughed. "Closed against a hurricane coming from the inside."

"You have your cell?"

She handed it to him and he put his number into it.

"Hate to leave this place, but I think I'll go to the quiet of power tools." He heaved himself up with his crutches.

"Why don't you take Aunt Sara with you?"

He started walking away from the doors. "I thought I would. I just need to find her. She's good at hiding. Anything else you want to know about me?"

She thought of asking about what actually happened the night Evan was killed, but she didn't. "How much of your father's personality did you inherit?"

"Much more than I'd like to have. Call me when the house is clear."

She watched him disappear behind plants, then went into her suite.

At the door, she took a few moments to gather her courage. With her shoulders back, she left her cozy apartment and went into the house. She called the people together and told them a whitewashed version of the plan. This was to be a memorial service, *not* some kind of undercover investigation. "The sheriff's department is looking into the deaths of these women, and they're handling it well. We just need to gather the people who share memories of them." She knew her words would be reported to Sheriff Flynn and it was better to keep him off their backs.

She explained about the stories they would encourage guests to write and how they were to be put in the box by the door. The messages would then be deposited, *unopened*, into the coffins with Cheryl and Verna. After that, refreshments would be served. It would be a simple, thoughtful memorial, and that was the message they should be sharing with the people they were contacting. Did they have any questions?

Hands shot up. Would there be wine? What about beer? Domestic or imported? What kind of food? Gluten-free? What about people with nut allergies? How about caviar? Maybe a bartender should be hired. Somebody's son-in-law was a bartender in a Miami nightclub. Could he have the job?

When Heather saw that Kate was about to drown in questions, she took over—and made the decisions. Wine, yes, no to beer and hard liquor. No caviar, but lots of hors d'oeuvres.

After lunch—ordered from the local pizzeria—a young woman showed up and Kate knew she was Jack's sister, Ivy. She wasn't dark like he was, but was fair like their mother, with streaky brown hair and big blue eyes.

They were two young people in a sea of oldies. "Love your dress," Ivy said.

"It's a Kate Spade knockoff. I find clothes I like online and my mother makes them for me."

"Wow! Really? That's a dream come true. By the look of it, she's an incredible seamstress. Where does she get the fabric?"

"She flies to New York four times a year and returns with piles of glorious fabrics and trims."

They smiled at each other, then ran to Kate's room to look at her clothes and shoes and bags.

An hour later, Heather pulled them back into the chaos and put them to work organizing who'd said yes and who'd said no.

Kate slipped away to text Jack. Okay to tell your mom and sister the truth?

The answer came back instantly. Yes.

"Don't wear your fingers out," she mumbled and went back to work.

The people didn't leave until 8:00 p.m., and Kate texted Jack that they were gone. Minutes later, he and Sara were back there—and the house was blissfully quiet.

Sara and Kate were bursting to tell each other all that had happened, while Jack sat at the kitchen counter and listened. They unloaded the casseroles from the fridge and reheated them.

When it came to eating, they were like the Three Bears. Jack ate lots of anything; Sara ate no carbs or sugar; Kate ate as low-calorie as she could manage.

Through it all, Sara and Kate talked while Jack smiled.

"Ivy was great," Kate said. "She's going to sit in the little room during the memorial and get the messages. She'll open them, read them, then text us if we should know something. We set up a group text so we all get every message." She glared at Jack. "Will you please stop grinning?"

"Just glad to see that you two hit it off. Did anybody bring any dessert?"

"A chocolate cake," Kate said, then she and Sara looked at each other and groaned.

With a great show of effort, Jack hobbled into the kitchen and cut himself what had to be a quarter of the cake: seven-layer chocolate with chocolate frosting.

He took it back to the family room and the women watched with longing as he ate it. "So what's for tomorrow?" He was licking the fork. "Who made this? It's really good."

"Janet," Kate said. "I think. Can you get the box done by Tuesday?"

"I used some moldings I had in the shop, so it can be installed tomorrow. This cake really is good. Wonder if I can get the recipe."

Kate couldn't take any more of watching the forbidden chocolate being devoured.

She stood up. "I'm going to bed."

"Don't forget what tomorrow is," Jack said.

"The day you go into a sugar coma and don't wake up for thirteen and a half years?" Kate smiled sweetly.

"It's your date with the Viking god."

"Oh, yeah. I would *never* forget that."

"Been thinking about it all day, have you?"

"Every minute." She had her hand on her bedroom door.

"Sure you don't want some cake? It's awfully good."

"I'd rather go to bed and dream about tall *blond* men." As she closed the door, she heard Sara laugh.

On Saturday, people seemed to think that the planning was to be continued at Sara's house. But she'd had enough. Every time the doorbell rang, she answered it. She told the person standing there, laptop in hand, that the house had been quarantined with cholera. Or typhoid. Or smallpox. When she got to leprosy, Kate told Jack to stop laughing and do something. He called the security guards back in and they finally had peace. Only Ivy and Heather joined them.

With the help of his sister, Jack prepared to cut a hole in the wall of the little study off Sara's bedroom.

Kate hadn't seen the room and she marveled at it. With the two-story ceiling, it was like a tower and it had bookcases all around and all the way up. A ladder rolled about on a brass railing.

"It's Beauty's library," Kate whispered. "I love it." There was a deep window seat with a dozen big, soft pillows.

"Thank you," Jack said.

"And I thank you, too," Ivy added. "He built it—I decorated it."

Kate turned to Jack. "You are *not* to make a hole in those bookcases! You do that and the floor will open up and the devil will grab you by the ankle."

When he laughed, Ivy looked from one to the other, wide-eyed. "It'll be all right. You'll see. Our dad taught him well."

Kate wasn't convinced, but when Jack finished, she was in awe. In the hallway it looked like an old shrine had been inserted into the wall. Jack hadn't mentioned that the moldings he was using were antique. There was no evidence that there was a camera hidden at the top.

Inside the little library, there seemed to be no change. When Jack pushed a book, a door—camouflaged by more books—swung open to reveal the back of the newly installed niche.

"Do I hear an apology?" His hand was behind his ear.

"Not from me." Kate walked away. "I expected perfection."

Behind her, he smiled at her compliment.

In the afternoon, the women worked on organizing what was needed to feed the people. Caterers, bartenders, more security. There was already too much interest in the event. Jack had brought in half a dozen boxes of Sara's books from the garage and she would autograph them.

At six, Kate escaped to her bedroom to begin to get ready for an evening out with Alastair. She was looking forward to thinking about something besides a murder scene.

She took time with her hair and makeup, then looked at her clothes, trying to decide what to wear. Not too formal, not evening wear. Casual but nice. She settled on a pair of black wide-legged pants and a white silk blouse with a band of sparkling beads at the shoulder. She pulled back one side of her hair, clipped it with a silver barrette, grabbed her clutch and left her rooms.

Jack and his sister were on the couch, Sara and Heather in the kitchen. They all stopped to stare.

"Do I look okay?"

"Gorgeous," Sara said.

"I agree," Heather said.

"Can I hire your mother to sew for me?" Ivy asked.

Jack said, "Glad to see you took a shower."

Sara and Heather insisted on driving her to the restaurant Alastair had chosen.

"That way you can drink. Later, you can call us to come get you."

Kate protested. She wasn't a teenager with a curfew, and if she drank too much, she could call a cab.

Sara looked at her in horror. "Somewhere, there's a murderer who I'm sure knows that we're investigating the case. No, you're not driving around after dark alone."

"Alastair will probably take me home."

"No!" Heather said, sounding almost near to panic. "I mean, he might drink, too." No one needed to mention the recent crash that had taken a life.

Jack was sitting on the couch and she called goodbye to him. "Have fun with your old man," he said.

Laughing, she got into the car with Sara.

Alastair was waiting for her at the restaurant, and he held out her chair. "Did I see that you were dropped off?"

"Yes. They worry about drinking and driving."

"Considering what the Wyatt family has been through, I can understand that." He poured her a glass of wine. "I hope it's all right that I ordered a bottle of white to start with."

She took a sip. "Lovely." She picked up her menu. "What's good here?" When he didn't answer, she looked at him. He was staring at her. "Is something wrong?"

"You're just beautiful, that's all. I keep thinking of the luck of meeting you. And then finding out that you're a mover and a shaker. You're turning little ol' Lachlan on its ear."

She put down her menu. "I haven't meant to. We just stumbled on—"

"I know," he said. "It's all anyone can talk about. Those poor women. What makes me angry is that back when it happened no one in this town gave a damn that they went missing." His voice rose, attracting a glance from the people at the next table.

"It's all right," Kate said. "We're looking into it."

He lowered his voice. "That's what I heard and I'm glad for it." He looked at his menu. "Maybe we shouldn't mention it again tonight. You must be sick of it all. What do you want to order?"

"Scallops. My favorite. What about you?"

"Calamari." He put down his menu. "I want to know more about you. Where did you go to school? For that matter, where—" He broke off as the waiter took their orders, then left.

"Now, where was I?" He was smiling, all blond good health. His blue eyes sparkled in the candlelight. "Oh, yes. You."

"Actually," she said, "I'd like to ask you some questions. Your picture was in the yearbook with Cheryl Morris. I know you were older, but what do you remember of her?"

"I've been thinking about that ever since they were found, but I only have a vague recollection of her. I know she was a pretty girl, and I remember that a couple of the guys on the team made remarks about her. It was just locker-room bragging."

"But not you?" Kate asked.

He gave a sheepish look. "I'm embarrassed to say that as a big-shot senior I was so full of myself that I would never have deigned to look at a thirteen-year-old. She—"

"Sixteen. Cheryl turned sixteen just before she was…"

"Murdered?"

They were silent as the waiter put hot plates of food in front of them.

"Do you think it was murder for both of them?" he asked. "Not murder/suicide?"

"Couldn't have been," Kate said. "The cold-blooded bastard planted a tree over their dead bodies." She swallowed. "Sorry. I've been living with this for a while now. You were telling me about yourself in high school."

"Don't apologize. I can't imagine what you've been going through. Anyway, that year I had a full-time girlfriend, Delia Monroe. Head cheerleader, prom queen, that sort of thing. Between school, sports and Delia, I can assure you that I had no time for anyone else. Besides, Delia was a bit jealous." He raised his eyebrows.

"Fiery temper, huh?"

"The worst. She was my first girlfriend and I had no sisters, so I thought that's how all girls were. She and I vowed to be together forever."

"What happened?"

"College. Life experience. When I got away from Lachlan, I met girls who were interested in something besides how they looked." He leaned forward a bit. "And I met young women who didn't demand to know where I was and who I'd spoken to every minute of the day." He leaned back. "Sorry. It still gets me. All that high-school possessiveness."

"Is she the reason you're not married?"

"Actually, I was married. But it only lasted three years. I came home early one day and she and a co-worker were... Well, let's just say that I never used that shower again. Anyway, it's an old, boring story. The divorce was quite civilized. I'm just glad there were no children. Why are we talking about me? I want to know everything about *you*."

Kate started to ask more questions but stopped herself. Since the moment a skeleton had seemed to reach out and grab her hair, all she'd thought about was misery. The murder of two women, Evan's passing, accusations about Jack, his angry father, et cetera.

She picked up her wineglass, drained it, then held it up for more. "I would really like to talk about something other than death."

Alastair filled her glass, then raised his for a toast. "What about not even mentioning the Wyatts?"

"Cal, Roy, Evan, even Jack," she murmured. "I'd very much like to have a Wyatt-free evening."

Alastair held his glass back without touching. "What would you most like to talk about?"

"Houses!" she said. "I have a career, one that I'd like to succeed in. Someday I want to see Medlar Realty on a door."

"Then here's to that," he said. "Medlar Realty." They clicked glasses and drank deeply.

"Actually…" Alastair said as he leaned toward her.

"Uh-oh. You look serious."

He didn't smile. "I *am* serious. I didn't answer your texts this week because I was in Atlanta."

"Makes sense. I've heard that up north they don't have the internet. Very backward people are those Yankees."

He laughed. "My father used to say 'If they can grow apple trees, then they're Northerners.'"

"I like that." Her scallops were delicious. "So you couldn't answer my texts because Atlanta isn't a technically advanced city. Right?"

"No. It was me. I was putting in sixteen-hour days and collapsing at night. Too tired to answer any form of communication. My mother is so angry at me that I have to take her to lunch on Sunday. Somewhere *very* expensive."

"So why all the work?"

"I completed what I needed to move my business here. Well, not here in Lachlan, but into a high-rise downtown on Broward."

"Ooooh. Big city. Why not Miami?"

Alastair held his fingers up in a cross. "Don't hex me with that name. Fort Lauderdale and Miami don't mix."

"I didn't know. I've been learning that Fort Lauderdale and Lachlan are separate."

"True. We just share utilities, taxes, public transportation and schools with them."

Kate finished her second glass of wine, while Alastair had barely touched his. "And we can't forget the Broward County Sheriff's Department that rules us both."

"With its state-of-the-art forensics department."

"Really?" she asked.

"Yes. Fort Lauderdale Police Department uses it."

"Wish they'd use Sheriff Flynn," she said under her breath.

"I wondered how you were getting along with him. Too bad you aren't a Kirkwood." He grinned. "Or a Stewart. Hey! Let's elope tonight and tomorrow you'll be a Stewart. That's one up from a Kirkwood. Ol' Sheriff Flynn will be kissing your rings."

Kate had already drunk enough wine that it seemed

like a hilarious proposition and she laughed hard. "You're my third marriage proposal."

He picked up a table knife. "If one of them was from Jack Wyatt, I'll stab myself in the heart now."

"Jack? Not a chance. He's more like my brother than a…than a…"

Alastair held the wine bottle over her glass. "Say he's not like me and I'll buy a hundred-dollar bottle of their finest."

"He's not at all like you," she said.

Alastair signaled the waiter and ordered a second bottle. "Now, seriously, Kate, my lovely, I need a house here in Lachlan. Can you find me one?"

"Oh, yes. Definitely. What are you looking for? Acreage? Old house? New? Something to remodel? Water view? In town so you can walk to the shops?"

He was grinning at her. "I like this Kate. Do you wear suits and high heels? Carry a briefcase?"

The way he said the words was so sexy that she felt herself sliding down in the chair. "I'm prim on the outside but I *love* lacy underwear."

He raised an eyebrow. "From that catalog?"

"The one teenage boys like so much?"

"And mature adults. How about something chocolate for dessert?"

"Too many calories."

"But also a reward for all the work you've been doing. Besides, we need time to talk about the house you're going to find for me. I've only lived in Granddad's house and in glass-walled apartments. I need something in between." He ordered the dessert. "I think it's time I settled down. What about you? Any plans for the future in the way of a family?"

"Two kids," she said. "Maybe another one later when the others become obnoxious teenagers. I like babies."

"Sounds like we agree on that. What kind of house do *you* like?"

"Regional," she said. "I like houses that look like where they've been planted."

"Like apple trees in Maine," he said.

"And corn in Iowa."

"And palm trees here."

"Spanish," she said. "I love Sara's house, the one you grew up in."

"Me, too, but half that size. We definitely don't need a room for Jack Wyatt to freeload in."

"We?" She was on her second glass from the expensive wine. It was by far the best she'd ever tasted. The waiter brought a large piece of chocolate cake and two spoons for it. Spoons were needed because hot chocolate fudge was oozing out of the center. "I am now going to sin." She picked up a spoon and tasted. Heaven! "You are an evil man, Alastair Stewart."

"Truthfully, Kate, you could stand to add a few pounds."

She groaned. "Those are 'get her into bed' words."

"Really? Do they work?"

"Always." As Kate put a bite of the deep, dark chocolate in her mouth, she closed her eyes. "Those words have *never* failed."

When she opened her eyes, he was smiling at her. "I would love to take advantage of your inebriated state, but I am officially declaring that I'm in this for the long term. How about if I pick you up tomorrow and we spend a Sunday afternoon looking at houses for sale in little Lachlan?"

"Great idea." Kate's mouth was full. "No. Wait. I can't. Jack and Sara and I are going on an adventure."

"What does that mean? Should I be jealous?"

"No. It's not a real adventure. The place just sounds like one. It's somewhere in Fort Lauderdale but far from Lachlan. I really need to study a map."

"Aventura?"

"That's it!"

"Mind if I ask why you're going?"

Lots of good food and way too much wine were making her mind blurry. "Someone—I think it was Janet from church—found a neighbor of the Morris women. She's in a nursing home, so we're going to visit her and ask her lots of questions. Aunt Sara says it's all becoming like one of her stories. Have you ever read any of her books?"

"Never. Your aunt is going with you? You won't be alone with that Wyatt kid?"

Kate smiled warmly at what could possibly be jealousy. Coming from such a lovely man, it was flattering.

Alastair put his hand over hers. "Just so you know, I don't want to give him more chances to steal my girl." He removed his hand. "Now, I think I should get you home."

Kate's eyes were drooping. "Maybe so."

TEN

JACK ARRIVED SO QUICKLY AFTER HER CALL
that she wondered if he'd been waiting nearby. She
hardly had the truck door closed before he said, "So
why didn't the Viking drive you home?"

She closed her eyes for a moment. The evening had
been a welcome respite from the last few days. She
didn't want any negativity associated with it. "I don't
know."

"Is he meeting someone later?"

She didn't answer but waved and smiled when
Alastair drove past them, and he smiled back.

Jack was behind him as they pulled out of the parking lot. They stopped, waiting for some cars to go by.
"Did you have a good time?"

"Oh, yes," she said. "Very good. He's a funny man.
And generous and kind. He's uncomplicated." The

wine was making her reveal more than she normally would. "He wants to settle down, have kids. My last boyfriend couldn't think past sex."

"Was the boyfriend late teens, early twenties?"

"Yes."

"At that age, that's all a guy can think of. The only thing Evan talks about is—" He stopped and for a moment his memories seemed to fill the cab of the truck. Evan was gone forever. "Stewart is what? Forty by now?"

"Based on the yearbook, I think he's about thirty-eight."

"He's thirty-eight and you're what? Twenty-one?"

"Three. I'm twenty-*three* years old." Jack's snide remarks were killing her good mood.

"That's quite an age difference."

She glared at him. "Alastair doesn't laugh at me."

Jack gave a smirk. "That's smart of him. Gets him more."

His insinuation of what Alastair was after was clear. Kate took her time before speaking and she changed the subject. "Is it still on that we're going to the nursing home tomorrow?" Her teeth were clenched.

Jack glanced at her, then back at the road. "You don't have to go. Sara and I could go alone. Maybe you and Stewart could have another date."

"He's taking his mother out to lunch."

"And it's not even Mother's Day. What a nice guy."

"He *is* a nice guy." Her voice came out angry; she didn't like having to defend herself.

They had reached the house. She started to get out but stopped. Damn him, but he'd ruined what had been a lovely evening. And for *no reason*! Was it spite? Jealousy? Or did Jack think that his grief gave him the right to take his anger out on others?

When she spoke, she looked straight ahead and her voice was calm. "You know, Jack, I truly believe that a person *chooses* whether or not to be happy. I've met people who are fifty years old and still whining that their parents didn't love them enough and that's why they're miserable."

She paused. "If you dig deep enough, we *all* have bad things in our pasts. My mother has debilitating fits of depression. By the time I was six years old, I knew how to open a can of soup, pour it into a bowl and heat it in the microwave. I—not my mother—set it up with a little mom-and-pop grocery that I could get food from them. When my mother came out of one of her depressions, she'd pay the bill.

"I did this because I love my mother and because the alternative was worse. If the State took me away, they would send me to my uncles. When I was seven, they were shouting at me that I was going to hell because my skirts showed my knees. I had to *learn* to enjoy the time when my mother wasn't depressed. I *forced* myself to see the good, not the bad." She took a breath. "Everybody has problems, Jack. It's just what you *do* with them that makes the difference." She got out of the truck and slammed the door.

ELEVEN

"OH, MY GOODNESS," MARY ELLERBEE SAID as she looked up at the man from her big easy chair, noticing what looked like a gray wig peeping out of his pocket. "I haven't seen you in ages." She was in her mideighties and quite thin. Her eyes weren't as sharp as they used to be but her mind hadn't dulled a bit. "How have you been? Is your mother well?"

"Yes," he said. "A few aches and pains, but nothing serious."

She had an idea why he was here and what he planned to do to her. She'd seen the news on TV and had shed tears over what had been found in dear little Lachlan. It was about her friends Verna and beautiful young Cheryl. Their skeletons had been found in a tree's roots! After her initial grief and shock, she remembered the young man she'd seen lurking about. It probably meant nothing, but she decided she should call the sheriff, though she hadn't got around to it yet. Why had she hesitated?

She glanced at the closed door. "Where is that nurse? She should be here any minute." She tried to control the shakiness of her voice. "Maybe I should call her."

He put himself between her and the call button beside her bed.

Mary immediately thought of that one night not long before Cheryl and her mother vanished, when that pretty young girl had been sitting on the back doorstep and crying. All summer she'd been practicing being a newscaster while the Wyatt boy filmed her. Mary had encouraged them. It was important for Cheryl to think about her future. And besides, that poor Wyatt boy needed to get away from his loudmouthed father.

But that particular day, only Cheryl was there. Mary put the pie she'd baked down on the porch and wrapped her arms around her. The girl was too often alone. Verna did her best to support them, but it meant that she was gone a lot. The Wyatt child made Cheryl laugh and Mary liked that.

The other boy, the older one, the one who skulked around, sniffing like a wild boar, bothered Mary. He made sweet little Cheryl indecently happy or, like now, left her in tears that came from deep inside her. Mary knew what the problem was. She hadn't lived sixty-plus years without seeing this particular kind of agony. She had to refrain from asking, "When are you due?"

"Now what?" Mary asked, her arms tightly around the girl. Her whole body was heaving.

"We'll have to get married. I wanted to wait, but…" Crying overtook her.

"You could do something about this," Mary said softly.

"No! Absolutely not!" Cheryl sat up and wiped her eyes, which spread makeup across them.

Mary had talked to Verna about how Cheryl dressed. "Let her be a child," Mary said.

"It's not me," Verna had said. "I want her to stay nine years old. It's her. She has dreams and ambitions. She wants a place in the world, and she wants it all to happen *fast*."

Mary knew from experience that Cheryl was everything to her mother. The center of her world.

That night Cheryl had gone back into the house to get her little red makeup case and repair her face. It looked like *he* was coming over. The Shadow Boy, as Mary called him. Skulking about and hiding.

Mary had encountered him face-to-face only once. No words were spoken. They just tripped over each other in the dark. She had the good sense to act like she didn't recognize him, didn't know why he was there. Later, when she saw him in church, she pretended that she didn't know who he was.

Not long after Cheryl had been crying, she and her mother abruptly left town. Packed up everything and left. Mary had been away that weekend, visiting her sister. When she got back, they were gone.

"So he refused to marry her," Mary said to no one, not in the least surprised.

She thought about telling the sheriff what she knew, but then what? He'd track them down? And do what? Cause a scandal? No, it was better to keep her mouth shut. But she missed them deeply. Several times she peeped through her curtains and saw the Wyatt boy over there. He looked as lonely as Mary felt. One time she saw him sitting in the back under what looked to be a newly planted tree and crying hard. She took some cookies to him but he didn't want any.

He was embarrassed at being seen crying. He wiped his eyes, sniffed and kicked the tree so hard that it fell sideways. Then he ran away.

Mary straightened the tree and stamped on the earth around it. The roof of the house leaked, the kitchen stove was twenty years old and there were rusty iron parts in the back, but the landlord planted a goddamn *tree*? She was tempted to rip it out of the ground.

But she didn't. She went home and watched TV and tried to calm down. She never saw the Wyatt boy there again and she never again crossed the road to the house. Even when it was rented, she never went over to meet the new neighbors.

So now she was looking up into the eyes of The Shadow Boy—and she knew what he'd done. Cheryl had told him about the baby and he'd killed her. And, of course, her mother had to go, too.

That he'd come back and planted a pretty tree over their graves made her feel sick. Did he think bright orange flowers made up for what he'd done?

She glanced toward the door. Maybe Nurse Jenkins would come in with her cheery smile—and her big shoulders. Mary thought about screaming but her voice was weak. No one would hear her. Part of why she'd chosen the place was because it was so well built. You couldn't hear what was going on in the next room.

"I'm really sorry," he said as he pulled what appeared to be a plastic dry-cleaning bag out of his pocket.

At over eighty, you'd think she'd be prepared for death. But she wasn't. She tried to fight him, but it was a baby rabbit wrestling against an eagle's talons. He slipped the bag over her head and tied it about her neck with her own bathrobe belt. He stood over her for a moment, watching her try to breathe, nodding, satisfied with his work.

Through the plastic, as she gasped for breath, she saw him sit down on the edge of her bed, phone in hand, as he answered his emails.

It didn't take Mary's soul long to leave her body. He finished the last email, then went to her. When he saw no movement, he removed the scarf and the terry-cloth belt, then the plastic. He picked her up and put her on the bed, taking time to arrange her naturally. The scarf and the belt were put back where he found them. He loosely stuffed the plastic into his pocket.

Once he was done, he went to the door and walked out with a firm stride. There were several people in the hallway and no one paid any attention to him. He was just another visitor saying hello to an old relative.

By the time he got to his car, he was smiling at a job well done.

TWELVE

KATE HAD BEEN TOLD THAT THEY WEREN'T leaving until eleven, so she was lying in the shade by the pool, a book across her bare legs. The weather was balmy warm and she liked the breeze in the exotic palm trees.

Jack clearing his throat made her open one eye, but she closed it again.

He sat down on the chair beside her chaise. "What do I have to do to make you forgive me?"

"Change your personality," she said.

"You're not the first person to ask that of me. Gramps made that suggestion every time I got in a fight with Roy."

"If you're trying to get sympathy from me, it isn't working."

"How about if I give a flat-out apology? I overstepped. I'm sorry. Alastair Stewart is a good guy."

"And?"

"I don't know what else to say."

She turned to look at him. "How about that you won't do it again."

"I'll try," he said. "But if you date some guy I know is bad, I'll—"

"You're Roy Wyatt's son, so that puts *you* on the 'bad guys not to date' list."

Jack laughed. "You got me there. But there are some guys in this town who have a worse reputation than I do."

"Think Sheriff Flynn would agree on that?"

"No. To him, I'm on the verge of turning into Roy."

"Did you tell Aunt Sara what I said about…you know?"

"Your mother's depression?"

"I shouldn't have said all that. I was angry at having my good mood taken away and I lashed out. I told too much."

"Don't worry, I didn't tell her. She might think it was her fault for not seeing you all those years. And before you ask, I have no idea what caused the rift between her and your mother."

"Where is Aunt Sara?"

"She went to pick up a filled picnic basket. It's Family Day at the nursing home and they said a lot of people bring lunches and eat on the grass. I hear that ants are a good source of protein. And the gators love the smorgasbord of old people who can't run too fast."

"Is that a Florida joke?"

"More of a tourist joke."

She looked back at the pool. "Do you know this woman we're going to see?"

"I saw her around a few times when I used to visit Cheryl. Sometimes she had pies that she said a neighbor had baked. And after Cheryl, uh…left, there was a day when a woman came over. She asked if I knew where they'd gone. I don't remember it very well. I'd been forbidden to go to Cheryl's house and…" Jack shrugged. "Anyway, it was a long time ago. So no, I don't really know her."

"What happens if Mary knows something about the murderer and tells us about him?"

"We tell Flynn and he'll know just what to do."

That was so absurd that Kate laughed. "I better get ready to go."

"I like what you have on. But that swimsuit covers too much skin."

"I didn't grow up in a bikini-wearing atmosphere."

"You could have put a couple of Ace bandages over your knees, then you would have been fine."

She smiled. "If I'd exposed my belly button, my uncles would have…" She sent her eyes skyward. "I'll put on something pretty. Mrs. Ellerbee deserves care being taken." She gave a pointed look at Jack's jeans and T-shirt.

"Yes, ma'am. I'll raid the ol' closet."

They separated, and after Sara returned, they met in the driveway. They were taking the MINI across Fort Lauderdale to Aventura on the far east side. Sara got in back.

"Because you're the only one who can fit in there," Jack said.

"I get MINI jokes from the guy who loves that zero to sixty in nanoseconds?"

Kate raised her eyebrows in question.

"The mighty MINI does have a bit of speed." He raised the door to the trunk. Beside the picnic basket was a big box with the name of Sara's publishing house on it. "A gift for Mrs. Ellerbee and her friends."

"How nice of Sara."

"It was totally my idea," Jack said.

Kate got in the passenger side, then watched Jack limp forward along the side of the car and get in behind the wheel. "When does that come off?"

"Three weeks and two days," he and Sara said in unison.

As Jack drove out of the driveway, he said to Kate, "If you can bear talking about anything but murder, I'd like to say that Ivy and I are working on a design for Cheryl's house."

"Tell her the rest of it," Sara said.

"I'm thinking about moving into the house when it's done. I can't keep living in someone else's place."

"Me, neither," Kate said. Her beautiful apartment in Sara's house went through her mind. "Maybe I'll buy one of the other houses."

"Me, too." Sara's tone made them laugh. It sounded like she was saying, "If you two are leaving, I'm going with you."

Jack didn't take any of the highways that criss-crossed Fort Lauderdale.

Instead, he used the roads with traffic lights to show Kate the big, beautiful city: wide, clean streets, enormous stores and businesses.

"Whatever you want, we have it here," Jack said with pride.

The nursing home was beautiful. One- and two-story buildings spread out over acres of manicured lawns. They parked and made their way toward the entrance.

"It's like a paradise." Kate admired a plant with big red flowers.

The main building had a two-story entrance with a desk to the right and hallways leading off in three directions. They went through the glass doors, but no one was in sight.

"Hello?" Sara called, but no one answered. "They should have a bell to ring."

There were cameras in three of the corners of the room and Jack waved at them.

Kate was looking at the papers on the desk.

"I'll get someone." Jack started off on his crutches.

"I'll go," Kate said. "You'll take too long."

Just as she turned down a hall, a woman wearing a white uniform entered. She had cake crumbs on her prodigious chest. Her name badge said Peggy Baker.

"I was…" She didn't finish her sentence. "Who was it you wanted to see?" The instant they gave Mary's name, her face fell. "I'm so, so sorry, but…Mary died just this morning. I'll call the director."

"No, please." Sara's voice sounded of tears. "Not yet. Tell us about her. It's been so long since I've seen her. What was she like when she lived here? Who were her friends?"

"Mary was here for eighteen years and she was *very* popular. Her mind was always sharp. She used to make us laugh all the time."

"Did Mary ever mention a woman named Verna?" Sara asked.

"Or her daughter Cheryl?" Jack added.

"Oh, yes!" Peggy said. "Verna and her beautiful

daughter." She lowered her voice. "When we heard on the news that their bodies had been found, Mary was really upset. We all think that the grief is what killed her. A broken heart."

"What exactly did she say about them?" Jack was looking at Peggy as if she were a beauty.

"Uh…"

Sara stepped forward. "Mary used to tell me about a boy who liked Cheryl. But I think it was a secret."

"Oh, yes, there was a boy she mentioned. Mary said he used to make videos of Cheryl." Peggy's eyes widened. "You don't think they were porno, do you?"

"No, they weren't," Jack said.

"Peggy!" a sharp voice snapped. "Are you talking to these people about one of our guests?" Behind them was a tall woman with pulled-back black hair that had gray streaks in it. Her name badge read Dr. Anita Talbot. She was an intimidating-looking person.

"Ms. Baker was offering us sympathy and understanding for the loss of someone we loved," Sara said.

"I assume you mean Mary Ellerbee?" She didn't wait for an answer. "I've not seen you here before."

Sara held out her hand. "Let me introduce myself. I'm Sara Medlar."

Behind the doctor, Peggy gave a little gasp, then said silently, *"I love your books!"*

The doctor shook Sara's hand, but not in a friendly way. "I never heard Mary mention you."

"That's because she was respectful of my privacy," Sara said. "I'd like to see her."

"I'm afraid the coroner has already taken her away. If you'll leave your name and address with Peggy, we'll tell you when the memorial service will be. Taking care of our guests when they leave this mortal plane is part of the service we offer here. Now, if you'll excuse me..." The doctor went down a corridor and was soon out of sight.

When they were alone, Peggy said, "I'm sorry about that. Dr. Talbot and Mary were friends and she's taking this hard. She's actually a nice woman."

Sara made a movement as though she was about to collapse. Kate started to help her, but Sara held her arm out to Peggy, who ran to her.

"This has been a shock to her," Jack said. "We brought lunch with us. Would it be all right if we had it here in this beautiful place?" He was smiling sweetly at Peggy.

"Of course. Several of the families are sitting on the grass." She looked back at Sara, who was leaning on her. "Did you really write all those books?"

"I did."

"There's something I've always wanted to ask an author—where do you get your ideas?"

"I look for them. I always keep my mind open and try to find ideas."

"I was wondering about these cameras," Jack said. "Where do you keep the films and could we see them?"

"Afraid not," Peggy said. "Dr. Talbot is fierce about that. Erik, our video guy, once demanded the police get a search warrant when all they wanted was to see how a man fell. But Dr. Talbot believes in privacy."

"Just like me." Sara gave a sigh, sounding like she was at death's door. "I wish I could see my friend one last time, even if it's on video."

"Sorry, but it's not possible," Peggy said. She looked around the room. "Erik keeps that room locked and

only he has a key. Not even Dr. Talbot goes in there."
The phone on her desk rang. "I have to go, but you can
picnic here as long as you like."

The three of them walked back to the car and immediately both women leaned against it and put their
hands over their faces. Their gestures were so identical
that Jack stood back and blinked at them.

"Do you think we killed her?" Sara whispered
through her fingers.

"I don't know," Kate said. "We talked too much, told
too many people, and everyone knew we had found her."

"Exactly." Sara dropped her hands to look at Kate.
"But who is going to believe us?"

"No one."

"Right," Sara said. "They'll just think she was another old woman who dropped dead for no reason."

Jack looked over the top of the car to the front of
the building. "Dr. Jekyll is watching. Let's go sit under
a tree and talk."

When he went to the back of the car to get the basket, Kate followed him, Sara close behind her. "You
think something is wrong, too, don't you?"

Jack lowered his voice. "My instinct says that doctor
is so protective of this place that if she found a body
with a knife in its heart, she'd remove it and sew up
the wound."

"To protect the reputation of her worthy establish-
ment." Sara's voice held disgust. "There were cameras
in that entry hall. Every visitor was caught on film. I'd
really like to see those tapes."

Kate pulled the picnic basket forward. "When I
went down the hall, I saw a room that said Video on
it. Maybe we could…" She didn't finish her sentence.

Jack looked from one to the other. "No." His voice was calm and very firm. "Whatever you two are thinking, it's no. Leave this to me and I'll figure it out."

As Sara and Kate took the handles of the basket, they headed toward the side of the building that contained the video room. But neither said a word. Jack stood over them as the women spread the cloth on the ground and began pulling food out of the basket.

It was only half-empty when Jack reached inside, withdrew a dark green notebook and handed it to Sara. "Why don't you write what's in your mind?" His voice didn't allow any argument, and he didn't step back until she was leaning against a palm tree, notebook in hand.

He picked up a couple of plastic-wrapped sandwiches and a cold bottle of white wine. He nodded for Kate to get the glasses and a corkscrew. Silently, they walked away until they came to a bench nearly hidden in the shade. It was on the edge of the canal that encircled the property.

Jack motioned for her to take a seat. He sat down at the opposite end of the bench, opened the wine and filled their glasses. "Have you changed your opinion of me yet or have I reinforced what you were told?"

Kate unwrapped a sandwich. Both halves of a thick French loaf were too many calories for her. She handed Jack the top half of the bread and he took it. "You think Aunt Sara will be all right?" she asked, ignoring his question.

"She will now." He leaned far to his left so he could see around the shrubs. "Writing calms her." He was staring at Kate, waiting for her answer, but she didn't know what to say.

"When you first got here, I asked you who you'd

talked to so I'd get an idea of what you'd been told about me. Stewart lived with a judge who despised Roy. Bessie used to work for the family. Tayla likes me but she's scared of Sara."

"Don't forget Melissa."

"How could I?" He gave a half smile. "If I piece it all together, my guess is that you were probably told that I'm a parasite who is after your aunt's money."

There was no answer Kate could give to that but affirmative, so she bit into her sandwich and looked at the water.

"I think I should tell you about Sara and me, about how we got together."

"You don't have to," she said. "I came on too strong last night. With the booze and negative words after a pleasant evening, I broke. You didn't deserve all that I said, and I can see that you and Aunt Sara care about each other."

"It's more than that," he said. "I owe my life to her. And so do my mom and Ivy and—and Evan."

When he paused, she said, "Go on. I love stories."

He smiled. "Runs in your family. I'll start by saying that Sara showing up in person when my family needed her the most was a cosmic happening. Fate. The stars aligning. Whatever it was, it all changed on Friday afternoon, the week of June the twenty-first, 2004. You see, Sara's mother died the same week as my dad and they were buried the same day. Half the town came out for his funeral."

"This was Henry Lowell."

He was pleased that she hadn't said *Roy*.

"What about Aunt Sara's mother? Were many people there at my—my grandmother's funeral?"

"Sorry, but no. Only Sara attended." He gave a small smile. "Afterward, she said that that was the only time her mother ever did—" Jack rethought telling that part.

"What did Aunt Sara say?"

"That it was the only time in her life when her mother did something good for her."

"Yeow! Not a nice lady?"

"No, she wasn't," Jack said. "But then, Sara's hate-filled mother and Cal's mean-tempered father were what bonded them."

"Every cloud has a silver lining, that kind of thing?"

"I guess," Jack said. "But that silver lining had some holes in it."

He smiled in memory. "Later, Sara told me the story from her side. It's much more interesting than mine. She knew from the beginning that I wanted something, but there I was, thinking I was being so subtle."

"Tell me every word," Kate said.

Lachlan Cemetery
2004

Sara listened to the young minister talk about what a loving, caring, generous and kind woman Ruth Medlar had been. But even he was having a hard time saying the words when the only people there were ones he'd found hanging around the church that day. The man who mowed the lawn had his head down. The secretary kept looking at her watch. The assistant minister had a new baby at home and seemed to want to lie down on the soft grass and go to sleep.

As for Sara, her hands were clenched so tightly she could hardly feel them. Ruth Medlar had never done or said a kind thing to anyone in her life—except for her beloved son.

If her good-for-nothing brother was available, Sara would have sent him money for the funeral—Randal was always broke—and let him handle it all. In lieu of that, she'd tried to dump the whole mess onto the church, but they'd refused. They'd insisted that Sara return to Lachlan and deal with it all herself. She understood, but it didn't mean she wasn't bitter about it. She wanted to be here as little as everyone around her.

The minister finally stopped his flowery lies—*and people say I write fiction*, Sara thought—and the funeral was over.

She gave a curt nod and left as quickly as possible. She didn't go down the gravel path with the others and have to listen to their fake words of sympathy. Instead, she cut across the lawn. There was a gravestone she needed to see. Or maybe she shouldn't see it, shouldn't remind herself that a man she'd loved so very much was forever gone.

As she rounded the little building that sat in the center of the cemetery, she halted. If she'd been hit by lightning, she couldn't have stopped more abruptly.

Another funeral service was going on. But unlike her mother's, this one was attended by what looked to be half the town. A big photo of Henry Lowell was on an easel.

Standing on the far side of a casket, like a vision from a nightmare, were three women Sara had known long ago. It was like a Lachlan High School reunion—something she'd avoided for so many years. Tayla Kirkwood, Donna Wyatt and Noreen Stewart stood there, side by side. They'd been close friends in high school and were widows now.

Ate your men alive and threw the bones away? Sara wondered.

But in the middle were two men who took Sara's breath away. She hadn't seen them since Cal had passed and they looked so very much like him. His dark looks, inherited from his Brazilian mother, had always made Cal stand out in a sea of blond heads and pale skin.

One was Cal's son, Roy, the bane of his father's life. Liar, cheat, thief. As bad as Randal but without her brother's finesse, his sense of showmanship, his likability.

For all of Roy's sins, he was still a very good-looking man. There was gray in his dark hair and he had unshaven cheeks, but they just made him look more interesting. His eyes hadn't lost the sparkle of his lust for life.

He was standing beside his ex-wife, Heather, who looked like she'd been crying for days. It was obvious how much she'd loved her husband, Henry. And as Sara watched, she saw Roy glance at the diamond on Heather's hand. Saw him stare at her pearl earrings.

On Roy's other side was a young man who looked so much like Cal that Sara thought she might faint. When Cal was eighteen years old, his senior year of high school, he had been a glorious creature: tall, dark, athletic, smart. He and his two friends had been dubbed The Magnificent Three—and they well deserved the title.

That Sara had been the girlfriend—the true love—of one of them had been a great source of pride to her. The world that she and Cal had outside of school, away from the spotlight of sports and school intrigues, was what fueled her entire life. It was what gave her the strength to survive her mother and the horror that was her home life.

That it had all ended badly didn't take away the seed that had rooted so deeply and strongly. Love lasts forever, even if the lovers are rarely together.

The boy who looked so much like Cal was his grandson Jackson, grown up now and bursting with health and energy—and, from the expression on his handsome face, anger.

When Sara saw Roy put his arm around Heather in a proprietary way, then saw the scowl on Jack's young face deepen, she knew that war was to come. She could foresee the future: Roy would move back in on his ex, now a rich widow, and Jack would do what he could to stop it.

I must get him away from here, Sara thought. When the funeral service ended, she went forward.

No one seemed to be surprised to see her. But then, news always spread quickly in Lachlan. Cal's widow, Donna, snake that she was, wisely slithered away through the crowd. She had always been one to do things in secret, never in the open.

Tayla still wore that "forgive me" look, but Sara ignored her. Noreen Stewart didn't deign to look at a Medlar.

Roy was so intent on leading pretty Heather away that he barely glanced at Sara.

Bet if I had on my Cartier watch and some pearls he'd run to me, she thought, then dismissed him.

Jack stayed by the coffin, watching as it was lowered into the ground. His eighteen-year-old eyes had a look of age and turmoil that were too much for him.

She didn't know if his grandfather had ever mentioned her to him. But she did know how close they'd been. Jack was what Cal had hoped his son would be.

She went to stand beside him. They were the only mourners left. "I'm Sara," she said softly and didn't know if he heard her.

For a long moment he didn't move, but then he took her hand in his and held it tightly—and that was when Sara's tears started. She'd never met Henry Lowell, but this tall, beautiful boy should have been her grandchild. Hers and Cal's.

They stood side by side, holding hands, a tall young man and a short older woman, two strangers who should have been family. Their tears fell as they stared at the coffin with the red roses on top.

It was a while before Jack turned away. He released Sara's hand. Without looking at her, he said, "Are you hungry?"

"Always." She was at her heaviest then. Years and years of sitting and writing and eating from deli delivery had packed on the pounds.

He turned to look at her, seemed to study her, then nodded. "You have a car?"

"A rental parked over there."

"Leave it and let's go in my truck."

"Sure," she said. At her age, it was always a pleasure when a young person didn't ask her if she needed help lifting her handbag.

Jack's truck was about two feet off the ground and her short legs had a hard time getting up into it, but she didn't ask for help. When he took off so that he left a strip of rubber, she laughed like she was again six-teen. Cal had been brilliant with cars and his engines rumbled as they rode.

Jack took her to a drive-through hamburger place and ordered for both of them.

"Onions okay?"

"Why not?" She was beginning to realize that what he was doing was courting her. The driving too fast and greasy burgers were a teenager's idea of caviar and champagne. *He wants something*, she thought.

Had it been anyone else, she would have said, "Let me out here." If success had taught her nothing else, it was that everyone in the world claimed to be the basis of all that she'd achieved—and so she should give them money.

But Sara didn't protest. Whatever Cal's grandson wanted, she would do her best to give it to him. She could feel the pain radiating from him, and something inside her felt called to heal him however she could.

He drove down a gravel lane and parked under a big oak tree. Sara knew it was one of the make-out sites for Lachlan kids. In fact, she and Cal had often made love on a blanket about twenty feet away from this very spot, hidden under the trees.

She leaned back against the door and took one of the huge hamburgers and a giant Coke. When he said nothing, she began. "So where are you going to college?"

"Can't. Gotta protect Mom from Roy. And Ivy and Evan."

He didn't say this in a "feel sorry for me" way, but as fact.

"I'll pay for your college," she said. "Ivy League. Anywhere you want. You don't have to worry about being away from your family—it'd just be for a few years. You'll be back in no time. Unless you go to law school."

"Nope."

"Medicine?"

He shook his head.

She chewed awhile. "You know exactly what you want, don't you?"

He nodded. "Granddad Cal told me that if I ever really needed help that you'd give it."

"Did he?" Sara's voice was hoarse. "So he talked about me? Bet Donna loved that!"

"He spoke of you only to me. He never mentioned you to anyone else. But he said that you and I are alike."

"How so?"

"I'd like to think that we're just plain lovable, but it's more likely that we're hardheaded and stubborn. Fight to the death when we see a wrong."

Sara turned away so Jack wouldn't see her tears. How deeply she missed Cal! The only person who saw her as she truly was and loved her anyway. She looked back at the young man beside her. "What do you need?"

"I want to take over my father's business. And by 'father,' I mean Henry Lowell. You see, he was…a kind and very generous man."

That his words were the same as the minister had said about her mother made Sara smile. Then grimace. "Died broke, did he?"

"Pretty much," Jack said. "He paid too much for materials and charged too little. If a customer gave him a sad story, he would lower the price of whatever he was selling."

"What about you?" she asked. "You have the same kind heart?"

"I have Wyatt blood in me. I don't over- or undercharge."

She waited for him to go on.

"Five years ago, Tayla Kirkwood returned to Lachlan and—" He broke off when Sara gasped. "Are you all right?"

"You want to go into business with her?" Sara's voice was angry.

"I want to go into business with you," he replied in the same angry tone. "If you'd just put those stupid high-school feuds behind you and listen to the deal Henry and I put together—"

Sara was laughing.

"You sound just like him! Cal was always calm unless I got angry, then he'd start yelling."

"Really?" Jack's eyes were wide. "I never heard Granddad yell at anyone."

"That's because Donna is too bland and boring to raise any emotion in a person. She—"

"She is my grandmother." Jack's voice was low, almost threatening.

"Shouldn't be," Sara growled, sounding just as fierce.

"Then you should have stayed and fought for him!" Jack yelled.

Sara started to defend herself, but instead she nodded. "Yes, I should have. But by the time I came to my senses, Donna had made her move and your father was on the way. Cal believed in doing the right thing. I didn't attend their wedding."

Jack reached across the truck seat and squeezed

her hand. "Sorry. I shouldn't have yelled. The last few months have been hard. Dad knew he was dying, so he and I worked to figure out how I could take care of everyone after he was gone."

"A plan that involved me."

"Yes," Jack said. "I need money, but it's an investment. I need backing to continue Dad's remodeling and construction business. Lachlan is coming back to life and I want in on it. And when it succeeds, you'll benefit, too."

"You could do that after college."

Jack frowned. "If I left this town for four years, Roy would divorce Krystal, then sweet-talk my mother into remarrying him. He would spend the little that Henry left her and Ivy. Roy would never pay child support for Evan, and Ivy would have to live with Roy, and—"

She put her hand on his arm. "I get it. No college. Do you have anything about this business on paper? And do you know enough to remodel houses? You're awfully young."

He picked up the empty wrappers and wadded them into the bag. "You have time to go see some houses?"

"Just you and me?"

"Just us. But it will take hours because I have a lot of ideas about what I want to do."

"My whole life is about ideas. I'd love to see what you have planned."

Grinning, he started the truck and pulled out...

"You went into business together," Kate said.

"We did."

"But if it's all so aboveboard, why do people think there's something underhanded going on?"

For an answer, he just looked at her.

"Your father's reputation."

"Right. And the fact that Sara wanted her part in it kept secret."

"Afraid Roy would hit her up for money?"

"Him and everyone else. And she wanted people to think I did everything on my own. Not many people believed that Roy Wyatt's eighteen-year-old son could run a business—and sometimes I thought they were right. But I managed." He gave a little smile of pride. "Anyway, after I took out for wages and materials, Sara and I split everything fifty-fifty. She loved doing it! We'd meet in New York twice a year and I'd show her floor plans of what was for sale. We'd spend at least a week together and she'd feed me until I could hardly walk. And we'd go to lots of Broadway shows. I have a weakness for them."

"And no one knew of this?"

"I didn't even tell my mother. I was afraid she'd slip and tell Roy."

"Did he, uh… Did he and your mother get back together?"

"He tried. He told her she'd always been the one he loved and that all the bad he'd done was because he was so angry at being fool enough to lose her. Et cetera. Et cetera."

"I could see how that would do it. She's a strong woman to be able to resist that." Kate looked up. "If you were buying houses, Roy must have thought Henry left you a lot of money."

"That's exactly what he thought. He tried to get me to 'help him out,' meaning to cut him in on the profits, but I refused."

From the way he said that, Kate guessed that there were some heated—maybe violent—arguments. She held out her glass and Jack refilled both of theirs. "Who knows what now?"

"The town only knows that Sara Medlar bought the biggest house in Lachlan, paid the town bad boy's son to remodel it, and now we're moved in together. Old-timers like Sheriff Flynn think we're trying to make people believe we aren't trash. To him, that's impossible to achieve."

"That must hurt." She looked at him over the wineglass. "Am I the only one who knows this?"

"Yes. Ivy thinks I paid for her schooling, but Sara did. And Evan thinks—" He drew in his breath. "Thought I was going to send him to veterinarian school. He'd only finally made up his mind about what he wanted to be when—when…"

Kate looked out at the water. "You said you were going to move out. Did you mean that?"

"At the moment I did. It was your eyes. I knew what you'd heard about me, so I asked Sara if she'd mind if I told you the truth." He lifted one side of his hip, withdrew his wallet and handed her a tiny flash drive. "All the paperwork of Wyatt Construction is on there, plus the name and number of our accounting firm. Sara's name is on everything, including payments. You can check it all out."

She took the little drive. "I believe you."

"You'll keep this to yourself? No telling your boyfriend?"

"He's not—" She stopped. "I won't tell anyone, even my mother. But if she thinks I'm keeping even the tiniest secret from her, she'll put me through an interrogation that will be torture. I swear I won't reveal this. I'll protect you and Aunt Sara."

"Thank you." He still had his wallet in hand, and he withdrew a card. "A school friend, Gayle Ashe, called me yesterday. Her husband got a job in Houston and they've moved out. They're going to put their house in Lachlan up for sale. Dad built the house and it was one of the first I worked on. Three bedrooms, three and a half baths on half an acre. Gayle wanted me to make some minor repairs before calling Tayla."

He handed her his business card with the address on the back. "I thought maybe you could show the house to Stewart before it comes onto the market. He might like the place. It would be your first sale in Lachlan."

"Thank you."

Jack leaned back over the bench. "Sara's putting her notebook away. You ready to go home?"

When Kate stood up, the two glasses of wine made her trip and Jack caught her arm. "Thank you for telling me all this. I feel honored that you trust me with it." She smiled at him. "You're like the brother I never had." She walked past him to return to her aunt.

"Your *what*?" Jack said under his breath, then louder, "Brother? You think I'm your *brother*?"

Thirteen

"HOW ABOUT IF I MEET YOU IN THE PARKING lot behind the tea shop?" Alastair said.

Kate held her cell phone to her ear as she looked around at the chaos of Sara's house. There seemed to be an endless stream of delivery people: food, drink, flowers, chairs, tables, cutlery. Sara had long ago escaped to the tiny courtyard outside her bedroom. Jack was hiding out in the garden with the fountain. Kate wished she could join either of them, but Ivy and Heather needed help with all the preparations.

"I don't think I can," she told Alastair. "Looking at houses is going to have to wait until all this is cleared up. Wednesday afternoon at the earliest."

"What did you have for lunch?"

"Tastings," she said. "Every person who has donated a dish has asked me to taste whatever he or she brought, then waited for me to give lavish praise. I've used the words *fabulous* and *extraordinary* a dozen times."

"They like to hear *amazing.*"

"Not in this house! Jack warned me that one utterance of that word and Sara might kick me into the street."

"Are you in love with him yet? Is my chance completely lost?"

It was the first genuine laugh she'd had all day.

"I have something I want to show you," Alastair said. "Something that I think you'll like. And it won't take long. Promise."

Kate looked around the big room. A man in a white chef's jacket looked like he was filling yet another spoon for someone to taste. "Ten minutes?"

"You can make it in eight."

"I'll take Aunt Sara's MINI and be there in six."

It took Kate a whole eleven minutes to get there because she had to maneuver the MINI around three vans parked in the driveway. But Alastair was waiting for her. Feeling like she was skipping school, she got out and gave a sigh of relief. She leaned on the side of the MINI beside him.

"That bad?"

"Worse. Noise and confusion and strangers."

"But aren't your housemates strangers? You haven't known them but a few days."

"I guess, but it doesn't feel that way. Jack says that Aunt Sara and I are so much alike that we're almost twins."

"Bit of an age difference, isn't there?"

"She's young and I'm old, so it evens out."

He smiled at her joke. "And you and Wyatt?"

Kate thought of what Jack had told her at the nursing home. It meant a lot that he'd entrusted her with that secret, and she wasn't going to reveal anything to anyone.

"Uh-oh," Alastair said in a way that made her laugh. They got into their cars and she followed him to a part of town she'd not seen before. When she saw the street, she drew in her breath. It was the same address as the house Jack had given her to sell. She pulled into the driveway beside his Bimmer, turned off the engine, then got out and waited for him to explain.

"You called Tayla and she called me. I saw the house this morning and I love it."

When Kate said, "Oh," the disappointment in her voice was clear.

"I screwed up, didn't I?"

"No, of course not. Good houses go fast and Jack said this one is a beauty."

"The ever-present Jack," Alastair mumbled, looking contrite. "Like to see inside?"

"Sure." It was very pretty on the outside and Kate's Realtor eyes checked the gutters, the windows, the concrete. It was all in good repair, well taken care of. Add a few flowers to the beds and it would be pristine.

She wasn't surprised when Alastair had a key to the front door. The inside was as well kept as the outside—and the floor plan was what everyone wanted: open, light, simple. The kitchen had cream-colored granite countertops and she recognized the documents on them. Alastair had already made an offer and it had been accepted.

Kate's name was on the papers. She was going to get the commission. She'd share a percentage with Tayla's company but the bulk of it would go to Kate.

"You and Tayla didn't need to do this. I didn't show you the house."

"You're the one who finagled it out of Wyatt."

"He volunteered it," she said. It was her first sale at Kirkwood Realty and she didn't feel that she'd earned it. Where was the chase? The agony of showing twenty houses and the buyers hating them all? Then at last she would open a door and they would fall in love. Never mind that the house bore no resemblance to what they'd said they wanted—love was love.

"Sorry I messed things up for you," Alastair said. "It's just that as soon as I saw this house, I knew that I wanted it. And Tayla said it would go soon. Come see the Florida room."

She followed him past the pretty kitchen to a big screened-in porch. There were two cheap aluminum chairs and a table with a white cloth. On top was a bottle of champagne, two glasses and plastic containers of food.

"Please forgive my decor," he said. "May I serve you lunch in my new home?"

He looked so repentant, so sorry, that she forgave him. Besides, it was difficult to stay angry at a blond Viking. "I would love it." She sat down, then he poured the champagne and filled her plate with little sandwiches and salads.

"Tell me everything you've been doing," he said. "The whole town is buzzing with talk of the memorial service. Is Miss Sara really giving out free books?"

"Oh, yes. Boxes of them. Jack opened them and—" She broke off as Alastair groaned.

"Wyatt again."

"He does live there," Kate said tersely.

"I don't mean to be disparaging, but you'd think a grown man would want his own place. Whatever happened to that newscaster he was dating?"

"Cheryl Morris?"

"Jack dated Cheryl?" Alastair looked shocked. "I had no idea. You don't think he…?"

"No, nothing like that." Kate quickly realized her mistake. "I don't know who Jack has dated or is dating."

"Foot in mouth," he said, "but then I've thought of little else besides the murders since our dinner together. I've tried hard to remember if anyone ever mentioned that poor girl. Or her mother." He took a bite.

"And?"

"You remember the guy who yelled hello on that first day that I met you?"

"Dan, wasn't it?"

"Yes. Dan Bruebaker. What a good memory you have."

"Part of my trade. Did he know Cheryl?"

"I don't know but I remembered that he used to talk about her a lot. But then, most of the guys did. She was a very pretty girl and she dressed like an adult. I remember some women at church making remarks about her being a 'painted harlot.'"

"Do you know who Cheryl went out with?"

"No one in the open, that's for sure. Maybe…" He looked down at his plate.

"Maybe what?"

"Did you ever think that she dressed up like that because she was trying to attract a man? I mean as opposed to a high-school boy. I think Cheryl—what with a mother like hers—might have been too much for us fumbling boys. I know I would never have approached someone like her." He paused. "I've made you frown. Sorry."

"It's just the concept of blaming the victim that I hate. Whatever she did, she didn't deserve what she got."

"Of course not. I apologize."

"From what we've found out, Cheryl was working toward getting the job she wanted. Maybe *that* was what she was trying to attract."

"And the boys' locker room was a by-product. Do you know when it happened? The date she was killed?"

"Not specifically. Early September, just before school started."

"When my class was heading off to college."

Kate looked at her watch. "Do you really think Dan Bruebaker was after her?"

"He and I weren't close, but I do know that he talked about her often. It was like she was some trophy he was trying to win. He used to tell all of us on the team in detail about what he'd like to do to her, that sort of thing. Locker-room talk. I dismissed it at the time." He paused. "So how was your adventure yesterday?"

At first she didn't know what he meant. "Oh, Aventura? The rest home. Mrs. Ellerbee wasn't… I mean… She'd passed away."

"Oh, no! I'm so sorry."

Kate put down her napkin and stood up. "I really need to get back."

He got up. "Give me a date if you hear about one and I'll do what I can to help you find alibis for the people in high school. I'm good at research and my mother kept every piece of paper about my high-school years.

Her scrapbooks are practically a daily diary. It could help narrow down the list. Anything I can do to help, let me know."

"That's very kind of you. By the way, why did your mother go to Henry Lowell's funeral?"

"I didn't know that she did, but it makes sense. Mr. Lowell used to keep our house from falling down around our ears. I think he and Mother became friends, and between you and me, I don't think he charged her very much."

"I think he did that with a lot of people." She glanced at the table. "Thank you for all of this. It was a nice treat."

"Would you like my help tomorrow?"

"It would be nice if you showed up at the service at the cemetery in the morning. Maybe it's vain of us but we'd like to show Sheriff Flynn that Cheryl and her mother were remembered."

"Now, that's something I can do. What about afterward?"

Kate started to say that he might be good at interviewing people, but she stopped herself. She'd already told him a lot, and officially bringing in a fourth person was something that needed to be discussed with the others. The thought made her smile. She was now part of a team. "I think we have it covered."

For a while, they talked of his new house and how he was going to furnish it. She suggested he hire Ivy to decorate it and he liked that idea. Then they exchanged the double-cheek kisses that were prevalent in South Florida and Kate drove home smiling.

By 7:00 a.m. the next morning, Kate was up and ready to go to the memorial service. It wasn't until ten, but she was nervous. She hoped lots of people would be there, but at the same time, she hoped they'd be respectful.

The house, so full of what was needed that day, was quiet. Aunt Sara was sitting at the kitchen counter with a big plate of scrambled eggs and bacon. She offered Kate some but she got out a box of sawdust cereal and skim milk.

"Ready for today?" Sara asked.

"I doubt it. What still needs to be done?"

"Jack can't get his dress pants on over the cast. You wouldn't mind helping with that, would you?"

"Not at all. Where are they?"

"With him. In his room. He's expecting you." Sara pushed away her empty plate. "I need to…" She shrugged.

You need alone time, Kate thought. "Sure. Go ahead. I'll get our boy dressed and ready." When she finished her cereal, she went in search of Jack's room. It was down a hall that led to the laundry room—a place she hadn't yet used. She knocked and Jack answered. He was wearing only a low-slung towel and a cast. His chest was covered with black hair that fanned out over well-toned pecs and abs.

She stepped past him. "Are you appearing half-naked to get me back for saying you're like a brother to me?"

"I am. Is it working?"

"Yes. From now on, I'll think of you as my *athletic* brother."

Jack gave a snort of laughter and went into the bathroom, but he didn't close the door.

His room was large, a bedsitter really, with a couch

and chairs, and big windows looking out at the front of the house. He'd be able to see who arrived and when they left. And being so near the garage would allow him to go and come without anyone knowing. His own guard post, Kate thought.

On the foot of the bed was a pair of dark trousers, which she picked up. "You have a pair of small, pointed scissors?"

"Here." He held a pair of nail scissors out to her.

"Thanks." She went to the bathroom door and saw that Jack had put white lather on his face. She leaned against the door as she prepared to trim away the stitching on his pant leg. But she didn't snip. Instead, she watched him.

He glanced at her in the mirror. "You look like you've never seen a man shave before."

"Just on film."

He halted, razor in hand. "No boyfriends?"

"Lots of them, but I didn't live with them."

"Mommy said no?"

"Kate said no."

Grinning, he kept shaving. "So what did you tell old man Stewart last night?"

"That I'm still considering his offer to elope."

"That's a joke, right?"

"Only on my part. He did make an offer. If you stop being a very hairy Mean Girl, I'll tell you what I learned."

"Think I should wax?" He ran his hand over his chest. "A lot of guys do now."

She ignored his question. "Tayla told Alastair about the house you gave me to sell and he bought it."

Jack rinsed his razor. "You didn't get to show him the house? Didn't get your ta-da moment?"

She ducked her head down to hide her smile at his perception, but she wasn't going to tell him that. Besides, she was rather enjoying looking at the back of him. Muscles under tanned skin...

"Do you know Dan Bruebaker?"

"He's more my mother's generation than mine. And Stewart's."

"Stop being a jerk."

"I will try," he said solemnly as he dried his face. "No, I don't really know the guy. He makes high-end wrought-iron fences. Good quality and expensive, but I've never needed to use his work. Which aftershave should I use?" He opened a medicine cabinet to show four brands lined up.

Kate stepped into the bathroom, opened them one by one and smelled them. "Alastair said that in high school Dan was obsessed with Cheryl. Bragged about what he was going to do to her. Sexual things." She handed him a bottle. "This one."

"Good choice. Guaranteed to drive women wild. Did you meet Dan?"

"No. He went after us on the day I arrived and Alastair nearly ran from him." Kate went into the bedroom, sat on the end of the bed and began taking out the inside seam on the trousers.

"Interesting. What else?" When Kate hesitated, he said, "Go on. Out with it."

"Ever since I got here, I've heard what a snob the Stewart family was, but Mrs. Stewart attended Henry Lowell's funeral."

"And he was just a building contractor."

"I didn't mean anything disparaging."

"Didn't think you did."

"Alastair said your father did a lot of work for her, and charged her too little, but still…"

Jack stepped into the room, hobbled over to a table by the window, picked up a framed picture and handed it to her. It was a black-and-white photo of three beautiful young men: tall, muscular, radiating good health. It was a candid shot. They had their arms around each other and were laughing. The one on the right was obviously Cal. He was a clone of Jack. The middle one looked enough like Alastair that he must've been his father—but he was better-looking than his son. There was something round and open and friendly about his features that Alastair didn't have.

"This guy?" she asked.

"Walter Kirkwood, Tayla's late husband."

"Could Mrs. Stewart have been there because her late husband and your grandfather were friends?"

"Possible. But not likely."

"What's she like?"

"Mrs. Stewart?" Jack limped into his closet. "As a person or your future mother-in-law?"

"Person."

"Cold, pinched woman. Granddad said Hamish—"

"Who?"

"Hamish Stewart. Named after some Scottish ancestor. Anyway, Granddad said Hamish was given a choice of marrying rich, smart Noreen or being disinherited. He was a very likable guy, but he wasn't strong in the brains department. And he didn't want to have to work for a living. He married her."

Jack came out of the closet wearing a white dress shirt and a tie, but no pants.

Thighs of a soccer player, she thought, then held up the pants with the open leg. "Try them on."

"I think I need help."

"I'll call Melissa."

"Spoilsport." He took the pants from her. "What else did ol' Stewart tell you?"

"Just that we need to get a date of when—when the murder happened. He has scrapbooks from high school. Maybe we can piece together something. Although, Alastair thinks we should look at men, not boys. He thinks that was why Cheryl wore so much makeup and dressed the way she did—she was trying to look older for some man."

Jack's jaw clenched. "She was trying to look older for the career she wanted."

"That's what I told him." He had pulled on his trousers and one pant leg flared out like a skirt. "That looks awful. You should sit down at the service and not get up again."

"Can't. I'm singing."

"You're what?"

"Singing. 'Ave Maria.' Didn't have time to rehearse something new. Don't look at me like that. I can do things besides hammer in nails."

"Velcro," she said. "Wait here." She ran to the cabinet by the kitchen, where she'd seen a roll of the adhesive-backed fastener. She grabbed it and a pair of scissors and went back to Jack. She went onto her knees behind him. "Stand still, and no smart-aleck remarks. I've got to stick a strip of this on the cast and more on the fabric. There may be a gap but it's better than wearing palazzo pants."

"I saw Cheryl on her sixteenth birthday."

"That was the day Roy showed up, yelled at both of you, then ran over your bike. Happy birthday, Cheryl."

"Yeah, that's the day. School started a few days later, but she didn't show up. By then she was... She was..."

"I know." Kate was peeling the backing off the Velcro and sticking it to his cast. "That's too big of a time window. We need to narrow it down."

"Then find alibis for everyone in Lachlan?"

Kate sat back on her heels. "Not possible, is it?"

"No. This isn't going to itch, is it?"

"It won't touch your skin. Stop moving!"

There was a knock on the door and in unison Jack and Kate said, "Come in."

Sara entered, paused a moment to ascertain what they were doing, then sat down on the end of the bed. She had on a black dress that Kate was willing to bet was by some Italian designer. "What's going on?"

"Our Kate is going to elope with Alastair Stewart and have Noreen for her mother-in-law."

"That's good," Sara said. "Three months later you can ride up on your Harley and rescue her and be the hero."

"Been writing romances again, have you?" Jack said.

"Sort of. Kate, what did you get out of Alastair?"

She and Jack told everything, talking together, interrupting each other.

"Not much, is it?" Sara said.

"No, but I have something." Jack went to a cabinet by the door and withdrew a DVD in a jewel case.

"It's a copy of the video of everyone who entered the nursing home."

Kate and Sara looked at him in awe.

"I called Gary—my security guy, remember?—and he knew someone who knew someone."

"How much?" Sara asked.

"Three hundred and fifty."

"Not bad," Sara said. "Have you seen it?"

"Yes. That's why I slept late this morning. There's no one I know on it. No one I've ever seen before."

"I'll have to look at it," Sara said. "Maybe some ancient old person is someone I went to high school with. Your pants look good. Great job, Kate."

She looked around his legs at Sara. "Can he actually sing?"

"Quite well. If I'd known that back when he graduated from high school, I would have kidnapped him and made him try out at Juilliard."

"Only if I could have taken Mom, Ivy and Evan with me."

They were silent for a moment. If they'd all left town then, maybe Evan would still be alive.

Fourteen

THEY LEFT FOR THE CEMETERY AT NINE. Sara and Kate were frowning in worry about the coming service. Would many people show up? Since few remembered the deceased, would they laugh and giggle? Stand around complaining about their bosses and spouses? Be disrespectful?

"You two are going to get wrinkles," Jack said.

"Too late for me to worry about that," Kate said. "And too soon for Aunt Sara." That she had purposefully said it backward made them laugh.

At the grave site, the two coffins were side by side and draped in roses. White for Cheryl; red for Verna. They wouldn't be covered until the notes had been put inside.

Four rows of chairs were on three sides and with no one there, they looked imposingly empty. There were two florist vans parked close by and they were unloading huge arrangements.

"They from you?" Jack asked Sara.

"Some, but not all of them."

Kate began to read cards aloud. "Raintree Bakery. W.G. Hall Jewelers. The Swiss Cork. Tangled Yarn." There was something from nearly every store in Lachlan.

Jack went to an enormous arrangement of white lilies. "It's from a place I've never heard of—Medlar Realty." He looked at Kate. "Something you haven't told us?"

Kate smiled. Alastair must have sent those. "Just an inside joke."

"The Great White Hunter goes after his prey," Jack mumbled and walked away, his crutches sinking into the soft ground.

At nine forty, people began to arrive. By nine fifty, there was a crowd, a couple hundred, at least. They lined up to speak to Jack or Kate or Sara, saying, "Tayla called me," or "Alastair Stewart invited me. Hope that was all right."

Kate couldn't keep from giving Jack an "I told you so" look.

At ten after ten, the service began. There were two pastors and they each said a few words. They weren't the usual bland, generic words, but personal, thoughtful comments about the two women. Sara had made sure the ministers were informed.

Cheryl's hope for the future was spoken of. Verna's deep, unwavering love for her daughter was emphasized.

The ministers finished and stepped to the side. Out

of the crowd came six young women, as thin as wraiths, with long, silky hair and black dresses. Three had violins and the others were standing in silence.

"Where is the sound equipment?" Kate whispered to Sara, but she didn't reply.

The people at the front of the crowd were quietly waiting, but in the background, children were getting restless and noisy. Parents did their best to hush them, but it wasn't working.

Jack walked in front of the young women and leaned his crutches against a chair. His clean-shaven face made her think of the little boy she'd seen laughing in the videos with Cheryl. She gave him an encouraging smile but he didn't seem to see her.

He nodded toward the violinists and they began the beautiful, mournful song of "Ave Maria." Beside them, the other girls began a slow chorus. Their voices were so soft, so low, Kate doubted if they could be heard more than a few feet back. Why, oh, why hadn't someone told her of this? She could have arranged for microphones and speakers.

Jack took a breath and began to sing.

His voice was clear and beautiful—and rich. Loud. The sound, the vibrations, got everyone's attention. Children stopped playing and listened.

The song had a sad feeling to it, but Jack's voice was liquid tears. Cheryl and her mother, Evan and Henry— the man he'd loved as his true father—were all there. The notes cried for them as they came directly from Jack's heart.

Ave Maria, gratia plena. Hail Mary, full of grace. Dominus tecum. The lord is with thee.

Kate reached out and took Sara's hand, and she covered it with her other one.

They were both crying. So much love given; so much love lost.

Benedicta tu in mulieribus. Blessed art thou among women.

Around them the other guests had stopped moving. Jack's sweet, strong tenor voice encased them and pulled feelings from inside them that they'd tried to bury.

Mothers, fathers, children, lovers, friends. All the grief that was hidden deep inside them was being drawn to the surface.

Ora pro nobis. Pray for us.

Kate saw tears on Jack's face and he closed his eyes, looking only at the memories within him. A young girl, so full of hope and life, had had it all taken from her.

Ora, ora pro nobis pecatoribus. Pray, pray for us sinners.

Nunc et in hora mortis. Now and at the hour of death.

Et in hora mortis nostrae. And in the hour of our death.

And in the hour of our death.

When Jack finished the last note, there was silence in the crowd. Someone started to applaud, but angry faces were turned toward him and he stopped.

Gradually, the people came back to life and began to move. But they were quiet, speaking in low tones. Jack's song had made them remember why they were there.

As for Jack, he seemed to disappear. Kate had seen him pick up his crutches and walk away. The six young women had surrounded him like a protective shield, allowing no one to get near him. Kate and Sara stood together, thanking the people for coming.

"Is he all right?" Kate asked Sara when the line began to thin out.

"I don't know. Go find him."

Kate smiled at the people before them, then turned away. Once out of sight, she began to run, looking everywhere for Jack.

She found him near the large headstone of his grandfather Cal. Close by was another stone for Henry Lowell and not far away was Evan. She looked around but didn't see Roy Wyatt's headstone.

Kate didn't say anything, just stood beside Jack as he leaned on his crutches and stared at his grandfather's name etched in granite.

They were quiet for a while, then Jack said, "You ready to face the masses? The hungry, teeming hordes?"

"I have my lamp lit and the golden door will be opened."

"For me or old man Stewart?"

"For the whole town," she said, then realized that his innuendo was sexual. She turned a bit red and they laughed together. "Aunt Sara will be waiting for us." She started toward the car.

"Wait," he said and held out his arm.

They'd known each other a very short time but they'd been through a lot together. She went to him and wrapped her arms around him, and he kissed her forehead.

"Thanks for all this," he said. "It wouldn't have

come about without you. Sara and I would have retreated to our rooms in silence."

She smiled as she knew that was true. "Your singing—"

Groaning, he released her. "How am I gonna get any girls now? I'll be known as the Singing Wimp of Lachlan."

They were slowly walking toward the car.

"Speaking of that, I've been meaning to ask you about some newscaster you've been seeing."

Jack gave a one-sided grin. "Jealous?"

"Insane with it. I want to claw her eyes out. Rip out her hair. Beat her with your crutches. I fantasize about—"

"Okay, I get it. You couldn't care less who I date." They were at the car.

Huddled in the back, looking tiny, was Sara. "Ready to get this over with?" he asked her.

"Oh, yeah," she said.

Kate got into the front passenger seat. "Come on, let's go sleuthing." With an eye roll, Jack put his crutches in the back, then got into the driver's side.

Two hours into the memorial at Sara's house, they were thinking they'd made a mistake. They hadn't learned anything.

Kate had settled Sara at a table in the big family room. Instantly, a long line formed to get a free autographed book. The first eager person to reach her said, "There's something I've always wanted to ask an author—where do you get your ideas?" Kate didn't stay to hear Sara's answer.

Jack had his back to the wall in the living room

and was surrounded by girls who were swooning over his singing and his… Whatever. He looked over their heads to Kate. "Do you need me?" he asked loudly, then mouthed, *Please*.

"No, not at all," she said sweetly.

She opened the doors into Sara's bedroom and went into the little library.

Heather was sitting beside a box full of folded papers. Everyone who was there today had some connection to the victims and they were supposed to have written down their memories.

"Anything?" Kate asked.

"Cheryl was pretty and Verna kept to herself," Heather said. "The same thing over and over. When I was married to Roy, we lived near them, but I don't remember them at all."

Kate sat down. "Did you get anything to eat and drink?"

"Lots. Ivy went out to talk to some of the people Cheryl went to school with. Not many people who knew Verna came."

Kate closed her eyes and put her head back. "No husband who committed adultery with her? No furious wife with an ax in her hand? What about Roy? Did he ever say anything about either of them?"

When Heather didn't answer, Kate opened her eyes. Jack's mother was standing by the receptacle that he'd built and was looking at a piece of paper with wide eyes. "What is it?"

She read the note aloud. "'I know someone who hated Cheryl Morris enough to kill her.' It's signed Elaine Pendal, then it says 'If anyone does read this, I'm wearing a red scarf.'"

"Red…?" Kate said. "I gotta go." She nearly ran out of the room. Jack was still pinned against the wall—not that he was making an effort to be released. Kate made her way through the girls, practically pushing them out of the way.

"Excuse me. Excuse me." She grabbed his forearm. "Come with me."

"Sorry, girls. I have to go." As soon as they were away, he said, "Thank you. With all my life, I thank you."

She handed him the note. "Go find the red-scarf lady and take her to your room—if she'll go. If not—"

"She will."

"What is it with you and women?"

"I don't know. *They* like me. Actually, *they* think I'm hot. As in sexually desirable."

"How strange. Anyway, I'll go get Aunt Sara and meet you."

They separated and Kate hurried into the family room. The line at Sara's table was still long, and there were many books left.

The next woman up spoke. "There's something I've always wanted to ask an author—where do you get your ideas?"

"She steals them," Kate said. "From her Facebook ladies. Sorry, but we have to go now. She'll be back later. Maybe."

A man stepped out of the line. "But I have a question I want to ask her. It's important. I'm going to be a writer and I need to know where she—?"

"Albuquerque," Kate said loudly. "She gets all her ideas from Albuquerque. Very spiritual place." She took Sara's arm and they hurried down the hall toward

Jack's room. When a woman started to follow them, Ivy stepped out of the crowd and blocked her.

"Love you," Sara said as she ran to keep up with Kate.

Inside Jack's room, he was smiling at a woman who was sitting in his big easy chair and holding what looked to be a gin and tonic. She had on a gray, soft-shouldered suit that looked vaguely familiar. A red scarf was draped around her neck.

"Elaine was in school with Cheryl." He said it with pride, as though she'd accomplished some great feat.

Kate couldn't help staring. *This* was the girl whose photo they'd seen in the yearbook? With the frizzy hair and the "woe is me" look? There was no resemblance. This woman was exquisitely made-up, and her clothing, even her demeanor, was so perfect that she was a bit intimidating. She looked like what every woman hoped her "after" photo would look like.

They sat down on the couch across from her, Jack in the middle. It was a bit tight for all of them, but they presented a unified front, as though they were one being.

"Excuse me if I'm a little jet-lagged. I just got off a plane from New York." Elaine looked at Jack. "Although I did get here in time to hear you sing. Ever think of doing anything with that?"

None of them answered her. Jack's singing wasn't what was on their minds.

"You came to Lachlan just for this?" Sara asked.

"Yes. You see…" She took a drink. "Everything I have in my life, I owe to Cheryl Morris. You can't imagine how hard I've tried to find her. Google searches. 'Find people' investigative services. I hired a professional investigator. I've called and written to everyone I know in Lachlan and asked about her, but no one knew where she and her mother went after they left town. The best I got was a cryptic and unfriendly reply from Captain Edison."

"What did Cheryl do for you? And your note—who hates her?" Kate asked. "We'd like to hear everything."

Elaine was looking at Jack. "You were there that day. Eating pie and drinking milk. I must say that you grew up rather well."

Before Jack could reply, Kate said, "He knows that. What happened at Cheryl's house?"

Elaine leaned back in the chair. "You want the long or short version?"

"Long," they replied in unison.

"Okay. It started near the end of my senior year on the day that I was bawling my eyes out in the girls' restroom of Lachlan High School."

"Young love," Sara said.

"Of course," Elaine answered. "What else makes a person so miserable? It was during class but I didn't care. In fact, I hoped I'd get caught and expelled. I never wanted to go to school ever again. Never wanted to see any of those kids again." She raised her hand. "It was teenage angst at its worst…"

May 1997

Elaine Langley was sitting on the cold tile floor of the girls' restroom and crying hard. When the door opened, she wanted to scream at whoever it was to get out, but tears were choking her throat too much to speak.

When she saw it was that girl who looked like a teacher, she cried harder. What was her name? Sherry? No, Cheryl. No one knew much about her—or wanted to.

Elaine tried to stifle her tears, but they kept coming.

Cheryl was using a wet paper towel to try to get a stain out of her blouse, but it wasn't working. "Silk is not a good fabric for high school," she said. "Certainly not something to wear around Gena Upton."

At the name, Elaine let out a howl and her tears increased to a veritable flood.

She was choking, nearly suffocating on them.

"Oh, hell," Cheryl muttered, then turned to face Elaine. "What's that bitch done to you?"

Elaine covered her face with her hands and shook her head. She could never, ever, never tell anyone what she—not Gena—had done. If she did, she'd die from humiliation on the spot.

Above her, Cheryl gave a deep sigh, as though she knew what she had to do but definitely didn't want to. She hiked up her straight black skirt to her thighs, sat down on the icy floor in front of Elaine, then pulled the girl's hands away from her swollen face. "Tell me."

Elaine shook her head. "Can't," she eventually said, barely managing to choke out the word.

"Anything to do with Jim Pendal?"

Elaine gasped. "How could you know?" She wasn't to the hiccup stage yet, but she could feel it coming.

"I watch people. And besides, you aren't exactly subtle. When he's around, you don't breathe."

Elaine put her hands back over her face. "Then he knows!"

"No, he doesn't. He's a boy. He only knows about food and sports."

"And Gena Upton," Elaine said loudly.

"She went after him. His family is rich and Jim is a hunk. My guess is that she's trying to get him to knock her up so he can't get away."

Elaine drew in her breath so hard that she started coughing.

Patiently, Cheryl waited until Elaine got herself under control. "Now tell me what you did."

Elaine shook her head. "No, I can't. It's too stupid. Today women are supposed to stand up for themselves. Find careers. But all I've ever wanted is…"

"Jim Pendal."

Elaine nodded.

Tenderly, almost motherly, Cheryl smoothed a strand of hair behind Elaine's ear. "You know," she said softly, "that's not really true. You pay attention to your clothes."

"Gena says I dress weird."

"Not weird but different. Not like everyone else."

"Not like you," Elaine said, then gasped. "I didn't mean anything bad."

Cheryl smiled. "I'm practicing for the life I want, but this isn't about me. What did you do to try to get Jim to notice you?"

Elaine hesitated. "I made a plan that took me a whole year to pull off."

"I do that, too!" Cheryl's eyes widened. "I'm making a plan for my entire life. But what did you *do*?"

"Do you know Dane Olsen?"

Cheryl groaned. "That leech! I despise him. He

stops by my locker and says he's going to give me the pleasure of going out with him."

"Out to the back seat of his dad's Lincoln."

"Exactly," Cheryl said. "So what about him? Did he proposition you, too?"

"Yes, but only to do his science work. We were assigned as lab partners. For the whole year."

"Gag." Cheryl's head came up. "Jim and Dane are best friends. I can't imagine why."

Elaine shrugged. "Jim is serious; Dane isn't. I guess it's sort of opposites attract."

"Ah," Cheryl said. "You did something for Dane in order to get close to Jim. From your misery, it doesn't seem to have worked."

"No, it didn't, but I was so honest and up-front with Dane."

"A mistake," Cheryl said. "He wouldn't know honesty if it bit him. What did you ask of him?"

"I said I'd help him with his science if he'd take me to the Spring Fling in May. Not the prom—that's too important—but to the small dance. He agreed."

"The Spring Fling is in two days."

Elaine drew in a trembling breath. "Today Dane said he doesn't remember agreeing to that and he's thinking about taking Theresa Lambert. They're going to double-date with Jim and Gena."

Cheryl looked thoughtful. "Since you and Jim graduate in June, this will be your last… Actually, your only chance with him. Unless you're going to the same universities?"

Elaine's tears started again and she could only shake her head.

"Okay, so we need to fix this now," Cheryl said.

"First of all, Gena won't go on a double date with Theresa Lambert. She has a cute face and triple-D boobs. Gena would be afraid that Theresa would get too much attention. Gena would much rather double-date with you."

Cheryl's meaning was clear. There was absolutely nothing about Elaine that would make any female jealous. She was plain-faced. Not pretty, not ugly. And she was tall and shapeless. Not curvy in that Marilyn Monroe way that high-school boys liked so much.

Having her flaws spoken of so coolly had a sobering effect on Elaine. When the tears seemed to draw back into her, she started to get up.

But Cheryl put her hands on her forearms. "Gena Upton is stupid. Clever but dumb. And blind. What's your dress for the dance like?"

"I made one. It's silk and strapless. I hand-sewed tiny silver sequins in a kind of sunburst on the skirt and bodice. It took me weeks." She sniffed. "But my mom made me buy a dress. Pink with tulle over the skirt. She wants me to wear it so I don't stand out."

"Screw your mother," Cheryl said. "Sorry. I envy your fashion sense. The dance is Saturday night, so bring the gown and shoes to my house about three that afternoon and I'll fix your face and dress you."

Elaine was still smarting from Cheryl's earlier comment. "You're going to perform surgery?"

Cheryl leaned forward so they were nose to nose. "Do you really not know? You have one of those faces that with the right makeup can be anything. And your skin is beautiful! Gena Upton, with her big eyes and thin lips, won't age well. But you... I can make you look like a model."

Elaine's jaw seemed to drop lower with each word she heard.

Cheryl leaned back, frowning. "I just realized that this could be bad. If you show up looking great, Gena will probably pull a Cinderella and tear you apart. You'll be left in your underwear with bloody claw marks on your face. And your ego will be destroyed."

"I don't..." Elaine whispered. "I'm not sure..."

Cheryl stood up. "Leave this to me. I'll take Gena out of this. At least for one night." She held out her hand. "I've been on the receiving end of that girl's venom too many times. Come on, get up and wash your face. Tell people your allergies made your eyes red. Don't talk to Dane today and please, please stop looking at Jim Pendal as though he's an angel come to earth."

"He is, isn't he?"

"Not my taste, but he's a nice guy." A bell rang. Classes were over and the restroom would soon be full of girls. When the door opened, Cheryl said, "Act like you don't know me. I won't do your reputation any good."

Elaine started to protest that, but Cheryl quickly left. For the rest of the day, Elaine did exactly as Cheryl had told her. She tried to keep her mind on what the teacher was saying, but really! Who cared about some whale defending itself against men with spears?

She did all she could to keep her eyes off Jim Pendal. In Spanish class, he sat three seats ahead of her and to her left. She'd arranged that so she could pretend to look at the chalkboard, but she really just stared at the back of Jim's head.

At the end of school, she was beginning to lose

hope. Nothing seemed to have changed. No one had said a word to her about the Spring Fling. Was it on or off?

As she got her books out of her locker, deciding what to take home and what to leave, she could feel her anxiety going from hope to depression. It was like she was standing at the top of a forty-foot-long children's slide and she was about to start the descent that would leave her at the bottom. Forever.

"Hi," said a male voice behind her.

Elaine turned so quickly she almost hit him with a book. It was him. Jim Pendal.

The most gorgeous, talented, smartest—et cetera— human on the planet. She couldn't speak.

"I want to apologize for my friend Dane. He said you helped him out with his science because you want to go out with him." Jim gave a small laugh at the vanity of that statement. "Is it him or the dance you want?"

"Dance." Her voice was weak. He smelled so good that she had to put her hand on her locker to keep from falling to the floor.

"I thought so. I like to dance, too. You mind if it's a double date?"

She managed to shake her head.

"Good. We'll pick you up at six on Saturday night. You live on Pine Grove, right? House with the red door?"

Again, all she could do was nod. He knew where she lived! *He knew where she lived!*

He stepped away but then turned back. "I think you should know that my girlfriend, Gena, is the one who arranged all this. Dane wanted to take Theresa Lambert but Gena said she liked you better."

"Thank…" Elaine cleared her throat. "Thank you. And her."

"You can tell her on Saturday. Oh! What color is your dress? For the flowers?"

"Blue."

He smiled at her. "Like your eyes."

Some guy yelled, "Hey, Pendal," and Jim caught a ball and ran down the corridor. As always, the students parted to let the sports gods pass.

On Friday, Elaine was so nervous she couldn't think. In each of her classes, she was the student the teachers could count on for an answer to any question. But this day, she just sat there.

One teacher, a nasty little man, said, "It looks like you have a date for the dance."

Not realizing that he was making fun of her, she happily said, "I do!" The whole class burst into laughter.

At home she stayed in her room, saying she had to study for a test. She knew her eagle-eyed mother would know that something was different.

On Saturday, she lied to her mother and said that she and some friends were going to get ready for the dance together.

Instantly, her mother looked like she wanted to cry in happiness. In high school in New Hampshire, she'd been a popular girl, invited to every social event. The only antisocial thing she'd ever done was fall in love with a shy nerd who wanted to become a tax accountant and live where he never again saw snow.

Her mother offered to drive her, but Elaine said no. She knew her mother would want to meet the other girls and chat with them, maybe even take them home-made cookies. She wouldn't like that her only child was going to a house in the worst part of Lachlan. And besides, there were whispers about Cheryl's mother.

When her mother kept pushing to accompany her daughter, Elaine sat down and said she wasn't going to go. It was the closest she'd ever come to throwing a temper tantrum.

Finally, her mother relented. Elaine put the dress she'd made into a long garment bag, her shoes at the bottom, and rode away on her bike.

When she reached Cheryl's house, she hesitated. The whole road was full of small houses in need of repair. Next door, empty cans littered the front porch and weeds grew through the old sidewalk. She'd heard people say this area was a "shame" and she could see what they meant.

Cheryl had slipped her a note earlier saying to come to the side door. Elaine hid her bike under a window, near a propane tank, then stared in shock at the backyard. It had rusty machinery in it and a big hole toward the back fence.

"Horrible, isn't it?" Cheryl had opened the screen door and was standing there.

She had on jeans but she looked as perfect as she did at school.

Elaine thought it was better not to lie. "It is awful. Somebody should clean it up."

"Mom and I agree but the landlord wants too much to do it. Come in."

Elaine was afraid the inside would be as bad as the outside, but it was nice. The house was clean and felt warm and friendly. The furniture in the living room was plain but it had been decorated with bright pillows, and a scarf tossed across the back of the sofa. There were many framed pictures on the wall, all of them looking to be original.

"These are pretty," Elaine said. "Who did them?"

"My mother. She likes to paint on weekends."

There were sunsets and old buildings and, Elaine's favorite, a beat-up old truck in a weed-infested field. "I really like them."

Cheryl seemed to be pleased by that and said thanks.

The kitchen was a separate room and Cheryl led the way. "We need to start by deep-conditioning your hair. It will help tone down the frizz."

To Elaine's surprise, there was a boy, eleven or twelve, sitting on a stool by the worn Formica counter. He was eating a huge piece of cherry pie. Nearby was a glass of milk and a big video camera.

Cheryl went to the old refrigerator and pulled out a jar of mayonnaise. "This is Jack. He's going to be helping me with a project this summer."

"Hi," Elaine said, but Jack said nothing. He just stared at her as though he didn't want her there.

"Jack." Cheryl's tone was of disapproval.

"Hi," he said reluctantly, then downed the last of the milk.

Cheryl handed him three one-dollar bills. "We need more milk, so you can go get some."

"I haven't finished my pie."

"Take it with you."

The boy looked like he was about to refuse, but he finally got off the stool, took the money and the rest of his pie, and left.

"Wow," Elaine said. "What's his problem? And who is he?"

"Roy Wyatt's son."

Elaine had to think where she'd heard that name. "Oh! Isn't he the guy who's always in trouble?"

Before Cheryl spoke, she looked outside to make sure Jack was gone. "Yes, he is. A couple of years ago, Jack's parents had a vicious custody battle. His mother hired a lawyer to have her ex-husband declared unfit, but then there was an accident at work." She motioned for Elaine to sit on a kitchen stool, and she put a towel about her shoulders.

"Was Roy hurt?"

"Heavens no!" Cheryl began slathering mayonnaise on Elaine's hair. "But Jack's stepfather was. He's a building contractor and a new wall that had been nailed down fell on him. When it happened, Roy was surrounded by men in a bar, but everyone knew he'd done it. Jealousy. But Jack's mother dropped her suit, so now the boy spends a lot of the summer with his father, stepmother and his little brother."

"I didn't hear any of this. Who told you?"

"I hear things," Cheryl said quickly, then was silent.

Elaine could tell that she'd overstepped. Looked like Cheryl's sources of gossip were off-limits. "Do you know the boy's dad?"

"No." She was massaging Elaine's scalp. "I met Jack when I got tangled up in a clothesline and couldn't get out. He was riding by on his bike and heard me call for help. He saved me."

Elaine still wasn't understanding the connection. "So why is the boy here now?"

"He brought the camera by. This summer his little brother is with his grandparents in Colorado, so Jack is going to film me doing some broadcasts." Cheryl

wrapped the towel around Elaine's hair, then told her
to stretch out on the kitchen table.

"Do what?"

"I want you to lie down with your head at this end.
I'm going to try my best to get some moisturizer into
your skin. What products do you usually use?"

"Soap and water?"

Cheryl groaned. "How do you expect to accomplish
anything in life if you don't take care of yourself first?"

Elaine was sitting on the old chrome-legged table
but it wobbled. "Don't worry. It's safe. I give my mom
facials every week."

Elaine stretched out and Cheryl put a rolled-up towel
under her neck. "What do you want to broadcast?"

"The news."

"You mean like on *Good Morning America*?"

"Yes and no," Cheryl said. "I just want to do the
local news." She was putting a nice-smelling lotion
on Elaine's face.

"But being a journalist could take you around the
world."

"I don't want to go around the world."

She said it so firmly that Elaine opened her eyes.
She knew little about Cheryl.

Until two days ago she wasn't sure of her name.
"What do you want to do?"

"Get respect," Cheryl said. "I want...normal, I
guess. A nice husband, two children, a lovely house.
I don't want to get stuck with one of the Roy Wyatts
of this world."

Elaine was beginning to understand. She'd read
somewhere, "Dress like what you mean to achieve."

"Is that why you wear what you do? So you don't attract people like the Wyatts?"

"Yes!" She smeared a clay mask on Elaine's face, then stepped back. "Clothes are powerful tools. They're a key that unlocks doors. I want my children to go to great colleges. I want dinner parties. When people see me, I want them to feel a sense of respect."

"A sort of Lady of the Manor."

Something about that made Cheryl laugh.

"I still think you should go to New York and get a job—"

"If I don't do it here in Lachlan, it won't matter. Being a broadcaster elsewhere would just be a job. I need to show people *here* that my family isn't what they think we are." She dried off her hands. "That's enough about me. What about you? What are you going to study at university?"

"English lit. My mom says that being a teacher is a good job for a woman."

"Where did you get that white jacket with the red piping?"

"I made it. When I was twelve, I spent the summer with my father's sister in North Carolina. She taught me how to sew. I loved designing things. I made whole new wardrobes for my aunt and me. We were a big hit at church."

"Then what?" Cheryl began taking the clay off Elaine's face.

"Nothing. I came home and went back to school. No more sewing. My mother doesn't believe in what she calls artsy-fartsy stuff."

"And your father?"

"He just wants me to be happy."

Cheryl began massaging moisturizer into Elaine's face. "I think you should pursue a job in fashion. I know! Change your major to business and make clothes on the side. Sell them on campus and take lots of photos. When you graduate, go to New York and present your portfolio of designs to some big shots at a design house."

Elaine was loving this fantasy. "And what about Jim?"

"Jim Pendal is so good-natured that he'll follow you anywhere. You just need to make him fall in love with you now so that he changes to UCF. You two *must* be together during college or some girl will snatch him up before he finishes the first year. Jim is pure husband material. He won't last long out there with all those hungry, grabbing girls."

Elaine was laughing. "So tonight I'm to stand up against the very strong personalities of Gena and Dane and make Jim like me so much that he decides to go to school with me and… What? Marry me and live happily ever after? While I'm some famous clothes designer in New York, that is?"

"Why not? Besides, I made a few calls." That seemed to be all Cheryl was going to say, but Elaine stared at her to tell all.

"I'm good at imitating voices. 'Our boys are gonna win! And if they don't, I'll nail their hides to a fence post.'"

Elaine was wide-eyed. Cheryl sounded exactly like their coach.

"Would you like some tea, ma'am?"

"That's English."

Cheryl quickly ran through half a dozen accents,

then mimicked three teachers. It was when she spoke so much like their common enemy, Gena, that Elaine nearly fell off the table laughing.

"I'm afraid to ask. What did you *do*?"

"My mother has a friend who owns a very nice Italian restaurant in Fort Lauderdale. Let's just say that, due to some phone calls that Gena and Dane received, there is going to be a major mix-up of who is supposed to be where. Those two are going to the restaurant instead of the dance. There might even be another misunderstanding about ages and they might be served bottles of champagne. Or maybe it's sparkling apple juice in a champagne bottle. I forget which."

"Are you saying that Jim is mine for a whole evening?"

"Or longer." She took Elaine by the shoulders. "I've seen you with other people. You're funny. You're creative. You're smart. But if you keep staring at Jim like he's something to be worshipped, you'll never see him again. Let him see the real you. Show him what he's missing by being chained to a dog like Gena."

Elaine was looking at her in wonder. "Why don't *you* have a boyfriend?"

"You think I don't?" She put her hands up. "I've said too much. I want you to get in the shower and wash that conditioner out of your hair now. We still have work to do and only a few hours to do it. Mark is going to get a workout tonight."

"Who is Mark?"

Cheryl nodded toward a red leather case on the table. "My Mark Cross is full of things that are going to show the world the beauty that is within you."

"Mark better put on his work clothes because he has a big job ahead of him."

Cheryl laughed. "Go on. Get cleaned up…"

Elaine looked as though she'd come out of a trance of memory, but there was a smile on her face. "Cheryl gave me one of the best nights of my life. Jim and I sat with his friends—the glamorous people of the school—and I was *on*. Like a spotlight had been turned on inside me, I lit up. I thought, *This is where I belong. With these people.* And you know what? They never said it out loud but they were glad to be around Jim without his little entourage of Dane and Gena. We laughed and danced and were full of the joy of being young and alive."

"And what happened afterward?" Sara asked.

"Jim went back to Gena and I took Cheryl's advice to act like I didn't mind. But that night at the dance had put a crack in the dam. The other girls loved the dress I wore and asked me to design theirs for the prom. A couple of times one of them would be talking to Gena and they'd leave her when they spotted me so they could show me a color they liked or a fabric. Sometimes just to chat. About two weeks later, Gena started throwing accusations at Jim and she broke up with him. He asked me to go to the prom with him—which I did. It was another magical night and that's when we started talking about going to college together."

"You started all this by saying that you knew someone who hated Cheryl enough to kill her," Jack said. "It seems like Gena would be angry at *you*."

"I thought she would be, but Gena was not only a control freak, she was also a spy. When we met that first time in the bathroom, Cheryl told me to act like I didn't know her. After she helped me, she still insisted I keep up the charade. I didn't like doing it, but I listened. Then, the first Saturday after graduation, I saw her outside the ice-cream shop and I asked her to go in with me. I was dying to tell her that her plan worked. We were sitting there with big chocolate malteds, laughing together, with Cheryl congratulating me, when Gena came to the table.

"I'd seen her at school and I thought she'd be furious at me for picking up the boyfriend she'd thrown away. She'd given me some dirty looks but she'd never said anything. I thought I'd misjudged her, that she was actually a gracious loser."

Elaine paused, as though what she was about to say was hard for her. "Gena came to our table and didn't so much as look at me. Her eyes were only on Cheryl and she said, 'You did this, didn't you?' She jerked her head at me and said, 'This one is too innocent to pull off what she did all on her own. All she knows how to do is make cow eyes at my boyfriend and cry herself to sleep.'"

Elaine paused. "When I look back on it, I know I should have stood up to her and defended my friend but she really scared me. Gena sneered at Cheryl and said, 'I knew that if I watched long enough I'd find out who really took my life away from me. There's nothing innocent about *you*. When you want something, you go get it. I had everything planned and you destroyed it.'"

Elaine looked at her hands for a moment. "What she said next haunts me. Gena said, 'I'm going to do the same thing to you. Whatever it is that you want, I'm going to see that you don't get it.'"

Elaine took a moment to calm herself. "Gena left after that. She walked out with her head up and her shoulders back, like she'd won a battle. Cheryl and I hadn't said a word. When Gena was gone, I reverted to a whimpering bag of mush and started crying. I was so afraid of her wrath. But Cheryl put her hand over mine and said I wasn't to worry. She said she had a secret weapon that no one, not even her mother, knew about, and that everything would be all right."

Jack, Sara and Kate were quiet for a moment, absorbing the story, then Sara said, "Your last name is Pendal, so I take it that you and Jim married. Still together?"

"Very much so. We have three beautiful children—two girls, and a boy born last year." Elaine paused for a moment. "When I said I owed my entire life to Cheryl, I meant it. Jim and I went to UCF and I told him what Cheryl said I should do. He thought it was a great idea. We both majored in business but he was much better at it than I was. My mind was mostly on designing and sewing and selling.

"After we graduated, we went to New York, and I got a job with a designer who eventually let me open my own label. Jim runs the business side of the company." She smiled. "Remember Cheryl's little red Mark Cross case? When I branded my line, I used half of that name."

Kate gasped. "You're Elaine Cross?" She stood up. *"Elaine Cross!"*

She smiled. "I am."

Kate turned, as though she meant to run to her own room, but she stopped. "Oh, no! You're going to hate me. I copy… I mean I…" She sat back down. "I love your designs."

"I'll send you this year's collection. Anybody who cares about Cheryl is my friend."

All Kate could do was nod.

After Elaine left, the three of them stayed in Jack's room. For a while, they just silently stared out the windows.

Kate was the first to speak. "Do you think this Gena murdered Cheryl?"

"Looking at it from a writer's point of view," Sara said, "I'd say no. She'd want Cheryl alive so she would suffer."

"But she didn't get a chance," Jack said. "Someone else wanted Cheryl out of the picture completely."

"Or Verna." Kate stood up. "I'm going to see what needs to be done with the other people. Wonder if your mom found any more interesting notes."

Kate left, then soon returned to signal that it was okay for them to come out. The girls who'd pestered Jack and the people waiting for autographs had left. There were no more notes that had anything but platitudes on them. On the kitchen counter were the names and addresses of people who still wanted their books. Janet from church said she'd mail them out once Sara had a chance to sign them.

"She's a godsend," Kate said absently as she started clearing up the debris from the party.

It was after seven when it was done. Heather and Ivy had left, both of them hugging Kate and Sara, and exchanging cheek kisses. Jack was filling a bowl full of ice cream.

Sara looked at her niece and said, "I don't know about you but I could stand some Kelly."

"As in Chicago?"

"Oh, yeah."

Smiling, the two women went to the big couch in the family room. Sara picked up the remote.

Jack put down his crutches, made his way to sit between them and took the remote. "What are we watching?"

"Severide," they said in unison.

Groaning, Jack turned on the TV and brought up Hulu. The women directed him to choose *Chicago Fire*.

"Yet another man," Jack mumbled.

He started to eat his ice cream, but when he looked at the women curled up at the ends of the couch, their legs drawn up, he lifted his bowl.

They stretched out, their feet in Jack's lap. He pulled a soft lap robe off the back of the couch, covered their bare feet and put the ice-cream bowl on top. They settled in to watch back-to-back episodes of the TV series they all enjoyed.

Sort of watched it. In their minds was the story they'd heard that day. Cheryl had done a very good deed for a girl she hardly knew. She had changed Elaine's and Jim's lives. And in a way, she'd changed the world. The Elaine Cross line of clothing wasn't necessary to the earth's health, but it provided jobs and gave pleasure. More couldn't be asked.

Yet Cheryl hadn't been allowed to live to see what she'd done. The question of "where do we go from here?" hung in the air.

During the credits of the first episode, Sara said, "We have to find Gena."

"Yes," Jack said.

"When we go, do we take arsenic or hemlock?" Kate said and the others smiled.

It was exactly how they all felt.

The next morning at breakfast, they agreed that the best thing would be to get back to normal.

"As if we've had any normal." Sara turned to Kate. "I still want to show you around South Florida."

"I'd like that."

Jack was moving eggs about on his plate and saying nothing.

Once Kate got to her office, everyone stared at her, but no one asked any questions.

Tayla gave her the listings and the code to the locks on the doors. "I want my agents to see a house before they try to sell it, so go look at them. If you see anything distinctive, put it in the specs."

Kate was glad to get out on her own. Her mind was so full of what had been going on that it was hard to think of small talk. "So how was your weekend?" wouldn't end in "Oh, fine. How was yours?"

She finally had a map of Lachlan and used it to find her way around town.

Tayla's specs included comments about each house. There were selling points, like walk-in closets, divine kitchen, new air-conditioning.

But there were also coded comments. "Make it your own" meant the house needed to be gutted. "Cozy" meant too small for more than three pieces of furniture.

But Kate's thoughts were so filled with the Morris women that it was hard to concentrate on what she was seeing.

When she left the bedroom of the eighth house and Jack was standing by the front door, leaning on his crutches, she wasn't surprised.

"The Matthews family owned this house," he said. "It needs a new roof and the plumbing is bad. There are three dogs buried in the backyard."

"Okay, Mr. Sunshine, what's happened?"

"We found Gena. She's in Miami."

Kate took out her cell. "I'll call Tayla and tell her—"

"Sara called her and they made up and they're going to spend today at a spa. Together. Talking about old times."

"I guess that really means that Aunt Sara is in the back seat waiting for us, and you called Melissa to flirt with her so *she'd* tell Tayla that I'd be gone."

Jack tried to repress his laughter but didn't succeed. "Exactly right. Can you imagine them suddenly being best friends? Hey, you want tacos? It's on the way and I'm driving."

"Think they have salads?"

"Ones with no calories at all. It's a miracle."

"Laugh all you want, but if you keep sitting and eating barrels of food, you won't keep that flat belly." She walked past him, her head high.

"Glad you noticed that I have one."

They locked the house and got in Sara's MINI, leaving Kate's car in the driveway.

On the long drive south through big, bad Miami, Kate described the houses she'd seen and Jack told the history of some of them. Sara knew a few of the families and their backgrounds.

They sat in the parking lot to eat tacos—with Jack eating the fried tortillas that the women wouldn't touch.

"So how did you find her?" Kate asked. "And what has she done with her life?"

Sara spoke. "Heather emailed us. Get this. Gena married Dane Olsen just out of high school and their baby was born six months later."

"Cheryl was right that Gena was trying to get knocked up to catch a man," Kate said.

"Cheryl was right about most things," Jack said. "Are you gonna eat that sour cream?"

With a pointed look at his midsection, Kate handed him the little cup. "Did they live happily ever after?"

"Dane left her before their child turned one," Sara said. "Five years later, he was arrested for dealing cocaine and spent three years in prison. After that, he wisely seems to have disappeared."

"And Gena?" Kate asked.

"At least three marriages. Takes any job she can get. Never stays with one for long. She had only the one child and he's nineteen now. He seems to like to steal cars."

In silence, they tossed their wrappers and Jack pulled onto the road.

He left the highway and drove into a neighborhood that needed work. The houses were small, close together and neglected. They made the Morris house in Lachlan look almost palatial.

Jack parked on the street. "Hope the hubcaps are here when we get back." When the women were silent, he stepped between them and put an arm across each set of shoulders. "You need to remember that whatever she says happened a long time ago. It's over and done with, and the pain was buried under a poinciana tree." Pausing, he looked from one to the other. "Let's stay polite. No anger. We'll get more out of her that way. And let's try to get leads of where to go next. Understood?"

The women nodded, then followed Jack up the weedy driveway. He knocked on the metal door. There was no answer.

"Did you call to make sure she was here?" Kate asked.

"And send her packing?" Jack said. "No, we didn't." He knocked again. Still no answer.

They were about to turn away when the door was opened by a woman who looked enough like the school photos that they knew she was Gena Upton. It was hard to believe she was under forty years old. Her bleached hair was dry to the point of cracking, and her skin was an illustration for how sun could damage a person's skin.

She looked like she'd been sleeping. There was black makeup smudged under her eyes and a bit of lipstick at the corner of her mouth. "You." She was looking at Jack and her voice was hoarse. "I've been expecting you." She gave a brief glance at Sara and Kate. "Looks like you still live in a circle of women."

Sara started to say something, but Jack put himself in front of her.

"Mind if we come in? We'd like to talk to you."

"I bet you would." She stepped back and they went inside. The furniture was old and worn. But what permeated the place was years of cigarette smoke.

Gena sat down in a wood-framed chair, while Kate, Jack and Sara took the couch. Gena lit a cigarette, took a deep draw, then said, "I saw on TV what happened. I figured it wouldn't be long before somebody came to me. I was never quiet about what I thought of Cheryl Morris. It's the innocent ones like me who always get blamed."

"Why don't you tell us your side of the story?" Sara's voice sounded caring and concerned.

Gena took another deep draw and let the smoke come out slowly. "Because of that girl, in one night I went from having it all to having nothing. She set me up to get drunk with a loser named Dane Olsen, and we slept together. And why not? The man I loved was in bed with that slut Elaine Langley. I've always wondered what trick she used to entice him."

"She made him laugh," Sara said. "And she was nice to him. She *liked* him." Sara's eyes were like an eagle with a rat in sight.

"Yeah, well, it wasn't real. That girl went around school wearing the stupidest clothes anyone had ever seen. She looked like a clown."

Kate started to say something but Jack put his hand over hers.

"Would you tell us more?" Jack sounded interested in what she had to tell.

Gena's sun-damaged face relaxed into a smile of pure pleasure. "I can't say I was disappointed when I heard Cheryl was dead. Murdered, wasn't she?"

"We think so." Jack showed no emotion, but he gripped Kate's hand so hard it almost hurt. But then, she needed that to keep from throwing the heavy glass ashtray on the old coffee table at the woman.

"Wonder who else hated her? Besides me, that is." Gena's voice showed that she was pleased by it all.

"We're only interested in *you*," Jack said.

Kate wriggled her hand from under his before he broke bones.

"All this—" she waved her hand around "—is due to Cheryl Morris. If she hadn't interfered, I'd now be Mrs. Jim Pendal and living in a nice house and wearing good clothes. She—"

"What did you *do* to her?" Sara was trying to conceal her anger. "How did you get her back for what you believed she'd done to you?"

"Heard about that, did you? Who told you? Wait. I bet it was that slut Elaine. What happened to her? Jim ever see through her and dump her?"

"Yes, he did." Sara didn't so much as blink at the lie. "He found out the truth about what she was like and left her. He's now lonely and looking. What did you *do*?"

Gena leaned back against the old chair and smiled as though her life was going to change for the better. "You may not think it, but I can make myself look good. I just need a little makeup. I'll get Jim back in no time." She looked at them as though expecting encouragement, but they said nothing. "The truth is that I've wanted to tell this story for twenty years, but I couldn't. Now that everyone is dead, I guess there's no reason to keep it secret." She smiled slowly. "It was a masterful plan and it worked perfectly."

She lit another cigarette. "I was in the bakery in town and feeling about as low as a person can be. I was supposed to leave for college in just a few days. University of Virginia. Jim and I were going to go there together. But because of what Cheryl Morris had done, Jim had changed schools, changed girlfriends, changed everything. And I was left alone. By myself."

Her frown changed to a smile. "But then fate took over. I was sitting in that bakery when Roy Wyatt's oldest kid came in." She gave Jack an up-and-down look. "You grew up as pretty as your father. But I think you're soft. Not like him at all." She said it as though it were a condemnation, a failure on Jack's part.

"Anyway, I saw you buy a birthday cake. I knew it was for *her.* You see, several times during that horrible summer I'd driven over there and parked in front of that rattrap of a house of hers and watched. I wondered how she felt at having destroyed a person's life. I saw a kid—you—go into her house, and I made it my business to see what you two were doing. I couldn't believe that she was planning for a career where she'd be on TV. She'd ruined my life but she was going to be a star on TV? She was going to have a life of nothing but *good*?" When Gena took a deep drag, her hand was shaking.

"I broke then. I drove away and cried for days. It was like there was no justice in the world. She got everything and I was to get *nothing*? That wasn't right."

"What did you do?" Jack asked.

She smiled at him. "I drove over to where Roy Wyatt was working on cars. With a whole lot of tears, I told him that I'd seen Cheryl Morris giving his eleven-year-old son a blow job."

The only sound was the sharp, angry intake of breath, but Gena didn't seem to notice.

"Of course, I didn't use those words. I just described the deed to your dad. And I asked him why Cheryl was doing such a thing to a little boy. Was it a cure for some illness?"

Gena was laughing at her own cleverness. "Your

dad, for all that he screwed half the women in town, fell for it. He kissed me on the forehead and told me he'd take care of it all."

Gena stubbed out her cigarette and lit another one. "And from what I heard, he *did* take care of it. What a *man* he was! He yelled at that bitch Cheryl, then he told old Captain Edison everything. I don't think he believed Roy, because the sheriff had me personally tell it all over again. I was a great actress. I acted wide-eyed innocent and described pants down around ankles and lipstick and… You get the idea."

She looked at Sara. "You write those books, don't you? I oughta tell you my life story, you write it, then we'll share the money. I bet it'd make millions. I could tell you lots about my second husband."

Sara's voice was low. "There's enough hate in the world. I don't need to add to it."

"Oh, well. You're probably so rich that you don't need more money. And why help someone else?" Gena paused, waiting to see if Sara would change her mind, but she was silent. "So anyway, I begged the sheriff to keep my name out of it. I told him I'd been traumatized by what I'd seen and I didn't want anybody to know. He was a nice old man and he said he understood."

When the three of them remained silent, Gena seemed to at last see the anger in their eyes. "Look, if you think I had anything to do with that murder, you're wrong. All I did was give payback for what she'd done to me. It was a high-school prank. Nothing serious. Besides, right after that, I left for college. But then I found out I was pregnant, so I had to drop out. I married that no-good bastard Dane and I—" She shrugged. "But you don't care about what happened to *me*, do you?

Only to that Morris girl. If you ask me, she got what she deserved. She asked for it. She—"

"Who else did you see at Cheryl's house?" Kate asked loudly. "Who else visited?"

"Arthur Niederman. I saw him there several times. But I think he went there for the mother—if you know what I mean."

"Who was Cheryl's boyfriend?" Sara's teeth were clenched.

"The only one I saw is baby boy here. And who knows what they did when I wasn't there? Maybe I guessed the truth."

When Jack made a movement, Sara and Kate each grabbed an arm in case he decided to leap on her.

"Did you see anyone else?" Kate asked. "Anybody at all? Male or female? Young or old?"

Gena's wrinkled face seemed to drain of color. "You think I saw the murderer, don't you?" She stood up. "If he's watching you guys, he'll connect you to me. Get out! Get out! Now! Go!"

They hurried out the door, Jack's crutches catching on a torn piece of carpet, but Sara halted. "On the night you went out with the Olsen kid, the 'champagne' you had was actually apple juice. And Elaine did *not* sleep with Jim. He was honorable and went back to you. But *you* broke up with *him*. Nobody has been at fault for your rotten life but *you*." Sara stepped outside.

With a sneer, Gena slammed the door.

When they got to the car, Sara took over. "You!" she said to Jack. "Get in the back. I'm driving."

He didn't protest. He handed Kate his crutches and she put them in the back.

Jack climbed into the rear seat, and Kate took the

front passenger. Sara quickly turned the dial on the GPS to direct them through the labyrinth of Miami to get them home.

She handed her cell to Kate. "Send a text to Gil to come over with full padding. He needs to get rid of some energy."

She didn't have to say who "he" was. Kate glanced over the seat at Jack. He looked like a cross between a volcano about to erupt and a man who was going to sink into a depression and never come out of it.

Kate sent the message and they went home.

FIFTEEN

KATE WAS SITTING ON A STOOL IN THE kitchen and she looked at the clock. Again. "How long have they been at it?"

"Two hours and ten minutes," Sara said. "Neither of them can take much more."

Behind them, coming through the open doors, was the pounding sound that Kate was beginning to recognize: leather hitting leather. Since they'd returned from Gena's house, Jack and Gil had been boxing. Or rather, Gil held the hand pads while Jack hit them.

For a while, Kate had watched them, but the anger on Jack's face had been too much for her. She remembered Sara saying that Jack's fights with his father had been sick-making. Scary. Kate could believe it.

She'd left the men and gone to her bedroom to have a long telephone chat with her mother. She heavily sugarcoated it all. Yes, everything was fine. Yes, she was working, had already sold a house. Yes, she was still seeing Alastair Stewart. Nothing serious yet, but maybe. No, Sara hadn't thrown one of her temper tantrums. Yes, Kate had been thinking about moving into her own place.

After she got off the phone, Kate took a shower and left her rooms. Jack was still pounding away or clunking about on the stone pavers in his cast.

"Gil will make him stop," Sara said. "And it's not all boxing."

Kate had seen that Gil was ordering Jack to do sit-ups, push-ups, hobble fast on his crutches. Anything to burn off the energy from what he'd heard.

Abruptly, there was quiet, and moments later, Gil walked through the house. He was sweaty and exhausted. He started to speak but then shrugged and went out the front door.

Jack came behind him, wearing only baggy shorts and his cast. His entire body was dripping sweat. It was cascading off him.

Sara handed him a tall glass of water, which Jack drained. She refilled the glass from the refrigerator door and he drank that one. Halfway through the third glass, he sat down on the stool beside Kate.

The women looked at him.

"Roy really did think he was protecting me," he said.

"That's what all this—" Sara motioned to his sweaty upper half "—was about?"

He finished the third glass of water. "Naw. This is about Gena. But I've been thinking about Roy. Any more of that fruit left?"

Kate got up and began preparing a plate for him.

Anybody who'd heard what he had today deserved to be waited on. "Cheryl wanted respect. That's what came through to me. She knew what people thought of her mother, so she was determined to get their respect." She pushed a plateful of orange segments to Jack.

"And she had a boyfriend," Sara said. She put a fat towel over Jack's head and began to rub his hair dry.

It was such a loving, mother-son gesture that for a moment, Kate looked away.

"But Roy…" Jack trailed off.

"Was protecting you." Kate started peeling a mango. "Maybe he ran over your bike to force you to stay away from a girl he thought was introducing you to too much, too soon."

"Yeah." Jack was smiling, his mouth full.

Kate glanced at Sara. It was nice to hear him say something good about his father.

"Respect," Sara said. "What Cheryl said to Elaine interested me. She couldn't leave Lachlan because if she didn't earn respect *here*—in this town—it didn't matter. Why do you think that was?"

Kate was eating a mango slice and Jack had a banana.

"You're the writer," he said. "So tell us why."

"A man," Kate and Sara said in unison.

"We know that," Jack said. "We just don't know who."

"I haven't eliminated that nasty Gena as a suspect," Sara said. "Anyone who can lie like she did could probably also kill. And she said she's kept this secret about Roy for twenty years."

"I can't see her planting a tree," Jack said.

"Of course she could!" Kate was splitting big purple

grapes, removing the seeds, then putting the seedless halves on Jack's plate.

"He can take his own seeds out." Sara took the knife away from her.

"Sorry. Habit. Sometimes it was hard to get Mom to eat, so I fed her grapes. She liked the purple kind but hated the seeds, so I…"

There was an awkward silence and Sara looked like she was about to ask questions about Kate's mother.

"If you want to peel them, too," Jack said, "that's fine with me."

Kate gave him a look to say thanks for covering for her.

"Speaking of skinless grapes," Jack said, "what about your old man Stewart?"

"I have no idea who you mean," Kate said.

"Alastair?" Sara said. "He would certainly fit the bill. Lachlan upper class. Cheryl would need to dress up to be considered good enough for his family."

"So would anyone from the Kirkwood family," Kate said. "And Alastair had a girlfriend. Who else in this gossipy little town is considered local royalty?" There was the beginning of anger in Kate's voice.

"Kitten got her dander up," Jack said. "Protecting her lover."

Kate reached for his plate, but Jack held on to it.

"Okay!" he said. "Sorry. I thought of him because he's always hanging around. I seem to see him at least four times a day."

"Give me a break," Kate said. "He's never even been inside the house. What about Dan Bruebaker?" She repeated what Alastair had told her, that Dan had been obsessed with Cheryl.

"I hope you two realize that we are completely ignoring Verna," Jack said.

"Arthur Niederman," Sara said. "I meant to look him up."

"I did." Kate looked at Jack. "While you were trying to hurt poor Gil, I found him and pinned his address on the bulletin board in the kitchen."

"That was fast work," Sara said.

"I did have some help."

"My mom?" Jack asked.

"Yes." Kate was smiling.

"Isn't there a song about wanting a gal like the one who married dear ol' dad?" Jack said.

"Eww," Kate and Sara said together.

He laughed. "So what's our next move?"

"You shower, dinner, then we'll make plans," Sara said. "Bruebaker and Niederman, for sure. Maybe we can find the landlord of their house. I'm with Jack and want to know who robbed the place."

"How do you shower with that cast on?" Kate asked.

Jack got off the stool. "Come on and I'll show you."

"You wish," Kate said. "Go on. You're beginning to stink."

Acting like he was hurt at her comment, he went down the hall to his bedroom.

"Tub," Sara said.

"What?"

"He gets in the tub with his leg over the side. He'll stay in there for at least an hour. What do you want for dinner?"

"Answers," Kate said and Sara agreed.

They had a much-needed quiet night. The repercussions of Gena's lies went through their minds. Like dominoes, one lie built on top of another one until they all fell down. Or in this case, two people ended up under a tree, their disappearance not even noticed.

The question they didn't speak aloud was "Did Roy kill the two women?"

The next morning, Kate and Sara were in the kitchen making breakfast. High-fiber cereal and skim milk for Kate; bacon and eggs for Sara.

A sleepy-eyed Jack, wearing only pajama bottoms, came in on his crutches and wanted some of all the food.

He'd barely taken a bite when the doorbell rang. Then rang again and again as someone began pounding on the door.

"Stay here until I see who it is," Jack said over his shoulder as he went to the door.

Ignoring his order, the women were close behind him.

Jack seemed ready to do battle, but when he looked through the glass panel beside the door, he said, "Oh, hell," turned away and went back to the kitchen.

Sara looked out. "Make that double hell." She followed Jack.

When Kate looked out, she saw a woman holding a newspaper, her thin face red with rage. She was older and had a hard look about her, as though she'd seen and done too much in her life. She had on tight shiny leggings and a red top with sparkles around the collar. Her shoulder-length hair was white blond.

She was still ringing the bell and kicking the door. Sara and Jack were nowhere to be seen. "Cowards!"

Kate called out, then took a breath, put on a smile and opened the door. "Hello!" she said cheerfully, her hand extended. "I'm—"

"I know who you are. One of Jack's. And a Medlar. Double curse on you. Where is he?" She didn't give Kate time to answer but strode ahead. "Jackson!" she shouted. "Come out and face me!"

It took him a moment, but Jack entered the living room. He'd pulled on a T-shirt. "What do you want, Krystal?"

Behind them, Kate nodded. She remembered. Roy's second wife and Evan's mother.

Krystal waved the newspaper in Jack's face. "*You* did this. To Evan's father! How could you do that to my son? How could you…do…that?"

The woman's energy was beginning to leave her. Kate went to her, put her hand under her arm and led her to one of the blue couches. Sara was peeping around the corner, so Kate motioned to her to get something to drink. Jack was reading the newspaper she'd brought.

When he finished, he sat down across from Krystal and put the paper on the coffee table. Kate knew him well enough to see that he was so angry that it was a wonder steam wasn't coming out of his ears. She sat down beside Krystal.

"This is your fault," Krystal said. "Flynn never tried to investigate your father. You must have told him—"

"You think he'd listen to me?" Jack said. "He hates me more than he did Roy."

"Not Roy. He's your *father*. You should call him Dad."

Jack's mouth went into a straight line of absolute stubbornness, and Kate knew she was seeing a glimpse of what Roy Wyatt's temper must have been like.

Sara appeared with a tray full of drinks. She'd cleaned out the fridge of cans and bottles, had poured a cup of coffee and made a mug of tea. Not fancy, but certainly plentiful.

"What's this?" Krystal glared at Sara. "You think you can shut me up with coffee?"

Sara suddenly looked as angry as Jack.

Kate leaned forward. Damn! This was like trying to deal with her uncles. She knew she'd only win them over by being on their side. "What did Jack do to you?" She heard his intake of breath but she ignored it.

Krystal's anger was taking on new life. "He's telling everyone that my husband killed those women."

"Actually," Kate said with exaggerated calm, "he's been trying to prove the opposite. We were told that Roy was the murderer and that, since he's passed away, we were to leave it alone. Jack insisted that we do whatever was necessary to prove his father was innocent."

Krystal leaned back to look at Kate. "You're a real sweet talker, aren't you?" The way she said it was *not* a compliment.

But Kate acted as though it was meant as one. "Thank you." She picked up the newspaper. "Mind if I read this?"

"Sure. Go ahead."

There was an adorable photo of Jack, younger than when he knew Cheryl, and a picture of Cheryl looking about twenty-five. It set the tone of the story that something was not right.

Tree Murders Solved
by Elliot Hughes

Rage. Lust. Child abuse. It's all there in the twenty-year-old double homicide that was recently discovered in the tiny, quaint town of Lachlan, Florida. When a giant poinciana came down, two skeletons were found tangled in the roots. Sheriff Daryl Flynn of the Broward County Sheriff's Department has now completed his intensive investigation.

The late Roy Wyatt was the town's bad boy: dark and handsome, quick-tempered, practically lived on a big black Harley. He was in and out of jail from the time he was a teenager. Never stayed inside for long and some said it was because he could coax a peacock out of its plumage.

But one thing Roy was serious about was his eldest son, his little Mini-Me, Jackson Charles Wyatt.

Back in 1997, when Roy discovered that a teenage girl was abusing his young son by... Well, no one really knows what happened—or at least isn't telling the sordid details.

What people do know is that twenty years later, the girl and her mother—who charged for being the town's good-time gal—were found buried under a tree. And the property had recently been purchased by Jack Wyatt, the aforementioned son. How's that for a cosmic coincidence?

Sheriff Flynn says there's no proof—and never will be—of anybody's guilt, but he now knows enough that he's closing the case. "Sometimes a man has to do what he has to do," he said, leaving it to the imagination of the listener as to what Roy Wyatt did or didn't do to protect his child.

It looks like the town bad boy may have posthumously redeemed himself. But we'll never know, will we? As Sheriff Flynn told us, "We should let the dead rest in peace."

I say that it looks like what goes around, comes around.

When Kate put down the newspaper, her hands were shaking. Sara had moved behind her and she took it.

"This isn't true," Kate said. "Not any of it."

Krystal shot a hateful look at Jack. "He's been sleeping with her."

Kate looked at Jack but he didn't react. "With Cheryl? All that about the child abuse isn't true. It was made up by—"

"Not her." Krystal grabbed the newspaper. *"Her!"* She was punching it.

"Elliot Hughes is female," Jack said but made no expression.

Kate gave him a narrowed-eye glance. So Elliot was the newscaster she'd heard he was dating? He should have told them of this complication. "That doesn't mean—"

Krystal cut her off. She was staring at Jack. "Donna is in tears. She's had to hear people say that her son is a murderer." She looked at Sara. "I bet you like anything that causes her pain."

"If you think—" Sara began.

Kate put her hand on her aunt's arm, then looked at them. For all the softness she saw, their faces might as well be on Mount Rushmore. "Oh, the hell with all this," Kate said, then turned to Krystal. "You have two choices. You can yell and scream and spit venom at us, or you can help us prove that Roy didn't do it. Your choice."

Kate got up and stalked into her room. She stood in front of the window, her arms crossed over her chest. She had to calm her own anger down. She'd spent a lifetime dealing with relatives who only knew anger. Orders. Decrees. Threats. Never any reasoning about anything.

After a few minutes, Jack came into her room. "Krystal has some things she wants to say to you." When Kate didn't react, he stepped behind her. "Come on," he said. "She's calmed down. I think she'll talk now."

Kate still didn't move.

He put his hands on her shoulders. "We can stop this anytime you want," he said softly. "My family is too much for me to handle, much less for an outsider."

She rubbed her upper arms. "It's not them. I think maybe it's the injustice of it all. That article was truly awful. It condemned innocent people. It assumed guilt of both Cheryl and Verna."

"And Roy."

"Yes. And him." She turned to face him. "If we figure this out, can you get that woman to retract what she wrote?"

"I think she'd love to write an in-depth piece about the truth."

"Is she the newscaster Alastair said was your girlfriend?"

"Probably. I met her when she interviewed me about

buying the houses. But it was just a one-night thing. We haven't gone out since."

"Think she had a good time with you?"

Jack blinked. "This happened before I met you. I didn't—"

Kate waved her hand. "A newspaper insider might be useful in helping us. But if you did some quickie that turned her off, she'll tell us to get lost."

Jack's eyes were wide. "No quickie. An all-nighter. Best she ever had. Her words, not mine."

"Good. Unless she was lying. Let's go talk to your stepmother."

Shaking his head, Jack followed her back into the living room. Krystal was still sitting on the couch and she'd poured her drink into a glass with ice in it. Cheese and crackers had been added to the tray.

Sara was on the opposite sofa but she looked ready to run away if the atmosphere again got angry.

"I want to help," Krystal said. "She said you want me to tell my side of what happened."

She, Kate thought. Looked like the air hadn't cleared enough that the names of her enemies were going to be used.

"I didn't know about the sex stuff," Krystal said. "Roy didn't tell me that part."

"There was no 'sex stuff,'" Jack said. "We didn't—"

"What happened?" Kate asked.

"When we heard about the, uh, tree, I looked back at my old calendars. I used to keep them so I'd know about Evan's shots. He needs—" She took a breath. "Anyway, I made a note about that house. And I remember it because of the camera." She looked at Jack. "And your bike."

She took a drink. "It was the last weekend before school started, and that Saturday morning we were going to the Sawgrass Mall to buy school clothes for Evan. Roy was in a foul mood, snapping at me, and we were about to get into a fight. I wanted to get there early, but he said he had to make a stop."

She looked at Kate. "He drove to the Morris house, parked across the road and told me to wait for him. In the front yard he picked up a bike that had been smashed. I knew it was Jack's." She glared at him. "Roy's first wife married a rich contractor, so Jack didn't have to take care of his things. If he lost or broke something, his stepfather could just buy him a new one. That bike cost a lot of money, but Jack had destroyed it."

Kate looked at Jack, but except for a darkening of his eyes he had no expression.

"Roy threw the bike down, then went around to the back of the house. I didn't know those people. I'd heard about Verna, so of course I had nothing to do with her. An old van was parked at the side, and it was packed to the ceiling. There were even things tied onto the back."

"What did Roy do?" Kate asked.

"He was out of sight for a while and later he told me that he went through the house. He said it was a mess inside, like they'd left in a hurry, but nobody was there.

"I saw Roy open the car door and take out a box." Krystal looked from Kate to Sara. "I guess he shouldn't have done that, but he was pretty mad about the bike. Those women shouldn't have destroyed his son's property no matter how mad they were at Roy."

"What was in the box?" Jack's teeth were clenched.

"A video camera and tapes. Roy said they belonged

to Henry Lowell and he was going to return them. I never saw them again."

She caught her breath. "Wait! That may not be true. I saw a camera just like that one at Donna's house, but that was at least a year later. I remember thinking that Henry must have recommended it. He was such a nice man." She looked at Jack. "I don't know why you couldn't have been more like him."

"Too much of my dad in me, I guess."

"Roy tried to make a *man* of you, but you were always ungrateful."

Kate said, "I think—"

"So how often did *you* leave him?" Jack asked. "And you got your nose fixed. It looks better than it did in the hospital."

Krystal came to her feet. "Everyone knows you killed my son. You were drunk and driving and—"

Kate put her hand on Krystal's arm, Sara went to the other side and they managed to get the angry woman to the front door.

"I'll talk to you two, but not to *him*," she said as they closed the door behind her.

Kate and Sara leaned against the door and both let out a breath. It felt like they'd just fought a fire-breathing dragon.

When Sara and Kate finally recovered enough to walk away from the door, they found Jack in the kitchen frying eggs. For all that he'd just been accused of a heinous crime, he didn't look disturbed.

"I'm going to go to work today." He sounded happy. "What are you two doing?"

The women weren't fooled. Sara glanced at Kate. "We're going with you."

"I need to—"

"See the sheriff," Kate said.

Jack gave a giant sigh. "Stop trying to read my mind. Flynn shouldn't have told the reporter all that."

"You mean your girlfriend?" Kate said. "Why aren't you calling her and bawling her out? But then, she's probably too proud of her own cutesy writing to be upset. What happened to printing the real news? Facts? Not hearsay about bad boys and motorcycles."

"Jack has Roy's Harley," Sara said. "It's in the garage at his old house."

"Yeah?" Kate's eyes lit up, but then she remembered that she'd declared she didn't like motorcycle-type guys. "You're going to go see the sheriff, aren't you?"

Jack didn't answer.

"Of course he is," Sara said. "And I'm sure the infamous Wyatt temper will help our cause." She looked at Kate. "How soon can you put on something nice? And short?"

"Are you pimping her out?" Jack sounded angry.

"I am." Sara smiled big. "Use your youth while you have it."

Kate looked from Jack to Sara, then back. "I have an Elaine Cross dress—a copy of one, anyway. I'll…" She didn't finish but hurried to her bedroom.

Minutes later, they were in the truck, Kate in the middle. "I think Krystal inadvertently gave us a date of when the murder happened."

"Yeah," Jack said. "Cheryl's sixteenth birthday. The day I gave her the necklace."

"And the day Roy ran over your bike." Sara sounded bitter. "I feel like telling Krystal the truth about that."

"She won't listen," Jack said. "She's martyred Roy so he's a saint."

"Do you think that Verna is the one who packed the car?" Kate asked. "Did what Roy said to Cheryl make them decide to leave town?"

A muscle in Jack's jaw was working. "Maybe Roy went back later. Maybe Verna got angry. Maybe he did kill them."

Kate looked at him. "Let's see what Sheriff Flynn has to say."

"After his 'intensive investigation'?" Jack sounded like he was gearing up for a fight.

He parked the truck in front of the sheriff's department and the women waited for him to get out with his crutches. "Let me have your car keys," he said to Kate.

"My—? Oh, no. I completely forgot! My car is still at the listing house." She dug in her Dooney & Bourke handbag for them.

"I thought that after we leave here I'd drop Sara off there. She can drive your car home, then you and I can go to the grocery. I'd go myself but with these things it's not easy."

He meant his crutches, but he was looking at Kate hard, letting her know he wanted to talk to her in private.

She gave him a nod of understanding and they went into the office. As before, the same young man was behind the desk. He spoke to Jack. "He's expecting you. Been on the phone for a day and a half. Watch your step or he might crack your other leg."

Sheriff Flynn was sitting behind his big desk and already frowning. There were three chairs lined up across from him.

"Good morning," Kate said, but the others were silent as they sat down. "Jack's stepmother, Krystal Wyatt, showed us a newspaper article and we were wondering if you—"

Sheriff Flynn put up his hand. "I know all about it. Krystal called and told me everything. And last night I got a call from a Lachlan girl, Gena Upton. Ever hear of her?"

"Yes, we have," Kate said.

"She's a lying little—" Sara began.

Again, the sheriff put up his hand. "I know. Bad actress. Lots of tears and no truth. I know Jim Pendal and his family. They were happy when he got away from that girl, and they are very proud of the one he did marry."

"Elaine," Kate said.

The sheriff stood up. "I want you three to stop what you're doing. Go back to building and selling houses and writing books." He looked at Jack. "And you can stop sleeping with every pretty girl who smiles at you."

Jack glowered. "You told Elliot that Roy killed the women. You have no proof of that."

Sheriff Flynn bent toward Jack. "Do you think I don't know what you people are up to? You're like a cyclone tearing through this town and leaving death in your path."

He had their attention now.

"You went on TV and made a fool of yourself over a pretty reporter and bragged to everyone how you'd bought a house. But there was *somebody* who knew that house hid his murder victims. The next thing you know, *somebody* cut the brakes to your truck. You ended up broken, but your brother is dead."

His crudeness made Kate gasp and Sara looked like she was going to faint, but Jack didn't so much as move a muscle. He was just staring at the sheriff.

"Then you snoops went to an old-age home to visit a neighbor of the murdered girls. What happened? When you got there, she was *dead*."

He picked up a file folder off his desk. "See this? It's an autopsy report of the late Mrs. Ellerbee that *I* ordered. Cause of death? Asphyxiation. She suffocated. I was told that she's old and accidents happen. Maybe she got twisted up in the sheets. But it's also possible that someone put a plastic bag over her head to keep her from talking."

He glared at Jack. "And *you* bribed the video guy to give you a copy of the tapes of who visited the home that day. Yes, that's right. I found out about that, too. A man who can be bribed isn't one to keep his mouth shut. It's quite possible that a *murderer* knows that you have him on film."

Sheriff Flynn went to the far side of the room. "I've got people calling me at home, in the office or wherever I am. I can't take a piss without someone reporting on something else your Scooby-Doo gang has done."

He turned around to them. "Not that you've waited for the results, but the skeletons found under that tree *are* Verna and Cheryl Morris. And yes, they were murdered. The girl was hit over the head—blunt-force trauma. Died instantly. Verna was stabbed. I guess that wasn't enough to kill her because she was also strangled so hard the bones in her neck were broken. Someone strong and really, really angry killed those two."

He looked down at his desk, then back at them. "Twenty years ago, something truly awful happened in this town and nobody knew it. The evidence was buried. It was all a real shame."

He leaned toward them. "But now you interfering busybodies are stirring up that evil. You're asking questions, making people remember nasty little things about their time in high school. It's like you're stoking a fire that's already burned people up. Four—*four!*—people have now died because of whatever happened at that damn tree." He glared at Jack. "Evan! Your little brother. I remember how you used to ride him around town on your bike. And Mary Ellerbee. I knew her. Very nice woman, but she must have known something about the killer, so she had to go."

For a moment the sheriff paused. "I want you to stop. I'm sorry the Morris girls were murdered. It's a tragedy. Edison shouldn't have believed that jealous Upton girl. He should have looked into it all and taken care of it back then, before it all escalated." He took a deep breath. "But that was a long time ago and it's done. I care about *now.* Today. I care about people who are still alive and I want them to stay that way. Am I making myself clear?"

Through all of this, Jack, Sara and Kate had said nothing, just sat there and listened. At the sheriff's question, they gave silent nods. Yes, they understood.

"That's it," the sheriff said. "I hope I don't need to come up with any threats to make you lot mind your own business. But if I have to, I will. Now get out of here. I've got a dozen calls I have to answer. Krystal and Donna are stirring up the town. And that girl Gena thinks she's going to be blamed for the murders—or be sacrificed to the murderer. She wants me to arrest Jim Pendal's wife, for God's sake. But if there are any arrests made, it will be your little Junior Detective group. For your own protection."

The sheriff stood there, waiting for them to leave. Jack took his time getting up on his crutches. Kate's heart was beating hard. Had Jack known the truth about his brakes being tampered with? Sara had told her that they believed brake fluid had drained when Jack drove over some rocky terrain, but now the sheriff said they'd been cut. Everything had just become much more serious—and dangerous.

Sara looked like she was about to collapse from shock.

Kate was the last one up. She reached for her handbag, which she'd set on the floor, but the sheriff did a deft little kick and sent it skidding under his desk. She looked at him in surprise but then understood. He wanted to see her alone.

Outside by the truck, Kate said she'd forgotten her bag and needed to go back to get it.

"I'm going to take Sara and your car home. I'll come back to pick you up."

With a nod, Kate turned and went into the office where the sheriff was waiting for her. He no longer wore his look of anger. Instead, he seemed to be a deflated balloon. She took a chair across from him and waited in silence for him to tell her what he had to say.

"That wasn't easy for me." He looked at her. "You're the only sane one in your little trio and I need your help on this. Those two have so much baggage hanging around their necks that they can't think straight."

Kate wanted to lighten the air—for her own sake as much as his. "To be fair, I have an equal amount of *very* annoying baggage. But the airlines lost mine. If it ever shows up, I'll be up that creek. No paddle has been made that can get me away from *my* baggage."

It took him a moment but the sheriff did manage a bit of a smile. "This whole thing started with Jack slobbering over that reporter. And now he's got *you* following him."

"Jack and I aren't an item, if that's what you mean."

"That's good. Saving yourself for a Stewart. Wise choice."

Why were the people in this town so obsessed with who she was or wasn't dating? Exasperated, she said, "Would it do any good to say that today women make their own futures? Men are just desserts? I believe in feminism, in women's power."

The sheriff had a full-on smile. "You are so much like your father."

"You knew him?"

"Anyone in Lachlan over…well, a certain age, knew him. Of course, he was a lot older than me."

"Of course."

"It's an old-fashioned word but he was charming. Made people laugh. Cheered them up. He and Roy and I—"

"Roy Wyatt? Jack's father? And you?"

Sheriff Flynn gave a one-sided smile. "I haven't always been a person dedicated to good. I sowed a few wild oats. Actually, it was your father who made me go into law enforcement." He laughed. "It was either that or jail. Roy went the other way."

"And my father?"

"He left town. Looks like he did a good job in making you."

"Thank you. Maybe I could take you out to dinner some night and you'd tell me about my father?"

The sheriff stood up. "I'd love to do that, but the gossip in this town would be that I made a pass at you."

Kate stood. "Then I'd have to say that I accepted. But that wouldn't be good for your reputation as a fighter of evil."

He looked surprised, then pleased. "Go on, get out of here." He sighed. "But please do what you can to get them to stop trying to be detectives. Go sell some houses. Help Tayla beautify this town. Leave the dead to rest in peace. You guys made a beautiful memorial service. That's enough."

She started to leave but turned back. "I didn't know about what happened to Evan...about Jack's brakes."

"Nobody does. But the day after those bodies were found, I was suspicious. I had a friend check that truck out. The line had been cut."

"Then why hasn't there been an investigation?"

Sheriff Flynn took a while to answer. "Jack kept saying he'd driven over some sharp rocks and they'd cut the line. But then, maybe somebody used a piece of flint to do the cut. Whatever, Forensics couldn't prove it was intentional." He shook his head. "Besides, there was a lot of alcohol involved. Evan was clean but Jack was saturated. And no one could prove who the driver was. If I'd pushed, it could have ended up with Jack in prison."

"And he is a Wyatt," Kate said and the sheriff gave a quick nod. "But you don't believe it was an accident?"

"I did at first, but since then, I've changed my mind. There's too much coincidence. Jack was the one who bought the house with the skeletons, so I think he was the target. But Evan paid the price. You need to make them stop looking into what isn't any of their business."

"I will do my best." On impulse, she kissed the sheriff on the cheek, and he turned the other one. Oh, yes. Cuban. As she left, she managed to smile, even if it was a bit weak at the corners. Outside, she saw that Jack wasn't back yet, so she sat on a bench in the shade.

Since the day she'd arrived in town, she'd been told that people believed Jack had been drunk and driving. Just this morning Evan's mother had accused Jack of murder. On the day the skeletons were discovered, the sheriff had asked Jack if he was staying sober.

But it seemed that it was possible that someone had wanted to kill Jack.

And Sheriff Flynn was beginning to see the *truth*. Even though he couldn't get his bosses to believe him, it was nice to have someone on their side.

When Jack arrived, he didn't get out of his truck. Kate got in and he drove away in silence.

He didn't go far as she'd seen that South Florida was rich in huge, well-stocked grocery stores. A Publix was in a strip mall and surrounded by necessary shops.

Jack pulled into a parking space and turned off the engine, but he didn't move. Nor did he look at her. He seemed to be waiting for something—and she had an idea what it was.

"Did you know?" she asked softly.

"Yeah. As soon as I got out of the hospital, I put my smashed truck up on a lift and examined it. Whoever did it didn't know squat about vehicles. Probably looked up what to do on the internet. I knew nobody wanted Evan dead—he was the good son—but Roy made a lot of enemies. They might want to take it out on me instead. It wasn't until after we found the bodies at a house I had bought that I began to think there was a connection."

"Does Sara know?"

"I told her about the brake fluid being drained, but I blamed it on some rough terrain I'd been driving. I didn't tell anyone I thought it had been done on purpose. Why should I scare you two?"

They still hadn't looked at each other. Kate's heart was pounding and she tried to quiet it. "You let everyone believe you may have been driving drunk."

"Wish I had been," he whispered. "Wish Evan had stayed home."

She turned to look at him. "I'm so sorry about all this. Your friend and your brother. You've lost the most from this."

He opened his door. "Which is why I plan to keep on searching for the bastard who did this. Flynn and his cowardice can go to hell for all I care." He paused. "But I want you and Sara to stop. I'll—"

She flung open the door. "Come on, let's buy you some fruit." She climbed out, then watched across the seat as he wrestled with his cast and crutches. "You think they have any pink grapefruits? I *love* pink grapefruit. Burt's Bees has a lip balm that smells like it and I would like to smear it all over my body."

"Can I help?"

She'd set him up for that one, but she was glad to see his teasing, smart-aleck, devil-may-care smile return. "Can you help choose fruit? Sure."

He gave a snort of laughter and shut the door.

They first went to the huge produce section. Jack

began filling plastic bags with fruit, while Kate went for the vegetables.

"Get the ones already cut up," he said.

"They're more expensive."

"I've got two houses you can list for me. We'll be able to afford them."

"We," she whispered as she grabbed bags of broccoli, green beans, brussels sprouts and peppers. All for her new family. Was there anything more soul-satisfying than belonging?

"So what did Sheriff Flynn want from you?" Jack put three colors of grapes—all seedless—in the cart.

"A date."

He gave her a half-hooded look.

"He told me that I'm sane, that you and Aunt Sara aren't, so I'm to reason with you and make you stop investigating." She left out the details of how Jack could have ended up in prison. "Did you know he and your father and mine ran around together?"

"Based on Flynn's wimpiness, my dad might have knocked him up."

"I'd laugh at that if you hadn't called my entire sex 'wimpy.' But it does say something about the preferences of your father."

Jack laughed. "You win. No, I didn't know. Roy and I weren't chummy. No fishing trips together. And no, I don't remember ever having met your father. What did Flynn say about him?"

"That he was charming. He said my dad made people laugh, cheered them up."

"Like you."

"Thank you." She put two bags full of yellow onions in the cart. "So what do we do next?"

"You and Sara stay home while I visit Arthur Niederman."

"You plan to visit him *alone*? Without *us*?"

"I take it you don't approve of that idea. How about if you and I visit Mr. Niederman while Sara stays home and writes?" He was putting tomatoes on vines in a bag.

"Aunt Sara won't like that."

"Then I take it that you don't want to protect her? You think she can stand up to whatever Flynn dishes out if he finds out we aren't quitting this case?"

The way he put it, it was impossible not to agree with him. And besides, he knew Sara much better than she did. She decided to change the subject. "I've been meaning to ask what you thought of Alastair Stewart when you were growing up."

Jack looked like he was about to make a joke but didn't. "I was in awe of him. Rich, blond, very tall, great athlete, four-point-oh average. When I was a kid, I wanted to dye my hair because everyone kept saying I looked like Roy."

"And Cal."

Jack picked up lemons and put them in the bag Kate held open. "Yeah, and Granddad."

"So what's your grandmother Donna like?"

Jack shook his head. "Grans is the opposite of Sara in every way."

"Except in her love of Wyatt men."

"No." Jack held up a big avocado. "Not really. Roy was her favorite. Granddad and I were a bit of a nuisance to her."

"The baddest boys get loved," she murmured. "Anyway, back to Alastair."

"Again." Jack headed toward the big glass seafood case, Kate close behind him.

"Do you think Cheryl would have been interested in Alastair?"

"Maybe. I was eleven; Stewart was a senior. We didn't exactly share lunches. But my guess is that all females like him. He called dibs on you ten minutes after you arrived and you said yes, yes, yes."

She ignored his statement. "You knew Cheryl. Who was her type? What fish do you want?"

"Sara likes the red snapper. Get whatever you want."

"Right. Real men eat whatever is put in front of them."

"Now who's being a Mean Girl?"

"Me!"

She spoke with so much delight that Jack laughed as he waited for her to give the order to the fishmonger.

They got shrimp and scallops as well as the fish, then started going up and down the aisles. Jack vetoed whole wheat pasta, calling it "extruded tile grout."

They were at the canned goods before he answered her question. "I don't know what kind of man Cheryl liked. I sure as hell wanted to be whatever it was. One day I showed up wearing one of Roy's leather motorcycle jackets and she thought it was funny."

"You were so cute that it would have been."

Jack groaned. "Cute. The death word for a man's libido." He put three cans of artichoke hearts in the cart. "If Cheryl liked Alastair Stewart, I never heard a hint of it. If I had, I definitely would have dyed my hair to look like his."

"What about Dan Bruebaker?"

"I don't remember him specifically. All those football guys hung out together. In their eyes, we little kids didn't exist."

"And when you were a senior, were you the same way?"

"Oh, yeah. My one and only year of being king of my realm." He ignored Kate's snort. "Have you learned anything that points to a murderer?"

"No. It's getting worse. Suspects are piling on top of each other." They were in the paper aisle and she was filling the bottom shelf of the cart. "Why wouldn't her boyfriend acknowledge a hottie like Cheryl?" When Jack didn't answer, she looked at him. "Oh. Her mother. He wouldn't have wanted to be associated with them—might've affected his reputation."

Jack nodded in agreement.

Kate paused with a big pack of paper towels in her hand. "I wonder who started the gossip? Who inflamed it? Who kept it going?"

"Yet another good question that we don't have an answer for." He took the towels from her, put them in the cart and started moving.

"Cheryl wanted to do better in life—but she felt she had to do it here in Lachlan. I think there was someone in this town who made her want to stay."

"And Verna was the same way. She could have left town," Jack said. "I mean, she had a good job in a big city but she gave it up to return to Lachlan. Why?"

Kate was putting packets of bacon in the cart and she halted. "I don't remember hearing about her having a good job and giving it up."

Immediately, Jack looked guilty. "Get the thick-cut kind." He swallowed. "Maybe Cheryl told me. I'm not sure."

"And you're just now remembering that important fact?"

Jack gave a weak smile. "Guess so. You want some hot dogs?"

"No. They're poison." Kate pulled her cell out of her bag.

"Calling anyone I know?"

"Your mother. You deserve a time-out. I cannot believe you forgot to tell us that. What else—? Hi, Heather. Could you help me find out something about Verna?" She told her what Jack had said about the job Verna had given up, adding in her annoyance with Jack for keeping it from them. From the look on Kate's face, Heather agreed with her.

When she hung up, he was smiling. "You and my mom get along well, don't you?"

"Better than you and I do. Wait until I tell Aunt Sara this. What kind of cheese do you want?"

"All of it. Did we get any crackers? I like it when you make a plate of things. You do it so it's very pretty. And tasty."

She knew he was complimenting her so she wouldn't be angry at him. She started tossing packets of cheese in the cart. "Come on, let's go. We need to get to Mr. Niederman before the sheriff talks to him and he runs away in terror."

"That would be difficult, since he can't use his legs."

She glared at him. "So help me, if you just remembered that, I'll throw that big round of Gouda at you."

"Somebody told me recently," he said. As Kate grabbed the end of the cart and began pulling, he added, "I think."

SIXTEEN

BY THE TIME THEY GOT HOME, KATE WAS seeing Jack's side. They must protect Sara. With the sheriff's threat that he was going to do what he could to stop their investigation, things could get very unpleasant.

"I don't want to see her locked up," Jack said as he drove them home.

It flashed through Kate's mind that her mother would love to hear that Sara had been thrown into jail. She made herself stamp down that idea. Of course her mother wouldn't be happy if that happened. But it was guaranteed that she would go into such hysterics that Kate would have to return home to calm her down.

Jack kept glancing at her, waiting for her answer.

"I agree. But how do we exclude Sara from this one thing?"

"She's been alone for a couple of hours, so she's writing. When she's absorbed by that, an earthquake can't disturb her. One time in New York she went into her bedroom to get ready to go out to breakfast. She didn't come out until it was time for dinner."

"I thought she retired from writing."

"I think trying to make a writer retire is like persuading a lioness to pretend she's a kitten. Can't be done."

"And irritates the hell out of the bear."

"What?"

"It's just a saying about talking to a man. Can't be done and irritates the hell out of the—"

"I got it. What if I called your uncles and told them you were using bad words?"

Kate didn't laugh. "Clever pirate," she mumbled as they pulled into the garage.

She didn't want to think about her uncles. "You think Lachlan residents will ever stop calling this the Stewart Mansion?"

"Nope. Could be flattened by a hurricane and rebuilt and it'd still belong to the Stewarts." Jack reached over the side of the truck bed and handed the bags of groceries to Kate. As she opened the door into the house, he gave a conspiratorial nod. They were going to talk to Mr. Niederman alone.

They were quiet as they put the groceries away. Paper and nonrefrigerated items could be left for later. It was better to come and go quickly.

It was when Kate looked at the bulletin board that she knew something was wrong. She'd pinned Mr. Niederman's address there but it was gone. When she tapped Jack's arm, he pivoted so fast on his crutches that he nearly fell. "It's gone," Kate whispered. "The address isn't there."

"I know how to get there. It's my town, remember? We'll—" Suddenly, Jack understood what Kate was thinking. His face turned red and he let out a yell that shook the house. "Medlar!"

There was no answer.

Kate ran to Sara's bedroom, threw open the doors and ran into the little library, Sara's writing room. It was empty.

"I'm going to murder her," Jack muttered when Kate found him in the garage. He heaved himself up into the vehicle.

She jumped into the passenger seat and shut the door. "You think she went ahead of us?"

"Oh, yeah. I saw that her car was gone, but she likes to park it under the palms on the far side. Says the car enjoys the view."

"Why did she go without us?"

"Because she figured out that we were going without her." He was backing the truck out. She'd never been in a vehicle doing fifty miles an hour in Reverse. She held on to the armrest and checked her seat belt—then noticed that Jack's wasn't on. But the look on his face made her stay quiet.

She'd never seen him so angry. In fact, she'd never seen anyone look as furious as Jack did. Kate remembered Sara telling about Jack's fights with Roy. The laughing, easy-tempered man she'd come to know wasn't in the truck with her.

This was what Cheryl saw that night, Kate thought. Roy Wyatt's dark good looks had been distorted into menacing, threatening rage. No wonder it was easy for people to believe that Roy had murdered two women.

Jack used back roads with little to no traffic to get to an area she'd never seen before. It was rural, with thick growth hanging down around them. Ahead of them was a crossroads with a stop sign, but Jack wasn't slowing down. There didn't seem to be any cars coming but the untrimmed shrubs made it hard to see very far. "There's a stop sign!" she yelled.

In the next second Kate saw the brilliant yellow streak of Sara's MINI Cooper coming from the side. She screamed. Jack turned the wheel so hard the truck skidded into a circle—and headed directly toward a palm tree with a trunk as thick as a stone pillar. He slammed on the brakes.

Instinctively, Kate threw her arm across her eyes. There was no way they weren't going to hit the tree.

There was another abrupt turn that threw her against the door, then the truck stopped. By the time she opened her eyes, Jack had already leaped out of the truck and grabbed a single crutch from the back.

"Sara!" Kate flung open the door and jumped to the ground.

The back of Sara's MINI was barely visible under trees and tall shrubs. Jack was fighting his way through to the door.

Kate was dazed but she was smaller than Jack and not hindered by a cast. She slipped in front of him to reach Sara's door first.

But her aunt was already out—and she looked as angry as Jack did.

"You were going to leave me out of all of it," she yelled at him.

He backed out of the bushes but his face was still like the person Kate had never seen before. "You're damn right I was! Flynn wants us to stay out of this. You—"

"If you say I'm too old for this, I'll hit you. I'll—" She gritted her teeth; her fists were clenched. "You were *leaving* me!"

The agony in her voice went right through Kate. She put her arm around her aunt's shoulders and began pulling her toward the road. As they passed Jack, she looked at him. "If you act like Roy Wyatt, we're going to treat you like him. Get it together!"

She escorted Sara across the road to a little clearing and helped her sit down.

The truck was nearby, turned around, and headed in the opposite direction they'd been going. There were skid marks on the pavement and a headlight was broken. The big palm was jammed against the side of the old truck. Another inch and they would have hit it hard.

Kate got three bottles of water out of the back, handed one to Sara and kept the other two. Sara was shaking so badly Kate had to open the bottle for her.

It was minutes later before Jack appeared with his single crutch. Pausing, he looked both ways before crossing the road, then dropped to the ground beside Sara.

Kate, still standing, opened a bottle of water and handed it to him. He drained half of it. As she stood there, looking down at both of them, waiting for them to start making amends, she realized she was furious. How close it had come to all of them being killed! It didn't take words to know that they were all thinking of Evan's recent death.

"You don't need me," Sara whispered.

Jack reached out an arm and pulled her to him so her head was on his shoulder. "Not true. We can't do without you."

Kate sat down on the other side of Sara and kept her mouth shut. This was Jack's bad and he needed to fix it.

"I saw what Flynn did with the purse," Sara said. "And you two went to the grocery to talk. I knew what was going on. You think I'm too old and fragile for this. But then, people think that old equals senile. I get asked if I'm 'afraid' to sit up without help. If I forget where I put something, I'm told I'm probably in the early stages of Alzheimer's. It's as though my age is all that's left of me. Nothing I've learned in my life counts. Just *age*."

"It was all my fault," Jack said. "I didn't see the stop sign, and I'm the one who didn't want you to go with us. But to be fair, I wanted to leave Red out, too. I thought I could do everything alone."

Kate kept looking ahead, saying nothing.

"Okay," Jack said. "New rules. We're in this together. We're stronger as a threesome."

He was still holding Sara against him, his face hidden from hers.

Turning, Kate looked at him. His voice sounded strong, but she saw how pale he was, and his eyes were full of fear of what had almost happened.

She stood up. As always, she wanted to lighten the misery. "I'm going to get the MINI out of the bushes before an alligator crawls inside and eats the seats."

Jack nodded thanks and put both his arms around Sara. Neither of them had recovered.

It took Kate a while to get the car back onto the road.

A side mirror was broken and there was some paint damage, but the car was drivable. She pulled it off to the side, fairly well concealed, and safe from traffic.

She locked the car, then went across the road to Jack's truck. He and Sara were still there, clinging to each other, but they looked better.

She needed to move the truck to the side. When Kate got behind the wheel, her hands were shaking. She put her head down on the steering wheel. She'd never been in a car accident before and the terror she'd felt had drained her of energy.

"Out," Jack said softly. He was standing in the open door, looking at her. Kate sat upright.

"I need to move the truck. I should…" Tears were starting. Jack opened his arms to her and she fell into them.

"I was really, really, really scared."

"I know." He stroked her hair. "It was all my fault. I'm sorry I got so mad."

"You were ugly-mad." She hiccupped.

"I know."

"You looked like Roy."

"I'm sure I did. But you weren't afraid of me."

"You love Sara too much to hurt her."

"I do. I— Holy crap!" He pulled away from her. "Flynn's car just went by. The idiot didn't even look this way. I bet that bastard's already been to see Niederman. I'm gonna—"

Kate didn't like that he seemed to have so quickly tossed aside his remorse. As hard as she could, with as much strength as she could muster, she kicked him in the shin. She hit his leg where the skin was the thinnest and where it would hurt the most. She was glad she had on her Coach pumps with their hard soles.

Jack hobbled backward, grabbing his leg. Between the cast and the one crutch, he fell flat on his behind onto the hard pavement, then looked up at the women in bewilderment.

Sara had stepped beside Kate and they put their arms around each other's waists. They were smiling down at him.

"You drive?" Sara asked Kate.

"Love to." She looked at Jack sprawled on the road. "Think you can get in the truck bed?"

He rolled his eyes. "Sure you don't want to tie me onto the bumper?"

Sara snapped her fingers. "I knew there was a reason I should have brought the chains." She got into the passenger side of the truck.

Kate stayed outside until Jack was in the back. He winked at her and she got in to drive.

Sara reached across the seat to squeeze Kate's hand. "I'm glad you're here."

"Me, too," Kate said. "Now, how do I get to Arthur Niederman's house? Not that the poor man will talk to us. Sheriff Flynn probably scared him to death."

"Or made him laugh in derision."

"Good point."

Jack slid the back glass open. "Are you two just going to talk all day?"

"How's your shin?" Kate started the engine.

"Bleeding. I may need stitches."

"I can sew," Sara said and the women laughed.

With a groan, Jack said, "Uncaring, unsympathetic. Is this where feminism has led?" When he turned away, he was smiling. With no thanks to him, they were safe. And they'd made vows to stay together. But then, a three-legged stool wasn't very strong with a leg missing.

SEVENTEEN

A MAN IN A WHEELCHAIR MET THEM AT THE front door of a very nice house set in a beautiful tropical garden. He was in his sixties, plain-faced, with sparse white hair. From the waist up, his body looked strong, but his legs were bone-thin.

"I've been expecting you," he said. "I assume you know that I'm Arthur Niederman. Please come in." He wheeled himself into a pretty living room and nodded toward a big couch and a couple of easy chairs. On the coffee table was a tray of sodas and water beside a closed metal cake tin. "I would have made coffee but you got here too soon after Flynn left."

When they sat down close beside each other on the couch, he looked startled. "What happened to you people? You're as pale as ghosts. Flynn scare you?"

"I almost caused us to crash," Jack said.

Arthur nodded. "Roy's son would do that."

Kate frowned. "Jack was worried about Sara, so he—"

Jack gave her a look to stop.

Arthur was staring at Sara. "You've aged well. But then, you always were the prettiest girl in the school."

"Was she?" Kate asked. "You knew our Sara?"

"Not really," Arthur said. "She was always running off home after school. And she was older than me. Not that you can tell that now." He smiled. "Anyway, you only ever talked to Cal, isn't that right?"

Kate looked at Sara and saw that she was wearing an expression like a bulldog. Her jaw looked to be made of iron. Kate thought that if talking to this man weren't important, Sara would leave. But at least her anger was making the color come back to her face.

Arthur was still staring at Sara. "What was the name of that brother of yours? The one you were always having to look after?"

"Randal." Sara's jaw was barely moving. "Do you know anything about Verna or Cheryl Morris?"

"I know lots," Arthur said, "and I've been waiting for you to come and ask me questions. Soggy Drawers Flynn ordered me not to say a word to you."

"Are you going to obey him?" Jack asked.

"Of course not. You can't obey someone who you've seen in perpetually dirty diapers." He was still looking at Sara. "So now you're a famous writer. I bet you have lots of contacts."

When Sara gave a little snort, as though she finally understood something, Jack and Kate looked at her in question.

"Give it to me." Sara sounded resigned to her fate.

Arthur smiled in triumph. "I knew we were like-minded." He wheeled himself back a few feet and took a thick envelope off a table. When he turned back, he seemed to have a spring in his wheels.

He handed the envelope to Kate, who passed it to Jack, who handed it to Sara.

She held it aloft. "Okay. You've given me your Great American Novel. Now tell us what we need to know."

Arthur's face changed from cocky to sadness. "I was really upset when I heard about Verna and her daughter. For the last twenty years I've wondered what happened to them. It wasn't until you guys found them and restarted the town gossip that I realized that I knew everything. I just don't know the specifics."

"What does that mean?" Jack asked.

"When it all happened, it made sense that Verna had run away. But I thought she'd at least send me a postcard, but she didn't. That really hurt. Now I'm sorry for my anger. I understood, but—"

"You understood *what*?" Sara blurted out.

"Still impatient, aren't you?" Arthur seemed to be amused. He looked at Jack and Kate. "When we were in school, I tried to talk to her, but she was always too busy." He turned back to Sara. "Tell me, do you remember me at all?"

"No."

Arthur grinned. "Thought not. I've never been someone who attracted women. 'Easily forgettable.' That's what some girl in high school called me. And that was *before* this happened." He nodded toward his legs. "Fell off a big company's roof. It was their fault, so their insurance paid me millions. Now women think I'm—"

Sara held up the envelope. "If you want this read by someone in the publishing world, then stop with the 'poor me' act and tell us about the Morris women."

Arthur's eyes lit up and he looked at Jack. "See what your grandfather had to put up with? She always did have a salty tongue." He looked at Kate. "By the way, who are you?"

"Randal's daughter, Kate."

"Good lord! Now, there was a boy who was loved by everyone. I remember—"

Sara stood up, loudly dropped the heavy envelope on the coffee table and said, "Let's go. He doesn't know anything."

"I know who killed them and why," Arthur said complacently.

When Sara sat back down, Arthur smiled as though he'd won a tug-of-war game.

"Would you please tell us?" Kate asked softly.

"When I say I know 'who,' I mean that I know everything except the man's name. And when I say I know 'why,' I know it all except how they were connected."

"In other words," Sara said, "you don't know—"

Kate put her hand on her aunt's forearm. "We'd like to hear anything you can tell us. Mind if I pour some sodas? And what's in the box? Cookies?"

"Yes. Help yourself." He smiled sweetly at her, then looked at Sara. "She's as well mannered as Randal, isn't she?"

Sara glared at him.

Arthur looked at Kate. "You need to find out who Cheryl's father was. You find him and you'll find the murderer. Verna came back to Lachlan because of her love for him and she stayed here because of her hatred of him."

Arthur leaned back in his chair, smugly smiling at their rapt attention. "I think the murders happened because young Cheryl was pregnant with somebody's baby." He was pleased at the shock on their faces.

He turned away to look out the window. "Those women had too many secrets. Verna with the love/hate relationship that ruled her life, and that beautiful girl who wanted to be somebody she wasn't. When the secrets were revealed, it's no wonder somebody exploded."

When he looked back at them, his eyes seemed to have aged. "Back then I was full of self-pity for what had happened to me. Little did I know how good I had it. I was getting around on two canes, and I had a specially designed car that I could drive. I was quite mobile. But I wasn't an example of virility like young Jack here, so I wallowed in my misery."

He looked at Sara. "I'm telling you this to explain why I didn't ask questions. I didn't believe that other people had problems because I was so involved in my own. When I heard about one, I turned away. I didn't listen. I…" He let out a breath. "When I saw that poor girl throwing up, all I wanted was to get away from her. I realized that she was pregnant and she hadn't even turned sixteen. But I wasn't concerned about who and why. I never even thought of actually helping."

For a moment he looked at his hands. "I guess you want to hear about that day when I found out."

"Yes," Kate said. "We would like for you to tell us everything."

Arthur nodded. "All right. It was near the end of the

summer and that day I had an appointment to spend a couple of hours with Verna. She…" Arthur smiled. "If you don't mind, I'd rather keep the physical part of Verna and me private."

"Of course," Kate said. "Just tell us about Cheryl's father."

"And who knocked her up." There was anger in Jack's voice.

Arthur smiled. "I saw you there that day. You looked like a lovesick calf. Big eyes staring at pretty little Cheryl."

"I never saw you."

"That's because I made myself invisible. And besides, a herd of rhino could have tramped through the house and you wouldn't have looked at anybody but Cheryl." Arthur lost his smile. "I can't imagine how bad you must have felt when she just up and disappeared. I'm sorry for your loss."

"Thank you," Jack said.

"So anyway, it was about a week before the girl's birthday. I knew because Verna was trying to get me to buy Cheryl a car. Verna saw no reason why I shouldn't spend some of my settlement on a nice secondhand Chevy for her daughter. Anything for Cheryl was her mother's motto. The love of her life."

"But that love wasn't stronger than her hate," Sara said.

"I think they were all one. Sometimes I saw it as a giant ball that was on fire inside her. Once that fire burned itself to the surface, it was all going to explode." He looked at Sara. "I used that in my book, so don't try to borrow it."

"I will do my best to restrain myself."

"Still spicy, isn't she?" he said to Jack.

"Would you tell us?" Kate asked, her voice soft. "From the beginning? Please?"

But before Arthur could start, Sara spoke up, her voice quiet. "I've written many novels, all of which required a great deal of research. In order to write about subjects like PTSD, I've read a lot of books about it." Pausing, she pointedly looked at his thin legs. "What we want to hear is the *truth*." She looked back up at his face. "It's time to tell it all."

Kate and Jack were looking at her curiously, having no idea what she meant, but the redness of Arthur's face seemed to show that he understood.

"Yes," he said. "It's time to tell the truth. Not what I wish were true and what the town believed, but what actually was..."

Lachlan, Florida
1997

Arthur Niederman did his usual trick of slipping around the side of Verna's house, making sure no one saw him. Since he needed two canes to walk and his balance was bad, it wasn't easy. *Damn the landlord and his laziness!* he thought yet again, working his way across the littered yard.

The owner of the house, Lester Boggs, wanted Verna—meaning Arthur—to pay three grand to clean up the place. But Arthur was holding out. He had enough trouble with every relative he had hitting him up for money. Just yesterday his mother's third cousin by marriage had called and asked for twenty grand.

Even this long after he'd received the settlement,

it still shocked him that people truly believed that if they just had X amount of money they'd be happy. At first, Arthur had yelled at them. "I've lost the use of my legs. You're healthy and you have a loving family, but you're the one *crying*?"

It hadn't done any good. Within four months of the money being deposited in his bank account, his relatives had labeled him selfish. Uncaring about his own family. That not one of them had visited him in the hospital or helped with his rehabilitation didn't seem to matter to them. Their demands had made him bitter and lonely.

He stopped at the corner of Verna's house and looked both ways. No one was around. He liked to slip through the back so nosy old Mary Ellerbee across the road wouldn't see him. She was like a mother and grandmother to Verna and her daughter. Always baking things for them, knitting useless little things. She would spend whole afternoons at their house, chatting with Verna for hours. And she was endlessly curious about their lives.

But then, poor Verna didn't have many friends in Lachlan. Actually, only him and Mary that he knew about. There might be some other men, but he didn't like to think about them. When you got down to it, he liked to think of Verna and Cheryl as his family. The one he never got to have.

When everything seemed to be clear, he leaned on his canes and started toward the back door. To his right were the remains of an old thrasher, something Boggs refused to move until Arthur paid him to do so. Farther away was what used to be a barbecue pit. Left over from the six college boys who'd rented the house for a couple of months. They'd dug the deep pit, cooked their hog, then hadn't bothered to fill in the hole.

Because Arthur was thinking so hard about other things, he didn't see Cheryl until he almost ran into her. He always tried to stay away from her. After all, what could he say to a kid who dressed like an adult? "How was work today? The traffic was bad, wasn't it?" She didn't look like someone you could ask, "Did you do your arithmetic homework?"

Cheryl was leaning over the concrete steps at the back of the house and throwing up her guts.

Arthur tried to leave unnoticed, but he didn't make it.

"Oh, Mr. Niederman," she said. "Sorry, I—" She couldn't finish but collapsed on the step.

He thought she was such an old child, a woman-child, really. So adult, so unflustered by anything. But right now she was just a girl wearing what looked to be her mother's clothes. Her usually perfect hair was messy and scraggly. When she looked at him, there was such misery in her eyes that he wanted to grab his canes and take off running.

He was pretty sure he knew what was causing her to vomit. She was about to pop out of the front of her blouse and four days ago he'd seen her nearly faint. Lord! Yet another pregnant teenager.

In an instant, Arthur could see his life ending. Verna wouldn't stay in Lachlan. She'd take her way-ward daughter and leave town forever. Arthur would be *alone*.

The horrible thought made him practically fall backward to sit on the steps beside Cheryl. She wasn't the only one who was depressed. Side by side, they were two glum-looking people. "What now?" he whispered.

"I'll get married," she said.

He turned to look at her. Ah, to be that young! There was no doubt in her voice that the boy would marry her and there'd be a happy-ever-after. "You're a bit young, aren't you?"

"I guess not," she said in a way that almost made him smile.

"So he'll take responsibility, that sort of thing?"

"Oh, yes. He's like that."

Again, there was that certainty. "What did your mother say?"

Cheryl's pale skin looked bleached. "She knows nothing."

"Verna must have some suspicions. When she met the boy—"

"No!" Cheryl took a breath. "I couldn't introduce her to him. To anybody. Never."

"You've kept all of this secret? In a town like Lachlan?"

"It hasn't been easy. I've—" She put her hands over her face. "Oh, Mr. Niederman, it's been awful. I've had to lie and sneak and hide. Lots of hiding! But if Mom had found out I had a boyfriend, she would have ruined everything."

Arthur's eyes were wide. His housekeeper was one of the town's biggest gossips, yet he'd never heard a hint of the Morris girl with any male. Suddenly, he realized what Cheryl was saying. Her mother would "do" something? And young Cheryl was having to keep it all secret? "How old is this guy?"

"Not much older," she whispered. She was looking at him with eyes filled with tears.

Arthur wanted to run away. He fumbled for his canes but one had fallen to the ground. He did not want to be involved in some scandal that would make little Lachlan a national laughingstock. Teen pregnant by…what? A man in his twenties? Thirties? Forties? Married with kids?

"I better go. Tell your mother I'll call her."

Cheryl clamped both hands on his forearm, her perfect pink nails cutting into his skin. "I want you to tell Mom for me. Find out how crazy she'll be when I tell her that I'm going to get married very soon. Tell her I'll stay here in Lachlan and I'll get a good job at a local TV station. A job like she used to have. I will not be throwing my life away."

Arthur could feel his heart in his throat. "I can't do that."

"Yes, you can."

Again, he tried to stand up.

Cheryl's look of pleading went away and was replaced by an expression he'd seen on Verna's face. Had seen it only once. About a year ago, he'd made a joke about how pretty her daughter was and maybe little Cheryl would start running around soon. It came out more vulgar than he'd meant it to.

Verna's face had changed to this, an expression of such rage that it made the hairs on his body stand up. Before he could apologize, she pushed him off the massage table. If he hadn't bounced onto the bed, he would have hit the floor. As it was, he had to pull himself across the old carpet by his arms to get to his canes. The fact that he was naked added to his humiliation.

When he managed to stand, he tried to cover his nakedness, but keeping his balance at the same time was impossible. He made an attempt to grab his boxers but she threw them out the open door.

Completely naked, he got outside, leaned against the house to pull on his boxers, then drove home. It was seven months before he was able to persuade Verna—with flowers, candy, lavish apologies and doubling his payments—to forgive him enough to start the massages again.

Right now, young Cheryl, with her tearstained makeup, was wearing that expression—and it scared Arthur half to death.

"The people in this town think you and my mother have sex for money," Cheryl said slowly. "You never contradict them because you like that people think you can still do it."

Arthur sat back down. She was right. He liked being teased about what he did at the Morris house. Young men driving big pickups tugged at the brim of their caps when they saw him. Their tributes made him feel young and whole.

As he looked at Cheryl's hard eyes, he thought of how his life would change if his secret was told. Pity instead of accolades. "I'll talk to her," he said. "I'll ask."

She stood up. "Good." She went into the house.

Minutes later, Arthur was lying naked on the massage table that Henry Lowell had made for Verna. Her hands were glistening with oil as she gouged and dug into his flaccid leg muscles.

"So why'd you come back to Lachlan?" he asked.

"Why do you want to know?"

"Just being friendly, that's all."

"You've never so much as asked me how my day was, much less about my life."

"So maybe I'm curious. Is that so unusual?"

"From you, it is."

Arthur took his time before asking again. "So I'm bored. Tell me your life story. Take my mind off my own problems."

"I thought you believed only you had problems."

Arthur gave a sigh. "How about that car for Cheryl? In exchange for a story?"

"The green one?"

"Sure. So tell me a story worth a car."

"Why not? It's not like I have a thousand friends in this town. It's simple, really. In high school all I could think about was getting away from this backwater town. I wanted to go someplace where the muggers didn't have four feet and teeth."

"What you got against gators?"

"Are you going to listen or not? So anyway, the day after I graduated from high school, I went to Baltimore. I loved it! Everything was fast and they had snow. I worked as a waitress during the day and went to school at night. I became a legal secretary."

"Good money?"

"Yes." She paused. "But then my father died and I returned to Lachlan for the funeral and to get my mother settled in a nursing home. That was the end of my life as I knew it."

"You look healthy to me."

"But then, you never believe that there are things worse than your own problems. Turn over." She waited until he was on his back. "I met a man."

"Ah," Arthur said.

"Right. Exactly. I knew him in high school. He was a jock and I'd never paid any attention to him, but—" She shrugged. "But when I came back, I fell for him. Fell really, really hard." She seemed ready to stop there.

"So why aren't you with him now?"

"He was already married."

"Never heard of divorce?"

"He wouldn't do it. Gave lots of reasons. So I went back to Baltimore, cried a lot and thought that was the end of it. But four months later, I realized I was pregnant."

"What did he say when you told him?"

"I didn't. I planned to wait until after the baby was born, then send him photos. I was sure that would make him come running. But when I held Cheryl in my arms…"

"That was it," Arthur said.

"Yes. I had friends, a good job and my daughter. I didn't want anything else."

"No man?"

"There were a couple of guys I dated, but…"

"But they didn't do for you what Cheryl's father did."

"You're making this into a cliché."

"Sorry. So, then what made you come back?"

"He did. He found us when Cheryl was eleven and begged us to return. He had business here, so he couldn't leave, but he showed the papers of the divorce he was going to get. He said he wanted to be part of our lives." She stopped massaging Arthur's legs.

"And you moved back to Lachlan."

"I did, but he didn't go through with the divorce." Verna gritted her teeth. "His wife said no, he couldn't leave his kid, his business would suffer. You name it, he gave it as an excuse."

Arthur watched as the red of rage seeped up her neck and into her face.

"You could have gone back to Baltimore."

"I wanted to, but Cheryl begged to stay here and—and I wanted him to see us. To see what he'd lost. I knew he was miserable in his marriage. He offered me money but I refused. That was probably a mistake. To stay, I had to supplement my income with you."

"And a couple of others," he added, trying not to smirk. When she said nothing else, he opened his eyes and looked at her. Her face had gone stone-cold. Everyone in town knew what she did, which was why Arthur had never felt bad about letting people think there was more between him and Verna than massages. Only he knew that Verna would have slapped him down if he so much as asked. Was she like that with her other clients? He'd always assumed that what the town whispered about her was true, but what if it wasn't? "The town thinks that you—" He couldn't say the rest of it.

"I know they do. At first I tried to set them straight, but no one believed me."

"Who started the gossip? Who keeps it going?"

"I'm not sure, but I have an idea."

He waited for her to say who it was, but she didn't. "So what happens now?"

"The minute Cheryl graduates from high school, we're out of here no matter how hard she fights me. The only temper tantrum she ever threw was when I said I wanted us to leave this town. I can't figure out what she loves about it."

"She certainly loved something here," Arthur

mumbled as he thought of Cheryl's predicament. The girl was fifteen and pregnant with some older man's baby—and she actually believed the guy was going to marry her. Arthur needed to lead into a talk about that. "If you leave, that Wyatt kid will be heartbroken."

"Yeah, probably. I stay away from that boy. He shows up and I hide. If I got near him, Lord only knows what Roy Wyatt would accuse me of. Not that he pays any attention to his poor son."

"He and Cheryl seem like a good match."

"Yeah. He's a smart kid. Helps my girl with her newscaster practice. Cheryl wanted me to do it but I don't have the patience."

"It's been a good summer for her. Mostly because of that boy." Arthur paused. "Maybe Cheryl will want to get married and stay here."

"Hell no! When she graduates, we're leaving. I'll have the car packed and ready. I'll be glad to see the last of this place."

"But what if Cheryl has other plans?"

"Like what?" Verna was getting angry.

"I didn't mean anything. I was just asking." He put his hand out and she gave him his canes. "What does Cheryl know about her father?"

"Nothing at all. I told her he was a man I met at a concert and that he played a killer guitar."

"What about when Cheryl gets a boyfriend here?"

"That's not going to happen. I keep too close a watch on her. I drill it into her that earning a living is what's important. She shows up with a boyfriend, and two hours later, we'll be on the road heading north…"

Arthur stopped talking.

"That's it?" Kate said. "But what happened?" She

looked at Jack and Sara. "Oh." She turned back to Arthur. "You never saw them again?"

Arthur looked out the window. "Only once. I knew it was Cheryl's birthday and I took the keys to the car I'd bought her to their house. It was late because I'd had the car cleaned and detailed. I wanted the girl to have something nice because of what was coming to her."

He looked down at his hands, then up again. "You know how sometimes you can just *feel* an atmosphere? Like going into a haunted house and you don't see anything but you can feel that there is something else there?"

The three of them nodded in unison but said nothing.

"That's how it was that day. I parked a few houses away. It was harder for me physically, but I was afraid of facing Verna. Afraid of what I was going to find at their house. If Cheryl had told her mother…" He paused. "It was worse than I ever imagined. I swear I could feel the misery inside that house as soon as I reached the driveway. Verna's old car was gone and there was a big black van parked there. The back doors were open and I could see that it was already packed with household goods."

He looked at Sara. "I'm ashamed to say that all I thought of was myself. They were leaving *me*. That's how I saw it. I felt no compassion for what they must be going through to make them pack up and leave. All I felt was anger that I was going to be utterly and absolutely alone." He grimaced. "And how was I going to keep up my image of being a stud? Of making people believe that I was still sexually active? Me. That's all I thought about. I put the car keys in my pocket and left."

"And that night someone killed them," Sara whispered.

Arthur's head was bent forward and they could see that he was softly crying. Kate looked at the others and they nodded. It was time to go. Jack picked up the manuscript, then quietly, they left Mr. Niederman's house. Outside, the air seemed fresh and clean.

They got into the truck and Jack drove them to where the MINI Cooper was parked beside the road. "I'll meet you back at the house," Jack said.

Kate nodded, then she and Sara got into the car.

Eighteen

ON THE WAY HOME, THEY DIDN'T TALK ABOUT what they'd heard. The day had been too long and too full of drama for them to fully digest it all. When they got back, Sara disappeared into her writing room "to make some notes."

Kate and Jack went to the kitchen. She put away the contents of the grocery bags they'd left behind when they'd run out the door. Jack began slicing peppers and onions for the grill.

"I'll get a couple of the men to take the MINI to the body shop tomorrow," he said.

Kate nodded but didn't speak.

"Actually, I need to buy a new truck. Maybe we can all go to the Chevy dealer and pick out one. You and Sara can choose the color."

Again Kate nodded. She was standing beside Jack

and peeling an onion for him to slice. The fumes were bothering her eyes.

He wasn't fooled. He set down the knife and put his arms around her. Her arms were hanging flat against her sides.

The tears came hard, wetting his T-shirt. "A baby," she whispered. "Three of them died, not two. They…"

Jack was stroking her hair. "I know. She was such a nice girl and she must have been in love and…" He was too choked up to speak.

Kate kept crying. All she could think about was what Arthur had told them.

Cheryl was going to have a baby and she thought she was going to be married and get a good job at a TV station and live happily ever after. "But her life was taken away from her," Kate said.

"And her mother's."

"And the *baby's*." Kate's tears strengthened and she clasped Jack about the waist.

"Now he'd be—" Jack broke off when the doorbell rang. "Ignore it," he muttered and clasped Kate tighter.

She pulled away and wiped her eyes. "It might be important."

With a grimace, he headed to the front door, Kate a step behind him. He looked out the glass panel, then turned to her in anger. "It's *him*."

"Mr. Niederman?"

Jack's eyes darkened.

She understood. It was Alastair.

"Don't ask him to stay. Don't tell him anything. Don't go out with him. You might slip up and tell him something."

"Jack," Kate said with a smile, "go screw yourself." Turning, she hurried toward her bedroom.

"Where are you going?" He was practically hissing. "Don't leave me alone with him."

"Man up and *talk* to him," she said over her shoulder as she closed the door behind her.

With the speed of light, Kate repaired her face and pulled on a cute cotton sleeveless blouse and midthigh shorts. Tasteful, not too revealing, but she hoped sexy.

As she stepped back from the mirror, she said, "What do you think, Cheryl?" For a moment she paused and blinked back more tears. How involved her life had become with those two women! She opened the door.

Sara had come out of her room and she was with Jack and Alastair in the kitchen. Alastair had a glass of cola and Kate would bet that Jack hadn't poured it for him.

Jack was still chopping things and he gave Kate a look as though he was being greatly imposed upon.

"Hi," Alastair said to Kate. His eyes swiftly moved up and down her in an approving way.

Kate smiled demurely. "It's lovely to see you again."

Jack rolled his eyes at her formality. Ignoring him, she went forward and exchanged double-cheek kisses with Alastair.

"Alastair brought something from high school to show you," Sara said.

"Honor-roll certificate?" Jack had been moving about the kitchen quite well, but now he made a big display of using his crutches.

"I didn't mean to just show up," Alastair said to Kate, "but I did send you some text messages."

"Sorry, but I didn't look at my phone. Today has been, uh, very busy."

"Bet your mother is frantic with worry," Jack said. "You should call her."

"She'll live," Sara said. "Alastair, please, let's sit down and you can show us what you brought. Jack doesn't need us to use a grill."

Jack mumbled something but they couldn't hear what it was. He stayed in the kitchen while Sara, Kate and Alastair went a few feet away and sat down on the sofa.

Immediately, Alastair's eyes went to the wall. On both sides of the big TV, they'd taped photos enlarged from the high-school yearbook, and the names of people they had talked to or wanted to interview. In large letters was printed Cheryl's Birthday.

"I see you've made some progress in your investigation," Alastair said.

Sara gave a little laugh. "'Fraid it has all come to a permanent standstill. Happened too long ago to find out anything now, and besides, Sheriff Flynn was threatening us that we had better stop. I've decided to use the work we did as inspiration for a new book."

Alastair was sitting between them and Kate looked around him to stare wide-eyed at Sara. She was certainly good at lying!

"So what do you have to show us?" Sara asked.

Alastair leaned back on the couch. "My mother found a high-school clipping that I'd like to show you." He turned to Jack, who was frowning in the kitchen. "Actually, I came to see you."

It was a moment before Jack looked up to see them staring at him. "Me?"

"Yes. Last night I had dinner with my mother and three of her lady friends. I don't mean to sound elitist, but they are all rich widows, and they don't like condo living. Too many young people, too much noise. They've decided that they'd like to buy your houses, all six of them. After you've remodeled them, of course. And they'd like to buy some more houses there, too. For more friends. They also want one of the houses made into a kind of gym-cum-spa and to put in a pool. Basically, they've dreamed up a retirement living community, but where they get their own homes instead of being cooped up in apartments."

Through all this, Jack had been listening with his knife aloft. He put it down and grabbed his crutches. "Kate! Finish this up. And add some more veggies. Alastair, would you please stay for dinner? It's not much but we'll do our best."

Kate got up, and as she passed Jack on her way to the kitchen, she murmured, "Money sings a new song."

Jack was smiling at Alastair too broadly to pay any attention to her snarkiness. Minutes later they moved to the outdoor kitchen and the big grill. Jack went with Alastair and left the women to bring out the food and drinks.

Once they were outside, Jack became the ultimate host. He crushed ice in a big blender and made a pitcher of margaritas. He served Alastair first.

"This is a nice layout." Alastair swerved around on his stool to look at the pool and covered lanai. "Mom and her ladies would love this. When I lived here—" He waved his hand. "You don't want to hear about the olden days."

Kate and Sara were sipping their drinks. "We'd love to hear."

"Everything in the house was very formal. Mom was raised in a family in Philadelphia that sat down every night to a dinner with three forks. To her, the Florida lifestyle was almost too informal to bear."

"And now?" Kate asked.

"She's adjusted well. Yesterday I had lunch at her condo and each plate had just one fork—with a bamboo handle!"

"Downright decadent." Kate was looking at him over her glass.

"And what about Hamish?" Sara was on a stool beside Kate.

Alastair shrugged. "You know what Dad was like. He was at home anywhere. Very easygoing, affable man. Everyone liked him."

"That's true." Sara was smiling in memory. "He used to visit Cal and me at our houses."

No one said it aloud but the thought that the man who'd grown up in the Stewart Mansion would visit the run-down houses of the Wyatts and Medlars said a lot about him.

"He sounds nice," Kate said.

"And so is my mother," Alastair said. "Except when she's nagging me to get married and give her grandchildren. Then she's a terror."

There was silence as Alastair and Kate smiled at each other over their drinks.

Jack's voice, so loud the birds stopped singing, broke the silence. "So how much say do you want in the remodeling? If you buy the houses, that is?"

Alastair whirled his stool to face him. "I'd love to

say none. From what I see of this place, I'd give you
carte blanche. But four rich widows with empty days...
Sorry, but I'm sure they'll drive you insane. Think you
can handle it?"

"Easily," Jack said.

"Mind if I look at this?" Sara asked. The envelope
he'd brought was on the bar.

"Please do," Alastair said. "I think I should warn
you that Sheriff Flynn has kept my mother informed
of everything he knows." He looked at Jack. "Sorry
to tell you this, but your stepmother and grandmother
have practically camped out in his office. They want
Roy's name cleared. And Gena Upton has come out of
the woodwork to set herself up as someone who needs
24/7 protection. She suggested Deputy Pete for the job."

"The hunk at the desk," Sara said.

"That's the one. Anyway, once the sheriff gave us a
date for the murder, it was easy to find out where I was
at the time." When Kate started to speak, he smiled.
"It's okay. It didn't take much deduction to realize that
every person in the school is a suspect. But then, everyone on the planet who was alive then remembers
that weekend."

Kate wasn't sure what he meant, but Sara's and
Jack's faces were also blank. They had no idea what
he was talking about.

"The funeral of Princess Diana," Alastair said. "I
remember it clearly. The team and I were in Naples
that weekend for a training boot camp. The coaches
were having fun seeing how much they could put us
through before we fell down dead." He looked at Jack.
"You remember those camps, don't you?"

"Oh, yeah."

Sara had pulled out the contents of the envelope. There were two newspaper clippings inside plastic slip-covers. Some of the players, like Alastair, were preparing for college in the fall, and they were the best from three counties. There was a banquet photo for the Friday night they were pretty sure Cheryl and her mother were murdered. The next morning Roy and Krystal had gone to the house. It was open and empty, the packed van in the driveway. It was possible that the bodies were buried just a few feet away. Had the tree been planted already?

Sara flipped through the pages. There was a copy of the week's schedule. It went hour by hour, from early to late. The last page was a certificate saying that Alastair Stewart had attended every class every day. It was signed and had a gold seal on it.

"I guess it's my alibi."

"You didn't need one." As she spoke, Kate looked at Jack.

"I think everyone in this town needs an alibi for that night," Alastair replied. He turned back to Jack. "Not to change the subject, but would you mind if I put dibs on the Morris house for my mother?"

"No, of course not."

"And we'd like to name the meeting place the CV Morris Clubhouse. You think anyone would mind?"

"I think that would be very nice," Sara said.

They had an enjoyable meal—Jack had wrapped the fish in banana leaves that Sara had pulled off a short tree in the garden—as they talked about Jack's previous remodelings. When he told what he wanted to do with the six houses he had purchased, Kate noticed that he never revealed that he and Sara were partners in the business. Kate had his flash drive of accounts but she'd not looked at it. She told herself that she hadn't had time. But what really kept her from looking was trust and a growing sense of loyalty.

The four of them sat at one end of the stone table near the outdoor kitchen. As Jack unrolled plans at the far end, Sara told them that he had designed the big table and had it made. The pride in her voice was almost embarrassing.

Alastair said he hated to be the voice of doom but his mother was going to want more: marble floors, glass-and-chrome built-ins, tiered ceilings, maple kitchen, gold bathroom fixtures.

"All that will cost you," Jack said.

Alastair smiled at Sara. "Thanks to you, she can afford it."

"All that glamour isn't good for resale," Kate said. "You're overbuilding the neighborhood."

"I know," Alastair said. "I told her that, but Mother has been so affected by the horror of what was done in her little town that she wants to do something about it."

"'Her' town?" Sara arched an eyebrow.

Alastair shrugged. "I know she wasn't born here, but she feels close to the place." He paused. "I shouldn't tell this because it's meant to be a surprise, but Mother has commissioned an Italian sculptor to make a double bust of the two women. She plans to erect it over the, uh, where the tree was planted."

"That's kind of her," Kate said. "And I'm sure Cheryl would have loved marble floors."

Alastair smiled. "From what I've heard of her, I agree. So, Jack, how about another bathroom on the side here? Mother may come to need live-in help."

"I'm not sure the property is big enough, but I'll work on it."

It wasn't until after the dinner, and after going over the plans, that Alastair turned his attention to Kate. "I don't mean to impose on your evening, but you promised to show me around the house."

The way he looked at her was so hot that her hair nearly stood on end. "Of course. We could—" She turned to Jack and Sara, feeling as though she was asking permission.

Sara gave a nod but Jack busied himself with rolling up the plans.

"I'll show you my gorgeous suite," she said, then led the way.

Kate felt a bit like a schoolgirl smuggling a man into her bedroom, but it was nice to think of something besides the murders.

She showed him her living room first, its big window looking out to the beautifully lit garden.

"This was my bedroom." He smiled. "I used to sneak out the side door to meet Delia. Ah, those moonlight meetings."

Turning, he drew her into his arms and gently kissed her. "I've wanted to do that since I rescued you on the street. A beautiful young woman with flowers and fruit. You were my fantasy."

"An almost dead one." She stepped away from him. They were alone but other people were nearby. "Want to see the courtyard?" She felt a bit awkward leading him past her bath and bedroom. She was glad she'd made up her bed.

Outside, the night was silvery dark and there were little lights on the fountain.

The girl dancing in the rain was beautiful.

"I am in awe," Alastair said. "This was part of the house where my mother never went. The maid's room was there and she hung out the laundry here where it couldn't be seen."

"That leads to Jack's room."

"I tend to forget that he lives with you."

"With us."

Alastair took both her hands in his. "Kate, I'm worried about you."

"Jack and I aren't—"

"No, not that. This afternoon Sheriff Flynn asked me if I could help persuade you to stop your very unprofessional investigation. He's worried about all of you. And so am I."

She dropped his hands. "It's not fair that Roy is assumed to be a killer."

"Then you *are* continuing to investigate!"

Kate clamped her mouth shut. She was doing exactly what Jack had feared: she was accidentally giving away information.

"I understand your feelings," he said. "From what I remember of Cheryl, she was a sweet girl. I'm like everyone else and want to know who really killed her, but the sheriff told us what may have happened to Mrs. Ellerbee. No one is sure if her death was an accident or intentional. Kate, the murderer may still be at large. And if he thinks you're onto him, he may need to commit more murders." His eyes were begging her to listen to him.

"We have stopped," Kate said. "Aunt Sara just wants to use the facts for a book. She's thinking of moving from romance to murder mysteries. She's really bored doing nothing all day. Jack and I plan to help her with the research. When we aren't working at our own jobs, that is. My mother wants to—to, uh, come here and…"

She trailed off. It looked like she hadn't inherited her aunt's ability to lie. From Alastair's expression, he didn't believe a word she was saying.

"You aren't going to stop until you dig up the truth, are you?"

She wasn't going to answer that.

"Okay, I understand. All I ask is that you please, please be careful. I don't want you to be hurt." He was quiet as he looked at her. "This is a waste of moonlight, but I think we should leave here. If we take too much time, Jack may show his true Wyatt nature. Think he'd use a sledgehammer to come through the wall?"

She knew he was trying to lighten the mood, but he had scared her. There *was* danger in what they were doing. And he didn't even know that the crash that killed Evan wasn't an accident.

He held out his arm for her to take. "Shall we?"

She slipped her arm through his and he put his hand over hers.

"If there is anything I can do, please let me know. Information you need, help in research, whatever, I'll do it. And Mother has a circle of friends who have nothing whatever to do. The sooner this is over, the sooner I know you'll be safe."

"Thank you," she said. "That's very kind of you."

The double bedroom doors had stayed open and they walked through them. Sara and Jack were in the kitchen, pretending to be interested in whatever they weren't doing, but they sprang to life when Kate and Alastair appeared.

At the front door, they exchanged good-nights, with many thanks from Alastair. He and Jack spoke of meeting with Mrs. Stewart to discuss the new plans that would have to be drawn up.

Alastair started to kiss Kate on the lips but she turned her head sideways so he reached her cheek.

After he was gone, Sara and Jack went back to the family room. Kate followed them. "Well? You two aren't going to say anything?"

"I'll be glad to sell all the houses," Jack said, but he didn't look at her.

She turned to her aunt. "You have something to say, so tell me."

"He sure is good at courting," Sara said. "First you, then Jack. I guess I'm next. Wonder what he has planned for me."

"I hope it's fruit," Jack said.

"I hope it's blank paper," Sara said. "I have a lot of things to write down."

"I hope it's an invitation to move in with him," Kate snapped. She went to her bedroom and firmly shut the doors behind her.

If she hadn't had such a long day, she would have had difficulty sleeping, but as it was, she was soon out.

NINETEEN

THE NEXT MORNING, THERE WAS A NOTE under Kate's door, and she picked it up.

> We apologize. Jack will behave…not sure if I can.
> —Jack and Sara

Kate laughed. Was this how real families worked? she wondered. Respect for each other's feelings? Apologies for making other family members angry?

Her uncles always made her furious, then they said her anger was a character flaw in her. If she was a well-adjusted person, she'd take their suggestions— i.e., their endless criticism—with a smile of gratitude.

When she opened her bedroom door, no one was about. But then she saw the toe of Jack's cast sticking out from behind the kitchen counter. She yelled, "I forgive you!"

Jack stood up. "Thank you. I think I've injured my good leg from hiding from your righteous wrath. And by the way, I love Alastair Stewart. Admire him immensely. Think he'll make a fine husband and father. Can I be your best man?"

By the time he finished, she was laughing. "Well, maybe he is trying too hard but I like the effort he's making. When this is done, I plan to see a lot more of him."

"He's so skinny you can't have missed much."

She narrowed her eyes at him and he threw up his hands.

"Sorry. I'm a sore loser, so shoot me."

Kate laughed.

After breakfast, they got into Jack's old truck and drove down to Pembroke Pines to the Chevy dealer. On the drive, Kate repeated everything Alastair had told her about what Sheriff Flynn said.

"He's telling everything he knows to outsiders," Jack said.

"Except about Evan," Kate said. "The sheriff doesn't seem to have told about your truck."

Jack nodded. "That's good. If the murderer thinks we know about that…" He didn't finish.

The dealership didn't want Jack's old pickup for a trade-in, but since he bought all his vehicles for his company there, they relented.

"I really do need to look at your finances," Kate said and Jack smiled.

She and Sara chose a beautiful truck: bright red, double cab, lots of chrome and fog headlights. Jack took one look at it, snorted, then told the dealer he wanted the black single cab.

"Sure glad we could help you choose," Kate said.

It took nearly two hours for all the paperwork. Sara said she'd pay cash if they'd do it quicker, but Jack refused her offer.

While they waited, Kate picked up a magazine. Sara went to the far side of the room and gave her full attention to her cell phone.

Jack took a seat next to Kate. "So when do you go out with him again?"

"We have an overnighter planned for this weekend." When Jack was silent, she looked up. "Someday you're going to have to deal with my having a real relationship."

Jack gave a little smile. "So this one isn't real?"

She put her magazine down. "I don't know. Alastair is lovely. A real gentleman, but there's something missing."

Jack leaned back in the chair, his leg in its cast stretched out. "Passion, maybe? That feeling where he so wants to touch you that he can't sleep? When he leans over you, the smell of your hair makes him dizzy? The way seeing you even talk to another man makes him feel so primal that he wants to hit, maim and kill? That's what's missing?"

She was blinking at him.

"Sir, your truck is ready," the dealer said.

Jack stood up. "You ready to go? We need to decide what to do next. Or if we want to stop."

Kate was still thinking about what he'd said. Jack held out his hand as though to help her stand up. She didn't take it but stood on her own.

"Let's let Aunt Sara decide."

"I'll tell you now that nothing stops her." He turned toward Sara. "Medlar! You ready to go or have you plotted a new *Game of Thrones*?"

She got up and went to them. "*Games the Children Plot* is more like it. What have you two cooked up that leaves old me out?"

"After what happened last time?" Jack said. "You'd probably drive your toy car up into the bed of my new pickup and ruin the paint job."

Kate smiled. "Her yellow, your black. You'd have a bumblebee truck. Hey! You could rename your company Bumblebee Construction. The motto would be Powerful and Fast."

"Or We Buzz to Please," Sara said.

Jack shook his head. "My two joke makers. Let's go home."

Sara lowered her voice. "Can't. We have someplace to go first. I found Verna's landlord, Lester Boggs. Or his widow, anyway. She lives in Hollywood."

"We take a plane?" Kate asked.

"Hollywood here," Jack said. "The real one. What are we supposed to find there?"

"Verna traded her nice car to Boggs for an old van, which she packed full of everything they owned," Sara explained. "We believed they were, uh, 'taken' on Friday. Roy saw the van there on Saturday morning. But when Jack and Captain Edison went there later, the van was gone. So who took it?"

Jack and Kate stared at her in silence for a moment.

"Come on," Sara said. "Let's go see if his widow knows anything." She hurried to the door, Kate behind her, Jack on his crutches coming up last.

As always, Kate sat in the middle. She enjoyed fiddling with the new truck's radio and its GPS system. Sara gave her the Boggs address and she fed it into the system. The female voice told Jack that he needed to make "a legal U-turn" and go back the way he'd come to get on I-75. The map showed the route as going south, then across Miami, then back up I-95. They were to make a huge U to get to someplace that was straight across.

"That's helpful," Kate said.

Jack ignored the GPS and drove them directly to an old, quiet suburb. Kate read the house numbers. The one they wanted was well kept.

"Not like his tenants' places, is it?" There was a muscle working in Jack's jaw.

As soon as he pulled into the driveway, the front door opened and a young man came out. "Hi. I'm Trent, Lester's son. You wanted to see the things Dad stored?"

Sara stepped forward. "I sent the text. Yes, we'd very much like to see what you have."

"I'd love to show it to you." They followed him to the garage. He punched in the numbers and the door slowly rose. Inside was a hoarder's paradise. Boxes, bags, a basket full of wigs, toys were all jammed together from floor to ceiling to form an impenetrable wall. The mass seemed to go all the way back but they couldn't see past the outer shell.

"How old is all this?" Sara asked.

"Older than me," Trent said. "My dad couldn't part with anything."

Jack put his hand on a box at the far end and leaned on it. Things were jammed together so tightly that nothing moved. He caught Kate's eye. There was one word on the box: *Morris*.

Kate nudged Sara and she saw it, but she didn't give away that fact to Trent.

"What are you going to do with this?" Sara asked.

"I…" He took a breath. "I don't want to sound callous, but my mother isn't well and as soon as… Anyway, we'll go through this, sell what we can, donate some and toss the rest. My wife wants to hire a big Dumpster and get rid of it now."

"I'll give you a check for five grand for the lot of it," Sara said. "Jack's workmen will clean it out for you this afternoon."

"My wife would like that," Trent said, "but I worry that my mom will find out, then—"

"Six," Sara said. When Trent hesitated, she turned her back on him. "Let's go. We have those storage units to bid on this afternoon."

She got only two steps before Trent yelled, "Yes! I'll take it. Clean it out. It'll be my gift to my wife."

It took only minutes for Sara to write a check and Trent to give them the garage code.

"I'll be at the hospital with my mother," Trent said, "so come at any time."

The three of them got into the new truck and drove away.

"Wow." Kate hugged her aunt and kissed her cheek. "You were wonderful. Wasn't she?"

"Totally brilliant. What do you think is in that box?"

"Photos of Cheryl with the boy who impregnated her," Kate said.

"And Verna with her daughter's father," Sara said.

"You two are real dreamers." He pulled his cell out

of his pocket and handed it to Kate. "Call Gil and tell him to get the men to pick it all up and take it to the Morris house. Put everything in the bedrooms and shut the doors. And don't flirt with my foreman."

"Even if he talks about my smelly hair?"

Jack glanced away from the road long enough to give her a warning squint.

"Let's lie about this," Sara said. "Too much info is getting out. We can tell Gil there's some good furniture in there, but we had to buy it all. And don't let him take any of it to the dump because that's what men with trucks like to do."

"Men with trucks, huh?" Jack murmured, shaking his head. "Talk about typecasting. Okay, I'll talk to him."

Kate held the phone while Jack told Gil what they'd decided, then hung up.

"By four today everything should be in the Morris house. We'll go over there and start going through it all. Text Gil to set up some stand lights so we can see."

"This should be interesting," Kate said.

Sara agreed eagerly. "I think so, too."

Jack said, "Let's stop at a Lowe's and get a lot of bug spray. Cockroaches love old boxes. Wait until you see a palmetto bug! The size of the palm of your hand."

Kate looked to Sara for verification that he was joking, but she nodded. Kate groaned and Jack laughed.

After they got back to the house, the three separated. Jack took off in his new truck to visit his work sites and to just plain be with men.

Sara said she wanted to write some things down. Kate had learned that her aunt Sara was like a watch that had to be wound daily. And her way of rewinding was to spend time alone with pen and paper. A true introvert.

Kate went to her suite and called her mother. It took a while to reassure her that Aunt Sara had shown no signs of a bad temper. Yes, she would soon go back to work.

Kate did her best to talk around what they were doing. Not lie but avoid.

She emphasized helping Jack choose a truck. But this upset her mother. Spending so much time with a Wyatt might cause "the young Stewart" to be lost. So Kate talked about Alastair and how he'd come to the house and had dinner with them.

"And my sister-in-law was nice to him?" Ava's voice was full of disbelief.

"Very, very nice. Aunt Sara is kind to everyone." At that, Kate crossed her fingers. Sheriff Flynn sent her aunt into a rage. But that was understandable.

There was a scary moment when she slipped and came close to telling how Jack and Sara had almost crashed into each other. Kate had to cover herself by saying that a tree branch had dented Aunt Sara's car. She just left out the fact that Aunt Sara was driving at the time.

When she finally got off the phone, Kate was so sweaty she took a quick shower. She wasn't used to lying.

At two, the doorbell rang and she met Sara in the foyer. Three big boxes had been left on the front veranda.

Kate drew in her breath. The label said *Elaine Cross*.

"Come on," Sara said. "Let's go to your room and see what she sent."

They carried the boxes into Kate's living room and opened them. Packed in tissue paper were glorious things: dresses, blouses, skirts, even shoes. Silks, cottons, knits, linen.

Kate flopped down onto the couch, totally overwhelmed. "I shouldn't accept this. It's too much."

"Don't be silly." Sara was holding up a striped shirt with a dozen tiny buttons down the front. "Think of it as your own personal Santa Claus come early."

"He never left anywhere near this much at *my* house."

"Oh?" Sara pulled out two dresses. One was white with black piping. The other was emerald green with a pale dragon on the back. "You and your mom had money problems?"

"We were always frugal. My father's life insurance policy didn't pay out too much. Mom got temporary jobs now and then, but her health didn't allow for much. Ooooh. That's nice."

The talk of Ava Medlar's finances stopped there. Kate asked if Sara minded if she tried on everything.

"Great plan and I'll find accessories."

What followed was an hour of laughter and ideas. Sara added scarves and jewelry and handbags from her own closet. She photographed every outfit Kate put on.

It was when they were putting the clothes on hangers that Sara said, "That Jack is getting back to work is a good sign. You've given both of us new life."

Kate decided to take advantage of that compliment. "Did you really take care of my father?"

"Yes and no. Randal was greatly loved by our mother. She took care of him while I took care of everything else."

"What about your father?"

"He didn't participate much with any of us."

Kate could tell from her aunt's closed jaw that she wasn't going to get more information than that. She changed the subject. "What do you really think we'll find in that stuff from the garage?"

"Old tax records. Probably that damn toaster Jack keeps talking about."

Kate paused, hanger in hand. "Do you think we'll ever find the killer?"

"The truth? No. It's been too long and the evidence has been destroyed. I think Cheryl and her mother kept their secrets so well that no one can find out now."

"What about Mrs. Ellerbee?"

"I think she knew at least one of the secrets. Probably the identity of either Cheryl's boyfriend or Verna's lover. Or both. With her gone, it leaves only the killer with the secret. In my opinion, he knows he's safe. We've found out a lot about the victims but nothing whatever about him."

"Or her."

"Killed two women, buried their bodies, then planted a tree? And this time around, disabled Jack's truck and killed Mary in her nursing home? I don't see that being done by a woman."

"Two killers?" Kate said.

"'A secret can only be kept by one person. More people than that know and it leaks out.'"

"Who said that?"

"Me in *Morning Stars*."

"Oh, yeah. They knew too much and it almost got them killed. I loved that book."

They heard a door slam.

"Looks like he's home," Sara said. "As soon as he's been fed and watered, let's go back to the Morris house and start rummaging through the old stuff."

"Great idea. What *are* palmetto bugs?"

"Uglies."

"Where is everyone?" Jack shouted.

Sara went to the doors, but Kate didn't move. "I better put on something for getting dirty."

"Good. I've saved some info to tell you both for when Jack got back. Come out when you're ready."

Minutes later, wearing a T-shirt and jeans, Kate went into the kitchen. Jack was on a stool eating jalapeño poppers that Sara had set out for him.

"I hear you got a lot of new clothes," he said.

"I did. Beautiful things. Enough for a hundred dates with Alastair."

"While I get *that*!" He nodded at what she was wearing.

Her T-shirt read Windy Refers to the Politicians. Chicago Weather is Zen. There was a picture of an angry man shoveling his car out from under snow. The shirt was faded from many washings. "This is—"

Sara interrupted. "Before you two get started on your *bons mots*, Heather called me today."

"What did Mom have to say?"

"That she'd had a long conversation—which she recorded—with Verna's best friend in Baltimore."

Both Kate and Jack halted, staring at her. "So?" Jack ate another popper.

"Aren't those things hot?" Kate asked.

"Kiss me and you can find out."

With a smile, Kate ate one. Then she grabbed Jack's glass of ice water and drained it.

Smiling, he turned to Sara. "What did the woman say?"

"Unfortunately, there was nothing new from what Arthur told us. The whole conversation is on my phone, so you can listen, but it's sad. Verna fell in love with some guy from Lachlan and had his child. Years later she left a very good life to return here with their daughter."

"And he dumped her," Kate said.

"We need a name," Jack said.

"Verna never gave one," Sara answered. "Kept it a secret even from her very good friend. The woman's name is Margaret Cheryl Wheeler. She named her son James Vernon."

"They named their children after each other," Kate said with a sigh. "It must have been some love affair to make Verna leave such a close friend."

"Something that struck me," Sara said, "was the question of this guy's wife. Did she know about the affair? If so, why didn't she let him go?"

Jack was holding up the last popper. "Like you did Granddad after he married my grandmother?"

"Exactly like that." Sara eyes were steely.

"Granddad used to go away on long fishing trips, but at home I never saw him touch a pole."

"He probably needed to get away from Donna's inability to carry on an intelligent conversation."

"I'm sure that's what it was." Jack put the popper in his mouth. He was staring at Sara but she didn't blink.

"Wow," Kate said to her aunt. "I wish I could lie as well as you. It's a real talent." For a second Sara looked like she might be offended, but then she laughed.

"Keep trying. It's a goal you can achieve because your father could outlie any person on earth."

"Yeah?" Kate's eyes were wide. "Did he—?"

"Are you two ready to go or not?" Sara hurried out the front door.

"That's all you get today," Jack said.

"I'm collecting every piece of knowledge. Another seven or eight years and I might have an eighth of a picture of my father."

"Better yours than mine. Help me with my crutches, will you?"

"You wish. Race you to the truck." She ran out the door.

"Don't touch that GPS system!" he called as he followed her out. "I don't want to end up in Orlando."

"Ooooh, Disney," Kate said back to him. "Can't wait."

TWENTY

WHEN THEY PULLED INTO THE DRIVEWAY OF the Morris house, the fading day showed that the back of the house was brightly lit up. "Damn it!" Jack said. "Gil must have sent the new guys. They left the lights on."

Sara got out of the truck, her camera around her neck. "I like it. I'm going to take some photos."

"Did you bring your flash?"

"Why would I need a flash? I have a Fuji." She practically ran to the back, where the bright lights from inside cast eerie shadows.

"You set her up for that one," Kate said.

"I did. Fanatics love their brands." His crutch was caught on something at the side of the truck.

Kate got out the other side. "I'll go get started."

"And leave me here alone to untangle this thing?"

"Yup." The truth was that she was curious to see what had been stored in the garage.

When she got to the door, she realized she didn't have the key. But a narrow crack of light was coming through. Looked like the new men had forgotten to lock it.

She pushed the door open, then threw her arm up to cover her eyes. The lights were on tall stands with three big bulbs on each, and the room seemed to be full of them. Their brilliance blinded her.

She lowered her arm an inch, blinking fast as her eyes adjusted. Through the windows, she could see Jack and Sara around the tall roots of the fallen tree. She was taking photos.

Kate wanted to turn the lights off but Sara needed them.

With both her hands up, Kate walked across the room toward one of the closed bedroom doors. She was only a foot away when she halted.

Very, very slowly, she turned to her left.

In the corner of the room was a man. He was hanging from a rope around his neck. At his feet, a chair was on its side.

Kate didn't think about what she did. She covered the distance to the man in two leaps, bent, threw her arms around his legs and did her best to lift him up. She put her head back and let out a scream that tore at her throat.

Sara and Jack were there in seconds, and they reacted quickly. Sara helped Kate hold the man up—he was quite large—while Jack lifted the chair and climbed on it, his cast-encased leg to one side. He soon had the rope undone and he managed to get off the chair without falling.

They gently lowered the man to the floor and Jack took his pulse, then shook his head.

He was dead.

"Take her out of here," he said to Sara as he got his phone out of his pocket and called 911.

Sara had her arm around Kate's shoulders and was leading her to the door. "Jack." Sara was nodding toward a piece of paper on the floor. It looked like a suicide note. He didn't touch it but quickly took a photo of it on his phone.

Sara led Kate outside, and they sat side by side on the concrete steps.

"We shouldn't have taken him down," Kate whispered. "The police will want to know—"

"We thought there was a chance he was alive."

Jack came out of the house and picked up Sara's camera. "Can you…?"

"Yeah, sure." She got up, took the camera and went inside to photograph everything—especially the man.

Jack sat down by Kate. "You okay?"

She held her hand out straight. It was shaking.

"We can't leave until after the police clear the scene."

She nodded. "I recognized him, Jack. He's the man I saw in town."

"Yes. Dan Bruebaker."

"The man Alastair wanted me to talk to. Why didn't I do it? Alastair was so sure that Dan knew something. I could have—"

Jack put his arm around her shoulders and drew her head onto his shoulder. "You are not allowed to blame yourself about this. You couldn't have prevented it or—"

She pulled away from him. "There was a note, right?"

"Yes." He held out his phone. "I didn't read it."

The sound of sirens reached them.

"Email it to someone," she said quickly. "If the sheriff knows we have a copy, he'll take it."

"Good idea." He tapped a name, sent the message, then erased it from his phone.

In the next second, they stood up because coming toward them was Sheriff Flynn. He had on black trousers, suspenders and a white tuxedo suit—and he was angry.

"Déjà vu," Kate said as she stood there, Jack beside her.

"I ought to arrest both of you!" the sheriff shouted when he was just a few feet away. "Lock you up and throw away the key."

"Just so we're together we can—" Jack began, but Kate elbowed him.

"We are so, so sorry," Kate said. "So very, very sorry."

Smiling, she took a step forward—then her eyes rolled back in her head and she fell rather prettily onto the grass. Kate had fainted.

TWENTY-ONE

WHEN KATE AWOKE, SHE WAS LYING ON A bed inside an ambulance and Jack was sitting beside her. He was jamming a long, stainless-steel stick inside his cast. She started to get up.

"No, you don't. I was put in here to make sure you don't move."

The doors were open and she could hear loud voices. "Is that Aunt Sara?" Her voice was raspy and her throat hurt.

Jack kept scratching. "Yeah, it is. She's having a three-way with Flynn and Cotilla."

"The detective?"

"That's him." Jack turned to her and seemed to inspect her face. "Flynn is mad at Sara, Cotilla is furious with Flynn, Sara is angry at both of them. They're having a screaming match, and by the sound of it, our Sara isn't winning."

Kate felt very weak and she suddenly remembered why she was there. Instantly, she started crying, the tears coming from deep inside her. "Did he kill them?" Her whole body was shaking.

Jack leaned over her, stroking her hair back as he motioned for the EMT to come. "We'll sort that out later. They can give you a shot to let you sleep. Okay?"

She nodded. She wanted time to get the image of that man hanging there out of her mind.

"Good," Jack said. "When I get you home, I get to undress you and put you to bed. I read about how to do it in one of Sara's books. I'll be gentle."

As she felt a needle in her arm, she tried to make a saucy reply to him, but her eyes were already beginning to flutter. "Take care of Aunt Sara."

"I will." Jack kissed her forehead. "Just sleep now and dream of chocolate ice cream."

"Strawberry," she whispered, then went to sleep.

When she awoke again, it was still night. She was in her bed in Aunt Sara's house and she could hear her phone. It was playing her mother's favorite song, Bette Midler's "Wind Beneath My Wings." Her mother was calling her. Some deep, primal command—inspired by having been her mother's caretaker for most of her life—made Kate struggle to stand up. Her clothes had been removed and she had on a cotton nightgown. Vaguely, she wondered who and how.

Her brain was foggy, but she stumbled toward the half-open double doors. She was still in the shadows when she heard Aunt Sara's loud, angry voice.

"Ava, I don't give a crap what you've read on the internet! No, you're not going to talk to her now. She needs rest." Sara paused. "Yeah? If I'd known what you were putting that child through for all those years, I would have had the law on you. No, I take that back— I would have made you get a *job*." She listened. "Stop it! Your melodramatics don't work on me. You're about as delicate as a Sherman tank. If you don't want me telling her the *truth* about all you've hidden from her, then you'll do just what I tell you. You are going to be compassionate *for her*. Sympathetic *for her*. For once in your life you're going to think of someone besides yourself and that worthless brother of mine. Do I make myself clear?" She waited. "All right. Now go rehearse what you're going to say to her. And I warn you that if it isn't loving and caring, tomorrow you'll be going to job interviews."

Kate's mind was so fuzzy that she wasn't sure what she'd just heard. Something about her mother and a job. But that made no sense. Her mother's nerves had never allowed her to hold any job for long.

As Kate yawned, she glanced into the family room and saw Jack, his hands full of papers and photos. When he looked up and saw her, he was shocked. With a frown, he motioned for her to go back to bed.

"Of all the gall." It was Sara's voice.

Kate turned away and went back to bed.

When she awoke again, Jack was in her bedroom and slinging the curtains back so the daylight could come in.

"You can't get in bed with me," she mumbled.

"Darn! And that's why I came in here. Other than that, I'm to tell you that you've slept the clock around and you need to wake up. Sara and Mom went some-where, so I thought you and I should catch up."

"I have to…" She motioned toward the bathroom.

She wasn't going to get out of bed in just her night-clothes.

With a shake of his head, Jack left the room. "I can't believe your uncles didn't see you as the prude you are."

"Only with you, Jack," she called. When she emerged from the bathroom, she went into her closet to pull on jeans and a T-shirt—and underwear.

He was in her living room with a pile of papers on the coffee table. And in a pretty glass dish were three scoops of strawberry ice cream with sliced strawberries and whipped cream on top. "For you."

"I can't eat that! The calories—"

He handed her the dish. "The doctor said you need to eat. Part of why you passed out was because you don't eat enough calories to sustain the energy needed for sticking your nose into the business of everyone in town."

"The *doctor* said that?"

"No. That was courtesy of Sheriff Flynn. He told Sara that *we* were the reason poor Dan Bruebaker died. If we hadn't stirred up so much trouble, he wouldn't have had to do what he did."

With the name came memory and Kate started to put down the dish of ice cream, but Jack wouldn't let her.

"What else?" she asked as she started eating.

"Flynn spilled his guts to Cotilla. Our sheriff knows when to retreat."

"Mary Ellerbee?"

"Yes."

"What about Evan?"

"The Broward County Sheriff's Department now

knows it all." Jack looked down at the paper with a grin.

"What are you smiling about?"

"It was a joy to hear Flynn being told that he was an idiot for ever thinking Roy Wyatt killed the Morris girls."

"That isn't what the detective said last time. What makes him so sure now?"

"The confession and suicide of the actual murderer." Jack hesitated. "We have been ordered off the case, though. Which is now officially closed."

Kate nearly choked on her ice cream—which she was enjoying immensely. "Again?"

"It was smart of you to tell me to send the photo of the suicide note to people, because Sara and I had our phones confiscated. And one of her camera cards was taken."

"What was on the card?"

"The pictures she took before you found Dan. The later ones were on a card she put inside her shoe."

"They don't know you took a photo of the note?"

"No. I sent it to my mother. And by the way, she came over here and undressed you. But I did offer to help."

"Kind of you." She held out her hand and Jack gave her a piece of paper. It was a copy of the suicide note.

I'd always thought Cheryl was beautiful, but she would never pay any attention to me. I knew it was her birthday, so I took flowers to her. She rejected them, then yelled at me to get away from her. I got so angry that I pushed her. She hit her head on the concrete steps and died. Her mother came out of the house and screamed that she was calling the sheriff.

I went berserk and strangled her. I threw both bodies in the pit in the back and kicked dirt over them. Right after that I left for the training camp in Naples. When I got back, I planted a tree over their graves. No one in town looked for them but what I did has haunted me for all my life.

I can no longer live with myself.

She put down the paper and looked at Jack. "He doesn't mention Evan or Mary. And what about the stabbing?"

"That's what Sara and I wondered, too. But last night all we did was nod and agree with every law-enforcement person that we'd behave and go back to our respective jobs."

Kate sucked in her breath. "Jobs! That reminds me, I heard Aunt Sara on the phone to my mother. She threatened her. Said she was… I don't remember, but it was awful. I have to call my mother now."

Jack reached across the table to put his hand over her wrist. "I think you should hold off on that."

"But—"

"I think there's something *big* between your aunt and your mother. Right now you need to decide whether you're going to stay out of it or put yourself between two armed warriors. You could get destroyed by both of them."

"Mom must have been hurt by Aunt Sara's words."

"Probably. So whose side will you choose?"

"My mother's, of course. She—"

"Want me to help you pack?"

His words made Kate visualize where her admission of overhearing and the resulting sympathy would lead. Of course, she'd have to immediately return to her mother's house. Then she'd spend weeks soothing her nerves. But to get ultimate calm, she'd have to agree that Aunt Sara was a terrible person. It would be years before Kate could get up the courage to again leave her mother on her own, so she'd have to take a job nearby. And probably continue living with her.

She looked at Jack. On one hand, she could be living with her aunt. And Jack. And the people she'd met in Lachlan.

Or she could go to her mother. And the three uncles and their families.

"Any decisions yet?" he asked.

Kate made a motion of zipping her mouth shut, locking it and throwing away the key.

"I agree."

They looked across the table at each other and made a silent agreement. The telephone call was a secret they'd keep between themselves. Besides, Sara would be horrified if she knew Kate had overheard her.

Kate motioned to the suicide note. "Do you believe this?"

"I don't know. It leaves out a great deal."

"Why would this man kill others so he wouldn't be found out, then suddenly give up?" she asked. "Because we were about to find out the truth?"

Jack shrugged. "Maybe. This note implies that Dan only went to the Morris house once. So why kill Mary? Did she see something and didn't know it?"

"And you," Kate said. "Why try to kill *you*? You keep remembering things—did you see Dan there?"

"Maybe he went after me because I bought the property where the bodies were buried. He'd know that I'd eventually find them."

"True, but maybe you did see someone. Mr. Niederman said you only looked at Cheryl. Maybe Dan was lurking in the corners. What was he like? I got the impression from Alastair that he was a real loser."

Jack's voice was soft. "His wife and his two teenage kids, a boy and a girl, were there last night. They were devastated. The girl was crying a lot. They didn't think he was a loser."

"So many tears," Kate said. "And *for what*?"

"You want something to eat? I was told I'm to make you a triple-decker club sandwich with lots of bacon and mayo. Sara even bought the bread for it."

"*Bread?* For me?" She started to get up.

Jack caught her hand. "I want to know how you feel. What you saw was traumatic enough to make you pass out. And when Sara saw you rolled up on the grass, I thought she was going to join you. There I was with two gorgeous women in distress, and with this damn leg I couldn't sweep either of you into my arms and rescue you."

He said it as a joke but his face was serious. She sat back down. "I'm all right. I still feel a bit out of it, but I'm okay. It was such a shock to see him there. I'd hoped he was still alive. I—"

Jack squeezed her hand. "You did exactly right, but he'd been dead for hours. Last night Sara and I were separated and questioned about who was where when. Someone went to Gil and asked him when he'd set up the lights."

"The lights! I forgot about why we went there. Did Sheriff Flynn confiscate everything from the garage?"

Jack leaned back on the sofa. "Odd thing about that. The deputies looked around the house. When they saw the bedrooms with all the junk in them, Flynn made some remarks about what a slob I am and closed the doors."

"They didn't realize that some of those things may have belonged to Cheryl and Verna. Not that we know for sure."

"And not that there's anything in there that we can use."

She stared at him in silence for a moment. "You don't think Dan did it, do you?"

"The truth?" He paused for a moment. "I think he may have paid the ultimate price to make us stop opening old wounds. Evan, Mary and now Dan. I don't want to see any more people hurt. I think it's time to let Cheryl and her mother rest in peace."

They looked at each other and didn't need to say that they were worried about Sara. For all that she was energetic and smart, she was still older and more fragile.

"I think I'll email Tayla to say that I'll be in the office on Monday."

"Sounds like a good idea."

"How do we get Aunt Sara to agree with us?"

"Easy. We just stop participating. And we start today. It's Saturday, so we'll do other things, like wash my new truck."

"Answer emails," she said. "And I need to look at new listings so I'm ready to go to work on Monday morning."

"Good idea. I might even make myself take care of the company's finances."

"You don't have a secretary?"

"She's on maternity leave."

"Yours?"

He grinned. "There's my Kate back. Jokes about everything. Come on, let's get you fed."

"But I just ate ten thousand calories."

"By this time tomorrow you'll be six sizes bigger, so what's a few bites more?"

"You are so not funny." She followed him into the kitchen.

TWENTY-TWO

SARA RETURNED JUST AS KATE WAS FINISH-
ing the huge sandwich Jack had made for her. After
they listened to Sara say that she and Heather had been
visiting people at the hospital, they told her they wanted
to stop investigating the murders. They were done.

Kate was standing close to Jack and almost reached
for his hand to hold. Like brothers and sisters standing up to authority.

"Cool," Sara said. "We can spend the weekend
catching up with our real lives. Who wants to hit the
gym?"

"Red, here, does," Jack said. "She's eaten so many
calories this morning that I'm sure she's gained ten
pounds. I tried to stop her but I couldn't."

"Needed the energy. I was exhausted from throwing you out of my bedroom."

Jack gave a chuckle.

"Great idea," Sara said. "I'll drive your new truck."

"You can't reach the pedals," Jack called over his shoulder as he headed toward his room. "I bet I can get ready to go before you two can."

"You win!" Sara and Kate said in unison. They laughed; Jack groaned. As it was, they beat him because he had three work calls.

Kate was impressed with the beautiful LA Fitness on University. After Sara signed her in as a guest, they went to the machines. Lifting weights was new to Kate but Jack was a patient teacher, and working out together came easily to them. While Jack took his turn, Sara and Kate talked about clothes and made plans for places to go. A couple of times they had to wait for Jack when people he knew came over to ask about his leg.

After an hour with the weights, they went to the basketball court. Jack pulled hand pads out of his big gym bag, and Sara gave Kate a set of red leather boxing gloves.

"I can't possibly do that." She backed away.

They didn't listen to her. Within minutes, Jack had her in gel protectors, then into the sixteen-ounce gloves.

Because of his cast, he had to back up against the wall to keep from falling as Sara hit the pads he held.

He spent a few minutes giving Kate basic instructions about twisting and using her body to power a hit, then held up his pads. She was timid, barely tapping, until Jack started softly saying names to her. Evan. Mrs. Ellerbee. Cheryl. Verna. Dan.

On the last punch, Kate hit so hard that Jack stepped

aside, removed his pad and shook his hand. "Got some anger in you, girl."

"A bit," she said. Hitting hard felt good.

When they got home, they sat in the living room, a pitcher of water before them. They didn't mention separating.

Sara took a chair, put a pretty bamboo lap desk across her knees and began to write on small sheets of paper. Jack took a couch and opened his computer. On the sofa across from him, Kate was his mirror image.

"Which house are you looking at?" he asked.

"Shhh." She glanced at Sara.

"She's fine as long as no one asks her questions. What house?"

"Twenty-three Kingfish Drive has just come up. It looks nice."

"The electrical needs work, but it's a great location. Let me have it for six weeks and I can increase the sell price by twenty percent."

"Yeah?" She made a note of it. "One eighty-two Redland Street?"

"That's a good one. Dad and I waterproofed the basement." Looking back at his computer, he groaned.

"What are you doing?"

"Downloading transactions from the bank, then categorizing them. I can't read Gil's writing." He handed her the receipt.

"Six two-by-fours. Eight two-by-sixes. Four pounds of wood screws, size seven."

For a moment Jack blinked at her, then handed her his laptop and put the plastic box of receipts on the coffee table.

She gave him her computer. "Write what you know

about each house and include the history. People like
to know about deaths and ghosts in the house."

"Where do I write it?"

She moved to sit beside him and Sara left her narrow chair to go to the other couch.

It was hours before they started moving about. Jack
went outside to lovingly bathe his new truck; Sara went
to her bedroom to turn on the TV while she typed; Kate
went to the kitchen.

It was while she was preparing a meal that Kate
began to think about the case. She tried not to. She
needed to go over the listings so she could answer
all the clients' questions, but her mind kept wandering. She thought of what Alastair had told her about
Dan—that he drank so much that he was rarely sober
and loved the glory days of high school when he was
a sports star. Alastair said Dan thought of Cheryl as a
trophy to be won, that he spoke of what he wanted to
do to the young woman.

As Kate put a stuffed chicken in the oven, she told
herself that Dan probably *did* commit the murders.
Just as he'd written.

But what about the others? she wondered.

Sara did say that they thought Jack's truck had
driven over rocks. Maybe that was really how the
brakes went out. As for Mrs. Ellerbee, maybe she actually *had* smothered in her sheets, and the timing of
her death was just a coincidence. A wild, cosmic con-
currence.

She was chopping zucchini. It was certainly nice of
Alastair and his mother to buy all of the houses from
Jack. And it might not hurt the resale value to add lux-
ury floors and ceilings. Besides, selling wouldn't hap-

pen until Mrs. Stewart left the earth. If she was still playing tennis, that was far away.

That thought made her think of Dan's suicide. What were the repercussions of it? What was going on now that the confession had been found? How was his family?

When Kate got to the carrots, Jack came in and sat on a stool on the other side of the counter. He took one and crunched it. "Sara won't eat those. No veg that grows underground."

She didn't respond.

Jack lowered his voice. "Been thinking?"

"Not at all."

He stared at her.

Kate glanced at Sara's closed bedroom doors. "Just a bit. I can come up with an explanation for everything."

"Of course you can. There's a logical explanation for all of it." He sounded sarcastic.

"Don't say it like that. I keep thinking of Dan's family."

"Mom called me. She and some of the ladies from church have been there. His wife is a mess."

"Her husband commits suicide and confesses to a double murder. How does she wrap her brain around that?"

"From what Mom said, Dan Bruebaker was an excellent husband and father."

"But—" She broke off when Sara came out of the bedroom.

"Are you two talking about anything interesting?"

"Nothing at all," Jack said.

Kate would have backed up his lie but her cell phone started singing. She took it to her bedroom and listened to her mother's heartfelt concern about what her daughter had been through when she found a man hanging. If Kate hadn't heard what her aunt Sara had said, she would have thought her mother had been told she had three days to live and was trying to create good memories.

There were no questions about Aunt Sara's bad temper, no prying into every minute of Kate's life. There was just loving concern about the ordeal her daughter had been through.

When Kate hung up and went back to the kitchen, she was in such a dazed state that her eyes seemed to be pinwheels. It was difficult not to throw her arms around Aunt Sara's neck and thank her.

As it was, she got behind Sara, looked at Jack and made faces and gestures of jubilation and being thankful. He looked down and didn't betray his amusement.

Kate awoke to the doorbell ringing like it was a fire alarm. *Not again*, she thought. What did Krystal want this time? The clock said it was 2:14 a.m. She waited for a moment, hoping someone else would answer Krystal's call, but the ringing kept on.

She pulled on a pair of jeans under the big T-shirt she was wearing and ran to the foyer, reaching it at the same time as Sara and Jack.

"I'm going to kill her," Jack muttered. "If she—" When he looked out the glass panel beside the door, he halted. "It's Dan's mother." He opened the door. "Mrs. Bruebaker, how—?"

She pushed past them, went straight to the living room and sat down. Her face was ravaged with tears and grief.

There was a wet bar around the corner and Jack went to it to pour a tall rum-and-Coke, then handed it to Mrs. Bruebaker. She drank half of it in one gulp.

Jack, Kate and Sara sat down on the couch across from her and waited in silence for the woman to speak.

"I was in Australia. Dream vacation," she said. "All my life I've wanted to hug a koala."

She took a sip of her drink. "I flew back as fast as I could. I was sure my daughter-in-law had made a mistake. Couldn't be Dan. Not *my* son."

There was no response they could make to that.

"I went to Sheriff Flynn and woke him up. He said his hands were tied, that the case was closed. I had to ask him what the hell he was talking about. What 'case'? He told me about finding skeletons and that *my* son said he'd killed those two women."

She got up and looked out the big windows at the garden in the outdoor lights. When she turned around, she was calmer. "Daryl Flynn and I used to date. I liked him, but then I met my son's father and…" She shrugged and sat back down.

"Daryl told me the case was officially closed and was never going to be reopened. And that under no circumstances was I to go to you guys and get you fired up again. But if I did see you, I was to tell you that he was really angry at having to go to the funerals of innocent people, and that he wants the killings to stop. And people should know the *truth* about those girls." She paused. "Daryl said every bit of that *three* times. Three! It was like he thought I'd lost my hearing. I kept telling him that my Dan would *never* commit suicide and certainly not murder! But all Daryl could talk about was how Sara Medlar and her troop of would-be detectives were finally off the case since he'd gone ballistic and threatened you."

She looked at Sara. "I've read your books. Everyone in Lachlan has, but I moved to Sunrise a few years ago. I didn't know you'd bought the Stewart house. I didn't know—"

Mrs. Bruebaker put her face in her hands and began to cry.

Kate went to her, put her arms around the woman and looked at Jack and Sara sitting rigidly on the other couch. Her eyes held a question. Did they get involved with this woman or tell her they were out of it?

Sara nodded first, then Jack. He seemed reluctant and Kate knew it was because he worried about their safety.

"Could we ask you some questions?" Sara asked softly.

It took a moment, but Mrs. Bruebaker finally managed to look at her. "Anything."

Kate spoke first. "Was your son getting help with his drinking problem?"

Mrs. Bruebaker sputtered. "His what? My son was allergic to wine. He never drank anything."

Jack was looking hard at Kate, his face blasting "I told you so."

Sara broke in. "We've been told some things about your son that appear to be false. Tell us about him in high school. Did he have a girlfriend?"

"Yes, but she didn't go to Lachlan High."

"Were he and Alastair Stewart friends?" Jack asked.

"No. Dan thought Alastair was a snob."

Kate shook her head. "But I saw Dan running after

Alastair. He said Dan wanted to reminisce about the good old days in high school."

"That lying bastard," Mrs. Bruebaker said. She took a moment to calm herself. "My husband was a good welder and he started a shop that makes decorative ironwork. The whole family was involved and we've done very well. After my husband passed, Dan took over, but I still keep the books. Noreen Stewart ordered ironwork for the entire balcony of her condo. She signed a contract for it, but when the bill came, she demanded a forty-percent discount."

Jack gave a low whistle. "You'd be in the hole for materials and labor."

"Yes," Mrs. Bruebaker said. "It's been four months and she's only paid sixty percent of the bill. She's threatened to spread it all over the internet that Dan is cheating her because she's a lonely widow on a fixed income. We do a lot of mail-order business and we can't withstand an all-out cyber assault."

She looked at Kate. "Dan wanted to talk to Alastair about Noreen. That's why he was chasing him down. When I called Dan from Sydney, he told me about it."

She looked Kate up and down. "Dan said Alastair was hovering over a pretty, red-haired girl like he was afraid she was going to run away from him."

"He always does that," Jack said. "Leans over her like his spine is broken and he can't stand up straight."

"He used to do that to Delia," Mrs. Bruebaker said. "Why are we talking about that awful family? Daryl was saying that you guys know something about all this."

"Not as much as we thought we did," Sara said. "Did you see the suicide note?"

"The what?"

"Dan's confession of guilt," Sara said.

Jack got up and went to Kate's suite to get the paper that was still on her coffee table. He returned but didn't show it.

"No," Mrs. Bruebaker said. "No one mentioned a note. My daughter-in-law told me Dan *said* he was the murderer." She put her hands over her face. "It's all been too much, too fast. I thought he confessed, then went…to wherever and did it."

"The Morris house," Sara said.

"Whose house?"

"That's where the skeletons were found. Cheryl and Verna Morris. We were told that in high school, Dan really, really liked Cheryl," Sara said.

Kate got the yearbook and showed the photo.

"Never saw her before. My son had school and sports. When he dated, it was with his girlfriend. They married right after graduation."

Jack handed her the suicide note.

When Mrs. Bruebaker read it, she seemed to relax. Surprised, they looked at her.

"Dan couldn't have written this. He is—was— severely dyslexic. That's why he didn't go to college. I had to read every school textbook to him and his teachers let him take tests orally. 'Went berserk'? Who talks like that?"

She paused. "Daryl knows about my son's dyslexia. They play…" She gasped. "Played basketball together. Daryl read the scores to my son." She looked at them. "Do you think Daryl knows that Dan didn't—didn't do that to himself? Do you think that's why he made sure I knew you'd been working this case? That he's somehow trying to ask you for help?"

"Yes," Sara said. "I do think that and we're going to do what we can."

"Thank you," Mrs. Bruebaker said. "I have to get back. You can't imagine what my family is like. My daughter-in-law. My grandchildren—" She broke off when she started crying again. When she stood up, she swayed on her feet.

Jack caught her. "I'm driving you home."

After Jack left, Sara said, "When he gets back, he'll be hungry."

Her tone was heavy and Kate well understood. Just this evening she'd told herself that there could be an explanation about everything, even the failed brakes on Jack's truck. But this was murder. They were all *murder*.

She went to the kitchen to make one of the cheese-and-fruit plates that Jack liked so much and was glad for something to occupy her hands.

She didn't want to think what it meant that Alastair had lied to her. Maybe he said that about Dan because he didn't want to be embarrassed in front of her. It would have been uncomfortable to hear about his rich mother trying to rip off a small local business.

She wondered if Henry Lowell had given Alastair's mother a forty-percent discount? Was that why she went to his funeral? To say thank you?

When Jack returned, he didn't say anything, just sat down on the couch across from them and began to eat from the tray Kate had set out.

"I didn't tell you everything," Sara said. "When I was at the hospital with Heather, I visited Mrs. Boggs."

"The landlord's wife," Jack said. "She remember anything?"

"She remembered everything."

"Tell us," they said.

Earlier that day...

Mrs. Boggs was in the hospital bed hooked up to tubes and beeping machines. Sara was old enough to know not to ask the woman what was wrong with her and what her prognosis was. That was what young people did. Sara might not know the details but she knew the woman was near her end.

Sara said that she and her two friends were investigating the deaths of Verna and Cheryl Morris and wondered if she could tell her anything.

Mrs. Boggs seemed glad to think of something other than her own pain. She even scooted up in the bed a bit. "I remember all of it." Her voice was raspy but clear.

"The rent check didn't come in Saturday's mail, so Lester went over there on Sunday morning to get it. He came back in a rage. He said they were moving out without paying. The house was empty, and the doors and windows were open. He closed the place up and put padlocks on the doors, then he took the van he'd traded to them. It was full of household goods and he said he'd give it back to them when they showed up with the rent."

"But they didn't show up," Sara said.

"No. We never saw them again. The van was parked beside the garage for months. Lester was so mad that he was going to take everything to the dump, but I liked Verna. I thought she got a raw deal in town. I never could figure out who spread all the gossip about her. I never saw any man at their house except that cranky old Arthur Niederman. He used to brag to everybody that he and Verna were lovers but nobody believed him. One time I saw that she was giving him a massage."

Mrs. Boggs's energy was fading. "Somebody was that poor woman's enemy. I don't understand why she stayed in Lachlan."

"Your son sold us the contents of the garage."

"Did he?" She gave a smile of irony. "Couldn't wait, could he? He always was like his father."

"Is what we bought from the Morris house?"

"Yes. Everything that was in the van is in there. I wouldn't let Lester throw it away because I knew he'd fill up the garage with more rubbish anyway. At least what those girls had was clean." She closed her eyes. "I think that now I need to…"

"Of course. I wish you well."

Mrs. Boggs didn't open her eyes. "I just hope that those books about Heaven are wrong. I don't want the first person I see to be Lester Boggs."

"I know what you mean." Sara squeezed her hand, then left the room…

For a while, they were quiet after Sara finished her story.

Kate looked at the other two. "I guess we should get some sleep. We can make decisions about what to do in the morning."

No one moved.

"The sheriff's department wouldn't let Gil take the stand lights. They're still there."

Kate looked at the tray full of food. Only Jack had eaten any. There was no question in her mind as to what they were going to do. They were going to start going through the garage contents *now*. "I'll put this food in bags. Aunt Sara, you get us water."

"Jack," Sara said, "get the box of gloves from under the sink. Kate, put on some solid shoes."

As the two women got up, Jack sat there smiling. "Am I allowed to make a remark about women changing their minds?"

"No!" Kate and Sara yelled.

"It was just a thought." He heaved himself up. "Do you really think Flynn sent Mrs. Bruebaker to us?"

"Oh, yes," Kate said from the kitchen.

"Definitely," Sara said.

At the Morris house, they were solemn as they entered. Maybe this was when they would find out the truth.

Jack went in first. He turned on one of the big lights and aimed it toward the corner where Dan had been hanging. Kate knew he wanted to make sure she saw that there was no longer a body there.

The image, still vivid in her mind, flashed in and out, but then it settled to show the empty corner. Sara and Jack were staring at her, waiting for her to reassure them she was all right.

With a small smile, she nodded and they let out their breaths. "Where should we start?"

"In Cheryl's 'haven of peace' as she called it." Jack opened the door of the smaller bedroom.

The room was filled with packages: sealed boxes, bulging shopping bags, a plastic laundry basket, a bucket, a big leaf bag. Everything had been stuffed with household and personal items.

The sight of it reminded them of how the two women had hurriedly thrown their belongings together so they could make a fast getaway. *Why?* Kate wondered. Because Cheryl had finally told her mother she was pregnant? By whom? The town bad boy?

That thought made her look at Jack. He was eleven then, but his father... When Jack glanced her way, Kate turned away in fear that he'd read her thoughts.

"Do we work separately or together?" Sara asked.

"Together," Kate said.

"I agree."

"Gloves on," Sara said.

The first box they opened held old lawn-mower parts. They closed it. Next was half-empty jars of motor oil.

They moved to another part of the room. Jack slit the tape across the top of an old Clorox box. "Bingo."

Inside were worn paperback books and the three on top were Sara's. Jack pushed aside a rusty old garden tool, took out a book and opened it. Inside was an inscription.

To Cheryl,
Hope you enjoy it,
Sara Medlar

"Nice." He put back the book. He looked to see if anything else was inside but there were only more books by other authors. "Just trash."

They opened three more boxes and unloaded two shopping bags before they saw *the* box. They hadn't seen it at first because it was buried under eight cartons of old canning jars. It was one of those sold in craft stores: shiny surface with pictures of pink roses and white ribbons.

Kate held it up. "I bet this belonged to Cheryl."

It was growing lighter outside but they still needed the big bulbs. They moved closer to a lamp and Sara slit the tape that was all around the lid.

When Kate looked up, she saw that, like her, blood was pulsing in their throats. Slowly, she opened it. Inside was a gray metal box, the kind that was used for cash. It was closed with a lock that needed a key. On the top, in red nail polish, was painted Private. CAM.

"Cheryl Ann Morris," Jack said.

With glove-encased hands, Kate lifted out the cash box and held it reverently. "Is there a key in there?"

Sara pulled out the contents of the decorative box: dried wildflowers, pink tissue paper, a snippet of blue silk. "No key."

"So what do we do?" Kate asked. "Pry it open?"

"Sure," Jack said.

But Sara put out her hand. "Don't freak, but I think we should take it to the sheriff. Unopened."

Kate thought of the ramifications of their opening the box now. What proof would they have that they hadn't tampered with it? She looked at Jack.

"Agreed." He sounded reluctant.

Jack called Gil, who was getting ready to go to work, and asked him to get security put on the house. Now that they were sure the contents belonged to Cheryl and her mother, it needed to be protected.

Even though it was very early Sunday morning when they got to the sheriff's office, it was fully lit up. During the night, all calls were transferred to the Broward County offices, so the office should have been empty.

"Think he knows we're coming?" Sara was making a joke.

"I just pray that another body hasn't been found," Kate said.

Jack snorted. "The bastard killer saves those for *us*."

The front door was unlocked and at first they thought no one was there. But then Sara saw Sheriff Flynn sitting at his desk, arms across his chest, eyes on them. She nudged Kate, who elbowed Jack.

Silently, they went into his office. Jack put the flowered box on the desk and they sat down and waited.

"I've been expecting you," Sheriff Flynn said. "I got to wondering what all those big lights were doing at the Morris house, so I called Gil and asked him. He said you'd bought a whole garage full of trash. Said he offered to take it to the dump but you laughed at him." He paused, waiting for an explanation, but Jack said nothing.

"Anyway, I figured things out. Captain Edison's report of his visit to the Morris house with an eleven-year-old Jackson Wyatt mentions a missing van full of household goods. If the women died and it was left behind, it figured that a penny-pincher like Lester Boggs would be the one to take it. I called his son and was told of you busybodies buying all the junk in his mother's garage. I gathered it had something Morris-related in it."

He leaned back in his chair. "Since you know what

you're looking for, I knew I just had to wait until you found it. I had to use poor Mrs. Bruebaker to nudge you along, but I had faith in you. My only worry was that you'd find something and keep it to yourselves."

Kate, Jack and Sara were blinking at him in silence.

"You got nothing to say?"

"What about the fight when Dan was found?" Sara asked. "You threatened us."

"In front of Cotilla? Of course I did. But since when did a Medlar ever take good advice? Randal would never—" He looked at Kate, then cleared his throat. "So what do you have for me?" He nodded at the box.

Kate spoke up. "Inside is a metal cash box that belonged to Cheryl. We're hoping to find out who her boyfriend was."

The sheriff stood up and started to lift the top, but Jack's question stopped him.

"When did you change to our side?"

"When I saw Dan's note. His mom and I are friends. I know the problems she's had with his schooling and he couldn't have written that." The sheriff took a breath. "When I saw that boy hanging there—" He looked to the side but they could see the tears in his eyes. Sheriff Flynn turned back and looked at Sara. "You got a camera with you?"

"Of course."

"It have video on it?"

"Four-K."

"I want opening this recorded."

"We couldn't find a key," Jack said, "so we're going to need a locksmith."

Sheriff Flynn looked at him. "You're Roy Wyatt's

son and there's a lock you can't open? He didn't teach you anything?"

"I don't know how to—" Jack began, then sighed. "Get me some paper clips."

Jack opened the lock while Kate got the camera bag out of the truck. They turned on every light available before Sara began recording the opening.

Inside was everything they'd hoped for: a girl's diary that professed her love to be greater than anyone else had ever experienced. There were four photos of her boyfriend. Alastair Stewart was asleep in each of them, his head resting against a car seat.

Kate sat down on a wooden chair hard. Sara sat beside her and took her niece's hand.

Kate's voice was soft. "I know how charming Alastair can be. He says what you want to hear. He asked me about my plans for the future, the children I want, my dream job." Her head came up. "He told me I needed to put on weight, then fed me chocolate." She looked up at Jack, still standing there with the photos spread out on the desk. She expected him to say something snarky but he didn't.

"I'm glad he was nice to you," Jack said. "And if it helps any, he had me drooling over houses he wanted to buy. He suckered all of us in."

"Not me," Sara said. "I never thought he was good enough for my Kate."

She smiled at her aunt. "Thank—"

Sheriff Flynn's face was hard-looking. "I hate to interrupt your romantic ditherings, but none of this means anything."

They looked at him in confusion.

"The only 'crime' this shows is that Alastair Stewart was this girl's love interest. She wrote about him, fantasized about him. She took photos of him while he was sleeping. The truth is that she could have stuck her camera in a car window when he was asleep after a basketball game."

Jack lifted a cheap locket on a chain with his gloved index finger. "Think there are fingerprints on this?"

Sheriff Flynn raised his hands. "I hope so. Pray that there are. But then what? He'll say he was in love with a girl and they kept it a secret because of her mother. That's not a crime."

"And his mother," Sara said. "Noreen wouldn't like her precious son dating Cheryl."

"A true *Romeo and Juliet* story," the sheriff said. "And that's all it is."

"You are going to arrest him, aren't you?" Kate asked. "Even if he is a Stewart?"

"Definitely," Sheriff Flynn said. "Stewarts should uphold the image. Impregnating a girl from the wrong side of town—" He looked at Sara. "Sorry, but it's true. I know he exploited that poor girl, used her, but that's not against the law. I have no proof that he did anything else."

"He killed them." Jack's voice was low.

"Maybe," the sheriff said. "But I don't know that. I need to question Alastair first. The only way he'll reveal anything is if he's trying to talk his way out of a murder charge."

He went to the door. "I want all of you to stop searching this out. I've got enough to reopen the case now, so the professionals will take over."

"They need to look into Evan's and Mrs. Ellerbee's deaths," Sara said.

"You better believe they will," the sheriff answered. "I'm going to hound them like it's the end of the world. I need the keys to the Morris house. They're going to go through everything in those boxes and analyze it. If there's anything in there, they'll find it."

Sara got up and went to the door. She handed the SD card that contained the video to the sheriff. "You'll let us know what you find out?"

"I will." As they left the office, he put his hand on Kate's arm. "Take care of them. And I'm sorry about you and Alastair. But then, he was probably just…"

"I know. Dating me to get information." She smiled. "At least I'll get to tell my grandkids that their decrepit old granny used to date a murderer."

For a moment the sheriff looked shocked, then he laughed. "You are so much like your father. Someday we'll have to have that lunch together. The stories I could tell you!" He squeezed her hand. "Make sure they stay out of trouble."

"I will do my best." Kate followed the others to the truck and they drove home in silence.

TWENTY-THREE

IT HAD BEEN TEN DAYS SINCE THEY'D TURNED everything over to the Broward County Sheriff's Department. They'd been interviewed at length, then told "Thanks, now go away."

They hadn't protested. Not even Sara made a quip. She'd smiled at Sheriff Flynn and said she knew he'd take care of everything. On the way to the truck, she'd said, "How can he screw it up when we did all the work for him?"

Kate had wondered how they'd get along, living in the same house, but with no unifying task to bond them, no murder to investigate. Now they had their separate jobs to go to. Actually, Aunt Sara was supposedly retired but Jack had laughed at that idea. "As long as she has paper and pen, she will occupy herself." Since

Aunt Sara spent most of her time in her little writing room, that appeared to be true.

Kate was glad to find out that her fears of living together in harmony were ill-founded. She and Jack shared an interest in local real estate. He brought home floor plans of the houses he'd bought and wanted to hear their opinions.

"I guess Mrs. Stewart won't be buying the houses," he'd said solemnly. They'd looked at one another and laughed hard.

It was easy for them to settle into a routine. Jack was the grill expert; Kate cooked in the kitchen. Sara was the organizer. Her years of plotting made her an expert on seeing what needed to be done and in what order.

The Medlar-Wyatt family formed an easy, comfortable existence—with Jack in control of the remote. Kate threatened him but he only laughed.

As for Alastair, he'd been released on bail almost immediately, but Sheriff Flynn called to tell them not to worry. They were building a case of proof. "He won't get away with this," the sheriff said, then hung up.

There was a small setback caused by the newspaper reporter—and Jack's former bedmate—Elliot Hughes. She'd been given her own column, where she vowed to "reveal injustice" wherever she found it. She had been granted an interview with Alastair in the few hours he was in jail before his powerful Miami lawyer got him out.

Ms. Hughes said the lawyer made it clear that there was no evidence against his client and that Alastair Stewart had a "rock-solid alibi."

"The whole charge is ridiculous," he was quoted as

saying, then Ms. Hughes went on to give her interpretation of the facts.

> Alastair Stewart, from the highest of the high families in elegant little Lachlan, and Cheryl Morris, bottom of the lowest, were childhood sweethearts. But sadly, every moment they shared, every kiss, was in secret because their parents didn't approve.
>
> When Cheryl disappeared with no goodbye, Alastair had to cry alone.
>
> Recently, Cheryl and her mother were found dead by notorious local bad boy Jack Wyatt—who was known to be a very, very close friend of the deceased. Jack says he bought the Morris house to remodel it. He swears that he knew nothing of the skeletons buried in the tree roots.
>
> But what happened was so long ago that maybe no one will ever know the truth. All I can do is keep my loyal readers apprised of the development of this tragic story.
>
> You can be sure that I won't let up until I am thoroughly satisfied.

When Sara finished reading the article aloud, she glared at Jack.

"I guess I should have called her," he said.

"You think?" Kate and Sara said together, then laughed and high-fived each other.

When Kate went back to work, she dreaded Melissa's endless curiosity and her silly questions about Jack. But they didn't come. She suspected that Tayla had threatened her job if she didn't back off.

Within hours, Kate was showing houses. Thanks to Jack's notes, she was able to honestly tell people the pros and cons of each place. Already, she had two possible sales. They just wanted to see the houses again. And again.

So now Kate was walking toward a house that had just come on the market this morning. "We already have a potential buyer," Tayla had said. "A Mrs. Richardson from Charleston. She said that with global warming, that town has become too cold for her and she wants to move south."

Kate had blinked at that senseless statement a couple of times and Tayla wiggled her eyebrows.

"I met her," Melissa said. "Cute little woman. Gray hair and blue eyes—and dripping gold jewelry. Tell her all about our pretty town and how your boyfriend can remodel the house any way she wants it done."

Kate knew she was prying about Jack. "Gil is *not* my boyfriend."

Tayla gave a little guffaw of laughter at the way Kate had deflected Melissa's gibe.

Kate had picked up her paper-filled tote bag—Prada, borrowed from Aunt Sara—and easily found the house. It was a two-thousand-square-foot, three-bed, two-and-a-half-bath that needed updating. She paused in front of the house for a moment. The shrubs were scraggly and sparse. There were bare areas in the grass. She'd have to sell it with the name of a good landscaper.

When she saw that the front door was ajar, she frowned. It had a Realtor's lockbox on it and she was supposed to open it with a code.

Cautiously, she pushed open the door. Ever since

she'd found Dan Bruebaker hanging, she'd developed a fear of what was behind slightly open doors. "Hello?"

Around the corner came a tall woman with hair too black to be natural, sun-darkened skin, and, as Melissa had said, dripping gold jewelry. But she wasn't little, cute or gray.

"Hi," she said. "I'm Barbara Richardson."

Even in those few words, her Southern accent was heavy.

"I bet you were expecting my sister-in-law, Charlotte. We married brothers, and since their passing, she and I tend to do things together."

Kate shook the woman's hand. It was a very firm grip. "I'm Kate Medlar. Did someone let you in?"

"A young man. Tall, brown hair. Not to be unkind, but his nose is a bit too big for his face."

Kate relaxed her shoulders. "Larry. He works in my office. I wonder why he didn't say something."

"Honey," Mrs. Richardson drawled, "if you want me to explain men, I haven't lived long enough." She slipped her arm through Kate's. "I brought some of my rose-petal tea from home and I want you to try it."

The woman was overly friendly in a way that Kate didn't like. "I don't think—"

"I won't hear a no."

Kate walked with her into the kitchen. Set up on the counter was a flowered teapot, two cups and saucers, a milk pitcher and a sugar pot. "How pretty."

"We do have some lovely traditions in our hometown." She poured the cups full of tea. "Milk? Sugar?"

"No, thank you. This is fine." Kate sipped. The tea was delicious. Fragrant and hot.

Mrs. Richardson started to drink, then put down

her cup and picked up her Louis Vuitton bag. "Oh, dear. I've misplaced my sugar tablets. I must have left them in my car. I'll just be a moment. Go ahead and enjoy your tea."

Kate finished the cup, then poured herself another one. It really was extraordinarily good. Just as she heard a door open, she felt a bit dizzy. The house was unfurnished but there was a deep windowsill. She sat down on it, her hand to her forehead.

"Oh, no!" Mrs. Richardson said. "You look awful. But I know that look. You're expecting a baby, aren't you?"

"No, I'm not. I just…" The room seemed to be going around and around.

"You can't fool me. I know the signs. We better get you to your doctor. Who is your obstetrician?"

"I'm not—" Kate began but couldn't finish. When she tried to get up, Mrs. Richardson put her arm around Kate's shoulders and helped her stand.

For all that she looked older, Kate thought she certainly felt strong. She leaned on the woman as they walked toward the kitchen door. "Don't have a doctor."

"That is too bad. I'll just take you to mine. My car is in the garage."

"Larry shouldn't…done that." Kate's words were slurred. Even to herself she sounded drunk.

Mrs. Richardson's black Mercedes was in the warm, dark garage and Kate gratefully slumped onto the tan leather seats. Instantly, she closed her eyes.

The next thing she knew, Mrs. Richardson had opened the car door and was pulling Kate out. Her head was swirling and all she wanted to do was stretch out somewhere and go to sleep. The grass looked so good that she made a movement as though she meant to lie down on it.

"Oh, no, you don't," Mrs. Richardson said.

As dizzy as she was, Kate heard the difference in her voice. "Accent," she mumbled.

"Comes and goes," Mrs. Richardson said. She led Kate to some stairs up to a cabin with a wide porch.

"I don't think…" Kate began and took a step back.

"Come on," the woman said and her accent seemed to have returned. "The doctor is inside. He'll make you feel much better."

Kate had a glimpse of what looked to be thick tropical forest all around the house. "Have a client…like… buy this," she muttered as they went inside. There was a couch and through a doorway she could see a bed. Ah, to lie down. To sleep!

But Mrs. Richardson led Kate to a stout wooden chair and practically pushed her down into it.

"Just sit there and I'll go get the doctor."

Kate's knees were so weak that she could do nothing but sit, and the moment she did, her eyes closed.

TWENTY-FOUR

WHEN KATE WOKE, IT TOOK HER A WHILE TO adjust. She was in a hard wooden chair, her body stiff from lack of movement, and her arms were behind her. When she tried to move, she found her wrists were tied together. From what she could feel, it was one of those plastic zip ties that could hardly be cut with scissors, much less by a human.

With her Realtor eye, she looked around the cabin. It was thirty or forty years old at least and seemed to be just two rooms. She was in the middle of the big, open living room facing a heavy wooden table with mismatched chairs. At the end was a kitchen with old cabinets and heavy iron hardware.

I bet Dan's company made those, she thought.

Twisting as far as she could, she saw two closed doors. She'd seen a bed, so the other one was probably a bath.

The place reeked of male. This cabin was a place where men gathered and smoked cigars and fried fish. There was no TV and she doubted if a cell phone had ever been allowed to enter.

By the light through the dirty windows, it looked to be early evening. Six, maybe. She was beginning to remember how she got there. The woman! Who was she?

She wondered if anyone was searching for her. Would Jack want to know where she was? Or would he say she'd probably run off with a pastry chef and would return in the wee hours? But Aunt Sara might make him get off the couch and go look for Kate. How long before they found her car? Before they asked Tayla? Before— Behind her, she heard a door open and footsteps. It took some willpower, but she didn't turn to see who it was. *Quiet!* she told herself. *Don't panic. Delay as long as you can.*

"A bath made me feel better," said a voice behind her.

Kate kept her eyes straight ahead while the woman came into view. She was the shape of the Mrs. Richardson Kate had met, but there was a drastic change in her looks. Her blond hair was pulled back into an elegant chignon, and the color looked natural. The dark tone of her skin was gone. Her plain clothes had been replaced with designer wear.

With the change of colors and attire, Kate knew who she was: Alastair's mother.

Norma? No. Noreen.

She stood a few feet in front of Kate and for a moment stared at her. "Do I need to introduce myself?"

"I think you're Mrs. Stewart."

"Yes. Alastair's mother."

At the name, there was a flash of anger in her eyes. With uncles like hers, Kate was experienced with rage. Her uncles expected to be obeyed, and when they weren't, they allowed their self-righteous anger to burst into flame. This woman was wearing the same expression as those men.

Whatever I do, Kate thought, *I don't want to challenge her. Don't want to send her over the edge. Time is what I need. Time to let Aunt Sara and Jack find me.*

Kate swallowed. "I'd really like to hear the truth of what happened."

"My son did not kill those women."

"That's why he was released. I think the evidence proves that he wasn't there when they died."

Mrs. Stewart nodded at that but kept silent. Casually, as though it meant nothing, she reached behind a stack of old magazines and picked up a pistol. It looked heavy enough to use in a weight-lifting class.

Mrs. Stewart tossed it from one hand to the other. "Isn't this thing awful? It belonged to my late husband. Made him feel like a man. As if anything could do that."

"You're saying he wasn't like Alastair."

"Like my beautiful son? Not at all." She took her cell phone out of the pocket of her white linen trousers. "My son is supposed to call me. I'm letting him decide what to do with you."

"Oh" was all Kate could say. The man they had turned in to the sheriff as a murderer was to decide her fate. "Who *did* kill the Morris women?"

"Oh. That." Mrs. Stewart put the big pistol down on the table. "No one killed them. Not really." She walked to the far side of the room and turned on two lamps. "I hate this place. Always did. Hamish wanted us to spend our honeymoon here. Can you imagine?"

Kate thought that with a good cleaning she'd love to stay there, but decided not to say so. "You've lived in Lachlan a long time."

"Too long, but in my day, children obeyed their parents. My father—now, *there* was a man! He told me where I was to live, who I was to marry, and I did it."

"But your husband wasn't the right man for you?"

"Hamish was a fool. Weak beyond imagining. I hated him. But he did give me Alastair. My beautiful son only made one mistake in his whole life, but I managed to repair the damage—until Jack Wyatt and you and…and that Sara Medlar came along. Did you know that in high school she used to make fun of me? She told Hamish not to marry me. Me! Can you imagine?"

"Tell me about the error Alastair made. I mean, there's nothing to do while we wait."

She toyed with the gun for a moment, seeming to try to decide what to do. "My son explained the truth of it all to me. They *willed* what happened to them. It was as though she—the older one—*wanted* me to finish it for her. It was like she was done. She'd had enough."

"I'd really like to hear that story." Kate's voice was sincere. "I want to understand."

Mrs. Stewart checked her phone again and gave a sigh. No calls. Kate wondered if there was a signal and if Mrs. Stewart knew how to tell if there was. Kate didn't know South Florida well enough to be able to guess how far they were from Lachlan. She'd slept through the drive and couldn't calculate. "Have you ever told anyone?"

"Of course not."

"Then the truth must be building inside you."

The woman sat down in a big padded chair near the window. "Actually, it's all been a relief. Before all this happened, I thought about the past a great deal. But afterward, with each one, I felt better."

Each one? Kate thought but didn't say out loud. "As hard as we searched, we could find out very little."

"Of course not. It was all taken care of long ago. There were loose ends but we managed to tie them off."

We? Kate thought. "Would you tell me the truth? While we wait? Please?"

Mrs. Stewart took a moment to decide. "I will tell you what my darling son told me." She took a breath. "Then me. It was not my fault. My husband… That woman…"

"Yes," Kate whispered. "I understand."

Noreen sneered. "No one can understand what was done to me. No one seems to think about *me* in all this."

"Alastair does," Kate said softly.

She smiled. "Yes, he does." For a moment she closed her eyes. "I guess I should start at the beginning of that night. Start with what my son told me."

TWENTY-FIVE

5 SEPTEMBER, 1997

CHERYL MORRIS'S SIXTEENTH BIRTHDAY

AS HE KNEW SHE WOULD BE, CHERYL WAS waiting for him beside that old rusty farm thing at the back of her house. For a moment he hid behind a big palm tree and watched her. She was a pretty girl but in a way that drew too much attention. She certainly wasn't the kind he could be seen in public with.

He'd tried to fix her. He'd tutored her, mentored her, did his best to tone her down while raising her up. He'd introduced her to silk, makeup, heels. But they hadn't helped much. He liked old movies and in his mind he compared her to Brigitte Bardot. You could put her in the most conservative clothes and she'd still ooze sex.

He leaned back against the tree. He'd leave for college soon, so he'd have to get away from her. She wasn't someone he could show to Mother. But maybe he could tell his father. Maybe this would change his father's attitude toward his son.

When Alastair turned back, he saw that she had her hand on something at her neck, and he recognized it. The local jeweler was making a mint off selling initial necklaces to the high-school males to give to their girlfriends. Alastair had been asked who he was giving one to and he'd made a remark about needing a half dozen of them.

Like he'd shell out two hundred and fifty bucks for a necklace for some girl.

He saw her move her hand. Damn if she didn't seem to be caressing the thing. So who had given her the necklace? One of the guys on the team? Hadn't he trained her better than to keep gifts from other people?

With a frown, he made his way across the street. Turning, he glanced at the house of that old hag Mary Ellerbee to see if she was spying. He'd bumped into her once and he didn't plan to do it again. But her house was dark.

Cheryl heard him approach and turned to him, her face welcoming. But he didn't miss that she slipped the necklace inside her blouse.

He allowed her to kiss him but he didn't return the gesture. Holding her at arm's length, he looked her up and down. "I saw you today and the back of your blouse was wrinkled. From now on, maybe you shouldn't lean back against the seat."

"Okay," she said, but she wasn't meeting his eyes.

He pulled himself up straight, to his tallest, and looked down at her. "What's the problem?"

"I have something to tell you." Her voice was soft, almost as though she was afraid of something.

"About the necklace?" He wanted her to think that he knew *everything*.

"The what? Oh." Smiling, she pulled it out of the inside of her blouse. She'd unbuttoned the top for him, something she wasn't allowed to do in school. "It's from Jack. Isn't it sweet?"

"That Wyatt kid gave you a gold necklace?"

She held it tightly in her hand. "Yes. He helps me so much. I wouldn't have accomplished all I've done if it weren't for him."

He stepped back from her. "And what exactly have you accomplished?"

"Oh, Allie, please don't do your jealousy thing now. I have something important to tell you."

"Don't call me that and what do you mean jealous?"

She put her hand on his chest and looked up at him. "We're going to have a baby."

Alastair couldn't say anything. He just froze where he was.

"It's all right." Her voice was urgent. "I've thought everything out. We've always planned to get married but we'll just do it sooner. I'll finish high school through correspondence and we—the baby and I—will make a home for you when you go to college. They have dorms for married students. I'll get a job and help with the expenses and…"

Alastair was backing away from her.

"Allie? I mean, Alastair?" She stepped closer to him. "Nothing has changed, just the date."

"Go," he murmured. "I have to go."

"I know. This is your training weekend. I won't see you again until Sunday night. We'll talk everything out then."

Alastair couldn't reply. He just walked away with as much composure as he could manage. He always parked his car far away, then made his way through side streets and backyards of people he knew weren't home. But this time, he went straight down the street and didn't slow down until he reached the good part of Lachlan.

His car was near the bookstore. He got in, shut the door and let himself breathe. What did he do now?

Mother was the only thought in his mind. She'd be angry but she'd know how to take care of this.

He took his time, trying to let it all sink in before he went home. He needed to present the facts to her in a way that showed he had reached manhood.

She was in the little sitting area off her bedroom. His father had his own set of rooms that were smaller and less lavishly decorated, but his mother loved silk and pearls and jade.

She glanced up from her book on the history of France in the sixteenth century—she did not believe in novels. There was only the tiniest flicker of annoyance when she saw his face, then she composed herself. She knew that he had something bad to tell her.

Alastair got his height and his blondness from her. Some people said that he was so much like his mother that it was hard to believe that Hamish had anything to do with him.

Noreen put down her book, nodded toward the blue brocade chair, then waited for him to speak.

In spite of his planning, Alastair didn't know where to start. At the beginning? Tell how he made such an effort to meet her through that dreadful Delia? No. Not there.

"She's pregnant."

Noreen seemed to be relieved. "That's easy to change. Careless of you but fixable."

"She wants us to get married."

Noreen laughed at that. "She couldn't be that stupid. Or is she? Who is it?"

"Cheryl Morris." The words almost choked him. Lowest of the low. The dregs. The type a Stewart didn't speak to, much less...

His mother's face had gone ghostly white. He'd never seen her look so upset. But how could that be? His mother was a rock. A solid, never-flustered person.

"Morris," she whispered, then stood up.

"I'm sorry. I—"

She whirled on him. "Why her? *Why?*"

"Dad said—" He'd never seen his mother look so angry.

"What did that father of yours say?" She was leaning over him, her face distorted with rage.

Alastair's belief that he was a man fled his mind immediately. He reverted to being a scared child, his voice full of tears. "He said she was a 'fine girl.' He said he was proud of the way she'd overcome her life. He said—"

She stood up and turned to the window. "No more. I can guess."

"I wanted to please him," Alastair sobbed. "Just once, I wanted to do something that he *liked*."

When Noreen turned back, she was calmer. "Are you packed to go to camp?"

"Yes."

"Then get your bag and leave. I'll take care of this."

"But how—?"

"Don't ask questions. If I need you, I'll let you know. Now get out of here."

He obeyed his mother.

Noreen went to the safe that was hidden under an antique carpet and withdrew twenty grand in cash. She also pulled out a diamond necklace that her beloved father-in-law had given her. It was a beautiful thing and she'd hate to part with it, but women like Verna Morris tended to like flash. As for the girl, she had no worries. After what Noreen had to say, agreeing to an abortion wouldn't be a problem.

As her son did, Noreen parked some distance away and walked to the Morris house. She certainly knew where it was. Not that she'd ever visited before, but she knew.

She wasn't recognized by anyone. But then, the light was low and she had raided her husband's closet. She had on his pants and shirt, a cap hiding her blond hair.

The house was well lit and she paused for a moment to see what was going on. There was an old van in the weedy driveway, all the doors open. Inside were boxes and bags of household goods. It looked like Verna had been told of her daughter's predicament and they were at last leaving town.

Good! Noreen thought, but she wanted to make sure.

She went to the back of the house. No matter what, she didn't want to be seen in this neighborhood, especially not at *this* house.

When she reached the back, the girl popped out of the shadows.

Of course, Noreen had seen her before—and been disgusted by her. She dressed above her class, above her age. Now her thick makeup was smeared.

Noreen couldn't conceal the sneer on her face.

"Oh, Mrs. Stewart, I knew you'd come. I knew Allie would tell you. I promise that I'll make a good daughter-in-law. I've studied everything, from drinking tea to how to dress to how to run a household. All of it. And I'm going to get a job as a newscaster. That's respectable, isn't it? I've done so much to prove that I'm worthy of being a Stewart."

Noreen's sneer reached epic proportions. One side of her upper lip almost disappeared into her nostril. "You stupid girl. You *are* a Stewart."

She shoved past her to go into the house, but Cheryl grabbed her arm. "What do you mean?"

Noreen jerked her arm away. She could see her husband in the girl. Her eyes had gone from begging to that stubbornness she so despised in him. Unlike Alastair, she couldn't always make Hamish obey her—and she was looking at the result of that. "Your father is Hamish Stewart."

"You're a liar." Cheryl's voice was calm and steely. "My father died before I was born."

"I wish that were true." Noreen took a step forward but the girl blocked her.

"I won't listen to your lies." The girl lifted her arm as though she meant to slap the older woman.

Years and years of rage that had smoldered inside Noreen came to the surface. Her upper body was strong from a lifetime of sports. She drew back her arm and hit the girl hard on the side of the head.

Cheryl fell backward, her head hitting a sharp corner of the concrete steps. She landed in the exact place where a few hours earlier she'd sat with young Jack Wyatt and received his birthday gifts.

As Noreen looked at the unmoving body of the girl, the blood already flowing across the step, her instincts told her that the girl was dead.

Part of her mind said she should *do* something, call someone. But the larger part felt some deep, primal satisfaction. She'd been married off at a young age to a man with half her intelligence, a man who just wanted to laugh and drink and help out his friends. A true waste of a human being. *She* had been the one to run their lives and their income. He'd repaid her with an affair that had produced…this.

She glared at the girl on the steps. So very much blood was coming out of her and was now running down to a lower step.

Noreen knew no one had seen her arrive. She could leave and no one would know. The girl slipped. She—

An eerie, high-pitched scream made Noreen look up. Verna Morris practically tumbled down the steps to her daughter and lifted her limp body.

"She fell," Noreen whispered.

"You shoved her. You hit her," Verna yelled.

"I did no such thing." Noreen's mind was beginning to function again.

"Call an ambulance," Verna ordered, her body cradling her daughter as she tried to find the spot where the blood was coming from.

Noreen went into the house as though to make the call, but she didn't. *Think!* she ordered herself. How to handle this?

She went back outside. "They'll be here in minutes."

Verna was rocking her daughter and making a low keening sound. "She is my life. All of it. I want nothing else but my daughter." Her voice became a whisper. "I can't live without her. I don't *want* to live without her."

She gave Noreen a look of calculation. "I'll see that you're put in jail." Carefully, Verna put her daughter on the steps and stood up. "I'll tell the world that your worthless son impregnated his half sister." She was advancing on Noreen. "You think you did a good job of spreading your lying gossip about *me*, telling people that I'm a whore, but wait until you see what I do to *you*. The Stewart name will be a laughingstock for the whole town. I'll—"

Noreen knew she didn't have much to be proud of, but the honor of her name was foremost. There was a flowerpot nearby that contained a dying plant. On the side was a plastic handle. She grabbed it and out came a weeding tool: long, thin, with a two-pronged end.

Without thinking what she was doing, she stabbed Verna in the stomach, then pulled out the blade.

With her hands over the wound, Verna staggered back to her daughter's body. Blood was coming out between her fingers. "I will recover from this, and I will tell the world your secrets. Hamish loved *me*, not you. I'll tell people what he said when we were in bed together. He wondered if the man you truly loved, your father-in-law, was Alastair's father. He said—"

Noreen wrapped her hands around the woman's neck and began to squeeze. Years of hatred, of being given a life she'd never wanted, were in her hands. Muscles she'd developed at tennis clenched around Verna's thin throat. Noreen heard the gagging sounds and they pleased her. How much pain this woman had caused her! She'd dared to return to a town that was owned by the family Noreen had been sold into.

When Verna's body went limp, she dropped the corpse on top of her daughter's body.

For a moment she enjoyed the silence. The lights from the house showed the two bodies piled together. "She *wanted* to die," Noreen whispered.

Her calm was coming back to her—and with it came relief. She remembered the divorce papers her husband had presented to her. He was such a fool that he'd told her the truth, all about the "love of my life" and the "darling daughter" she'd given him. Noreen had given Hamish a perfect son but he had never spent much time with the boy. "He's just like you" had been Hamish's excuse.

Noreen looked about her. It had all taken a very short time. No one had seen or heard. No one knew anything.

She looked back at the bodies. They were small females and Noreen had little trouble dragging them to the back and dropping them into some disgusting pit. Enough dirt fell down that she didn't bother trying to cover them. That the hole was there, that the dirt fell down, seemed to be an omen. She'd done what was supposed to happen.

When the bodies were hidden, she used the nearby garden hose to spray the blood off the concrete steps. If anyone came by, she didn't want them to see the obvious.

She thought about how to more completely conceal the bodies, but that would involve manual labor, work that was beyond her inclinations.

When she got back to her car, she called her son at his basketball training camp. They had finished dinner and were doing whatever it was that teenage boys did when together.

"You have to do something for me," she said, then told him everything. He would leave as soon as his roommate was asleep, return to Lachlan and do what needed doing. He'd be back at camp before the boy woke up.

The next morning, Noreen was smiling. She felt better than she had in years. So much of the bad of her life was gone. Forever out of her life. Only her husband remained.

When Hamish came to breakfast, she smiled at him. "Don't you think aconites would be beautiful in the garden?"

"Whatever you want," he muttered, "I'm sure you'll get it."

Aconite. Also known as monkshood. Deadly poison. She called the gardener and made the order.

TWENTY-SIX

WHILE MRS. STEWART HAD TOLD THE STORY, Kate had twisted and pulled on the bindings around her wrists until her skin was raw. In a way, the pain helped her deal with what she was hearing. The cruelty, the total lack of empathy, made her feel sick.

It was when Mrs. Stewart told about killing Cheryl in such a cool, detached way that Kate thought her fate was sealed. There was no way the woman was going to let someone hear the story and then continue to live.

When she told of planting the aconites, Kate stopped pulling against the bindings. Even she knew those plants were poisonous. Alastair had impregnated his sister and it was highly likely that his mother had poisoned her husband. No, she wasn't going to risk that story coming out.

The woman was looking at Kate as though expecting a sympathetic response for what she'd told her. Kate drew in her breath. "I can see what happened. It was just like now, with you and Alastair. A mother will do anything to protect her child."

Mrs. Stewart gave a small smile. "That's exactly right. It was Alastair's one mistake and I had to fix it."

"But then, the whole thing was his father's fault."

Mrs. Stewart gave a genuine smile. "You *do* understand."

Kate blinked. The woman sounded as though an orangutan had just solved a calculus problem. She glanced at the window. It was dark outside. No streetlights. No car headlights. No humans with flashlights. *Sympathy!* Kate told herself. *Give the insane woman understanding, pity, and agree with every terrifying word she says. And keep her talking!*

"I bet Alastair had trouble finding out about those brakes."

Mrs. Stewart gave a dry laugh. "Did he! He said I had confused him with a gardener and now a truck mechanic. My son has a delightful sense of humor."

The tree he planted, Kate thought. "So Evan wasn't…?" She couldn't think how to phrase her question.

"He wasn't supposed to be there. That Jack Wyatt always did cause problems. I knew where he came from. No one could believe that he'd grow up to own a business. I told people he probably stole the money."

Just as you spread gossip about Verna, Kate thought. Aunt Sara was right in hiding her involvement with Jack's finances. If that had been known, this vindictive woman would have made it into something dirty.

Suddenly, Kate remembered something in the woman's story. The gardening tool she'd used to stab Verna. She remembered opening a box of books at the Morris house. On top was a rusty old weeder. Rusty or covered in twenty-year-old blood? "That was nice of Alastair to plant that beautiful tree. It was a memorial."

"That's how we saw it."

"I guess Mrs. Ellerbee knew too much."

"I didn't think anyone would believe her story of having seen a Stewart at that house but I wasn't sure."

"Better safe than sorry."

Mrs. Stewart's smile left her and she looked at Kate as though to ask if she was making fun of her. "I bet you think I'm the bad person for telling people about that Morris woman. All I wanted was for her to take her Lolita of a daughter and leave the town. But she wouldn't go away—and worse, I had to see them all the time. At church, at fairs. Whenever there was anything going on in the town, there she was. Flaunting that odd daughter of hers. Verna Morris may not have been sleeping with a lot of men, but she *was* a slut, so I told people that. Where's the harm in that?"

"None at all." Kate nearly choked on the words.

For a long, nerve-racking minute, Mrs. Stewart stared at Kate. "You're clever, aren't you? The question is if you're more like your aunt or your father?"

Kate's eyes widened. "You knew him?"

"Everyone knew Randal Medlar—and liked him. His sister always thought she was smarter than everyone else, too good to join in with people. But Randal! Now, there was a lovely young man. So kind and thoughtful. He used to send me flowers on my birthday, and I invited him to all my parties. He was like you and got me to tell him all my secrets. But he *never* betrayed them. If your aunt heard of a secret, say a messy old tool that was accidentally left behind, she'd run to the police. But Randal would have taken a bullet to the head before he told. So which are you?"

"A clone of my father," Kate said with so much sincerity that her head nearly exploded.

When Kate saw her aunt Sara's face appear at the window, she had a hard time not crying out in pure happiness. How had they found her? But now was not the time to think of that.

She kept her eyes on Mrs. Stewart. "I don't think anyone could convict you of murder. It was all an accident."

"Are you patronizing me?"

"No! Not at all." In the background, Aunt Sara was making gestures but Kate didn't dare look to see what they were. Instead, she quickly turned her head to the side. "Is that Alastair?"

When Mrs. Stewart hurried to the window, Kate looked at her aunt. She was holding up three fingers and making a sideways motion. Kate nodded. She understood. She was to get out of the way of whatever was about to happen.

Mrs. Stewart seemed to sense that something was happening. She turned just as Kate pushed hard with her feet and made the chair slam on its side to the floor.

Besides the boom of the chair, there was a sound she wasn't quite sure of, but she thought maybe it was a gunshot.

From the floor, Kate looked up at Mrs. Stewart and saw that she was halfway across the room, her hand outstretched as she reached for the pistol on the table.

But the woman stopped abruptly and looked down at her white blouse. Blood was on her upper arm and she looked at it in disbelief. She seemed to be thinking *"Who in the world had the audacity to do such a thing to me?"*

In the next second, her eyes rolled back and she hit the wooden floor so hard that dust went flying up.

At the same moment, Aunt Sara ran through the front door, Sheriff Flynn behind her, Jack on his crutches and cursing in the rear.

Sara knelt down to Kate. "I need a knife!" she bellowed and both men handed her one. She took Jack's and cut the plastic ties around her niece's wrists.

"You—you... We didn't know..." Sara was choking on tears.

"Not now!" Jack snapped. "Save it for later." He looked at Kate. "Can you walk?"

"Better and faster than you can." Kate stood up.

For a moment Jack looked like he, too, was going to cry, but he recovered to give a smirk. "Sounds like you're fine."

Sheriff Flynn was putting handcuffs on Mrs. Stewart, who was facedown on the floor.

"I think she's been shot," Kate said. "Shouldn't she—?"

"Ambulance is on its way," the sheriff said. "Right now I just want her secure." He pulled the woman up.

"How dare you—" Mrs. Stewart began, but the sheriff cut her off.

"Shut up, Noreen. Oh, but I wish Hamish had had the balls to tell you that when he was alive."

"So do I," Noreen growled at him.

"I think you need to exhume him," Kate said. All of them stopped and stared at her.

"You didn't by chance get any info out of her, did you?" the sheriff asked.

"Lots," Kate said. "A huge, enormous amount."

"She's a liar," Mrs. Stewart said. "Just like her aunt, she makes up stories that have no basis in reality." She sneered at Kate. "You aren't at all like your father."

Sara put her arm around Kate's shoulders. "I guess you mean all the parties Randal went to at your house. I don't know for sure, but you better have a jeweler check your diamonds. My brother probably switched them for glass."

Jack and Kate and Mrs. Stewart looked at Sara in disbelief but Sheriff Flynn laughed. "I sure do miss that man."

Chuckling, he gave Mrs. Stewart a shove in her lower back and pushed her toward the door. In the distance they could hear a siren.

"Isn't he worried about charges of police brutality?" Kate asked. "Treating a wounded, alleged criminal like that?"

"She isn't really hurt," Sara said. "That's why he gave the rifle to Jack."

Jack gave a modest shrug. "I do tend to hit where I aim. You ready to go home?"

"Yes, I am." Kate's adrenaline was waning and she could feel the shakes coming on. "I just…" She nodded toward the bathroom.

She was out in a few minutes and there was an EMT waiting for her.

"I need to test your vitals," he said.

"I don't want to stay in a hospital."

"And we don't want to make you." He was a very nice-looking young man.

"I saved you," Jack said, "but you're flirting with *him*?"

The EMT stepped back. "Sorry, Jack, I didn't know—"

"Could you act like a grown-up for even one minute?" Kate said as she went to the door, Jack right behind her.

"Old enough to shoot my way in and save your ungrateful neck. And *I* was the one who saw that your car was parked on the street but you were nowhere to be seen."

"You were stalking me?"

They left the cabin and went down the stairs together. Jack helped Kate because she was still wobbling from her ordeal and she helped him with his crutches and cast. They bickered all the way down.

"Wow," the EMT said. "They're…"

"Yes," Sara said. "They are."

TWENTY-SEVEN

"HI." JACK SAT DOWN ON THE SIDE OF KATE'S bed and held out a plate piled high with blueberry pancakes oozing butter and maple syrup.

She was still mostly asleep. "I can't eat—"

He put a bite in her mouth.

"Just this once." She sat up and took the plate from him.

Jack got up and opened the curtains. It wasn't full daylight yet.

"I take it that you have something to tell me."

"Flynn wants us to come in early so he can tell us things he's not supposed to. Seems that our, uh, contributions to the case are going to be ignored. They don't think we need to know anything."

"They're going to take the credit?"

"Oh, yeah."

Kate held up her fork. "That will keep lookie-loos from wanting me to show them houses just so they can ask murder questions."

Jack smiled. "I like how you find good in bad places."

"Like how my father stole good diamonds from a bad lady?"

"I'm not getting into that." He started to sit down on the little couch, but instead he told Kate to move over, then stretched out on the bed beside her. "I meant for you to scoot this way. Toward me."

She put a bite of pancakes into his mouth. "Tell me what Sheriff Flynn is going to say."

"What they've found so far. We have to do it early because you are to be interrogated all day. Under glaring lights, with nothing to eat or drink for twenty-four hours."

"Bathroom breaks?"

"None."

"Sounds like a day spent with my uncles."

"I've been meaning to ask about them. Why—?"

"One set of psychopaths at a time."

Sara stuck her head in. "Is this a private conversation?"

"Wish it was," Jack said, "but it's not."

"Daryl just sent me a text. They caught Alastair."

"I take it they found some real evidence against him?" Kate said.

Both Sara and Jack looked at her. It wouldn't be good if the only evidence they had was Kate's testimony. Stewart money; Stewart connections; Stewart cold-blooded-killer instinct. They wouldn't have any hesitation about making sure Kate didn't show up to testify.

Sara ran Jack out of Kate's bedroom and told her niece to dress comfortably. It was going to be a long day.

When they got to Sheriff Flynn's office, it was only 7:00 a.m., but he was waiting for them. They took their seats in the chairs on the other side of his desk.

He looked at Kate. "You okay?"

"Never better." She was only lying a little bit. Aunt Sara squeezed her hand. "You didn't by chance do any DNA testing, did you?"

Sheriff Flynn leaned back in his chair and gave a big smile. "And here I thought I'd be able to surprise you with that. We found a red leather makeup case that—"

"Mark Cross," the three said in unison.

Sheriff Flynn looked at a paper on his desk. "That's the brand name, yes. It contained lots of hair samples." He paused for effect. "Hamish Stewart was Cheryl Morris's father." When no one showed surprise, he sighed. "Damn! I was hoping for gasps of shock. At least from two of you."

"Sorry," Kate said, "but last night I kept them up for hours telling them everything."

"She's a very good storyteller," Sara said. "Succinct. Organized."

"I'm not sure if I can follow up what is surely an unbiased opinion," Sheriff Flynn said, "but here's what we've found out. First of all, Evan. Three days before the crash, Alastair Stewart signed in at the library to use a computer. He spent an hour researching how to sabotage the brakes of a 2015 three-quarter-ton Chevy pickup.

"We called Dan Bruebaker's former coach, the one who ran that training weekend in Naples back in 1997. He remembers Alastair Stewart very well. 'Arrogant SOB' is what he said. Dan Bruebaker told him Alastair had been out all night. Seems Dan had a tummy ache and woke up every few minutes. He saw that his roomie was gone and he told the coach about it. The next day the coach worked Stewart out doubly hard but he never let on that he knew Stewart had been out all night with, they assumed, a girl."

"Good thing the coach said nothing or he might be dead now," Jack said.

"Unfortunately, that's probably true. We ran the video you bought from the guy at the retirement home through facial-recognition software. The gray-haired old woman in a wheelchair and the old woman pushing her were—"

"Alastair and Noreen," Sara said.

"Right. We called Stewart's high-school girlfriend, Delia Monroe. If you guys had called her, you would have found out that she and Cheryl were at one time BFFs. Did I get that abbreviation right?"

Kate nodded.

"They were forbidden friends, so not many people knew. Delia was from a good family, while Cheryl was...you know."

"That's the link," Kate said. "We couldn't find it."

"Stewart sucked up to Delia to get near Cheryl," Jack said.

"Exactly," Sheriff Flynn said. "Then he bullied the poor girl into dropping Cheryl."

"So he could have her all to himself," Sara said.

"I guess he liked Cheryl because she dressed like an adult."

"The other way around. He wanted her to dress like that and she did."

"The sick bastard," Jack mumbled.

"The *Story of O*," Sara said but didn't explain. "I bet you called his ex-wife."

"We did." Sheriff Flynn held up a paper. "Here it is. She sure does hate him! She called him the coldest bastard on the planet. Said he went after her because her father is the CEO of a major corporation. She didn't leave him because she was having an affair as he said she was. She ran away as fast as she could because he wanted her to wear a lot of makeup, silk blouses, tight skirts and four-inch heels. And he was clear that he wanted her to dress like that *all the time*."

He was disappointed when no one seemed surprised.

"Did you find anything in the box of books?" Sara asked.

"Yes." Sheriff Flynn sighed. He'd been saving that for last. "On top of your books was the tool that Noreen used to stab Verna. She must have tossed it on the ground. Greedy Lester Boggs must have picked it up on Sunday when he took the van. I'm sure the fingerprints on it will match hers." Sheriff Flynn put down the paper. "I've already put in an order to have Hamish's body exhumed, and there will be a lot more searching for evidence. We're building a solid case." He looked at Kate. "You'll have to testify."

She nodded. She dreaded it but she'd do it.

There was a noise behind them and they turned. The Lachlan office was filling with men in uniforms and suits.

"They're going to ask you a lot of questions," the sheriff said to Kate. "You ready for it?"

"I think so. But between us, I feel bad that I didn't see through Alastair. I've tried to remember what information I gave him."

"Nothing that kept him from being found out," the sheriff said. "Now go out there and get some doughnuts. Bessie at the bakery sent them over. She says she owes you big-time for vouching for Alastair Stewart."

"News travels fast," Kate said.

"In Lachlan it does," Sara said with a mix of admiration and disgust. "Come on, let's get this started so we get it over with."

As soon as they entered the main room, Detective Cotilla went to Kate. Jack and Sara put themselves so close to her that they were like pillars holding up a roof. They could collapse on top of the man at any moment.

The detective didn't apologize for the things he'd said before, but he didn't meet Jack's eyes. "We'd like to talk to you, Miss Medlar. If that's all right with you."

"Certainly. But I'd like my aunt to be with me."

"Of course. You've been through a trauma and—"

"And me," Jack said.

"I can't—" Detective Cotilla gritted his teeth. "I will try to get permission."

With a smile, Jack slipped a card into the breast pocket of the detective's suit. It was from the clinic that worked with sexually abused children. "Never needed that." Jack patted the man's pocket.

Detective Cotilla still refused to look at him.

They took only a few steps when the double glass front doors burst open and they heard voices. In came half a dozen officers in uniform. In the middle of them was a handcuffed Alastair Stewart.

He was perfectly groomed, neatly dressed...and furious. His eyes were pits of blue fire. He halted only a few feet from Kate. "You!" he said.

The officers went to the long desk to deal with paperwork, leaving only two men with Alastair.

The roomful of tall, broad-shouldered people paid no attention to five-foot-tall Sara. Only Jack and Sheriff Flynn saw her slip away and disappear behind two lumberjack-sized men in brown.

"You thought there could be something between a Medlar and a Stewart," Alastair said to Kate. "I couldn't even bear to allow you inside my car."

As Sara silently walked past a deputy's desk, she picked up his heavy motorcycle gloves and kept going.

Sheriff Flynn elbowed Jack to quit staring in wide-eyed fascination at whatever the little woman was doing. *Don't draw attention to her*, he seemed to be saying.

"That's enough," one of the deputies said to Alastair and started to pull him away.

But Sheriff Flynn shook his head. "The man should be allowed to have his say."

Alastair smiled smugly. "Kirkwoods were always our friends." He looked back at Kate. Even though Alastair's hands were handcuffed behind him, he still managed to look triumphant. "Your mundane, plebeian wishes sickened me. To create more Medlars! The earth should be cleansed of people like you."

Behind him, Sara went to the water fountain and picked up a wooden two-step stool. She put the gloves on top and carried the steps to place them just behind Alastair.

One of the bewildered officers started to stop her, but a look from Detective Cotilla made him step back.

Alastair sneered at Jack. "You should have known that I would *never* have a Wyatt's used goods."

Jack slipped his arm around Kate's shoulders but no one said anything.

Sara climbed up the two steps, put the gloves on, turned sideways, hands up in boxer position. "Hey, Stewart!" She was on his level and very close to him.

When he turned, Sara drew back her arm and used every ounce of muscle she had, from her toes to her neck. She hit him in the face with a right cross powered by rage. The sound of Alastair's nose crunching was so loud that people winced.

With his hands behind him, Alastair was unable to balance and he hit the floor hard. When blood came gushing out of his nose, he couldn't wipe it away.

Like a miniature Rocky at the top of the steps, Sara stood there, her small hands covered in the big leather gloves.

Jack started for her, but Detective Cotilla got there first. He went to help her down, but instead he raised Sara's arm. Sheriff Flynn raised her other arm. She was a fighter who had won the match.

The room erupted in laughter and applause—and a dozen cell phones snapped a photo.

Alastair was on the floor and shouting, but the cheering was so loud that no one heard him. For all that, publicly, no credit was going to be given to them, they all knew the truth. These untrained amateurs had solved a twenty-year-old double homicide and had stopped the killing spree of the Stewart duo. Already, the evil mother and son were becoming infamous.

Jack pushed past Detective Cotilla, put his hands on Sara's waist and swung her down. She threw her arms around him. He hugged her back and kissed the top of her head.

Finally, someone helped Alastair stand up. But no one blotted the blood off his face. "Better let a doctor do that," Sheriff Flynn said.

"I'm going to sue all of you," Alastair said. "I'll destroy this entire department." His eyes were already beginning to blacken, and his voice was thick from the smashed nose. Blood covered the lower half of his face.

The room grew quiet.

"That's your right," Sheriff Flynn said solemnly. "And I'm sure you'll win. Just last month we had our camera system upgraded." He pointed out the eight cameras aimed at the room. "We'll be able to show the jury in high-definition color how this young woman—" he nodded toward Sara "—flattened your ass with one of the best punches of this century. The audio is good, too, so I'm sure they'll enjoy hearing your views on genocide. They'll definitely agree that a murdering Stewart is a better-quality person than a justice-seeking Medlar."

Alastair gave Sheriff Flynn a look of hate but he said nothing.

"Take him somewhere to get cleaned up," the sheriff said to a deputy. "And by the way, Alastair, you are very welcome to sit in *my* car."

Still chuckling, everyone watched the prisoner being escorted out.

Sheriff Flynn and Detective Cotilla turned to the

three of them standing so close together. Sara looked a bit sheepish, but Jack and Kate were smiling so wide their ears were in danger.

"Come on," the detective said to Kate. "Let's talk."

She didn't move.

Detective Cotilla gave a sigh of defeat. "Yeah, okay. *All* of you."

As they walked toward the room, behind their backs, the detective made some shadow-boxing punches in the air. He grinned all the way to the interrogation room.

* * * * *

Turn the page for an exclusive preview of
A Justified Murder
the next Medlar Mystery story from
New York Times *bestselling author*
Jude Deveraux
Available soon from MIRA Books.

ONE

DORA FOUND THE BODY—AND ALL SHE FELT was annoyance. Now she'd have to find someone else to clean for to fill out the week. Mrs. Beeson—as she insisted on being called even though there was no evidence that she'd ever had a husband—had been a good employer. She always left a hundred-dollar bill, always said thanks. At Christmas, she left an envelope containing three crisp, new one hundreds and a card that wished her a merry holiday.

Now here she was, slumped forward in the chair, face on her knees. There was a hole in the back of her head. Blood and...*stuff* was on the wall behind her. Dora didn't see a gun but she guessed it was squashed between her belly and thighs.

Dora knew she ought to call the sheriff. But if she hadn't cleaned the house yet, would she have a right to take the envelope on the desk that had her name on it?

She could almost hear her late husband, Herbert,

chiding her. "Shouldn't you feel sorry for her?" he'd say. "Poor thing was so sad that she took her own life. Didn't she have friends who could help her?"

"Not that I know of," Dora said aloud, then caught herself. She tried to keep Herbert's voice to herself and not let anyone know how often she heard it.

She went around the body, picked up the envelope, and put it in her pocket. For a moment, she looked out the window at the palm trees and thought of what her beloved Herbert would advise. She knew she needed to work up some sympathy, maybe even some tears, for Mrs. Beeson. It wouldn't do to call Sheriff Flynn sounding like she couldn't care less that her employer had just offed herself. With her shoulders braced, Dora made the call.

Deputy Beatrice answered.

"Oh, Bea." Dora was nearly choking on the memory of Herbert's funeral. "The most awful thing has happened."

"Take a breath," Bea said, "and tell me what it is."

"Janet Beeson killed herself."

Bea didn't hesitate. "We'll be right there and don't touch anything. Absolutely *nothing*."

"I won't." Dora clicked off the phone, and her tears dried immediately. "Damn!" she muttered and put her pay envelope back on the desk. With a resentful glare at Mrs. Beeson's body, she sat down in the living room to wait for whoever was going to show up.

Sheriff Daryl Flynn was the first to arrive on the scene. After Bea told him what happened, he hadn't gone tearing away, sirens blaring. It wasn't a criminal act, but the suicide of a sad old woman. He knew that

Janet Beeson lived alone. He didn't think she'd even had any pets. Maybe the Lachlan website should include that article he'd read about how pets are good for old people and prisoners.

As he drove, taking his time, he realized he hadn't been this far out on San Remo Avenue in a while and he saw that the local super-Realtor, Tayla Kirkwood, had been at work here. The houses looked as manicured as the ones inside those fancy gated communities down in Plantation. For himself, sometimes he missed the days when Lachlan front yards had old cars on concrete blocks. Pretty as the place was, it lacked a sense of personality. It was as though everyone was just alike.

Janet Beeson's house was at the edge of the town limits. To his left, down Kirkwood Lane, was Tayla's ridiculously big, gaudy house.

On the right were lush palm trees. When he neared the address, there was a tall, solid steel fence that seemed to go on and on. *When did that go up?* he wondered. A wide metal gate was standing open, but he saw the lockbox nearby. The place looked like the home of some California movie star, not suited for sleepy little Lachlan. Why had no one told him about this?

He pulled into the drive that was shaded by overhanging trees, with flowering shrubs along the sides. He knew professional landscaping when he saw it. All this had taken time and a whole bunch of money.

He parked his Broward County Sheriff's car to the side, got out, and looked around the place. The house was long and low, with a red tile roof, blue-and-white Spanish tiles under the portal, expensive outdoor furniture, and a quietly splashing fountain with iron birds on it. He thought: *wealthy widow.* South Florida was

full of the dears. Work-exhausted Yankee husbands
died and left it all to their widows. The women moved
south to Florida's divine climate and tarted up some
house, then...

Then lived in isolation, Sheriff Flynn thought. Sad,
unhappy, lonely women.

Dora met him at the front door. She'd lived in Lachlan all her life and he'd gone to school with her. She
was a little out of it since her husband died and tended
to still talk to him, but she was a good person.

"What was it?" he asked. "Pills?"

Dora didn't say anything, just turned and led the
way to the back of the house.

As he followed, he saw lots of marble—cool in Florida's warm climate—and things that glittered. Tables
with gold-colored legs, shiny wood, heavy curtains that
shimmered. His wife made fun of the style. "Might as
well put up wallpaper that says 'I am rich,'" she said.

When the sheriff entered the last room, he was almost smiling. But one look at Janet Beeson's body and
he halted. Holy crap! The woman had blown the back
of her head out. On the wall was...

He turned away, not wanting to see what was there.
For this, he was going to need backup. He took out his
cell to put in a call to the main office, but then the body
started to slip to one side.

Without thinking that he was changing the scene, he
made a leap forward and caught poor Janet before she
hit the floor. When the body fell back against the chair,
what he saw so stunned him that he dropped his phone.

"Oh. My. God," Dora said.

They both stood there, paralyzed.

Janet Beeson had a gunshot in her head and a large

knife sticking out of her chest. Green vomit was on her chin and down the front of her shirt. Poison, maybe?

Sheriff Flynn recovered first. "Somebody really, really wanted her dead," he managed to say. It took a while to find his phone, but he hesitated in calling the main office. What would it matter if he took a few minutes to collect himself?

He couldn't take his eyes off the body. Janet Beeson, of all people! He couldn't remember anything significant about her. If her name was ever mentioned, it was always in good terms.

As his senses came back to him, it was as though he could see the future. He was just the local sheriff, so the big shots at Broward would take over this case. The fact that he'd lived in Lachlan all his life would mean nothing to them. They'd push him out completely. That he'd been instrumental in helping solve the last murder would mean nothing to them. He doubted if they'd even let him have a set of the photos they'd take. How could he investigate—on his own—if he couldn't study the crime scene? He needed those photos!

Before he could think about what he was doing, he called Sara Medlar's private number. She answered on the first ring. "I need you to take pictures of a dead body. Now. 2012 San Remo. It's—" Sara had already hung up.

Sheriff Flynn smiled. It was lunchtime so Jack might be home. He'd want to get here fast, so Sara just might arrive with young Jack on his dad's big Harley. About six minutes later, he heard the roar of the bike and his smile widened. At least he'd get photos! And if he manipulated the Medlar trio right, he might get more.

Yes, it would be better to call the downtown office *after* Sara had done her job. He went outside to meet them.

A Justified Murder
by Jude Deveraux
Available February 26, 2019, from MIRA Books.

Copyright © 2019 by Deveraux Inc.

Get 4 FREE REWARDS!

We'll send you 2 FREE Books **plus** 2 FREE Mystery Gifts.

FREE Value Over **$20**

Both the **Romance** and **Suspense** collections feature compelling novels written by many of today's best-selling authors.

YES! Please send me 2 FREE novels from the Essential Romance or Essential Suspense Collection and my 2 FREE gifts (gifts are worth about $10 retail). After receiving them, if I don't wish to receive any more books, I can return the shipping statement marked "cancel." If I don't cancel, I will receive 4 brand-new novels every month and be billed just $6.74 each in the U.S. or $7.24 each in Canada. That's a savings of at least 16% off the cover price. It's quite a bargain! Shipping and handling is just 50¢ per book in the U.S. and 75¢ per book in Canada.* I understand that accepting the 2 free books and gifts places me under no obligation to buy anything. I can always return a shipment and cancel at any time. The free books and gifts are mine to keep no matter what I decide.

Choose one: ☐ **Essential Romance** (194/394 MDN GMY7)   ☐ **Essential Suspense** (191/391 MDN GMY7)

Name (please print)

Address   Apt. #

City   State/Province   Zip/Postal Code

Mail to the **Reader Service:**
IN U.S.A.: P.O. Box 1341, Buffalo, NY 14240-8531
IN CANADA: P.O. Box 603, Fort Erie, Ontario L2A 5X3

Want to try 2 free books from another series? Call 1-800-873-8635 or visit www.ReaderService.com.

---

*Terms and prices subject to change without notice. Prices do not include sales taxes, which will be charged (if applicable) based on your state or country of residence. Canadian residents will be charged applicable taxes. Offer not valid in Quebec. This offer is limited to one order per household. Books received may not be as shown. Not valid for current subscribers to the Essential Romance or Essential Suspense Collection. All orders subject to approval. Credit or debit balances in a customer's account(s) may be offset by any other outstanding balance owed by or to the customer. Please allow 4 to 6 weeks for delivery. Offer available while quantities last.

Your Privacy—The Reader Service is committed to protecting your privacy. Our Privacy Policy is available online at www.ReaderService.com or upon request from the Reader Service. We make a portion of our mailing list available to reputable third parties that offer products we believe may interest you. If you prefer that we not exchange your name with third parties, or if you wish to clarify or modify your communication preferences, please visit us at www.ReaderService.com/consumerschoice or write to us at Reader Service Preference Service, P.O. Box 9062, Buffalo, NY 14240-9062. Include your complete name and address.

STRS19R